INCARNATION

INCARNATION

Emma Cornwall

G

Gallery Books

New York   London   Toronto   Sydney   New Delhi

G

Gallery Books
A Division of Simon & Schuster, Inc.
1230 Avenue of the Americas
New York, NY 10020

First Gallery Books trade paperback edition September 2012

GALLERY BOOKS and colophon are registered trademarks
of Simon & Schuster, Inc.

For information about special discounts for bulk purchases, please contact Simon
& Schuster Special Sales at 1-866-506-1949 or business@simonandschuster.com.

The Simon & Schuster Speakers Bureau can bring authors
to your live event. For more information or to book an event
contact the Simon & Schuster Speakers Bureau at 1-866-248-3049
or visit our website at www.simonspeakers.com.

Designed by Akasha Archer

Library of Congress Cataloging-in-Publication Data

Cornwall, Emma.
    Incarnation / Emma Cornwall.—1st Gallery Books trade pbk. ed.
    p.   cm.
    Summary: "Lucy Weston, from Bram Stoker's Dracula, hunts down the
ancient vampire who turned her in order to regain her humanity"—
Provided by publisher.
    1. Vampires—Fiction. 2. Stoker, Bram, 1847–1912.—Appreciation—
Fiction. I. Title.
PS3603.O76855I53 2012
813'.6—dc23
                                                                2012009229

ISBN 978-1-4391-9035-7
ISBN 978-1-4391-9040-1 (ebook)

Manufactured in the United States of America

10 9 8 7 6 5 4 3 2 1

Listen to them—the children of the night. What music they make.

—Bram Stoker, Dracula

PROLOGUE

1897

On the stage of London's Royal Opera House, Verdi's *Aïda* was approaching its dramatic conclusion. Shortly, the bold warrior and his princess would suffocate in the impenetrable darkness of the tomb to which their illicit love condemned them. But not before the tenor sang his poignant farewell.

> *To die! So pure and lovely!*
> *And through the yearning of thy heart*
> *In the flower of youth to part . . .*

Held breathless by the soaring music, I leaned forward so far as the constriction of my corset would allow. The box seats were a special treat for my twentieth birthday, the indulgence of my passion for opera that the other members of my family did not share. Beside me, my sister, Amanda, kept her lorgnette trained on the glittering audience. She was my elder by two years, and her cool, blond beauty contrasted with the untamable auburn curls, overly large mouth, and catlike slanted eyes that were my lot. Yet I loved Amanda all the same and would miss her when she wed. At the same time, I envied her impending matrimony, not because of her betrothed—a stolid, boring sort whom I could never have tolerated—but because marriage would presumably bring the solution to the great mystery of sensuality, a subject that distracted me far too often.

Nearby, our father snored softly, his neatly trimmed white beard and mustache fluttering with each exhalation until our mother poked him with her fan. He started but pretended not to wake. Mamma looked very well turned out in a violet silk gown from Worth, acquired during our annual trip to Paris the just-past spring. No doubt she would remonstrate with Papa later but only gently, for their marriage was one of true affection. For the moment, she sighed and resumed her own study of the audience.

My family's presence—so constant and commonplace in my life—did not divert me from the performance about to reach its tragic climax. I was gripped by the lovers' plight. Surely no one deserved so terrible a fate as to be sealed away alive, condemned to eternal night. I would pay any price, make any sacrifice to escape so hideous a death. My skin crawled at the thought, as though a thousand ravenous worms moved just below the surface, feasting on me.

Even as I shuddered at so macabre a notion, the air turned dank and chill. An odor—not unpleasant—hinting at loamy earth, ancient stones, and old fire—teased my nostrils. I heard, as though far off, the wind as it moaned over wide, empty places. The torches on the stage flickered and went out. Darkness swept over all.

When the shadows parted moments later, a solitary figure commanded the stage. The stocky Italian tenor was gone. In his place stood a tall, lithe being draped in black. His pale skin was luminous as the moon, radiating light. Ebony hair framed a high forehead above the straight blade of a nose, a chiseled mouth, and a square, firm jaw. His eyes beneath sweeping brows were wide, dark, and aglow with fierce intelligence. His appearance struck a chord deep within me. I knew him . . . somehow. But that knowledge was as yet so faint and fragmentary that I could make no sense of it.

Startled, I turned toward Amanda to see what she thought of so odd a bit of stagecraft, only to discover that my sister was gone, as were our parents and the entire rest of the audience. Their absence shattered the illusion of reality. I was dreaming, nothing more, a dream odder than any I had ever known yet from which I could not wake.

A strange lassitude gripped me. I seemed capable only of fascination—and surrender as the singer's voice, so seductive, wrapped around me.

No, thou shall not die.
Thou treasure, too high!
Thou art too lovely!

The power and beauty of this being who commanded my attention banished all else. He reached out, opening his arms to me in a gesture that found its echo in my deepest soul. I could think only of him, respond only to him. Obey only him.

Compelled to mirror his movements, I reached out in turn. My arms, bare above long white gloves, glowed pale as the pearls that bound me tightly from wrist to elbow. The tips of my fingers extending to their fullest seemed almost to brush the air around him. A little more and I would be able to touch him . . . be drawn into his embrace . . .

But instead I encountered a rough barrier pressing down close upon me. It had the texture of wood, and felt coarse and cold to my touch. Confused, I strained harder. Abruptly, the stage and the being upon it vanished. There was only darkness, the smell of earth, a creeping chill, and the sense that something was terribly wrong. What madness was this? What travesty of twisted reason?

I must have been taken ill; a fever most likely, casting up such nightmarish phantasms as the mind is prone to under duress. But no, that could not be true. It was all real . . . all of it. Yet it was not. The performance of *Aïda* had taken place a few months before; I remembered it clearly. But no otherworldly singer had appeared to preempt the stage. The opera had ended as it always did, with applause for the dead lovers and a rush to get on to the rest of the evening's entertainment.

A few days after that performance, my family and I had returned to our country home by the sea in Whitby. Shards of memory flew together and I realized that it was there I had encountered the luminous being. At a party on a neighboring estate, our eyes had touched, nothing more, but enough. From that moment my sense of knowing him began.

Several nights later, as we came from Christmas Eve Mass into the chill darkness around the country church, I saw him among the gravestones, leaning against the side of a tomb, a cheroot burning in his hand.

And once more, on the eve of the new year, I opened the window of my bedroom, intent on catching the snowflakes that fell so softly over the hushed world, only to find him sitting, seeming at his ease, on the roof nearby. He bestowed a smile on me before I retreated, certain that I was dreaming, to the safety of my virgin bed.

Memory pressed against the barriers of my mind. I resisted, clinging to the image of myself inviolate as I had then been, but the truth would not be denied. That same night, I ventured out, drawn by a compulsion I could neither deny nor comprehend. On a cliff above the sea, he awaited me. I went to him without hesitation, heedless of the chilled air and the sharp stones beneath my feet. In his arms, I accepted his embrace, breathed in the tantalizing scent of his cool skin with its hints of cedar and sage, and felt the touch of his mouth along the pulse of my neck where my lifeblood coursed.

Ecstasy swept over me, but too swiftly thereafter terror struck. Others knew what had happened . . . were hunting me . . . determined to destroy what I had become. Moonlight glinted on a stake held high, about to be driven into my breast. . . . The earth opened to receive me. . . .

A scream swelled in my throat, only to be silenced by the lyrics of *Aïda* drawn from my memory even as the singer drew me from the tomb of my unnatural sleep.

Ah, could my utmost pains
Remove this fatal stone!

Reaching out frantically in all directions, I faced the terrifying truth. I was not within the bosom of my indulgent family. Instead, I lay within the rude embrace of a narrow wooden box. Unlike Aïda, no lover shared my confinement; I was alone. Nor had I merited a gracious burial. No silk-lined, pillowed casket for me, far less a regal tomb. Dirt drifted through cracks in the crudely hewn boards. The decay of vanished summers settled in my nose. . . .

Buried alive! Condemned! With only the voice and the

luminescent memory of the being to awaken me to my terrible peril and compel me to save myself. I curled my hands into fists and punched the plank directly overhead. Again. Again. Shards of wood cut into my flesh, drawing blood that trickled down my raised arms and splattered onto my face. I licked the coppery taste from my lips and redoubled my efforts, fueled by urgency that flared against the all-encompassing darkness. Again. Again. The skin of my knees tore as I hammered with them, mixing blood and dirt into a sanguinary mud. I bent my legs and pushed with my feet against the lid of the coffin that confined me, straining with all my strength. Abruptly, a section of the wood gave way. Cold, dank earth caved in. I clawed upward, choking, retching, until at the limits of my endurance, I at last broke free into air glittering with diamondlike shards of frost.

Even then the grave was reluctant to give me up. I had to drag myself from it inch by inch, torn and bleeding until finally I hunched, exhausted on the ground. Nearby, a copse of trees rattled skeletal fingers against the cloud-swept sky. A road wound nearby, vanishing across a moor rippled by low hills and sluggishly stirring marshes. Scattered knuckles of stone glowed whitely in the darkness, slashed by shadowed clefts wherein something roosted fitfully. The wind carried a cascade of scents—the sweet rot of loamy earth, the dry perfume of moor grass and bracken, the salt tang of the sea not far distant. And more . . . raw, hot, pulsating life that stripped away the last of my strange lethargy even as the voice of the being from the opera house of my dreams soared on a final, triumphant note—

Opens the sky on a glorious tomorrow
That in its brightness eternal shall glow!

A thousand razor-sharp teeth bit deep inside me, as though an unborn monster was suddenly intent on gnawing its path into the world. I moaned and bent over, my arms wrapped around myself in a desperate effort to ease the pain. A faint rustle in the nearby bushes jerked me upright. I stiffened, listening intently, and heard the sound again. From beneath a gorse bush, darkly purple in the silvered light, a hare darted. *Feed,* my mind said. *Feed,* my body yearned, and I obeyed. Without hesitation, I seized the animal and sank my teeth into its throat.

Hot, salty blood filled my mouth. I groaned in relief but did not pause until the last exquisite drop was drained. Tossing the husk of the hare aside, I savored the sense of well-being flowing through me. It would not last; that much I knew already. But for the moment, it was enough.

With my most immediate need seen to, I was able at last to take account of myself. Looking down, I saw that I wore a silk bed gown that might once have been white but was now so begrimed with dirt and blood as to render its hue indiscernible. The neckline was beaded with small pearls, as were the sleeves, and finished with lace. My hair, strewn with clots of dirt, tumbled loose below my shoulders. I was shoeless, my feet much battered by my struggle to escape. Just as I had foreseen, a wooden stake protruded from between my breasts.

At sight of it a memory stirred more strongly—two men bending over me, talking between themselves. *Terrible business, but the old man wants it done,* one said. *Right enough, guv'ner,* the other replied, *and sooner the better.*

The shock of pain stunning me, the scream bubbling in my throat. The falling away, spiraling into darkness in which I floated unaware until the singer invaded my memory to call me forth.

I examined the stake cautiously. It had been hammered in with such force that the wood where the blows had fallen was softened to pulp. Grasping the wood, I found it thick and smooth between my hands. Slowly, I attempted to ease it out. A strange, dark anguish rippled through me. I tried again, with the same result. Again. My body became rigid, my back arching. I pulled harder and gasped as the stake came free. I cast it onto the ground where it burst into flames briefly before burning out and vanishing. Nothing was left but a small pile of ashes that blew away quickly on the wind.

In the distance, hounds bayed.

I ran for I know not how long, plunging through bracken and gorse, through pools of stagnant water and across rocky stream beds, running without thought or plan, heedless of the winter chill, driven only by the most primal need to escape. The moon was low in the sky before the baying faded behind me and I found a cave familiar to me in the life I dimly remembered before my present, calamitous existence. It was close to the shore, within sight of the dark water stretching away endlessly to an unseen horizon. I crawled inside and lay against a lichen-covered rock, my knees drawn up to my chin. So I remained, staring out through the narrow opening until night faded and the first gray herald of day began to wake the world. Only then did I sleep, drawn well back from the entrance where the darkness was eternal and nothing save myself stirred.

Sleeping, I drifted through splintered dreams and memories. Faces flitted before me and were gone—my parents, Amanda, others I knew though just then I could not name them. The companions of my former life, what had once been all of life to me. But more than all the others, the singer came to me, his presence at once a torment and a comfort. He was there in the darkness, in my terror, refusing me any respite yet also, I sensed, refusing to abandon me.

Who are you? What do you want? Tell me!

The only reply was the echo of my desperation across the dark water. My mind reeled away in confusion only to recall suddenly that moment of incandescent pleasure, the flowering of it all . . . that instant when he had eased away the collar of my gown and bared my throat . . .

I woke again screaming. I must have flailed on the ground of the cave, for the skirt of my gown was twisted tight around me. For a moment, I thought that I was trapped and reacted with rage, tearing myself loose. Only when I finally stood did I realize that I was alone and that it was no longer day.

With the coming of darkness, I instinctively ventured out to hunt. So keen were my senses that I found prey readily, then and in the nights to come. The first time I brought down a deer, I gorged so greatly that afterward I was ill, but the discomfort passed quickly. What was left of the gown fell away in tatters before disintegrating entirely. Neither modesty nor cold troubled me for I did not feel either. From time to time, I heard the baying of hounds but they never came close enough to concern me. I existed in a perfect state of nature and in so doing, I grew greatly in strength. Soon nothing could withstand me.

Yet that is not to say that my existence was idyllic. I was haunted by the dreams that grew steadily in vividness and power. Some were tormented recollections of the life I had known in a house I saw clearly in memory, but others had an entirely different quality. They resonated with the sense of *him*, the singer from the opera house. The conviction began to grow in me that I had been summoned from the grave for some great purpose, but I had no idea what it could be.

In my confusion, I hesitated. The cave had become a refuge, but I could not remain within it forever. The dreams intensified. In their grip, I began to venture outside during day-light. The sensation of the sun on my skin never failed to wake me. I found it startling at first but ultimately not unpleasant. Before long, I relished it, even though it provoked unsettling thoughts.

Sitting in the sun, watching the plovers dart along the foam-tipped waves at the water's edge, I wondered, Who was he? Why had he come to me? What did he want?

I tasted salt and discovered that I could still weep. My tears carried the flavor of the sea, as blood does in its essence.

The next night, after feeding, I did not return to the cave. Instead, I ventured farther, following the silver ribbon of the road that wound across the moors. When I spied the cottage, hewn of stone with a thatched roof, I stopped and hid behind a hedge. Wisps of smoke curled from the chimney. Through a window, I glimpsed the banked embers of a fire. I crept closer, catching the coppery scent of blood.

Hunger stirred, yet I was drawn not so much to feed on the family that lived there as simply to see them. Standing there in the dark, I felt for the first time a hollow sense of loneliness. A little closer and a dog began to bark. I could have killed it eas-ily, but I lacked the will to do so. Instead, I withdrew and re-sumed my journey, unsure of where I was going but determined to get there all the same.

A few miles on, I came upon the house of my memories.

It rose above the surrounding landscape, a pile of stone dark against the moon-bright sky. Not a single light shone in any of the tall windows. Staying in the shadows of the trees that lined the drive, I approached slowly but with undeniable eagerness. When my gaze fell on the broad double doors of polished oak, I imagined them open, light and sound pouring out, people coming and going up the wide stone steps, and I among them. A girl, laughing.

I climbed the steps and laid my hands against the doors, securely shut against intruders. They did not yield, nor did I try to force them, but a smaller door around the back, close to the wild tangle of an abandoned herb garden, gave readily enough.

Entering, I paused and looked around. I was in a kitchen with a high, vaulted ceiling from which copper pots hung. A wood and coal stove with three ovens held pride of place near a long worktable topped with a zinc counter. Wood and brass ice closets taller than myself were built into one wall. Opposite it was a door that when opened revealed an ingenious contrap-tion fitted out with multiple shelves and suspended by ropes: a dumbwaiter intended to ease the delivery of dishes to the din-ing room above.

All this I knew when I knew so little else. From the depths of my memory even more tantalizing fragments of a lost life arose unfolding as though before me—

Lucy, we can't! If we're caught—

Don't be such a ninny, Amanda. It's just for a lark. No one will know.

What are you children doing? Come away from there! Miss Weston, you know better!

Feet slapping against a slate walkway, gangly legs pound-ing, hurtling ourselves behind bales of straw in a stable where horses whinny softly and motes of dust dance in beams of light. Giggling so hard that we fall across each other, tangling like puppies until at last we lie, side by side, gazing up at the beams where swallows nest.

Lucy, I could never be as daring as you—

Slowly, I turned, and without pause, mounted the stairs I knew were there, climbing step by step until I emerged into a narrow passage, straight and dark, without decoration of any sort. I continued along it unhesitantly until I came to a door. Opening it, I stepped out into a columned entrance hall rising three stories to the domed roof of the house. To either side were vast rooms filled with shrouded furniture. At the far end, a marble staircase curved upward. I followed it to the top where I stepped out onto a landing.

Lucy, where are you? Lucy . . . ?

So clear was the voice in my mind that I felt compelled to answer it. "Amanda—? Amanda, are you here?"

My voice, so long unused, cracked. My throat was parched, my tongue thick. I was trembling. No one answered me.

The house lay wrapped in silence. Even the mice had fled at my coming. I was entirely alone, yet I was not. Memories crowded in, fragments flying together to form the bare outlines of understanding.

I passed one room, then another, until at the far end of the hall, I came to a door that I felt compelled to open. Standing on the threshold, I stared inside. As with all the other rooms, the furniture was shrouded, but I could make out a large, canopied bed, a dressing table, an armoire, and several other pieces. The high windows overlooking the garden had been stripped of their curtains, wooden shutters were drawn across them. The Persian rug with its intertwining pattern of vines and flowers where I saw myself suddenly—a child, dreaming of faraway places—was covered with a muslin drop cloth. But I remembered—

I . . . Before *he* claimed me. Before the stake and the grave.

In the days of sunlight when I had a heart that beat and lungs that drew breath.

When I was human.

Furiously, I moved about the room, yanking off the concealing shrouds.

When I came to the armoire, I jerked it open and plunged my hands inside, encountering a sea of silks and fine wools, linens and lace. I gathered them to my face and smelled . . .

Her. Her perfume, the scent of her skin, the lingering trace of her energy, her vitality . . . her life.

Her. Me.

Lucy, where are you?

Here! Oh, God, I am here! Let me out!

The next few hours passed in a blur. I ran frantically from the room in an effort to escape the hideous creature who had invaded it, only to recognize at last that there could be no escape from myself. She and I were one, Lucy and the being who had clawed her way from the grave.

We inhabited the same body, shared the same mind, had the same memories.

Little else was clear until I stumbled on a bathroom with its large, claw-footed tub at the center of its white-tiled floor. Turning a brass knob, I discovered that the water still flowed, though the pipes shuddered and sputtered when I turned it on. I think initially I had some notion of ending my agony by drowning myself. I may even have tried. Of course, there was no point. A heart that no longer beats cannot be stilled. I spent the remainder of the night in that tub, draining and refilling it until at last the filth of the grave and all that had followed was washed from me.

When I rose again, it was almost dawn. In the pale light, I discovered that despite everything that had happened and all I had done, my skin was unmarred by a single scratch or bruise. My body possessed a remarkable ability to heal itself. It remained to be seen if my mind could do the same.

I lived in the house for several months, leaving it only to hunt. The remainder of the time I strove to learn all I could about the life that had been mine. Nor was I alone. Memories of my parents and most especially of my sister, Amanda, clustered round me. In the airy music room where we had often sat after dinner, I discovered that I could play the piano passably well and the harp somewhat. Among dozens of well-thumbed musical scores, my favorites were Chopin's haunting nocturnes so evocative of moonlit landscapes. But I also returned again and again to Debussy's more daring harmonies. Music, it seemed, had been and still was important to me. Yet it could not engage me exclusively.

The library held many books; I devoured them. But the book that fascinated me the most was the diary I found in Lucy's—my—old bedroom. In it, I had recounted the small triumphs and disappointments in the life that had been mine. That lost self showed herself to be of a generally sunny disposition, optimistic, and resilient. But I had also nurtured a yearning for adventure and a conviction that the world held far more than I had yet discovered. The life planned out for me—marriage to a proper young man, children, the fulfillment of my role in society—elicited expressions of impatience and even, I must say, of fear.

Is that all there is? I had written. *Does life hold nothing more? People say we are at the beginning of a brilliant new age, yet I seem to have no part in it.*

And finally, just days before the end—

I went up to the old nursery today. The puppets I used to play with are all still there behind the little stage. They look so dusty and forlorn. How tempted I was to snip their strings.

In addition to my other pursuits, I resumed the habit of wearing clothes. The armoire was filled with them, but there were more in an adjacent dressing room. I spent hours trying on garment after garment—chemises, camisoles, drawers, corsets, skirts, shirtwaists, dresses in modest pastels or whites, gowns equally virginal, riding habits, boots, belts, bonnets, and on and on. But I never ventured near a mirror; something about them repelled me. In the process, I discovered that I had grown more slender and, oddly, a few inches taller, as though the experience of dragging myself from the grave had stretched my bones. My hair, once I had completed the laborious process of untangling it, proved to be auburn and possessed of a natural curl. I took to wearing it tied back by a simple velvet ribbon so that it did not get in my way as I read. Or hunted.

Throughout this time, the dark figure of the opera house and my tormented dreams in the cave did not return. Yet his presence hovered in my mind, leaving me oddly unsettled, as though there was somewhere else I needed to be, something else I should be doing.

Occasionally, I saw a carriage or wagon pass by on the road

beyond the end of the drive, but no one approached the house. Once, during a fierce storm, shutters in the back parlor banged open and water flooded in.

Had I not been there to close them hastily and mop up the damage, the floor would have been ruined. More and more, the house had the air of having been abandoned suddenly.

That troubled me, but I was undecided what to do about it until one day, exploring beyond the rooms where I had become comfortable, I found what was clearly a man's study. The shutters were still drawn, the chamber cast in gloom. A faint scent of cigar smoke, discernible only to my greatly heightened senses, lingered over a desk of burled wood and leather. On that desk, tossed as though in anger or despair, I found a bundle of typescript pages. The first page bore a title and the author's name: *Dracula: A Novel by Bram Stoker*. I settled in a nearby chair and began to read.

At first, I thought it no more than a tale of adventure. But to my dismay, I quickly discovered that it was something else entirely. Shockingly, Mr. Stoker's tale of hapless Lucy Westenra, as he dubbed her, and the creature he called a "vampire" turned out to be a sensationalized, cheapened version of what had befallen me. That this could be so astounded me. How had the author come by such information? Why had he twisted and perverted it as he had done? And why had I found the evidence of his fabrication on my father's desk?

By morning, I had absorbed all that the book had to tell me as well as all that it could not. When I stood at last, I knew where I had to go. And what I had to do.

CHAPTER 1

The London fog carried the sharp bite of sulfur from the coal dust that shrouded the city. Spectral fingers drifted along the Strand, winding around the hackneys and private carriages waiting for the theatres to let out. The yellow glow of the new sodium lights reflected in the black puddles left by a storm that had passed over a few hours before. It had brought not the freshening scents of the countryside, as Dickens remarked, but the foul, stale, wretched addition to the gutters that was a London rain.

Stepping carefully, I moved in the direction of a cobblestone alley near the corner where the Strand meets Wellington Street. A young whore with hennaed hair and rosy tits peeking above a soiled lace bodice occupied the spot and clearly meant to keep it. Her first reaction was to sneer at my modest appearance. I could not blame her. My hair was piled high on my head in a loose bun. I wore a simple shirtwaist beneath a fitted jacket, with a matching pleated skirt that brushed the tops of my boots. A wide belt, clenched around my narrow waist, held my purse. The style had been popularized by the American artist Charles Dana Gibson, who saw it as the personification of the ideal woman—bright, pretty, and capable. Once it had suited me well. Now it was merely a disguise.

The whore opened her carmine-painted mouth to warn me off, only to freeze when my eyes met hers. The monster I had become stirred within. The whore turned ashen and darted away into the night.

I sagged a little in relief when she was gone but I did not let down my guard. Surrounded by the hot, coppery fragrance of pulsing blood, the warmth of living flesh, the beating of collective hearts, the effort needed to restrain myself was almost more than I could muster. Hunger gnawed at me. Had a rat appeared just then, I would have swallowed my revulsion and drained it in an instant. But London rats are wilier than the country prey that had sustained me thus far, wilier even in some regard than the humans with which they must contend. Nothing stirred in the alley.

I drew back into the shadows, but kept my gaze on the Lyceum Theatre across the street. Its columned façade gave the appearance of an ancient Greek temple. The play advertised on placards out in front was one I had seen with my family the previous year during our visit to Paris. That seemed a lifetime ago—the life I had known having effectively ended on the windswept moors near Whitby when I fell under the spell of the seductive being who had so transformed me.

Thinking of him, I was startled by the arrival of the black-uniformed Watchers gliding along on their upright Teslaways, their faces invisible behind the visors of their helmets. A few years before, such vehicles would have been restricted to the pages of novels by H. G. Wells, Jules Verne, and the like. But the luring to England of the brilliant scientist and inventor Nikola Tesla had brought about a technological revolution, the implications of which were only just beginning to be felt. At the same time, fear of anarchists and others deemed "subversives" had prompted broad new laws that gave the authorities unparalleled powers over ordinary citizens. Not everyone was entirely happy with the results. My father, for instance, had worried that civil liberties were being undermined by the government's ever-expanding ability to observe and control its citizens.

As the guardians of the public safety took up position outside the theatre, the ushers threw open the doors and light poured into the street. First out were the upper-class patrons of the private boxes and the dress circle, the gentlemen in their evening dress or military uniforms and the ladies in their gowns and jewels. When they had been taken up into their carriages, the decent professional men and their wives who occupied the stalls were let out through one door, while the rowdy students, tradesmen, and foreigners from the balconies were made to wait before exiting through another.

All along the Strand, theatregoers were departing. Hundreds thronged the road under the gaze of the Watchers, calling farewell to friends, hailing cabs, exclaiming over the evening's entertainment or complaining of it. All was ordered and proper until a tall, somber-looking man suddenly cried out in alarm and slapped a hand to the pocket that moments before had held his wallet. A Watcher took note, spied the fleet-footed thief, and promptly pursued him. Weaving his scooter in and out of the crowd, he quickly overtook the miscreant, rendering him insensible with an electrical cudgel.

Other Watchers arrived on the scene and the boy was tossed into the back of a police van. His case would be heard in one of the summary judgment courts set up to deal with matters of civil disorder. Within hours, he would be tried, sentenced, and committed to serve his term without the possibility of appeal.

The streets of London were safer than they had ever been, but the prisons were fuller. There was talk that more such institutions needed to be built quickly.

The brief flare of excitement faded away as the streets cleared. In my mind, I went over my plan once again. I would approach the Lyceum Theatre, enter through the back, and seek out the author of the deceitful version of my life. I would not kill him; on that I was determined. But I would compel him to tell me why he used me as he had.

A clutch of young men hovered at the stage door, praising the attributes of the female lead, a certain Belgian actress who was linked romantically to the Crown Prince. When the cast finally emerged, the lady smiling in sables and diamonds, a cheer went up. Invitations were offered, accepted, or declined. Finally, the last of the stragglers departed.

Still, I waited. The lights in the theatre dimmed. The ushers let themselves out, offered muted good nights to one another, and vanished into the darkness between the pale pools of the sodium lights. The stagehands followed. Quiet, in startling contrast to the recent clamor, descended. The life of the city had moved on into the nearby streets crowded with restaurants and pubs, far enough away for my purposes.

The time had finally come. I stepped forward, only to stop suddenly when a flicker of movement near the theatre caught my eye. Was my quarry departing already? Was I in danger of missing him? But no, the shape I glimpsed between wisps of fog did not resemble the man identified as Mr. Bram Stoker, whose sketch in *The Illustrated London News* I had studied with such care. Instead, the figure appeared strangely garbed in a long robe such as a monk might wear. A hood concealed the head and face. Even as I puzzled over this, another identical figure appeared, followed by a third. Together, they took up position in front of the theatre.

I am not given to flights of fancy, but just as the whore had sensed danger when she looked at me, I knew that the hooded trio was a threat. They had the shape of men, but they moved with the lumbering heaviness of beasts, and even when they stepped into the light, darkness concealed their faces.

Although I had been in London only a short time, I had sensed the presence of beings that were other than human. But I had no wish to discover anything about them or, indeed, to allow any distraction from the dual forces that drove me. I was torn between the compulsion laid upon me by the singer in the opera house, so powerful that it had drawn me from the grave, and by my own yearning for the half-remembered human life that I had known. Both compelled me to find the one who had transformed me and demand from him both an explanation for his actions and a means of undoing them.

I stepped again into the street. At once, the trio of hooded creatures moved forward. Almost too late, I realized that they meant not simply to block my passage but to seize hold of me. Anger warred with disbelief. I dropped the valise I carried, hoisted up my skirt, and lashed out with a booted foot, catching one of the assailants in the chest. Such was the force of my kick that he should have collapsed. But after staggering for a moment, the creature righted himself and came at me again.

My recent transformation had endowed me with vastly greater strength and speed than normal, the extent of which I was still discovering. I flung one of the creatures against a nearby wall and another into a lamppost even as the third tried to grab hold of me. He was strong, but I was stronger. Whirling, turning, a blur of motion and fury, I scarcely knew when my feet left the ground and I soared, unfettered by gravity. That had not happened before and for just a moment I was distracted. The assailants seized the opportunity and came at me all together. I heard their hissing breath, saw their gnarled hands reaching out to pull me down, and realized that one was holding a chain finely wrought from silver links. As it brushed against my skin, a burst of pain convulsed me. For an instant, I was helpless. Two of the creatures bore me to the ground. The third, holding the chain, advanced. In a moment, I would be bound, engulfed in agony, and unable to defend myself.

The monster within me lifted its head and howled. I turned and sank my fangs into the nearest creature. The bite should have drawn blood, but mercifully I tasted nothing. I did, however, hear the high-pitched, keening cry that broke from the assailant as he struggled to free himself. Letting him go, I leaped to my feet and turned on the others. The one with the chain started forward again. I extended both my arms, knit my hands together, and struck him so hard a blow that he flew across the street and landed up against the alley archway. Just then, the moon emerged from behind high threads of clouds. Throwing my head back, fangs gleaming in the cold white light, I howled defiance.

The creature I had struck down did not move, but the other two did. They seized his arms and, dragging him, ran with all speed toward the shadows beyond the Strand. In an instant, I was alone. Only the silver chain, lying in the gutter, remained as mute evidence of the attack.

Giving the weapon a wide berth, I willed myself to be calm

and straightened my ensemble. My hair had come down during the struggle. It tumbled in thick auburn waves around my shoulders. I pinned it up again before recovering my valise and crossing the street. Swiftly, I found the door I sought. It was locked, but that was of no consequence. With care—there having been more than enough disorder that night—I lifted it off its hinges and leaned it up against the side of the theatre.

Just beyond lay a dark passage. My eyes, keener than they had ever been during my human existence, made out trunks and baskets, backdrops, and bits of scenery stacked along the walls. At the far end, a sliver of light shone. I moved toward it, alert to the possibility that more of the strange creatures might be lurking, but none were in evidence. When I reached the light, I paused. An inner door stood partially ajar. I could see a cluttered office and a man working at a desk illuminated by a small gas lamp. I recognized Mr. Bram Stoker at once.

Without hesitation, I pushed the door open and entered. Stoker looked up. His broad face with its thick brows and neatly trimmed brown beard appeared surprised but in no way alarmed. To him, I was simply an unknown young woman whose overall appearance suggested good breeding. My sudden presence in his theatre at night was certainly strange, but not an immediate cause for concern.

"Have you lost your way, miss?" he asked courteously, apparently taking me for a patron incapable of finding the exits.

My eye fell on a pile of identical leather-bound books stacked on a corner of his desk. To my horror, I saw that the spine of each was luridly inscribed with the title *Dracula*. I had not considered that he could have contrived to publish his hash of mangled truths and absurd fantasies so speedily, but apparently I had arrived too late to prevent him from doing so.

"To the contrary," I replied. "It appears that I have come to the right place." I gestured at the books. "You are the author of this . . . work?"

With misbegotten pride, he said, "Indeed, I am. I take it you are a fan." He rose from his chair as he gestured me into one facing him. "Do sit down. I will be most happy to sign a copy for you, if that is what you wish."

I resisted the impulse to roll my eyes at his eagerness to claim such tripe. Still standing, I said, "That isn't why I have come." Moving closer to him, I said, "My name is Lucy Weston, not Lucy Westenra, as you so lightly veiled me in your so-called novel."

Stoker paled and fell back into his chair with the look of a man who has come face-to-face with his own worst nightmare. His eyes wide and dilated, he stared at me in horror.

Holding his gaze, I tapped a finger on the topmost copy of his execrable book. "You will explain how you learned what happened to me and why you twisted the facts as you have done to conceal the truth."

It is said that in extremis, humans have one of two possible reactions—flight or fight. Apparently, Stoker knew better than to try to oppose me physically. Therefore, he took the only other option available to him. Barely had I finished speaking than he leaped to his feet and attempted to dash around me in the direction of the door.

Hoisting him in one hand, I returned him to his chair.

"This will go much better for you if you simply tell me what I want to know," I said.

Stoker was a big, burly man. The experience of being lifted off the floor by what appeared to be a slender young woman undid him. I could quite literally smell his fear.

Staring at me in frozen horror, he said, "You can't be her. She is dead. They told me so."

I thought of the dank earth, the coffin, the grave, the stake. My pounding against the wood until it shattered. My clawing my way out, gasping and straining, rising beyond death's clutches to be born again into the world as the new, strange creature that I was. My hand lashed out to close around his throat.

"Who are 'they'? Who did this to me? Tell me everything from the beginning."

Against the constriction of my grip, he gasped, "I can't! I don't know!"

Fury rose in me. "You are lying. The story you wrote is a distortion of the truth, but it is still far too close to be coincidence. You must know what really happened to me."

He did not attempt to deny it, but said instead, "I only learned about it afterward."

"Who told you of it?"

When he refused to respond, I squeezed a little harder and insisted, "Tell me!"

His fingers clawed at mine, yet surprisingly he continued to resist. "I cannot. These are matters that involve the security of the realm."

Taken aback, I hesitated, but only briefly. Nothing he said, no lie he told, would spare him. "You are Irish, are you not, Mr. Stoker?"

He stiffened and for the first time I saw anger in him. "That does not make me any less loyal, Miss Weston."

"As you will. I do not believe for a moment that what was done to me could have anything to do with the safety of the British Empire." Indeed, I took it to be the feeblest of excuses. Truly, patriotism is the last refuge of scoundrels.

With more courage than I would have expected under the circumstances, he said, "That is because you are not in possession of the facts."

Slowly, I released my grip. My arms fell to my sides. I took a step back and stared at him. He flinched, but appeared unable to take his eyes from me. Terror held him captive, but so, I perceived, did fascination. He struck me as a man who dips a toe into the water in the half-hope that the current will take hold and carry him to distant, enchanted realms.

Right then, in the cluttered office at the back of an empty theatre made to resemble an ancient temple, I was the most seductive temptation the author of *Dracula* had ever encountered.

"You are the remedy for my ignorance, Mr. Stoker. Tell me what I want to know and I will not harm you."

I gave him a little time to come to terms with that. The delay allowed me to get myself under better control. Being so close to Stoker, touching him, roused my hunger to a level that frightened even me. For all my threats, I needed him alive. And yet I also desperately needed to feed. The journey from Whitby to London had taken scarcely four hours thanks to the new piston-driven locomotives of the Great Northern Railway that were knitting the country together more tightly than ever. But it had also put me in close proximity to humans while availing me no opportunity to assuage the appetite they provoked.

Stoker may have sensed something of that, for abruptly he said, "What do you think would happen if ordinary people discovered that creatures such as yourself exist and that the authorities have kept the knowledge of them concealed for centuries? Can you imagine the anger and the fear, not to mention the loss of faith in our ruling class that would result? All that would play into the hands of those who are determined to harm this realm."

"Why should I care about any of that?" I demanded.

"Because rumors of your fate could have sparked a panic that would have raged out of control," Stoker replied. "Before that could happen, a decision was made to create the impression that it was all no more than a fanciful tale."

I had to admit that it was an ingenious ploy. With the publication of his book, any claim that a young woman really had disappeared from Whitby under terrifying circumstances would be dismissed as the foolishness of those so gullible as to believe a work of fiction. As for my family, they were—like Stoker—loyal British subjects. Had my father been persuaded that my fate was somehow entwined with the safety of the realm, I had no doubt that he would keep silent even in the depths of the most terrible grief. Moreover, he would go to any lengths to shield my mother and sister from such a hideous truth.

"These 'intermediaries' of whom you speak," I said. "They asked you to do this extraordinary thing, create a novel to their specifications and bring it to the world, and you simply . . . agreed? With no knowledge of who sent them?"

"They did not say . . . I swear it!"

He was parsing words in the way of lawyers, writers, and others who would hang the world on a turn of phrase. Shakespeare had his Henry VI muse over the benefits of killing all the lawyers. Conscientious parents forbid the reading of fiction. Neither was entirely deluded.

"But you suspected, didn't you, or you would never have listened to them."

"I cannot say . . ."

Regret rippled through me. Of the two of us, Amanda had always been graced with the more delicate sensibilities by far. I recalled her kneeling in the garden at Whitby, weeping copiously over a dead bird cradled in her hands while I looked on dry-eyed, an unsentimental child who saw death as merely one more of life's endless curiosities. Yet surely the Lucy I had been was not incapable of compassion.

"I do not want to hurt you," I said.

Far from relieving Stoker, my attempt at reassurance seemed to alarm him even further. He turned from gray to a shade of red that could not possibly be healthy. Sweat beaded on his forehead, dripping into his eyes as his breathing became even more agitated. Yet he remained stubbornly insistent.

"I cannot tell you, for your sake as well as mine! You should go far away from here. No one need ever know that I saw you. I won't tell, I swear! You can find others of your kind—"

"Others?" My surprise was so intense that I could not even attempt to conceal it. Bending down, I seized his shoulders and shook him hard. His head lolled back and forth, and for a moment I feared he might lose consciousness. Even so, I persisted. "There are others? Beyond the being who took my humanity and transformed me into . . . whatever this is that I have become?"

He sputtered and was overcome by a spasm of coughing that wracked his entire body. Abruptly, I realized that my actions were at odds with my objective. Unconscious—or dead—Stoker would be of no use to me whatsoever. I released my grip, leaned him back in the chair, and made haste to fill a glass with water from a carafe on the desk.

"Drink this . . . slowly. There is nothing to be afraid of. I mean you no harm. All I ask is the truth. You can manage that, can't you?"

A deep sigh escaped him. He swallowed a little of the water and stared at me. In his gaze I saw the struggle of a man of genuine principle confronted with a reality so far outside his experience that he had no context for dealing with it. Yet I left him no choice but to do so.

Taking a breath, he seemed to come to a determination in his own mind. "Perhaps it would be better to tell you. You must make your way in the world, after all, and ignorance is no fit state for anyone."

With care, so as not to alarm him unduly, I lowered myself into a chair facing him. "Tell me . . . please."

My stab at courtesy, however belated, seemed to calm him. He nodded once more but seemed not to know how to begin. Finally, he asked, "What is it that you want to know?"

"The truth. Not what you wove from your imagination but what you know to be real. The term you used in your novel, vampires, how did you come by that?"

Presented with a direct question, Stoker seemed better able to manage. With hesitation, he said, "It is what beings of your kind call themselves. They have existed for millennia and are spoken of by various names in legends throughout the world, but that is the name they prefer."

Even as I struggled to absorb this astounding information—and to wonder how Stoker possessed it—I plunged on. "The way you described them, how much of that was true?"

"They have many of the characteristics that I recounted, although not that business about turning into a bat. They don't do that, at least so far as I know, although they can defy gravity so as to appear to fly."

"Fascinating . . . and that creature 'Dracula,' did you draw him from life . . . so to speak?"

"Not really. In fact, making him foreign was part of the deception. Still, the public seems to find him appealing."

"But I did encounter someone, the one who transformed me . . ." The singer in the opera house. The being in my dreams. He who called me forth from the grave.

Stoker's gaze, which had been wandering in his agitation, abruptly sharpened. "What do you remember of him?"

"Very little . . . fragments . . . impressions, nothing more. I only know that I must find him."

"Why? To what purpose? After all, he left you to your fate, did he not?"

"Yes, he did." Left me to the stake and the grave. But he had also returned in some manner that I could not understand to call me forth. As he was still calling me, a summons from which I could not turn away. Rather than reveal any of that, I said, "As you are so knowledgeable about my kind, tell me, where should I seek him?"

"Paris," Stoker said too quickly. He was sweating again. "Numerous reports attest to the presence of vampires there. Also in Vienna and points east. In fact, now that I think of it, your best course would be to book onto the Orient Express and take the train all the way to Istanbul. I have heard stories about vampires there that—"

"I have no intention of leaving London."

He looked aghast. "But you must! Surely, you understand . . . I explained, a matter of the security of the realm." He paused a moment, then added, "If it is a question of funds,

I can be of assistance. The book is proving to be very lucrative and—"

"How kind," I interjected. "But did you not say that you made Dracula a foreigner as part of your deception?"

"I don't know . . . I shouldn't have . . ."

"Then the one I seek is English, isn't he? Before I hurry off to the ends of the earth in search of him, wouldn't it be more prudent to look first right here in London?"

Stoker's expression made it clear that he regretted having told me anything. But it was too late. He had revealed sufficient knowledge of my kind to convince me that he possessed far more. Rather than attempt to choke it out of him, I tried a different tack.

"I will be glad to leave you in peace, sir. Only tell me where in this city a vampire is to be found."

"How would I know that?" he protested. "I told you, I was approached by intermediaries. They—"

"Then where are they rumored to be? Where do the stories place them, the legends, if not your informants? You have knowledge of that, do you not?"

Reluctantly, he nodded. I stood as though preparing to leave, my hope being that he would do whatever he must to speed me on my way. I was not disappointed.

"I have heard of a place—" he admitted.

"What place?"

"A club, a gathering spot of sorts, called the Bagatelle." With trembling hands, he scribbled an address on a piece of paper and handed it to me. "It is off Fleet Street, near the boundary between the old City of London and Westminster. If the rumors are true, you will find others of your kind there."

I took the paper, glanced at it briefly, and nodded.

"But be duly warned," Stoker said. "There are those who will tell you that the place is a veritable cesspool of intrigue and treachery."

I scarcely heard him. Whatever he meant to say, my course was set. Before caution could get the better of me, I turned and went quickly down the cluttered passage to the door through which I had entered. At the back of the theatre, I peered out, mindful of the need to avoid the Watchers, but none were in sight. Fog lay heavily over the city. The smell of sulfur was strong. Of the hooded creatures, there was no sign. Stepping out into the night, I turned in the direction of Fleet Street.

CHAPTER 2

Subterranean waters murmured beneath my feet where the ancient river still ran, long buried by the street that had taken its name. Nothing else moved. The newspaper offices that crowded both sides of Fleet Street were shuttered, as were the shops squeezed between them. To the east, where the sun would rise in a few hours, I could just make out the dome of St. Paul's Cathedral wreathed in the ever-present fog. A dirigible floated nearby, but otherwise nothing moved.

A quarter mile behind me light and noise still poured from the pubs and restaurants, but here silence hung over all. I was alone, or so I hoped. For a being possessed of the skills that had so terrified Stoker, I was remarkably uneasy. And not only because I felt compelled to keep an eye out lest the hooded creatures appear again brandishing their silver chains. For all that he was genuinely afraid of me, the Irishman had given in too easily. Stoker's promise to keep silent about my presence in the city would likely prove as false as the story about me that he had foisted upon the world.

Yet I had no choice but to rely on the information he had provided. Referring to the scribbled address, I searched for the vampires' lair. Though I went slowly and looked everywhere,

I failed to find anything other than darkened windows and sealed doors.

Walking the empty streets alone, far from the comfort and company of others, a hollow longing took hold of me. Not for the first time, I reflected how much I had taken for granted in my previous existence. The domestic routine of family life had chaffed on more than one occasion, but I would have given almost anything to be nestled within it once again, seated around the table debating the news of the day with my father or laughing at one of Amanda's stories about her society friends.

Where had my family gone? How had they coped with my disappearance? What did they make of it? The Whitby house had the air of sudden abandonment, as though they had not been able to bear being there after what had happened to me. Were they now in London or had they fled to the Continent in search of solace? Had Amanda married as planned? I had been "dead" for not yet six months, scarcely enough time to allow for her to emerge from mourning. But was so unnatural a demise subject to such considerations? Whether she had married or not, I could not see her floating down the aisle, the happy bride she should have been.

And what of my parents? My mother despised black, claiming that it aged her horribly. She would cross over to the other side of Regent Street rather than pass in front of Jay's, the leading emporium for all mourning requirements. How was she coping? How was my father?

When I thought of them, I missed them terribly. Yet I had to admit that there were long stretches of time when I did not think of them at all, as though they no longer existed for me. Even as I longed for the life I had known, I could not deny that in my new incarnation the world was brighter, sharper, more intense, as though I was truly experiencing it for the first time. Nor was that all. My senses were keener, my strength greater, my stamina unlike anything I had ever known. The workings of my mind were swifter and more decisive, unfettered by the complex and often contradictory tug of human emotions.

The temptation to accept what had happened to me, even to rejoice in it, was very strong. Yet I resisted. Some contrary part of me still clung to my humanity that, for all its innate fragileness when compared to my new state, seemed more precious the further I became from it.

But for the moment nothing mattered so much as finding others of my kind. Only through them would I have any hope of finding the one who seemed to call to me more powerfully with each passing hour. Since my arrival in London, the sense of *him*, the singer in the opera house of my dreams, had only grown stronger. I was convinced that he was nearby, yet where? Why did he withhold himself from me? When I did find him— for I could not conceive that I might not—what would he require of me? Would I obey him willingly or would I resist, and at what price?

All this and more swirled through my mind, round and round without cease, even as the seemingly simple task of finding a particular address continued to elude me. Again and again, I retraced my steps, my heels ringing sharply against the cobblestones, the sound echoing off the surrounding buildings as my frustration mounted. Finally, the sheer futility of my actions brought me to a halt. Standing in the middle of the empty street, I fought a sense of hopelessness. I had to find the one who had done this to me. I had to—but what if I could not . . . ?

"Penny for a poor old woman, dearie?"

I jerked around. The voice came from deep within the shadows of a doorway, but I could see no one.

"Who's there?"

The whisper of shuffling, the flutter of movement. A hunched figure emerged slowly from the darkness, leaning on a twisted cane.

"Why, dearie, it's only Little Alice. Ye know me." She smiled, revealing pointed yellowed teeth.

The creature stood scarcely higher than my waist. Her face was gnarled like the bark of an old tree. Tendrils of matted gray hair trailed from her balding, splotched skull. I could not make out her eyes; they were buried within folds of wrinkled skin, but I could smell her. The miasma of dank, fetid odor made me gag.

I am not so shallow as to be repulsed by the natural effects of age. But Little Alice was, in a word, hideous. Yet there was also something undeniably pitiable about her. She seemed not entirely whole, as though her very being was clinging to this world only by the thinnest of threads. When I looked more closely, I saw that she was almost transparent.

Stiffening my spine, I said, "You mistake me for someone else. We have not met."

The creature cupped a hand to a pointed ear from which bristled tufts protruded. "Heh? What's that ye say?"

I tried again, more loudly. "We haven't met."

She pulled back and squinted at me. Her thick brow furrowed. "Who are ye then? And while we're at it, where's me penny?" Glaring, she thrust out a filthy fist. "Don't think yer crossin' me bridge without ye pay the toll first."

I found a penny in my purse and dropped the coin into her hand. "What bridge?"

"The one used to be here 'fore the humans buried the river, and may the old gods curse them for it."

Bridges . . . tolls. I had sensed the presence of others in the city who were not human, but I had not considered that I would confront them. "You're a—?"

"Troll, of course. I can still say that, though for how much longer is anyone's guess. As for ye—"

"I'm . . ." I hesitated.

There was a time not long before when I could have blithely said who I was. A beloved daughter, a future wife, a girl with no responsibilities and no cares beyond what gown to wear to the next gala. I remembered what it had meant to be that Lucy, but increasingly those memories had the gossamer quality of dreams. The thought that I might lose them entirely terrified me.

"I know what ye are," the troll said. "I can see those baby fangs yer tryin' to flash. What I don't know is why yer roamin' about alone."

Her derision stung, but I contained myself. If I could keep her talking, perhaps I would learn something of use. "Shouldn't I be?"

"'Course not. They train ye up before they let ye out on yer own. Least that's the way it's always been. What makes ye different?"

"I don't know." Until a short time before, I had not known that there were others of my kind apart from the one who transformed me. If I truly was set apart from them in some way, what hope did I have of ever finding the help I needed?

"Well, ye best figure it out, dearie. Take it from me, somethin' t'ain't right." She leaned a little closer, her nostrils flaring. "Off yer feed, are you? Is that the problem?"

Quickly, I said, "Never mind about that." I fumbled in the pocket of my skirt and held out the crumbled paper Stoker had given me. "I'm looking for this place."

She peered at it. "Aye, the Bagatelle. I know it right enough, but ye want to think twice before ye go waltzin' in there."

"Why?"

"It's not exactly an ingénue ball, dearie. It could go badly for ye."

"Even so, tell me how to find it."

"Or ye'll what?" She laughed harshly. "Believe me, if ye ever tasted what flows in my veins, ye'd never want to do it again."

The mere thought was enough to send a wave of nausea through me, momentarily overwhelming even my constant hunger.

Little Alice chuckled. "Maybe yer not so dumb after all. Right, then, on yer head be it. Go past the temple and find the griffin. In its shadow, ye'll see a narrow passage that gives on to a wee court. Look for the amber light."

Hope, so recently all but extinguished, brightened once again within me. I was sincerely grateful to her. "Thank you."

"Let's hope ye still feel that way once ye've found what ye seek. If ye take Little Alice's advice, ye'll go carefully. I've nothin' against yer kind; they always have a penny for me. But I'm not fool enough to ever turn me back on one of ye neither."

I nodded and bid her a good night. Before the words had left my mouth, she vanished into the darkness. I moved on through the hushed streets, retracing my steps yet again until I stood once more beside the gated entrance to the ancient church of the Templars set in an oasis of medieval courtyards and gardens that were now sealed for the night. Not far beyond, I looked to the left and saw, rising on top of a tall stone pedestal, a winged lion with the head of an eagle. This griffin kept watch on the boundary between the old city and the outer borough of Westminster. The sprawling growth of London had long since merged the two, but the ancient barriers and the traditions associated with crossing them still existed. The monarch herself was expected to pause at the boundary and ask permission of the mayor of London before entering.

I felt no such constraint. But as I stepped toward the pillar, I stopped abruptly. In the glow of gaslight diffused by the fog, I saw a sight that I could scarcely credit. Half a dozen extraordinarily large, powerful wolves circled the pedestal, their golden eyes gleaming with intelligence that looked human and more. They paced, muscles rippling, round and round, giving every appearance of being on guard.

The hairs rose on the back of my neck. The fear I felt was primal, but the hatred . . . that was something new. Blood lust rose in me. I wanted nothing more than to attack without reason or purpose except to kill. Never, even with the worst of the hunger, had I felt anything like this.

The wolves sensed my presence. They turned as one, their teeth bared. Their growls made the ground tremble. Their leader, the largest and most powerful, lifted his head and stared at me. I only just managed to hold myself in check. Not moving, I met his gaze.

We stood for what seemed an eternity but likely was mere moments. Contradictory impulses warred within me. I wanted to kill and I did not. I wanted to surrender entirely to what I had become and I was determined to fight that temptation with all my strength.

The other beasts pawed the ground impatiently. One made a move toward me. The leader turned his head and growled a warning deep in his throat. The first hesitated but did not retreat until the leader lunged, driving him back. The pack startled, clearly shocked by such behavior.

I stood, rooted where I was, as the leader turned again and stared at me. I bore his scrutiny until I thought that I could endure it no longer. In the instant before my control shattered, he threw back his noble head and howled. The sound echoed down the narrow street, reverberating against the stone walls. Before it had faded completely, the wolves were gone. I stood once more alone in the dark.

CHAPTER 3

Not far from the griffin, I found the passage. It was lined in brick with a low ceiling. As the troll had said, beyond lay a small court so lost in shadow as to be easily overlooked. To its rear, barely visible through the fog, I could just make out the amber glow of a small lamp. I moved toward it slowly, mindful that the night could hold yet more surprises.

No other light was visible, nor did I hear any sound until I was almost in front of a small wooden door surmounted by an arch. At first I thought my ears were playing tricks, but I halted all the same. A low hissing filled the air. Steam escaping from a generator? Did such great grinding, mechanical monsters exist here in the very heart of London?

I took a step closer and halted again. The arch appeared to be . . . writhing?

I was tired, exhausted even. It had been a tumultuous few hours. My eyes could not be trusted.

The hissing grew louder. What appeared to be two burning coals shone from the shadows above the door. I heard . . . slithering?

A forked tongue flicked out of the darkness. I gasped and jumped back. The head of an immense snake, its skin an iridescent armor of black, purple, and green, darted toward me. Its vast, sinuous body coiled all around the doorway, blocking the entrance to whatever lay beyond.

I had seen such a beast once before at the London Zoo, an anaconda captured in the wilds of the Amazon. It measured a full thirty feet long, was as thick around as a man's chest, and was fed a pig every few weeks, which it swallowed without difficulty.

Not to compare myself to any sort of porcine, but it could do the same to me easily enough. Was that among the ways a vampire could die? Somehow I doubted it, and being trapped for however long in the stomach of a snake held no attraction.

My first instinct was to flee, but to where? The trail I had followed since coming to London had led me to this place. If I turned away now . . .

The snake stretched out toward me. Its entire body writhed and flexed. Again, its tongue flicked, coming very close to my face.

I had bested the hooded creatures, but I was unsure whether it was their strength or their resolve that had proven weaker than mine. Could I hope to defeat the snake? Did I dare try?

Even as I debated what to do, the door opened. The sudden rectangle of bright light stabbed my eyes. Two elegant gentlemen in evening dress emerged. They appeared young, pale skinned, and undeniably handsome. One was laughing at a sally offered by the other.

At sight of me, they stopped.

"Who is this?" the taller of the two asked his friend. The speaker's golden curls were artfully arranged around his noble brow. His eyes were startlingly blue and had the look of arctic ice. He tossed back his scarlet-lined cape and looked me over far too thoroughly.

"I don't believe I have had the pleasure," he drawled.

In my human days, I had enjoyed flirting. It was a game, nothing more, and the young men in my social circle understood that full well. But this was not that. They were both beyond the bounds of courtesy, standing too close, staring too frankly. An air of intimidation—or at least an attempt at it—hung over the encounter, reinforced when my interlocutor flashed a smile that revealed his bared fangs.

Excitement rippled through me. I had succeeded in finding others of my kind—vampires, as Stoker had called them. Yet they seemed too callow and foolish to be able to provide me with the information that I sought.

Tartly, I said, "How unfortunate that there is no one to introduce us." I made to go around him before the door could swing shut.

The other moved to block my way. Dark haired, he put me in mind of a young, smoldering Heathcliff and reminded me once again why I had never enjoyed *Wuthering Heights*.

"You're new here, aren't you?" he said. "Who is your patron?"

Lacking any idea what he meant, I could not answer. I glanced over my shoulder to discover that his companion was also closing in, blocking my retreat. Darting forward, I tried again to reach the door. A hard hand closed on my arm.

"Who is your patron?" the taller one demanded, tightening his grip. "And where is he?"

Whatever I said, I was certain to be wrong. Moreover, whatever the consequence of being without a patron might be, I suspected that I would not enjoy discovering it.

Caught between them, I recoiled in disgust when together

they began to run their hands over my person, along my arms, across my breasts, coming ever closer to my throat.

"She's rather pretty, don't you think?" the golden one said.

The other laughed. "Not in whatever this is that she's wearing. Get it off her and she might do."

Fury swept over me. I yanked my arm free and was about to lash out at them when a spine-chilling howl tore through the air. At once, the assailants froze. At the far end of the passage, near the griffin statue, the alpha wolf stood, his head thrown back in stark defiance. Before the echo of his challenge faded, I was released. The wolf turned and vanished into the darkness.

Roaring in rage, both vampires made to give chase only to stop abruptly when another figure stepped from the shadows near the passage.

Before I saw him properly, I felt the heat of his skin, heard the steady beat of his heart, smelled the copper aroma of his blood, but tasted, too, the iron tang lingering just beneath, warning of his strength.

Human then, but unlike any I had ever encountered. If I had still possessed breath, it would have left me in a rush. Strictly speaking, he was not classically handsome in the manner of the singer from the opera house who possessed my dreams. This one's features were too broad and strong boned for that, his sun-kissed skin taut with no hint of softness. He was taller than I, even in my new incarnation, and wide shouldered, with thick brown hair shot through with silver and brushed back from a high forehead. His dark bespoke suit announced his familiarity with the tailors of Savile Row, but the civilizing veneer could not disguise his raw vitality. He was quite simply . . . magnificent.

And yet he was also strangely familiar. We had met before, this paragon of manly virtues, but where? When? I searched my memory, fragmentary as it was when it came to recalling my human experiences. A ballroom . . . an unseasonably warm spring night . . . tall windows opening onto a balcony and me . . . walking alone under a swollen moon. Until a murmur of voices across the width of the lawn betrayed two . . . men? The one hidden in shadows so that I could scarcely see him but the other unmistakably the man who stood before me now.

What was it I heard him say? "You know I can't let you near her."

Was that it? I really couldn't remember, but I had no such problem recalling what happened next. The one in the shadows sketched a faint bow and was gone. The other walked back toward the house, stopping when he saw me.

"Miss Weston," he said. "How nice to meet you. My name is Marco di Orsini."

The memory of his voice returned me to the present reality. My attention was drawn to the heavy gold chain around his neck. Suspended from it was a large red stone that glowed even in the faint light as though it possessed an inner source of energy. The effect was gaudy and out of keeping with anything a gentleman would normally wear. But it also had a barbaric splendor that made it quite riveting.

With a mocking salute to the two who had been giving me difficulty, Marco di Orsini said, "Nothing else to do this evening but chase wolves and importune young women?" His voice was deep and strong, the sound sending a startling ripple of pleasure through me.

"I can offer you better occupation." With a flick of his hand, he slashed his walking stick through the air.

I froze, certain that it concealed a blade he was about to reveal. In the same instant, I thought how extraordinary it was that a human would challenge two vampires. But what sort of human? He was unfazed by the presence of wolves roaming the streets of London at night. He had made his way to the entrance of the Bagatelle, where nothing he saw appeared to surprise him. To the contrary, he seemed completely at ease as he confronted the scurrilous pair. Stoker had at least possessed the sense to be afraid of me. This man seemed to fear nothing.

"She has no patron and she is here," the golden one said petulantly even as he backed away. "That makes her fair game. You have no right to—"

Again, the walking stick flashed. "She is one of you, you idiot. If you spent less time pickling what passes for your brain in the stews of Southwark, you might have realized that."

"She isn't—" the other began, only to stop abruptly as he stared at me. "That is . . . we didn't realize . . ."

The golden-haired one was frowning, no doubt wondering how they could possibly have made such a mistake. Shoving his companion, he said, "Let's go."

They fled down the passage and were quickly lost to sight.

"No harm done, I hope?" my rescuer inquired when they had gone. He did not come closer to me but remained where he was, affording me the chance to depart as well. Yet his gaze remained as intent as that of a hunter on his skittish prey who might break cover and flee at any moment.

Truly, my imagination was running wild.

"No harm at all, but thank you nonetheless, Mr. di Orsini."

Had I not been watching him closely, I would have missed the look of surprise that flitted across his face. As swiftly as it appeared, it vanished behind his pose of imperturbable politesse. Truly, he did not show his emotions lightly, assuming that he possessed them in any abundance.

This challenger of vampires might have the most noble intentions, but if I had learned anything of the strange world in which I now found myself, it was that nothing was quite as it seemed. Reality was far more complex and intriguing than I had ever suspected.

"You recognize me. I wasn't sure that you would, Miss Weston. We have met before."

"Under very different circumstances, I presume," I said. I had to pick my way carefully through the fog of memory, but I was certain of one thing. "Surely you are aware that the Lucy Weston you knew is said to have died under bizarre circumstances. But that is only fiction, isn't it?"

"I think you know better."

Abruptly the little dance of feint and parry in which we had been engaged ended. He knew who—and what—I was. About him, I was far less certain.

"As apparently do you," I said. *How* he knew was another matter. Was his presence in front of the Bagatelle at the same time as myself a coincidence or something more? Was he merely aware of Stoker's deception or had he had a hand in bringing it about? Who precisely was Marco di Orsini and how had he acquired the power that he appeared to have over vampires?

"What happened in Whitby," I said, "—what *really* happened—should be repellant to all human sensibility. Yet *Dracula* trivializes those events as no more than vicarious entertainment for the gullible public."

He shrugged. "Tragic events that afflict someone else— whether fictional or otherwise—tend to be a source of enjoyment, whether we wish to admit it or not. They prompt a pleasant frisson of relief. One's own friend or relation—or oneself—has been spared . . . this time. The shadow of death has passed over, the sun is out again. People step over tragedy and go on with their lives, as they must if our society is to continue to function."

"Whereas if they knew the truth about the dark powers among us, they would . . . what?" I said, thinking of what Stoker had told me. "Panic? Run amok? Demand explanations that those in charge do not wish to give?"

He shrugged. "All that and likely more. Tell me, Miss Weston, what brings you here?"

As he declined to answer my question, I saw no reason to answer his. Instead, I posed another. "Shouldn't I be asking you that? This is a haunt of vampires, I am told. No sensible human should come anywhere near it. So why have you?"

I did not go so far as to ask how he had managed to run off two vampires who should have been at his throat. But my gaze drifted pointedly to the pendant glowing against his chest, just above his heart.

Far from being nonplused, Marco di Orsini took my observation in stride. "You have unmasked me, Miss Weston. Clearly, I shall have to be on my guard around you."

I frowned. "What do you mean—?"

"No one has ever accused me of being sensible. But I assure you, I am not altogether lacking in other useful attributes, as I hope you will discover."

"You presume we are to be acquainted . . . again." The arch of my brow signified my extreme skepticism that any such association between us was likely.

He refused to be discouraged. "Let us say that I hope we

will become friends, and based on that I presume to dispense a small bit of advice. The Bagatelle is undeniably popular, but it is not to everyone's taste. Humans come here hoping to be chosen for transformation into vampires. You were mistakenly taken for such a supplicant."

I could not conceal my shock. "They actually want such a thing?"

"Indeed, some do. Should I gather from your response that you did not?"

He was studying me far too closely for comfort. Rather than reveal so much of myself to him, I ignored his question and said, "I have been warned already that it isn't an ingénue ball."

He took my reticence with good grace, replying, "You've met Little Alice, I take it."

What else did he know, this human who walked with apparent ease in the netherworld of hidden London?

Not taking my eyes from him, I said, "And paid a penny for the privilege."

"Wise of you. She's not what she used to be, but she still isn't one to cross."

"Neither am I, Mr. di Orsini. I have my own reasons for being here and I will not be dissuaded from them."

A flash of surprise darted behind his eyes and was quickly gone, but not before I had the satisfaction of knowing that I was not entirely what he had expected.

"I assure you, Miss Weston, that was never my intention."

He bowed and, with a slight flourish, stepped out of my way.

I proceeded quickly, before I could think better of it.

Above the door, the snake hissed.

CHAPTER 4

I stepped over the threshold of the Bagatelle to find myself in a dazzling salon. The walls were covered with trompe l'oeil paintings depicting beautiful gardens bathed in moonlight, populated with frisky nymphs and satyrs. Finely woven Persian rugs lay over the floors. Hundreds of slender white candles burned in crystal and gold chandeliers suspended from the high ceilings. Porcelain vases so thin as to be translucent were filled with rare lilies and orchids that released a heady perfume into the room. The furniture was inlaid wood, marble, and gilt in the lavish Louis Quinze style. But all that was as nothing compared to the splendor of the room's occupants. Male and female alike, they were all seemingly young, exquisitely dressed and jeweled, and beautiful beyond compare.

Few paid me any heed, occupied as they were with one another. I passed through the first room into the chamber that lay beyond. It was larger and incredibly even more glorious. With my family I had strolled through the Sun King's creation at Versailles, visited the magnificent Hermitage in Saint Petersburg, and marveled at the Sistine Chapel, but never had I encountered so much beauty in a single setting. So dazzled was I that some time elapsed before I realized that among the gloriously garbed vampires there were humans, men and women both.

I consider myself far from a prude, but their appearance was startling in the extreme. Both sexes were scantily clad, often with no more than a small triangle of cloth to preserve the illusion of modesty. Some of these humans were elaborately tattooed with intricate designs that flowed down their bare torsos and thighs, and around to their backs. They wore heavy gold bands covered with intricate carvings at their wrists and ankles. Bejeweled collars encircled their necks. Trailing behind the vampires, who drew them along on leashes, they kept their eyes lowered submissively.

As I watched with mingled shock and fascination, a female vampire of surpassing beauty beckoned her human with a crooked finger and a smile that displayed her fangs. He came eagerly. Together, they slipped onto a low couch. Her long nails, lacquered a brilliant red, trailed along his supple chest, tracing the pattern of his tattoos. Their limbs entwined. The human moaned and fell back, his throat bared. As she sank her fangs into him, his back arched in ecstasy. Watching the trickle of his blood that escaped her sucking, I felt as a voyeur would, intruding upon an act of the greatest intimacy. Yet I could not bring myself to look away. Hunger raged in me, for sustenance, for power, for pleasure. All this could be mine if only I embraced my fate.

My clothes were suddenly far too constricting. I longed to cast them off for the glorious garb of the female vampires, their silks and satins in the most vivid hues, the bright plumes in their hair, the jewels that adorned their necks and limbs. Yes, I was tempted. I wanted all that and so much more. I looked again at the pair on the couch. The female had released her grip on the young man. With the tip of her tongue, she licked the excess of his blood from her lips and murmured a word to him. At once, he slipped from the couch and knelt before her, kissing her hands in obeisance. Watching them, I was at once fascinated and repelled.

Humans were being bled all around the room, seemingly to their delight. Others were being displayed like trophies, while here and there they were being traded. I watched as a lovely flame-haired girl was handed over from one vampire to another in return for several gems. She went eagerly and was soon stretched out on a couch with her new patron.

The scene was both shocking and confusing. A single encounter with the luminous being on the moor had been sufficient to change me utterly. Yet here it seemed that humans could be fed upon repeatedly while remaining human. I could not begin to understand why my own transformation had proceeded so swiftly unless it meant that the being I had encountered was different in some way from other vampires.

Even as I puzzled over the matter, I became aware that I was being watched. A tall, slender male in a burgundy velvet lounging suit was leaning up against a nearby column. He had a long face framed by waves of dark hair that flirted with his shoulders. His mouth was full and soft but it was his eyes that struck me most, appearing both keen and sympathetic. He reminded me of a young Oscar Wilde, the writer who had been released from prison only the month before, having served his sentence for crimes of an intimate nature that proper young ladies such as I had been were not supposed to know anything about.

"First time here?" the young man in velvet asked with an amused glance at the valise I clutched.

I had come to meet others of my kind, yet confronted directly by one of them, I had to fight the impulse to flee. Cautiously, I replied, "Yes, it is."

He straightened and held out a hand. I could not fault his manner; he touched only my fingers as he bowed graciously. "I am Felix Deschamps and you are—?"

I hesitated, uncertain whether or not to reveal my real identity. I had no idea how the vampires would react to my arrival in their midst. Would they accept me as one of their own or would they view me as an interloper? Upon my ability to gain their confidence rested what hope I had of finding *him*.

When the silence had dragged on long enough to provoke a questioning look from my new acquaintance, I said, "My name is Lucy Weston."

Felix released my hand and took a step back but continued to stare at me intently. A single raised brow was enough to tell me that he recognized my name. However much Bram Stoker and his "intermediaries" had succeeded in fooling the human public, they had managed no such subterfuge among the vampires.

"By any chance, are you acquainted with a human named Bram Stoker?" he asked. When I did not reply at once, he went on, "Irish fellow, manages the Lyceum Theatre, dabbles in writing. I haven't read his novel myself; not to my taste. But we've all been speculating as to how he learned enough about us to write such a strange mélange of accurate details mingled with the most absurd, exaggerated notions. You wouldn't know who or what informed him, would you?"

"If you are asking whether it was me, no. But I do know that whoever gave him that knowledge wants what happened to me concealed. Hence the decision to present it as fiction."

"Interesting. . . . So what brings you to the Bagatelle, Miss Weston?"

Before I could respond, a cry of mingled delight and anguish interrupted us. We both looked toward the alcove where a large male vampire who had just fed was rising from a couch on which a nearly naked young woman lay. Her head was thrown back in an spasm of pleasure even as blood gushed from the gaping gash in her throat.

The couch under the woman was rapidly becoming soaked. She was clearly bleeding to death. I knew this yet I could rouse no feeling for her at all. She was merely a curiosity. I understood full well that I *should* care. Indeed, the Lucy I had been, whose ghost seemed to haunt me, was filled with horror at my callousness. Nonetheless, someone had to act and very quickly or the young woman had only minutes to live.

Suddenly several hooded figures identical to those I had encountered outside the Lyceum appeared. At once, I stiffened, readying myself to fight once again.

"Is something wrong?" Felix asked.

"Those . . ." I gestured toward the figures, who were clustering around the woman on the couch. "Those things, they—"

"They're thralls, servants of a sort. They'll take care of her." Mistaking the source of my concern, he added, "Thralls are unpleasant to look at, I know, but they're useful. She'll be fine, and in the end, she'll get what she wants."

I heard him clearly enough but kept my guard up all the same. "What do you mean, what she wants?"

He appeared surprised that I did not know. "To become one of us, of course. It's what all the supplicants want. That's why they're here."

Despite my own experience, I had not fully grasped the

process by which a human was transformed into a vampire. Now as understanding dawned, I said, "The humans submit themselves to be fed on so that they can become vampires?"

"Why else would they? There was a time when we hunted humans, but only with great restrictions. We knew hunger then, but not any longer. All that is passed now. With the promise of what we can offer, we have more candidates than we need to amply sustain ourselves."

"What brought about such a great change?"

He waved a hand dismissively. "Therein hangs a tale, but it will have to wait. You were about to tell me what brings you here."

"I am seeking the one who transformed me."

It occurred to me that as Felix knew my true identity, he might also know the being responsible for my state. But instead of revealing it, he shot me a look of surprise that was less than credible. I had to conclude that whatever he knew, he was not willing to share it, at least not right then.

"How odd that he is not with you," Felix said. "That is not at all how things are done."

"I can't speak to that. I only know that I would like to find him."

The hooded figures were carrying the woman away. They had stopped her bleeding. She was unconscious but breathing, as she would until the moment when she passed from life into . . . whatever the strange state was that I found myself in. Not alive, not dead, yet not in any sort of limbo either. In truth, I had never experienced existence so keenly. All my senses were exquisitely alert. I was aware of every sight, sound, smell, and movement around me, but above all, I felt the one who had created me in my new form, calling to me.

"Not to worry," Felix said. "Your incarnator is bound to show up here eventually. Everyone comes to the Bagatelle."

I remembered Marco di Orsini's remark concerning the club but did not speak of it. Felix seemed inclined to befriend me; I would be as foolish not to take advantage of that as I would be to trust him.

"Have you met any of us yet?" he asked.

"You are the first."

He made a little bow and smiled. "I am honored and I bring good tidings. Lady Blanche would like you to join her for a little tête-à-tête. "

"Lady Blanche?"

My ignorance earned a chiding glance. "Our proprietress. She doesn't extend herself to newcomers as a rule. You should be flattered."

So I might have been if it hadn't occurred to me just then that the proprietress of the Bagatelle might have sent the hooded figures to the Lyceum Theatre. If so, she would be pleased that after eluding them initially, I had walked directly into her lair.

Swallowing my concerns, I found a smile. "I would be delighted to meet her."

Felix offered his arm. We proceeded toward a set of curving steps at the far back of the room. He gestured for me to go first. Gingerly, not knowing what I was about to encounter, I began my descent into the lower reaches of the Bagatelle.

CHAPTER 5

So close to the Thames, I expected the air to be damp, but it was instead dry and pleasantly scented with fresh herbs. The stairs came out into a wide gallery, the stone walls of which were covered with worn but still beautiful tapestries visible in the light of gas lamps set in sconces. Felix and I walked a little way before coming to a wooden door studded with iron. He pressed the latch down and stood aside for me to enter.

The chamber I found myself in was less gaudy than the rooms above, yet it lacked nothing in luxury or elegance. More tapestries lined the walls, depicting medieval lords and ladies at the hunt. Iron braziers set on tripods gave ample light. In the center of the room, seated in a thronelike chair, was a woman of unparalleled beauty. Her hair, the silvered hue of moonlight, tumbled down her back. Unlike the female vampires in the club who seemed to vie with one another in the brightness of their array, she was garbed all in white. A magnificent rope of pearls encircled her lovely neck and looped to below her waist.

She appeared to be studying a ledger on the table before her but looked up as we entered. "Ah, Felix, you found her."

Her voice was pleasant, soft and melodious. The sort of voice that drew the listener to it.

"I did indeed." Taking me by the arm, he guided me forward. "Lady Blanche, may I present Miss Lucy Weston."

A perfectly arched eyebrow rose. "Lucy Weston? How extraordinary. It is said that everyone comes to the Bagatelle but I never expected a fictional character to walk in the door."

"Clearly, I am not—"

She cut me off with a languid wave of her bejeweled arm. "Of course you aren't, my dear. I said from the moment that awful book came out that Stoker was up to no good. I did say that, didn't I, Felix?"

"Repeatedly, my lady and, as usual, you were absolutely right."

Without taking her eyes from me, she continued to address him. "Darling, leave us alone for a bit, will you? Oh, and tell Chef to send in a plate of nibbles and a bottle of the Veuve Cliquot '86, would you?"

He bowed, cast me a final look, and departed.

"Sit down," Lady Blanche invited, waving me into a chair opposite her. "Please believe that I mean it kindly when I say that you appear rather done in."

She, on the other hand, looked exquisite. The more I gazed at her, the more I was struck by her luminous beauty. Like the pearls she wore, light seemed to glow from inside her. I had never seen a more breathtaking woman.

Lady Blanche smiled as though she guessed my thoughts. "It's been a very long time, but I still remember how confusing things can be in the beginning."

How old was she? I would have guessed no more than thirty but for her eyes. In their depths, the wisdom of centuries seemed to lurk.

"Is that how I appear, confused?"

She shrugged. "You appear to be alone, and that is, to say the least, highly unusual. Frankly, it's enough to raise concern. How long have you been . . . as you are?"

"A few months."

"And you've been on your own all that time?" She looked genuinely appalled.

I nodded. "I'm trying to find the one who . . ." I hesitated, uncertain how much I was prepared to reveal. Clearly, I would have to explain what had happened to me, as best I was able to recollect it, if I were to have any hope of finding *him*.

"The one who transformed you? Yes, I imagine you would want to find him. It's really quite extraordinary that he left you to your own devices."

"Is that not how it is usually done?"

"Certainly not. In fact, I don't believe that I have ever heard of it happening before. But we can hash all that out later. How fortunate that you found us."

A snake, much smaller than the one earlier on the door, slithered across the desk and twined itself around her wrist. She stroked it absently while keeping her attention firmly on me.

"Yes," I said, trying not to stare at the snake. "Fortunate indeed."

She studied me in silence for several moments. I was about to squirm under her scrutiny when a knock at the door saved me. A white-jacketed chef, who but for the extreme pallor of his complexion could have stepped from the kitchens of London's finest restaurant, appeared. Bowing, he placed a gold platter before Lady Blanche and removed the lid. She nodded her approval.

With an expert hand, he uncorked the champagne and filled a pair of tulip-shaped glasses. Leaving the bottle in its gold ice bucket, he bowed again and, with the merest glance at me, took his leave.

When he was gone, Lady Blanche said, "I stole him from a French baron he'd been with forever. Everyone says he's a genius." She nudged the platter toward me. "Tell me what you think."

The hunger I had fought since leaving Whitby was becoming more than I could bear. With my hands clenched in my lap, I stared at what the chef had brought.

"That is fresh stag heart," Lady Blanche said. "And that . . . let me see . . . that is the heart of a swan. Both are still warm, of course."

When I hesitated, she placed the stag heart on a small plate. "I always think this tastes of the deep forest and rushing water. Do you agree?"

I succumbed. The scent of the stag blood was sweet and thick. Already, I could almost taste it. Forgetting myself entirely, I seized the heart and bit clear through it. Blood spurted into my mouth. I groaned in delight. At once, I felt intense relief followed by a desperate need for more. Heedless of my manners, I devoured the stag's heart greedily, not pausing until it was entirely gone. Only then did I look down at myself in dismay. Blood stained my hands and I could feel it around and in my mouth. In the next instant, I all but gagged.

"Drink," Lady Blanche ordered and pressed one of the crystal tulips on me.

I took it and drank the contents in a single swallow. The cloying taste of blood eased, but only a little.

Refilling my glass, she said, "Should I take it that you have had some difficulty feeding?"

There seemed no point in attempting to conceal a truth she could learn easily enough. "I cannot feed on humans. I want to . . . I just can't actually do it."

She sipped a little champagne and said, "That's because you haven't been brought along properly. My first time was . . . messy."

I scarcely heard her. All my attention was on the swan's heart still lying on the platter.

"Please," Lady Blanche said and urged it on me.

I ate with marginally more decorum. When I was done, I cleaned my hands on the linen napkin she handed me and drank more of the champagne she poured.

"It is good to indulge in this sort of thing occasionally," Lady Blanche said. "But you still must have a proper diet. After all, there is hardly any point in living forever if one doesn't stay in good health, is there?"

Whether from the nourishment I had devoured or the champagne—or perhaps both—my head was swimming. I stared at her. "Living forever?"

She shook her head in dismay. "Did he tell you nothing, whoever he is? The cad! The villain! Be assured that I will hold him to account for his shameful behavior. But yes, theoretically, we live forever. Not that there aren't ways that our existences can be ended, but fortunately they are rare."

It was on the tip of my tongue to ask her what those ways might be, if only for my own use. But before I could do so, Lady Blanche asked, "Do you have a place to stay?"

I shook my head. "I have only just arrived in London."

"It will be morning soon. You do understand about sunlight, don't you?"

"Yes . . . of course . . ." In fact, I did not understand it at all. Since my emergence from the grave, I had been in sunlight often and had suffered no ill effects from it. But I thought it ill-advised to say so lest I raise suspicions about my true nature.

"Only the strongest of us can risk exposure," Lady Blanche continued, "and then only on a very limited basis. You will have to avoid it entirely until you are a good deal older and more experienced. For now, I think it best that you stay here."

Given that I had nowhere else to go, I said, "You are very kind."

She finished her champagne and smiled. "It is agreed then." She rang a small gold bell. Felix reappeared so quickly that I had to assume he had been listening at the door.

"Lucy has been so good as to agree to stay with us," Lady Blanche told him. "Do see that she is properly comfortable."

He inclined his head. "Of course, my lady."

I rose to go, not entirely certain as to the wisdom of my actions but convinced that I had no better choice.

"Have a good rest," Lady Blanche said. She gave me a long, level look before returning her attention to the papers on her desk.

"After you," Felix said and drew me away, back through the iron-studded door and down through the hall where long-dead lords and ladies gazed at us sorrowfully and unicorns shed tears of blood.

CHAPTER 6

Felix led me to an elegantly appointed chamber not far from the one where I had met with Lady Blanche. There I found not a bed but a platform draped in black, without pillow, mattress, or covers. Having removed my outer clothing, I hesitated before lying down. The bier proved surprisingly comfortable, but despite my fatigue and the relief from hunger that feeding had given me, I was wakeful.

Memories of my human existence glittered like rare gems in the darkness of my mind.

The boat train from Dover to Calais, my parents sitting close together in the first-class compartment we shared, recalling their journey along the same route years before when they had spent their honeymoon in France.

Amanda and I giggling as we strapped on skis, the pair of us greatly amused by the blandishments of a handsome Swiss instructor. Huddling afterward in front of a roaring fire in the chalet, sipping cocoa with our heads close together, laughing at our own antics.

How lovely it was to feel warm. Or so I imagined, for even the memory of what that was like had slipped away. Already it was beyond my reach.

At last my lids grew heavier, and I saw myself once again on the moors at Whitby. In my dream it was night, but a full moon rode high in the sky, illuminating a stark landscape devoid of all color. Sharp-edged shadows loomed on all sides. I could hear the distant roar of the waves coming ashore. The tang of salt lingered on the wind.

Behind me was the high brick house that was my father's pride, standing as it did in its own parkland and signifying how far he had climbed from his humbler origins. The night was cold and damp. Nonetheless, I felt compelled to wander out into the darkness, past the wrought iron gate and the road beyond until I came to the narrow track leading along the moors toward the sea. I followed it with no thought as to where it might lead until, suddenly, I was no longer alone. No murmur of sound, no flicker of movement heralded the luminous being's presence, but I sensed him all the same. Elation filled me. Without pausing to think, I held out my arms to him.

The night tilted around me. An owl screeched. I saw his face, imprinted forever in my memory. Powerful, brilliant, the ruler of the night. His beautiful mouth shaped my name, "Lucy." At the very last, I thought I heard faintly, a murmur only, "Forgive me."

Ecstasy and pain . . . the flash of fangs and then . . . terror and the womb of the grave holding me until he came again and I was reborn into the world.

Surely it must all be a fantasy of my own dark imagining? Yet as I drifted deeper into sleep, ravens cawed and wolves howled, vampires showed their fangs and humans bared their throats to be bled while off in the distance great engines roared and steam shot into the sky where soot fell as tears, baptizing the new age.

Through it all *he* sang of love and the triumph over death, but when I glanced away from the stage, I was startled to find that I was not alone in the velvet-lined box. Marco di Orsini shared the dream with me. In the darkness, the glowing red pendant burned as though lit by inner fire.

I woke a few hours later alone and with the sense of being summoned stronger than ever. I had to find the one who had transformed me before his song was done. If I did not . . . The mere thought of failure sent a wave of nausea through me. I had the sudden uncanny sensation that I stood on the edge of an abyss into which I and everyone else might plunge at any moment.

Spurred on by so unsettling a thought, I made as good a toilette as I could manage. My valise held a few basic changes of clothes and other necessities, enough for several days. Beyond that I could not think.

I donned a fresh chemise and shirtwaist, smoothed the wrinkles from my skirt and jacket as best as I could, and rearranged my hair before ascending the circular stairs to the club.

As I had hoped, no one else was about. The debris of the previous night had been cleared away and quiet hung over all. Beneath the door leading outside, I saw a crack of daylight.

Without hesitation, I put a hand on the door, pushed it open, and stepped outside. A quick glance was enough to determine that the snake was not in evidence, nor was the amber light lit. Instead, I looked out on a seemingly ordinary scene in everyday London.

The ever-present band of coal smoke hung above the rooftops, but here and there patches of blue could be glimpsed. The stench of the tidal flats along the Thames was greatly diminished, a certain indicator that the river was running high.

But the aromas of manure and diesel fuel made for a nasty mélange on the back of the tongue.

Although I was mercifully free of any need to breathe in
the acrid air, I could not avoid tasting it. Peering down the
passage, I saw vehicles of all sorts thronging Fleet Street. As I
watched, the liveried driver of a large black automobile bearing the crest of the Cabinet Office shook a fist at a recalcitrant
lorryman who refused to give way. Almost at once, Watchers
appeared, surrounding the lorry and clearing a route for the
government worthy concealed behind darkly tinted glass. Pe-
destrians were forced to scamper out of the road as the vehicle
sped off.

A spindle-thin paperboy shouted the morning's news.
"Subversives bill passes Commons! Anarchists to be held without trial!"

The subject seemed to be of great interest. Men and a few
women clustered around, thrusting money into the hands of
the grinning boy as they snatched up newspapers. Quite a few
walked only a short distance away before stopping to read. As
they did, I noted that some appeared well satisfied, nodding
emphatically as they absorbed what their elected representa-
tives in their collective wisdom had chosen to do. But many
others were frowning, shaking their heads, and hurrying away
with grave expressions.

My father had believed that the natural state for Britons
was one of freedom founded on the twin pillars of the Magna
Carta and the common law, which he regarded as England's
gifts to the world. I had to wonder if he still felt that way,
wherever he was.

The morning sun was pleasantly warm on my face; I felt a
temptation to linger outside the Bagatelle, but I told myself

that I should use what time I had before the other vampires awoke to go back and search the club. With luck, I might discover a clue to the whereabouts of the one who had transformed me. At the very least, I would gain a better understanding of the strange beings among whom I found myself.

I was about to return inside when a flicker of motion nearby stopped me. A man was leaning against the passage wall near the entrance to the club. He looked up from the newspaper he had been reading.

"Miss Weston," Marco di Orsini said. "What a surprise."

He had exchanged his evening dress for the elegant apparel of a gentleman of business, but he still wore the glowing red pendant. I could not help but notice that he looked every bit as formidable and compelling by daylight as he had in darkness.

My unwonted awareness of him put a tart edge on my tongue. "Have you nowhere else to be, Mr. di Orsini?"

Far from being put off, he looked amused. "I thought I'd make sure you were all right."

"While everyone was asleep?" I asked. The notion of him looking in on me as I lay unaware on the bier was disquieting, to say the least, yet I did not doubt that he was capable of doing just that. A human who could confront vampires when they were fully awake and eager for blood certainly would not hesitate to do so when they were asleep and unaware.

"Not everyone apparently. You're up and about. I hope you had a peaceful rest?"

"Peaceful enough." I made to go around him. "Now if you will excuse me . . ."

He shifted away from the wall just enough to block my path. "The sunlight doesn't trouble you?"

I recalled what Lady Blanche had said about the perils of exposure to full light and hesitated. "As you can see, I am well covered."

My assurances did not convince him. He came closer and studied me intently. I drew back as he reached out a hand but not before I felt the light stroke of his fingers along the curve of my cheek.

The effect was electrifying. Apart from my struggles with the thralls and with Stoker, no one had touched me since that night on the moors when *he* had transformed me. Until that moment, I had not realized how much I missed such simple human contact. Surely that, rather than any quality unique to the man himself, explained the deep, undulating pleasure that rippled through me.

"Your skin is cool," he remarked. I drew some satisfaction from the fact that his voice was not as steady as he no doubt wished. Imperturbable though he might look, Marco was not immune to the unexpected attraction between us.

"You are not breathing," he continued after a moment, "and if I move my fingers down just the slightest degree to the vicinity of your carotid artery, I dare say I will find no pulse. And yet—"

Abruptly, I regained control of myself. "And yet what?" I demanded, jerking away from him. More than his effrontery at touching me, I was alarmed by my own reaction. Pleasure still strummed within me, a siren song I was determined to resist.

"I am all too well aware of my state; you do not need to inform me of it."

He looked at me curiously. "Are you? Unless I am very much mistaken, you do not seem to have embraced it fully."

I remembered the supplicants vying to be fed upon for the

chance of receiving what had been given to me through no effort of my own. They both horrified and fascinated me.

"I did not ask for this existence . . . whatever this is. I am neither alive nor dead. I am trapped somewhere in between."

He nodded thoughtfully. "So you appear. No longer human, yet perhaps not entirely vampire. That would explain why you can tolerate exposure to the sun. And why those two last night didn't recognize you as one of them."

The thought that some human part of myself might still survive was more than I dared to hope. Before I could stop myself, I asked, "Do you really think that it is possible to be both human and vampire?"

"I would not have thought so . . . until now. I have never known vampires to exhibit lingering human traits or spare a moment's thought for their lost humanity. To the contrary, they delight in being rid of it."

"Is that so?" I could not hide my skepticism. My transformation engendered many emotions—shock, disbelief, curiosity, a certain animalistic exhilaration—but delight was yet to be among them.

"How could it not be?" Marco countered. "You are endowed with powers no mortal possesses. Your strength and speed are without equal. Your senses are stronger by far, allowing you to experience the world in a way no human ever will. You need never know illness and you need never age. Do all these attributes of your kind count for nothing with you?"

"The price is very high, some might even say that it is too high," I reminded him. When he appeared unconvinced of my regrets, I continued, "Right now, I can smell your blood. The scent is tantalizing . . . enrapturing. I have been tormented by hunger because I have refused to feed on humans, as I perversely yearn to do. But I have no idea how much longer I will be capable of such restraint."

My gaze drifted to the portion of his throat visible above his high collar, there where the life force pulsed. I swayed a little toward him. "Do you have any notion of how easily I could—"

Far from appearing concerned by my desires, Marco seemed much more interested in my unwillingness to act upon them. "You do not feed on humans?"

"The notion repels me, yet I yearn to do so."

As I spoke, my gaze was drawn to the glowing red pendant on his chest. Why did he wear it? How had he come by it? Did it play a part in his ability to confront vampires without fear?

I felt no danger in his presence, but perhaps that was due to my own ignorance, which I had to acknowledge was considerable. Apart from what I had gleaned from the mishmash of Mr. Stoker's lamentable novel and my brief contact with the vampires of the Bagatelle, I knew nothing of my own kind. By contrast, I remembered enough of what it had meant to be human to be keenly aware of all that I had lost.

"Does humanity really count so much with you?" he asked.

Before I could reply, he went on, "As we speak, the Greeks and Turks are killing each other. The Spanish and Americans are pounding their chests and baring their teeth at one another. As though all that weren't enough, there are rumblings that we have a second Boer War to look forward to in Africa before very long. None of that is unusual. Humanity has been in a state of perpetual war for centuries, if not longer. Is that something to be proud of?"

"Of course not," I said, "but there is much more to being human."

"Indeed? Look in the skies above you," he said. "With each passing day, we are under ever more surveillance for no better reason than that men live in fear and suspicions of one another. Our technology outstrips our ability to reason or even to care. Walk the shortest distance beyond the better areas of this city and you will find degradation and suffering that defy description. The inhumanity of man is also part of being human."

"You astonish me. I could almost believe that you would prefer to be something else yourself."

A look I could not decipher passed behind his eyes. After a moment, he said, "Perhaps that explains my fondness for occult studies."

"You have such a fondness?" That, at least, would explain why he was not shocked by me.

"I do, as does Mr. Bram Stoker." At the mention of the Irish author and playwright's name, I stiffened.

Marco ignored my reaction and said, "We are both members of an organization known as the Golden Dawn that is dedicated to exploring such matters. That is why Bram was charged with helping to conceal your fate."

So they were on a first-name basis—Stoker, who had sent me to the Bagatelle, and Marco, who had found me there. More than ever, I was convinced that Marco's appearances the previous night and again that morning could not be coincidence.

The most prudent course would be to walk away then and there. I would be far safer on my own, but I would also be no closer to finding the one I sought. What was it Stoker had said? *Ignorance is no fit state for anyone.* On that at least, the Irishman and I were in agreement.

"I can be of assistance to you," Marco said, as though he had sensed what was in my mind. "If you will allow me."

"And if I will not, what then?"

He hesitated but only for a moment. "It is your choice, of course. I will do nothing to hinder you. But if I am right about what is happening, we are—human and vampire alike—at great risk. Unless you and I cooperate, the outcome is likely to be grim for all concerned."

His urgency echoed my own and went a considerable way to persuading me. But one concern remained.

"You are asking me to trust you," I said, "when I have no idea who you are other than an associate of the man who played a key role in the conspiracy to conceal my fate."

Regret flitted across his face as he said, "Then may I suggest that we become better acquainted?"

The Lucy I was before my transformation would have been swayed by this man's quiet strength, the soothing timbre of his voice, and above all by the mixture of pleasure and anxiousness that his presence evoked. I was determined to ignore any such human considerations. Nor were they necessary, for the plain fact was that I had no good alternative.

Slowly, not taking my eyes from him, I nodded.

CHAPTER 7

Having left the environs of the Bagatelle, Marco and I proceeded to the headquarters of the Golden Dawn Society. Located in an elegant townhouse, the organization maintained an outward posture of discretion. The entrance, through double polished oak doors set with inlaid glass panels, was marked only by a simple plaque inscribed with the letters GDS. The ubiquitous eyes—magnifying periscope lenses ever more popular in government office buildings but beginning to make their appearance in private homes—were absent. Yet I could not help but sense that we were being spied on by means not immediately apparent.

At first glance, the interior appeared similar to those of the more exclusive gentlemen's clubs—Oriental rugs, crystal chandeliers, leather smoking chairs, and the like. I half expected an ancient butler to appear and remind us that ladies were not permitted. Instead, we were greeted by the aroma of burning sage and the pounding of drums accompanied by chanting.

"What on earth is that?" I asked. Vampire though I was, the occult was still very new to me.

Marco grimaced. "We have a bit of a demon problem at

present. It's being dealt with. Shall we go through to the library?"

We continued down a long, oak-paneled corridor lit by wall sconces set within inlaid glass shades that cast shadows in the shapes of runes across the ceiling. As we neared, double doors at the far end opened, and a tall, slim man emerged. Elegantly dressed, he had a full head of silver hair and a long, hawkish face. Seeing us, he stopped. His gaze flicked from Marco to me and back again as his nostrils flared.

My heightened senses captured a flood of impressions—the rigid set of his shoulders, the tightening of his mouth, the elevation of his heart rate, even the sudden alteration in his scent—a combination of musk and copper that I associated instinctively with violence.

Yet he inclined his head with apparent civility. "Di Orsini, nice to see you again. Keeping well, I hope?"

So smoothly that he scarcely seemed to move, Marco blocked me from the other man's view. With icy courtesy, he said, "I thought you were still in Berlin, de Vere."

"I've only just returned." Attempting to peer around his shoulder, with very limited success, he said, "I don't believe I've had the pleasure . . ."

Without stepping aside, Marco volunteered, "Miss Devinia Blanderkamp is assisting me in an inquiry."

"Indeed . . . ?"

"A bit urgent, I'm afraid. You understand."

Before de Vere could reply, Marco ushered me into the library and shut the doors behind us.

"What was that about?" I asked when we were alone.

His face tightened. For a moment, I glimpsed how very

daunting he could be when he was so inclined. The impression passed quickly enough but it lingered in my memory.

"I would prefer that Sebastian de Vere not be aware of your presence here," he said.

"Why? Is he a danger of some sort?"

"He is a renowned Darwinist and an expert on human cell structure."

"Surely that must be counted to his credit?"

"As it would be if that were all he is. De Vere is a member of the Golden Dawn because of his obsessive interest in all things occult and his connections to powerful people in the government. But he has skirted close to the wind on more than one occasion in matters regarding his research. Under no circumstances is he to be trusted."

His vehemence surprised me, but I gave it little thought except to be amused by the notion that he needed to protect me from the likes of Sebastian de Vere or, for that matter, anyone else. The library was large, stretching the full length of the building on the ground floor overlooking the garden. Despite its spaciousness, it was dominated by a larger-than-life-size portrait of a stern man with a long white beard and glittering eyes that hung directly opposite the doors, commanding the attention of all who entered. The personage wore a black velvet robe in the Elizabethan style, with a heavy silver chain of intricate design hung around his neck. Silver rings also adorned his fingers. Even the buttons of his robe and the subtle patterns of embroidery on it appeared crafted of the same metal.

"Dr. John Dee," Marco said when he saw the direction of my gaze. "Our sixteenth-century founder. He was a mathematician and astrologer, as well as a magus of rare talent."

"I've read about him, but I did not realize that his interest in the occult extended to founding a society for its study."

"A great many learned people of his time recognized the need for a better understanding of the unseen realm. Her Majesty, Queen Elizabeth, supported our founding. Indeed, she went so far as to generously endow the society."

I had long been fascinated by Elizabeth Tudor, whose ability to reign in her own right went against all the traditions of her age, but I had never suspected her involvement with anything as esoteric as the Golden Dawn.

Still gazing at the renowned magus, I said, "He favored silver."

Marco nodded. "Dee was morbidly afraid of vampires."

"He encountered them?" I had accepted that Lady Blanche was likely older than any human could be, but I had thought no further than that. Now, struck by the notion that vampires had been in England for centuries, I was taken aback. How had two species—humans and vampires—both so powerful in their own ways and so at odds with each other, managed to coexist for so long?

"Vampires have played a significant role in this realm," Marco said. "I think it would be helpful if you had some understanding of their—your history."

Impatience stirred in me. All I truly wanted was to find the singer and discover why he had done what he had to me. The need to do so was growing stronger with each passing moment. Even so, I had come to the Golden Dawn to learn. Schooling myself to patience, I said, "If you insist."

Marco drew a large, leather-bound volume from a nearby shelf and laid it on the table. "This is a history of the vampires in England as compiled by Queen Elizabeth's Dr. Dee over several decades of intensive research," he said. "Dee had access to"—he hesitated—"unusual sources of information, with the result that the work is very detailed and highly accurate."

I scarcely heard him, for by then my attention had been captured by the illustration on the first page of the dusty tome. With growing disbelief, I studied the drawing of a mighty warrior riding beneath banners emblazoned with the image of a bear and carrying a great sword beside which was penned the name *Excalibur*.

Slowly, I said, "That cannot possibly be—"

"Arturus Rex," Marco said. "The king who was and who shall be. At least that's what the legends say."

"What could King Arthur possibly have to do with vampires?" I demanded. Arthur was the very heart and soul of fantasy, the chivalrous knight seen through the kindly mists of vanished time. Even his death, tragic though it was portrayed, held within it the promise of redemption and rebirth. Darkness could not touch him. Could it?

Marco turned the page. Quietly, he said, "There is your answer, as recorded by one who saw all and had every reason to understand it only too well."

I bent closer and read what Dee had transcribed in his own hand but in another's words.

The vampires came into England when I was a child. Their leader was Damien, not a bad sort, kingly in his own way. The Christian priests spewed spittle at sight of them, so frightened were those men of God by what they called devil spawn. You would think they would have had sufficient faith in their own deity to be unworried, but no. The Druids took the vampires much more in stride, understanding as they did that the real danger came from the Saxons.

With the fading of Roman order, the way lay open for rapacious tribes to fall upon our fair isle. The old Anglo-Roman families—my father, King Arthur's being first among them—banded together and held off the invaders for a while, but the floodtide that washed up against Britain could not be long repulsed. We were overrun and in danger of extinction when King Arthur raised his banner. My royal father swore that he would do all that was needed to protect our families, our fields, and our hearths. He vowed to leave no measure untaken, no effort unfulfilled.

He lied.

When Damien proposed an alliance with his kind, King Arthur—under the influence of the Christian priests—refused it. In his arrogance, he said that he preferred to die, and have all his kingdom die with him, rather than make common cause with demons.

I was with the king's ward, Morgaine, in the great hall of Camlann when the High King announced his decision. In a fury, I challenged him, demanding to know by what right he could choose death for all of us. We quarreled bitterly. My royal father called me a faithless son and sent me from him. I went gladly, vowing that if he would not save us, it fell to me to do so.

Morgaine went after me. We stood just beyond the timber hall, the night filled with the scents of winter pine and smoke, the swollen moon so bright that I could see her as well as if by day. Better perhaps, for moonlight always became her well.

"I will go to Damien myself," I declared.

"No!" She cried out and made to grasp my arm. "You must not! We will find another way."

Later, I came to believe that her effort to stop me stemmed, at least in part, from her sense of what she was becoming. If the arrival of the vampires in England had not fully awakened her as a Slayer, the process had certainly begun. But by the time I discovered that, it was too late.

She followed me and we argued further, then made up on a bed of sweet moss beneath a sacred oak. I stole away before dawn and sought out Damien. My plan was to reach an accord with him, then gather a combined army of vampires and mortals to stand against the Saxons.

It almost worked. Morgaine, having followed me by some Druid means known only to her, burst in upon us. Although as a Slayer she yet lacked the power to kill Damien, she wounded him grievously. Well aware of what the coming of a Slayer meant to his kind and desperate to protect them, he passed his power to me before giving up his light.

What shall I say of the years that followed? Morgaine loved me still even as the hunger to kill me grew within her. I do not underestimate the battle she waged inwardly. Arthur continued to insist on fighting the Saxons alone, with little success. More and more, he turned to the Christian priests, who grew in power.

So, too, did the Saxons who benefited from the conflict between the vampires and the Britons. Ultimately, Morgaine succumbed to the force within her. She attacked my kind with wanton abandon, finally becoming strong enough, she thought, to challenge me.

Against all evidence, driven by my love for her, I let myself believe that if I could only put a stop to my father's bloody folly, I could keep both my kingdom and my beloved safe for all time. I truly did not want to kill my father, but urged on by his priests, he had no such reluctance regarding me. In the end, I had no choice.

Arthur fell and Morgaine came against me. The rest is too dark and tragic to dwell upon. I will say only that she and I both left the field of battle sorely wounded. I survived; my beloved did not.

The entry concluded with Dee's own words:

Thus did he whom I fear above all the rest explain the coming of his kind and the terrible bargain he made for what he claimed was his love of this realm, even beyond his love for she who sought to defend it against him and everything he represented. Twisted and dark are the ways of such love, and bitter its fruit.

Startled and uncertain of what to believe, I looked up. Marco was standing very close. Over the ancient book, his gaze met mine. For the first time, I saw that his eyes were a tawny shade of gold I had never seen before. Heat poured from him, intense, vital heat so powerful that it seemed to push against the coldness filling me, even to the point of threatening to crack the ice around what had been my heart. For a moment, the world seemed to tilt and shift, and I with it. Barriers slipped away and I was at once who I had become and who I had been, both parts of myself existing at the same time. But that was impossible. Surely no one could be both human and a vampire. And yet for that breath out of time, the contradiction evaporated like rain striking a fiery surface, rising as mist to hang briefly in the air before vanishing altogether.

In a room nearby, someone coughed, perhaps the effect of too much sage smoke. The world righted itself. Time moved on and we with it. With a great effort of will, I dragged my attention back to the vital matters at hand.

CHAPTER 8

King Arthur himself is a legend," I said. "We cannot know whether he really lived or not. But even if he did, to think that vampires could have played such a role in our history . . ." Confusion filled me. Was such a thing remotely possible?

"Dee's research was impeccable," Marco said. "And nothing we have learned in the centuries since suggests that he was wrong."

I looked down again at the book. "Whoever is speaking here . . . he names himself King Arthur's son. In the legends, he is called Mordred. Is that who this is about?"

"So it seems."

"And you believe this? That King Arthur's son became a vampire in order to protect England?" As extraordinary as that sounded, upon reflection I had to admit that it might not be so unthinkable after all. I had seen for myself the powers a vampire could possess. Against human foes, this Mordred would have been formidable indeed.

"I know of no reason to doubt it. The evidence in the centuries since supports Dee's account of what happened and why."

I looked down at the passage I had just read, trying to understand all that it revealed. After my initial shock, I felt as though I was peering into a hidden yet fascinating version of history that cast an entirely new light on much that was happening in the present day. Yet it all seemed to have begun in darkness and deceit.

"He speaks of Morgaine as though she was his lover, but I thought—"

"That she was Arthur's half sister?" Marco asked. "Who laid with the king by trickery and bore Mordred as a result?"

Well-brought-up young ladies are not supposed to know of such things and gentlemen are not supposed to speak of them. Apparently, Marco and I were beyond any such restrictions.

"That was my understanding," I said.

"The present British government is not the first to engage in such deliberate subterfuge. Morgaine was the daughter of one of King Arthur's high lords. When that man died, Arthur made her his ward. That is how she and Mordred came to know one another. Who they all were and what happened to them has been concealed behind a mask of lies."

As my own fate was being concealed, with Bram Stoker's able assistance and to his considerable financial benefit, I could not afford to forget that any more than I could forget that he and Marco were members of the same society with presumably the same shared aims.

"What is your part in this?" I asked.

"To do as Dr. Dee did," Marco said without hesitation. "He called on us to open our minds to the world as it really is, to see what is to be seen regardless of our personal desires or fears. He enjoined us to serve the greater good, no matter how difficult that may be."

"How noble," I murmured. Of course, any such sentiment depended on general agreement as to what constituted the "greater good." Clearly, Morgaine and Mordred had not seen eye to eye on that.

Slowly, I asked, "What is a Slayer?" Even as I spoke the word, a dark current of fear moved through me, as though I had some instinctive understanding of a deadly danger that terrified my kind.

"A mortal endowed with a preternatural ability to kill vampires. The coming of a Slayer is nature's way of righting the balance. Without that sort of corrective action, vampires might have wiped out humans long ago."

My eyes flicked to the chain around his neck and the stone secured by it. He smiled faintly.

"I am no Slayer, be assured of that," Marco said. "One is born once every thousand years, no more. Morgaine was the first here in Britain. She laid waste to the vampires before she finally perished. Only Mordred was left."

Doing my utmost to conceal my relief even as I still wondered how he was able to move among my kind with such impunity, I said, "But there are many vampires now."

"Indeed. You will find the explanation here." He pointed again to the book. Leaning forward, I resumed reading where I had left off. Mordred continued:

In the months after Morgaine perished in battle against me, leaving me sorely wounded but alive, I cursed the cruel fate that condemned me to be a cheerless wanderer in a world of perpetual darkness. With virtually all the vampire clan in Britain slain, I was truly alone. Had I understood the means by which I could contrive my own death, I would have gladly used them. But for all my power, I remained ignorant in the ways of my kind. I had no choice but to endure.

That is not to say that I did not attempt to end my life. In those as yet early days, I tried every method I could think of—poison, the knife, fire—everything, all to no avail. Yet the effort was not wasted, for by it I began to discover the extent of my own powers. I traveled for a time on the Continent—several centuries in all—finding my own kind, learning from them, and growing in strength. At length, I returned to Britain and began creating a new race of vampires to serve as my court.

"Mordred succeeded in his intent," Marco said, "but he also showed great wisdom in restricting the number of vampires he created. He understood that if there were too many, they would overfeed on humans, who would realize what was happening and respond violently. Both species would be doomed."

I thought of what I had witnessed at the Bagatelle, humans competing for the chance to become vampires. "Judging by what I've seen, the vampire population is about to increase."

"That is a new development."

A thought was forming in my mind, really no more than the flicker of a notion. I was ready to dismiss it out of hand but instead I asked, "How long ago did Arthur die?"

"Fourteen hundred years have passed since the great king was among us."

But Lady Blanche had said that vampires could live forever. "What of Mordred then?" I asked. "Is he still—"

Marco leaned over, so close that I felt the hard strength of his chest pressed against my back. His breath brushed the nape of my neck. I tried to remember that he was a human, therefore, strictly speaking, prey. But the thought dissolved into confusion borne of my own conflicting emotions.

"Remember," he said, "what Dee asked of us, to see the world as it truly is rather than as we assume or even wish it to be." As he spoke, he flipped through several pages of the book until he came to the one he sought. It contained the drawing of a man, or so he appeared. Only his face was shown, that taking up the entire page. Dark hair framed a high forehead, the straight blade of a nose leading to a chiseled mouth and a square, firm jaw. His eyes beneath sweeping brows were wide, aglow with fierce intelligence. Even in the simple pen-and-ink sketch, his pale skin appeared luminous as the moon, radiating light.

"This is Mordred," Marco said. "Do you recognize him?"

I had to force myself to speak, so fierce was the sudden constriction of my throat. A hot wave of yearning rose up within me, so powerful that the world itself seemed veiled in the hue of blood. That compelling face, the intensity of those eyes, the lips that smiled in the instant before they parted to reveal . . .

The singer in the opera house, the being of my dreams. He whose summons I had no will to resist.

My voice sounded as though it came from a great distance, yet the truth I spoke resonated within me. "I should do so for he is etched into my memory. I can never forget him."

Marco sighed deeply, the sound hinting at genuine regret, but also of acceptance.

"I thought that might be the case," he said. "As far as the Golden Dawn has been able to determine, Mordred disappeared about the time you were incarnated as a vampire. In fact, it now appears that you were the last one to see him."

"I don't understand . . ." My mind reeled from the discovery that a vampire of such ancient and powerful lineage existed and even more that he had inexplicably chosen to make me one of his kind.

"He said nothing to you? Gave you no explanation for his actions?"

I strained to remember. The moor . . . the night . . . the sense of compulsion that I had been unable to deny. All remained starkly clear in my mind, but beyond that . . .

"He said nothing or if he did, I have no recollection of it."

"That is unfortunate," Marco said. "Mordred's disappearance has very serious ramifications for the realm. Since returning to England and re-creating the vampire kindred here on our shores, he has ruled as its king. No one has ever been able to challenge his power and only a very few have been foolish enough to try. He is supreme among all the vampires in strength and will. Or at least he was."

"What could have happened to him?" The being I knew in my dreams was undeniably formidable, but I also had the impression that he was trapped and weakening. If I did not find him soon, his voice would be stilled forever.

"I don't know, but understand this," Marco said. "As the son of King Arthur, Mordred has a better claim to rule this kingdom than any other sovereign who has ever sat on the throne. But long ago, during the time of Elizabeth, he put his royal rights of inheritance aside and struck a pact that has endured to this day. In times of greatest distress, the power of Mordred and his vampires has been placed in Britain's service. Although the vast majority of humans are completely unaware of it, we owe him a great deal."

Stumbling to understand an insight into history that I would never have thought possible, I said, "He has fought to protect this realm?"

Marco nodded. "More than once and decisively. We would not be what we are today without the role he has played."

"Even so, surely that does not excuse everything he has done?"

"Perhaps not," Marco said. "But Mordred never transformed anyone who did not want to become a vampire, and most of those who did want it, he rejected. Over the centuries, he refused vast sums of money from the highest and greatest who longed to join his court."

"I never asked for this."

True, yet not the entirety of truth. I had not asked, but neither had I resisted. Some hidden part of my nature had led me to Mordred. Had I understood what he intended, perhaps I would have found the strength to fight, but the fact was that I had not. Loathe though I was to admit it, I was complicit to at least some degree in what had happened to me.

"Which raises the question of why Mordred made an exception where you are concerned. Why did he violate the principles that had guided him for centuries in order to incarnate you as a vampire?"

"If you are asking me to explain it to you, I cannot. I have no more insights into why he did what he did now than I had at the first moment I returned to awareness."

"Is that why you have come in search of him?"

"Yes . . . no, not entirely."

"Which is it?" When I did not reply at once, Marco persisted. "Do you seek revenge, perhaps? Or do you harbor the notion that what was done to you could be undone?"

"Could it?" Until that moment, I had not allowed myself to consider the possibility that my lost humanity might be restored. I longed for my family, when I happened to think of them, and for the love and closeness I had taken too much for granted. So, too, I yearned to feel warm again, to know the pulse of my own lifeblood and feel the beat of my own heart measuring out my allotted time. And yet the power I now possessed—and was only just beginning to explore—was a siren's song that surpassed even the compulsion that Mordred had placed on me.

"I have never known any of your kind to give a moment's thought to being human again, far less long for it. You are a puzzle, Miss Weston."

"That does not answer my question." When he remained silent, I persisted. "Do you think it is possible for a vampire to become human again?"

He hesitated, but I could see that the question had piqued his interest. Slowly, he said, "The incarnation of a vampire involves fundamental changes at the cellular level. Your greater strength and stamina, for example, are the result of more efficient energy production within the structures known as mitochondria. Your vastly increased longevity is a result, at least in part, of your heightened immune system. The changes are so profound that I don't believe any serious thought has been given to the possibility that they could be reversed, at least not under ordinary circumstances." A faint smile tugged at the corners of his mouth. "But as it seems that you, Miss Weston, are far from ordinary, we would be wise not to assume anything in your case."

Despite myself, I smiled in turn, yet I harbored no illusions as to why he had replied as he did. "Whatever my reasons for seeking Mordred, you want me to help you find him, is that not so?"

"It is," he said promptly. "Together, we have a far better chance of succeeding than either of us does alone."

"Perhaps. . . . Who do you think is behind his disappear-ance?" If I were to trust this human who had such unexpected power over vampires, I would know what he knew.

"Someone deluded enough not to understand or care what the consequences will be. Or someone who does know and thinks to profit." He hesitated a moment, then said, "You've already met one of the prime suspects."

I did not have to stretch my mind very far to guess who he meant. "Lady Blanche?"

Marco nodded. "She has lived in Mordred's shadow, so to speak, for centuries. He has kept her close but refused to grant her the power for which she yearns. With him gone, she may believe that she can step into his place."

I thought of her wrapped in pearls, holding court in the subterranean chamber. Her chill beauty hinted at a formidable will that would not be denied.

"Could she be right?" I asked.

"If she tries, there will be a war for control among the great vampire families. Of course, that will happen anyway if Mor-dred doesn't return."

"What about humans? Are there any who might wish him gone?"

With obvious reluctance, Marco said, "There have been rumors . . ."

"Tell me."

"Some of those in the highest levels of government take our ever-growing power over the forces of nature as proof that humans no longer need to share this world with vampires ex-cept on our own terms."

A wave of coldness moved through me. "What terms?"

"Some would offer no terms at all. They argue that vampires

should be exterminated. Others acknowledge that vampires have been useful to humans in times of crisis when we have stood together against mutual enemies; the Spanish, for example, in the time of Elizabeth I. They argue that a way can be found to enslave vampires so they will exist only at our sufferance to serve our purposes. Neither plan is realistic because neither takes into account the vast numbers who would die on both sides if conflict broke out between us."

"Both sides?" I asked. Admittedly, my experience was very limited, but I had the impression that a vampire was very hard to kill.

"Humans have been developing ever more powerful weapons," Marco said. "Not even a vampire can survive being blown apart. In the end, there would be no winners, only mutual destruction."

Far off in the recesses of the club the drumming had stopped. Perhaps whoever had been trying to expel the demons had succeeded. But other, likely far greater dangers remained.

The thought of a war between humans and vampires was horrifying. In centuries past, the struggle would have been unequal, but with the new weapons that humans possessed, such a conflict could rage on and on while the toll on both sides mounted steeply. Nor would the cost be measured in lives alone. The very fabric of civilization could be torn apart as society descended into a mad orgy of violence and bloodletting that could end only with the extermination of both races.

"If human arrogance does not bring on this war," I said, "then the increase in the number of vampires that is already occurring will make it inevitable anyway. Isn't that so?"

Marco nodded. "Regrettably, it is. The only hope of preventing both sides from falling upon each other is to find Mordred and restore him to his rightful place. Do that and we restore the balance between humans and vampires that has protected us all for centuries."

Through the sudden constriction of my throat, I said, "We had best hurry."

He looked at me closely. "I agree, but do you have a particular reason for saying so?"

I hesitated, reluctant to speak of a matter that felt so strangely intimate. Yet I could see no other choice.

"I am . . . in contact with Mordred in some manner, although I have no idea how or why. I can sense him well enough to know that he still exists, but he is growing weaker with each passing hour. If we don't find him quickly, it will be too late."

Marco nodded slowly. "Mordred must have realized that he was in danger. Likely he sought you out because something about you makes such a connection possible."

"I assure you that cannot be the case. I was an entirely unremarkable young woman." Albeit one bedeviled by a indefinable yearning for something hovering just out of sight, just beyond reach, drawing me out onto a moon-swept moor to confront a fate beyond any I could ever have imagined.

"Besides," I continued briskly, "I don't know where Mordred is. All I can say is that he feels closer here in London than he did in Whitby." A sudden thought occurred to me. "If Lady Blanche is responsible for his disappearance, she may have managed to confine him somewhere within the Bagatelle. I should return there at once and search the place while the others are still at rest."

"*We* should return," Marco corrected. As though that settled the matter, he closed Dee's book, put it back on the shelf, and crossed the library to open the door. Ever the gentleman, even when he was being dictatorial, he stood aside for me to exit first. Instead, I stood rooted where I was.

"If I am found wandering around the Bagatelle, I can claim to be acting out of simple curiosity. However, if we are caught there together, our presence will be regarded in a far more sinister light."

A long moment followed during which I observed him wrestling with himself. Clearly, he did not want to agree, but neither could he escape the fact that I was indisputably right.

Even so, his acquiescence was not as graceful as I would have wished. With obvious reluctance, he said, "Very well, but I have two conditions. We will make a stop on the way back to the Bagatelle. There is something I must show you. And you will agree without fail to meet me at the griffin statue tomorrow at noon. If you do not appear, I will assume that you have either betrayed our alliance or fallen victim to it."

The shadows near the doorway had deepened while we were in the library. I could only just make out the hard planes and angles of his face tinted darkly sanguine by the red pendant. For a moment, he looked more like a creature of the netherworld than I could ever be. Yet I had no choice but to trust him.

Quietly, I said, "I have a condition of my own: My family may be in London. Should we fail to find Mordred and prevent this war, will you try to get them to a place of safety if I am unable to do so?"

A look of surprise flitted behind his eyes. "You still care for them?"

Confused by my own feelings, but reluctant to admit as much, I said, "Apparently."

So softly that I had to strain to hear him, he said, "You have my word."

Thus was the bargain between us struck. I could hope only that I would not have cause to regret it.

CHAPTER 9

As we emerged from the club, Marco hailed a passing hackney. Handing me up into it, he said, "We should get off the street."

I did not understand his urgency until, glancing through the narrow window on the far side of the carriage, I glimpsed half a dozen Watchers gliding toward us. Their Teslaways cut a swath through the crowd as men and women alike hastened to avoid them. Marco joined me inside, closed the door, and called instructions to the driver. The wheels were rolling as the black-uniformed guardians of public order—their visors reflecting the rapidly emptying street—bounded up the steps of the Golden Dawn.

Raids on the homes and businesses of ordinary people were becoming distressingly commonplace, but importuning gentlemen within the sanctum of a private club was another matter entirely. Something must have greatly emboldened the Watchers for them to behave in such a way.

"De Vere may have been more suspicious of you than I realized," Marco said as he sat back beside me. "We will have to take greater care."

"You're suggesting that he has the ear of someone with sufficient authority to order a raid on the society?"

He nodded. Showing a disturbing ability to anticipate my train of thought, he added, "However, you should not conclude this means humans are responsible for Mordred's disappearance. If that leads you to let down your guard around Lady Blanche—"

Before he could continue, no doubt to issue dire warnings, I broke in. "What do you know of her? You said she has existed in Mordred's shadow for centuries. But how did she come to be a vampire in the first place?"

His mouth tightened. "Dee records that she came from a noble family of ancient lineage that rose in rebellion against the crown in the thirteenth century and was destroyed. She was the only survivor, and then only because she begged Mordred to transform her. He had his reasons for agreeing, I suppose. She is, after all, very beautiful. She aspires to be his consort, but he has always kept her at arm's length, perhaps because he does not trust her thirst for power."

Was that what lay at the heart of all of this, a spurned woman turning on the lover who had failed to give her what she regarded as her due? I thought it unlikely, but I understood Marco's warning not to underestimate Lady Blanche.

"Could she have taken him unawares?" I asked. "Overcome him in some way?"

"I would not have thought that possible, but then I didn't anticipate any of this."

I was silent for several moments, staring out the window of the carriage. Everywhere along our route, men and boys were up on ladders hanging red, white, and blue bunting in preparations for the Diamond Jubilee celebrations that were almost upon us. Sixty years Victoria had reigned, an eon by human standards. She had come into a world still largely lit by fire and powered by muscle, where wealth was won by sword and sail. She would ride to her Jubilee past electric streetlights that were steadily replacing the gas variety and within sight of steam boats plying the Thames. The time needed to cross the Atlantic had shrunk from weeks to days, and as for the new weaponry . . . I preferred not to think of the carnage it could wreak. Or of what another sixty years would bring if conflict did break out between humans and vampires. What would London be then? The wreck of a haunted city in which only ghosts and vanished dreams still dwelled?

How much did the queen empress know about the danger confronting her realm? She emerged so rarely from the magnificent Crystal Palace in Hyde Park, built by her beloved consort, Prince Albert, for the Great Exhibition of 1851 and preserved ever since by his widow as a monument to their love. Mired in permanent mourning, seeped in the rituals of death, she likely had no concept of the threat hanging over all. But she was an old, fallible human woman whereas I was . . . something new, different, even possibly unique. A weapon forged by Mordred for a very specific purpose and yet for all that still my own self. The clarity of that truth shone in the darkness, guiding me onward.

Turning back to Marco, I found him watching me not with the cold assessment I would have expected from a man forced into an alliance with a creature such as myself, but rather with what gave every appearance of genuine concern.

Against the sudden tightness of my throat, I said, "I have begun to wonder if Mordred may have created me as a means of saving himself." Before he could reply, I went on quickly.

"I am possessed by a compulsion to find him as well as by the ability to sense his presence. I cannot explain either, but I suspect that he could."

Rather than dismiss the notion, as a part of me hoped that he would do, Marco surprised me. Nodding, he said, "I have had the same thought. For him to transform you without your agreement, in contradiction of the principles by which he has existed for centuries, he truly must have regarded his situation as desperate. From what you have sensed of him, we must do the same."

For the first time, I heard behind Marco's strength and confidence a hint of his own dread of what would happen if we failed to prevent war between humans and vampires. As though he anticipated the final moments of his life crushed beneath the anguish of all humanity, the crying out of so many lost souls that his own would be lacerated by their suffering. On impulse, I put my hand over his. At once, his warm, strong fingers curled around mine. At his touch, such longing flowed through me . . . I cannot give words to it—not for lack of them, poetry sings in my spirit as it does in all of my kind even those who wish to be deaf to it—but because even now, after all that has transpired, some things are so fragile, so perfect, so necessary to the fabric of existence, that to speak of them risks that they will shatter like crystal struck by a single, soaring note whose very beauty is destruction.

The chill that had accompanied me out of the grave from which I had crawled to my rebirth and had hung about me ever since, a taunting shroud reminding me of all I had lost, abruptly vanished. In the space of his heartbeat, I was warm again.

The carriage swayed around a corner onto Fleet Street. Our

bodies touched, resting against one another until too soon we were righted once again. Recalled to ourselves, we moved a little apart, our fingers the last to yield. I looked away, forcing myself to concentrate on anything other than the yearning his nearness provoked.

Moments passed before Marco slid open the window behind the driver, admitting a breath of sooty air, and gave instructions to stop in the next street. Having descended from the carriage, we walked along a short passage adjacent to the Temple Church until we came to a two-story structure that, alone among the surrounding brick and stone buildings, still retained the plaster and crossed timber exterior of its Tudor origins. A sign in front read Serjeant's Inn, the term referring to an ancient order of civil servants charged with managing the courts.

Black-robed barristers came and went through its low, arched door, stopping to chat with one another. An aura of great age hung about the place. I wondered if Dee had frequented it.

"If you ever need a place of safety," Marco said, "or to get word to me, come here. The proprietor is . . . trustworthy."

His nearness, the warmth of his powerful body, and his voice all combined to distract me mightily. In an effort to regain some modicum of self-control, I forced myself to study the inn, but with scant result. Behind its deep-set windows, it gave away few secrets. That I might turn to it as a place of refuge seemed unlikely. That I would find a welcome there seemed even less plausible.

We walked past the arched door and turned down a narrow lane that ran alongside the inn. A few yards in we came to a second door. Marco produced a key. Moments later, we were standing in a small but pleasantly furnished office. The light within had a greenish tinge, filtering as it did through windows with leaded panes that were filled with bubbles, the breath of glassmakers now long dead. I looked around slowly. In addition to a plain but functional desk and tall bookcases filled with legal tomes, a cot was set up to one side next to a wardrobe.

"Someone lives here?" I asked.

"My brother, Nicolas. I had hoped to find him in, but he may be in court at this hour."

I had not known that he had a brother, but then I suspected that there was a great deal I did not know about Marco. I was drawn to him in ways I could scarcely understand, a yearning not merely of the flesh but of the heart and spirit as well.

Determined to conceal my unseemly thoughts, I asked, "He is a barrister?"

"Among other things. He also owns this inn."

Where he apparently chose to live rather than occupy lodgings more in keeping with a man of his stature.

As though anticipating my question, Marco said, "Nicolas likes his privacy. We should be going. Another time, I'll introduce you."

Leaving, I noticed a photograph on a small side table. Two young men stood side by side, their arms around each other's shoulders as they smiled for the camera. One was clearly Marco, yet he appeared so carefree that I had trouble reconciling him with the determined man I was coming to know. The other was—

"Is that your brother?" I asked.

Marco hesitated before glancing at the photograph. His tone was softer than I had heard before. "Yes, that's Nicolas before—" Abruptly, he caught himself. His face hardened. "Never mind. We should go."

I stepped back into the lane, but my thoughts remained on the two seemingly untroubled young men. What had happened to change at least one of them so drastically and why did the other choose to isolate himself in the back room of an inn away from family and friends?

At another time, I might have been so bold as to ask Marco, but graver matters weighed on us both. We continued on foot, keeping alert for the sudden appearance of any Watchers, until we reached the griffin statue. There we parted, but not before Marco took my hand and, looking deeply into my eyes, said, "Tomorrow at noon without fail, all right?"

A rush of warmth coiled through me. It was gone as quickly as it had come, but the memory lingered.

"I will be here." I made to draw away, but he was not quite ready to release me.

Without warning, he said, "Do you remember anything of the night we met?"

I hadn't, but just then the memory flooded back, momentarily overwhelming all else. His hand at my waist, the music soaring around us, and myself, smiling, laughing. He had said something amusing, but that was not the source of my pleasure. It was him, the sensation he evoked, trembling on the edge of a cliff, about to unfurl my wings and somehow knowing that he would not let me fall.

"I remember waltzing," I replied. "It was Strauss, I think."

"'Danube Maiden,' one of his better efforts. What else do you recall?"

"Very little. Fragments. When I try to fit them together, they fly apart again."

"I am sorry to hear that. . . . Sorry for all of it."

My fingers curled around his. "I don't understand."

He took a breath and let it out slowly. Softly, he said, "I was there that night because I had learned that Mordred was stalking you. I had no idea why, but I went to warn him off. It was arrogance on my part. I should have known that no mere warning from me would stop him. If only I had realized—"

If only he had. We could be standing there as a man and a woman without the shadow of all that lay between us. But also without any real means of defeating the danger that threatened to destroy everyone and everything.

"What if you had? What hope would there be now of finding Mordred?"

"You can't just forgive him like that. Think of what he took from you."

Resentment rose in me. Of Mordred and what he had done, but equally of Marco and his unwillingness to see beyond the limits of humanity.

"I do think of it, far too often. But I am also aware of what he gave. Nothing is as simple as we might like, but perhaps that is all to the good."

Before he could reply, I turned and hurried toward the Bagatelle. Near the stone passageway, I paused and looked back. Marco had not moved, nor had he looked away. I continued to feel his gaze until I pushed open the door and once again entered the confines of the club. I was greeted by a heavy stillness that suited my mood all too well.

Determined to take advantage of the remaining hours of daylight, and equally resolved not to think about Marco, I hurried to explore the premises, quickly discovering that the large main room gave way to numerous other gilded chambers. Many of these were given over to card playing, roulette, and other forms of gambling, but some seemed intended for pursuits of a more private nature. Moving on, I was surprised to stumble across a small library lined with floor-to-ceiling cases that were filled in turn with leather-bound volumes. Lady Blanche had not impressed me as one inclined to intellectual pursuits, but perhaps I had done her an injustice.

At quick glance, the books seemed to have to do mainly with history and science, the latter including Charles Darwin's controversial work *On the Origin of Species*. Almost four decades after its publication, the theory that species are created through a process of natural selection favoring those fittest for survival remained the subject of much debate. My father, for example, found the idea entirely reasonable, whereas my mother thought it was appalling. I had possessed no opinion of the matter whatsoever, but now, in my new form, I saw it in a different light. Ruthless though it might be, Darwin's theory was all too evidently correct. Vampires—beings stronger, swifter, and vastly longer lived—might already have driven humans into extinction had they not needed them to feed upon. Was that what the future held, a world devastated by war in which the remaining humans were kept as cattle to be bred for slaughter?

The thought sickened me. I shoved the book back onto the shelf with such force as to dislodge another nearby. Straightening it, I noticed the engraving on the spine. *Comparative Longevity of Diverse Species* by Dr. Sebastian de Vere. Next to it was another volume by the same author: *Cellular Degeneration: Catalyst of Mortality.*

The titles of the books meant nothing to me beyond the fact that I recognized the name of the man Marco and I had encountered at the headquarters of the Golden Dawn, the same man who had sent the Watchers after us.

Before I could ponder that too deeply, I recalled that time was passing swiftly. From what I had seen, the club possessed many more rooms. If I was to have any chance of determining whether Mordred was present, I would have to act quickly.

Yet I got no farther than the door when it opened suddenly. Dapper in a suit of burgundy velvet so dark it looked almost black, Felix Deschamps stared at me in surprise.

CHAPTER 10

"What are you doing here?" Felix asked.

I stepped out of the library, closing the door behind me. Resting my back against it, I mustered a smile. "I couldn't sleep so I thought I would look for something to read."

"Is there a problem with your chamber?"

"No, not at all, it's lovely. The problem is me, really. This is all still so new." I made a vague gesture of confusion that I hoped would explain why I was wandering about the club unescorted.

To my great relief, he nodded. "One forgets how startling incarnation can be. And, of course, you have not had the benefit of a mentor. Shocking, really, that you were abandoned in such a fashion."

"So Lady Blanche indicated. She has been very kind."

His gaze narrowed as he assessed whether or not I was sincere. After a moment, he said, "Yes, of course, which is why I came looking for you. Her ladyship has charged me with assuring that you have everything you need, including a proper diet."

"I'm not sure what you mean . . ." In fact I understood all

too well. A wave of nausea swept over me. The thought of feeding as I had seen the others do . . .

"Come along." Felix took a polite but firm hold on my arm. Rather than raise suspicion, I had no choice but to accompany him. As we returned to the main room of the club, he said, "I take it you didn't find anything to read?"

Absorbed in what I was about to confront, I stumbled to answer. "What's that? Oh, no, I didn't—"

"Hardly surprising. I don't think anyone's read a single book in there."

Belatedly, I realized that all the bindings had appeared untouched, the pages unturned. "Then why have a library at all?"

Felix pulled out a chair and waited until I was seated at one of the small round tables topped in marble with a gilded filigree edge. Empty but for ourselves, the main room of the club appeared even larger and more luxurious than it had the night before. Silence reigned over all, yet I could not shake the impression that just beyond the range of my hearing the air vibrated like the surface of a deep, dark pool beneath which one might find anything . . . hidden wonders of enthralling beauty or horrors too hideous to contemplate.

"Lady Blanche thought it would appeal to a certain someone who did not patronize the Bagatelle," Felix replied. "Unfortunately, he proved immune to any such seduction."

I did my utmost to appear only mildly interested even as I considered the possibility that the library had been intended for Mordred, whose consort she had aspired to be. But if it had not drawn him to the club . . . Did that mean he had not been trapped there after all?

"How curious," I said. "Judging by what I saw, he must be a highly erudite gentleman."

Felix settled into the chair across from me. "Indeed, absolutely brilliant. Shall we have coffee? I never feel quite awake until I've had a cup."

"Coffee? I thought . . ." The possibility of a reprieve, however temporary, made me almost sag in relief. With an effort, I managed to keep myself upright.

A smile flickered across Felix's face. I wondered if he wasn't enjoying drawing out my anticipation. Yet his intent seemed entirely benign.

"I'm from New Orleans originally. Did I tell you that? We have the most delicious coffee there. It's flavored with chicory, very beneficial to vampires. If I had my way, all humans would be fed on it to improve the quality of their blood."

I ducked my head, pretending interest in the swirling marble of the tabletop. The thought of blood unleashed a desperate craving in me at the same time that I was repulsed by my own longing. Part of me was screaming in refusal while the other, increasingly stronger part of myself wanted to thrust the contemptible human side of my nature back down into the grave and silence it forever.

No wonder my head felt as though it was about to split open and all the demons of hell come streaming out.

Through the pain, I murmured, "What an interesting idea. Perhaps we should explore ways to improve the health of humans in general. Strictly for our own benefit, of course."

Felix raised a hand, summoning a thrall who appeared from behind the bar. The creature shuffled toward us. Its face— assuming that it possessed one—was concealed deep within the folds of its hood. When it had heard our order and gone away again, Felix said, "I hope you'll accept a bit of advice, Lucy. Don't talk about helping humans, not for any purpose. The old families tend not to like it."

"Do they not?" I spoke absently, still staring after the creature. Its kind possessed great strength and ferocity, as I had experienced all too well, yet it appeared entirely tame, not to say beaten down with no flicker of will left in it.

"No," Felix said so emphatically that he succeeded in drawing my attention back to him. "They most definitely do not. You would be wise to do nothing more to draw their interest."

The suggestion that I had already done so surprised me. "More? What have I done already?"

He shrugged as though the answer was obvious. "You appeared here alone, without a mentor. Naturally, there are questions about who incarnated you and why it was done in such an unorthodox manner."

"Questions that no one wants answered more than I do." Abruptly, the constraints of caution and discretion became intolerable. My skin was prickling and every nerve I possessed felt on edge. Heedless of the consequences, I asked, "Do you know who is responsible?"

Felix started in surprise and as quickly frowned. "Of course not. How could I possibly?"

His protestations notwithstanding, I was certain that he was lying. The sudden shift of his eyes and the stiffening of his shoulders spoke more clearly than any words he uttered. I tried again. "Do you suspect anyone in particular?"

He leaned back in his chair and regarded me gravely. "Are you so determined to discover who he is?"

"How can I not be?" When he did not reply, I pressed harder. "Wouldn't you be driven to find the one who stole your humanity, transformed you into a creature unlike any you had ever imagined, and abandoned you to deal with that as best you could?"

Felix shrugged. He would have appeared bored with the subject were it not for the sharpness of his gaze. "Perhaps, but then what? Do you want to thank him or accuse him?"

I wanted to save him; indeed I was compelled to do so. But rather than say anything of that, I replied, "I want to understand why this happened to me. Until I do, I don't think I can ever fully accept it."

I was reprieved from saying more when the thrall returned bearing a golden tray set with a pot of fine Meissen china and matching cups. Felix dismissed the creature and poured for us both. We sipped in silence for several minutes. The coffee reminded me of that served in the cafés in Paris, only with a richer, deeper flavor.

Yet I could scarcely enjoy it, not while the hunger for blood was rising so inexorably.

Felix drew a jeweled case from an inside pocket of his jacket, chose a cigarette, and lit it. Looking at me over the glowing red tip, he said, "This is a tricky situation."

I nodded but did not speak. If he was, as I hoped, on the verge of deciding how much to tell me, I could not risk saying anything that might dissuade him.

"Before we go on," he said, "I must know you better."

I was about to ask how that might be accomplished when a thrall—whether the same or another I cannot say, for all the faceless apparitions looked alike—appeared bearing a crystal goblet filled with a bright red liquid.

"It is fresh," Felix said, as though that would somehow reassure me. "Best not to let it sit too long."

Slowly, aware of how closely he was watching me, I lifted the goblet to my lips. My hand shook so powerfully that I feared the crystal would shatter. Or, at the very least, I would spill blood all over the table.

"Whose is it?" I asked, rather stupidly, really, for what difference did it make? Warm, coppery human blood was just that and did not need to be anything more. The scent was enticing. The color when I held the goblet up to the light was perfection . . . the shimmer of the light striking it. . . . Never had I seen anything so seductive. My hunger, already so intense, surged suddenly, becoming a ravenous craving I had no hope of controlling.

"A supplicant's," Felix said, "thrilled, like all of them, to be of service. It doesn't matter where it came from. Drink."

Consumed with need though I was, I hesitated.

"Fresh, you said?"

"Very, drawn minutes ago. Once you have accomplished this, we will begin accustoming you to what is really the very simple process of feeding. But first—"

First, all I had to do was drink the blood already presented to me. Drink it from a lovely goblet rimmed with gold. Drink to satisfy the voracious craving that gnawed at my very soul.

"What are you waiting for?" Felix asked.

I put the goblet to my mouth. The scent, so tempting moments before, was suddenly thick and cloying. Even so, I persisted. A drop . . . another entered my mouth, slipped down my throat . . .

I gagged. The reflex was sudden and fierce. My throat closed. Another moment and I would be retching. That was my damnable human side, contemptibly squeamish. I could not allow it to control me. Mustering all my newfound will, I lifted the goblet again and drank.

Drank deeply, ravenously, with exquisite enjoyment, savoring every nuance of flavor and texture until not a drop was left. My father had tried to teach me to appreciate fine wine, what he called "educating the palate." But no complexity of soil, water, grapes, and fermentation could come close to equaling what the human body itself produced. As I set the goblet down, I ran my tongue over my lips, capturing the last enticing traces of blood. Only then did I become aware that Felix was staring at me. The fine lines around his eyes were more in evidence than ever. Suddenly, he did not look quite so boyish.

"You must have been starving."

I nodded, hoping to give the impression of composure that I was very far from feeling. The experience had shaken me deeply. I was at once disgusted and elated. I ignored the former and concentrated on the latter. Strength flowed in me. I was powerful beyond the comprehension of mere mortals, soaring far above all fear and doubt, liberated from every restraint.

"Is it always that good?" I asked.

He laughed. "Far better when taken properly from the source, as you will discover. But for now, I must say that I am relieved."

"Why so?"

"Lady Blanche, who as you know has only your welfare in mind, expressed a concern that the unorthodox manner of your incarnation might have led to a regrettable result."

"What are you saying?"

"That you might be caught in an intermediate state, half human, half vampire. Both identities in one form, each fighting the other, neither able to win. A halfling, as such a being is called."

"There are such creatures?" What he was describing fit my own circumstances too perfectly to be a coincidence. Were there others caught in the same indeterminate state as myself?

Scarcely had that hope begun to stir than Felix dashed it. "Only in myth . . . and prophecy."

Myth did not concern me, but prophecy was another matter entirely. People had been known to take prophetic warnings very seriously, even when they proved to be sheer bunk. I knew of no reason to think that vampires were any different.

"Some believe," Felix said, "that a halfling will come into the world to destroy our kind."

"I thought it was Slayers who destroyed vampires." Scarcely had I spoken than I knew that I had made a mistake, revealing knowledge that I should not have. If I could have taken the words back, I would have done so, but it was too late. There was nothing left but to brazen my way out.

Felix's gaze narrowed. "What do you know of Slayers?"

"Stoker mentioned them when I confronted him." I felt no compunction about blaming the Irishman for my knowledge. As far as I knew, he had no regrets for how shamefully he had misrepresented my fate.

"You have met the author of *Dracula*?"

I looked at him innocently. "I came across his book. Recognizing it as a distorted version of my own experience, I sought him out. Did I not say as much?"

"No," Felix said, "you most certainly did not. What else did he tell you?"

"He mentioned someone with an odd name . . . rather Arthurian. . . . What was it?" I pretended to search my memory.

"Oh, yes, Mordred. Stoker claimed that might be who had incarnated me. Or I think he did. I had my hands around his throat at the time so it was all rather garbled."

"How odd that you did not tell Lady Blanche about this."

"Should I have? Does it mean something?"

He hesitated, but I knew that I had him. Whatever loyalty he felt to the formidable Blanche, Felix was far too worldly not to understand that information is the only currency that really matters. It can be hoarded, traded, used as a weapon, and—if only very rarely—offered as a gift. Properly deployed, nothing else is as powerful, not for a human or a vampire.

"Mordred," Felix said slowly, "is the gentleman for whom the library was created."

"To lure him here to the Bagatelle? Did he come?"

"No . . . in fact, he has not been seen in months."

"What a shame. Is Lady Blanche very disappointed?"

"Rather more than that." He hesitated, clearly still uncertain how much to tell me, but as I already knew the name . . . slowly, he said, "Mordred is the king who created us all and who ruled over us until his sudden disappearance early this year. His fate remains a mystery. If you know anything of it—"

"What could I possibly know?"

"That, too, is a mystery. Who you are, why you are here, what you intend or are intended for. He must have had a reason for incarnating you." His gaze narrowed on me. "Perhaps you are the one who can find him."

A universal hope apparently, afflicting humans and vampires alike. I had to hope they would not all end up gravely disappointed.

"I would certainly like to do so. There must have been some place he frequented. If not here, where?" Even vampires needed somewhere to escape the sunlight, rest, and rejuvenate themselves. But a being who might be tempted by a library, surely he had needed more?

"Since we realized that he was gone," Felix said, "we have kept watch on all his residences—the house here in London, the estate in Kent, the manor in Scotland, the villa near Rome, the apartment in Paris, everywhere. All to no avail. But there is one other possibility. Are you familiar with Southwark?"

As was the case with all of London, the part of the city that lay along the south shore of the Thames had grown hugely in recent decades. What had been a haven for actors, prostitutes, and the like had become a teeming mass of factories and mills belching black smoke at all hours of the day and night. Proper young ladies, even those who liked to consider themselves modern thinkers, did not venture there.

"I know very little about it," I confessed.

"For centuries there was a walled manor on the hill at the top of the high street, overlooking the river. Mordred kept his court there. I never saw it for myself, but by all reports it was a remarkable place, a true palace enticing beyond compare. But these days, if you go to that spot, you will find not the home of a king but a huge, dirty, clamorous foundry. Like all of its kind, it produces a great din, belches foulness into the air, and is populated by humans who look to be little more than brutes laboring among fiery pits and rivers of molten metal. Those who have seen it say that it resembles hell itself."

"Go on," I urged.

"But there are also those who say that appearances are deceiving and the manor is still there, if you know how to find it. Further, they believe that Mordred still frequents the area."

"Surely Lady Blanche and others of the old noble families can find the manor? They must have looked for him there."

"Rumor has it that they have tried but failed. Whatever deception the king worked, it is deeper and darker than even they can penetrate."

Which left little hope that I would succeed, yet I had to try and very soon. Searching for Mordred had made me all the more vividly aware of how swiftly the very essence of him was draining away. Time was running out.

"Why are you telling me this?" I asked. "Did Lady Blanche instruct you to do so?"

He pretended to be hurt, although perhaps it was not entirely pretense. Everyone has his pride, even when he can ill afford it.

"You think I'm her toady, don't you?"

"I do not—"

He brushed aside my protestations. "Don't deny it; everyone thinks that. It's true to a certain extent, but this is also true: Mordred kept the peace between vampires and humans for centuries. With him gone, war is a certainty. I'm more afraid of that than I am of Lady Blanche, but she fears it as well, whether she is willing to admit as much or not."

He was taking a risk confiding in me as he had done. Lady Blanche might come to agree with what he had done, but not before she exacted a price for it.

Softly, I said, "I thank you for your candor. I will do my best to find him." I began to rise only to stop when Felix grasped my hand.

"You cannot leave now. Lady Blanche's doubts about you must be erased. If they are not, she will do everything in her power to destroy you." Pointedly, he added, "And anyone she thinks has helped you."

Slowly, I sat down again. "How can I win her confidence?"

"I doubt that you can, at least not quickly. Just try not to do anything that could lead her to see you as a threat. You are a newly incarnated vampire struggling to find your way and profoundly grateful for the interest she has taken in you. Let her believe that you regard her, not Mordred, as your true mentor. Nothing will please her more or make her more inclined to assure that you survive."

"Do you think that I should tell her that Mordred was the one who incarnated me?"

"You must," Felix insisted. "Your arrival in the wake of his disappearance is simply too coincidental. She already suspects and by admitting it, you can counter any concerns that she has about you."

"That I could be a halfling?"

He nodded. "Or a rival." When I looked at him in bewilderment, he added, "It is not unusual for newly incarnated vampires to desire the one who turned them."

Hastily, I said, "I do not. To the contrary, I only want to know why he did this."

"Tell her that . . . just like that. He has been her passion for centuries. If she thought for a moment that you—"

"Be assured, I will disabuse her of any such notion." Indeed, I would do so without even the need to lie. The truth was that though I felt a compulsion to find Mordred, it was of Marco that I found myself thinking all too often. Of the human who knew more about my own kind than I did, who went among us without fear, and who was willing to ally with a vampire to prevent a war that could destroy everything I still held most dear.

When her ladyship emerged from her chamber a few hours later, I was there to greet her. I wasted no time telling her of what I had discovered about the one responsible for my incarnation, stressing how greatly his abandonment upset me even to the extent of causing me to loathe him.

"Truly," I said, "I do not know what I would have done if I had not found you. I have so much to learn and I believe you are the only one who can teach me, yet I dare not assume upon your favor . . ."

Had I been speaking to a human, I might have feared that I was laying it on a bit thickly. But I was learning that vampires took flattery at face value, regarding it merely as their due.

"You have it, child," Lady Blanche said. In contrast to her gentle words, her smile was chilling. The pearls at her throat gleamed cold and hard. She twisted them around her hand as she regarded me. "But in return, you must promise to never betray our friendship. Do you understand?"

When I assured her that I did, she seemed satisfied. Yet I felt her gaze upon me all through that night as I remained at her side. Lady Blanche introduced me to the many guests who thronged the club, leaving no doubt that I had her approval. The outpouring of attention and, I must say, respect was gratifying as far as it went, but I did not forget for a moment how quickly it all could change. A single misstep and I would find myself receiving attention of a far different sort, more in keeping with the dark, vibrating tremors I felt emanating from the club itself.

Felix hovered nearby, ever watchful as the hours wore on

until finally, just when I thought I could bear no more, dawn sent the children of the night to their rest.

I seized a few hours on my bier but found little ease. At noon, while the club slumbered, I slipped past the snake and walked quickly through the passage to where the griffin kept watch.

CHAPTER 11

A s promised, Marco was waiting for me on the border between the old city and the new. He looked as handsome and compelling as ever, but there was a hint of strain around his eyes that suggested he had not slept. When he saw me, a smile flashed across his face, stripping years from him. For a moment, he looked like the boy I had seen in the photograph.

"There you are," he said. "I was becoming worried."

As he spoke, the nearby church bells began to toll the noonday hour. Restraining the impulse to point out that I was not a moment late, I said, "I have news about Mordred. Lady Blanche knows that he incarnated me. She means to keep me close and assure my loyalty, although why exactly I cannot say."

I had tried over the course of the night to determine the lady's intentions but without success. She might hope to use me to draw Mordred back or to assure that I could not fulfill the purpose for which he had created me. Either seemed equally possible.

Marco frowned. "Do you think she has any idea where he is?"

"If she does, she has not told Felix Deschamps. He is her—"

"I know who Deschamps is. He's not a bad sort, really. I can't say that I envy him having to deal with her."

Under other circumstances, I might have asked how a human had become so well acquainted with the vampire kindred. But time was passing all too swiftly. Mordred's presence was still strong enough in my mind for me to believe that I could find him, yet he was also undeniably weaker than he had been even the day before.

"Felix shares our dread about the potential for war between humans and vampires," I said. "He wants to help. He has told me of a place where Mordred might be found." Quickly, I related what I had learned about the manor.

Marco was nodding before I finished. "I know the place. That is, I know the foundry. There have been rumors of strange events that bore investigating."

"What sort of events?"

"Men frightened by things glimpsed out of the corners of their eyes but invisible when looked at straight on. Odd sounds, soft and faint yet somehow audible over the clamor of the workings. The brush of wind where there should be none. Daily, someone puts down his tools and flees. The others hang on only because they're desperate for jobs and the pay is good."

"Then you think it is possible that the manor really could still exist in some way?"

Marco looked doubtful. "The hidden world exists but it is part of this world. Most humans can't see it because of their own limitations. They see something entirely ordinary rather than what is, and if they ever do become curious, they are discouraged from looking deeper by the use of glamours. But that isn't what you're describing, is it?"

Slowly, I shook my head. "A foundry is real. People work

in it, things come out of it. The same space cannot also be occupied by a centuries-old manor fit for a king."

"By all we know, that is true," Marco agreed. "However, we
could be dealing with some sort of palimpsest."

I looked at him quizzically. "What is that?"

"Layers placed one on top of another, usually involving
writing. The practice comes from the days when most writing
of any importance was done on parchment, which was expen-
sive and hard to come by. Scribes developed the habit of scrap-
ping the surface clean so that it could be used again. However,
impressions of the earlier writing remained below. Some can
still be detected."

"Then we should take a closer look." He hesitated and I
saw that he was about to refuse, no doubt to insist that he go
alone. Some nonsense about it not being safe for me. Quickly,
I added, "I will hazard a guess that you've already been there,
drawn by the reports of strange goings on, and that you discovered nothing."

He did not deny it but said, "Probably because there is
nothing to be found."

"Perhaps, but given what I am, it is likely I will be able to
see things that you cannot."

Moments passed before he said reluctantly, "Very well, but
promise me that you will stay close beside me at all times and if
I say we must leave, you will do so immediately."

I saw no reason to accept his authority to such a degree, but
neither was I disposed to argue, not then. He took my curt nod
for acquiesce.

"Stay close to me," he said. "The streets are chaos, all to
the good as that will protect us from the Watchers."

Only then did I notice that the spot where we stood, and

everywhere that I could see in all directions, teemed with people. Every byway leading to St. Paul's Cathedral was so filled as to be virtually impassable. Men, women, and children of every class had turned out to welcome Her Imperial Majesty Victoria, by the Grace of God, of the United Kingdom of Great Britain and Ireland Queen, Defender of the Faith, Empress of India, as her procession made its way to the cathedral where a service would be held to give thanks for the grace and wisdom of her long reign. Her grateful subjects packed the sidewalks, spilled over into the streets, and hung from windows and balconies. The more agile among them had climbed lampposts for a better view, shouting down to those below what they could see. The few carriages that had wandered in among the masses were trapped. The horses for the most part stood placidly, perhaps glad of the rest. Drivers and passengers might fume, but they had no way to free themselves except to wait.

We managed—by dint of great effort, more than a little patience, and Marco's strong arms—to reach King William Street on foot. There we came upon a lavish mini-pavilion in the Brighton style much loved at the beginning of the century by the prince regent, set incongruously in the center of busy London. A white dome gave way to a palatial entrance, which in turn yielded to a long staircase leading down into the bowels of the earth.

"The Tube?" I asked with mingled excitement and trepidation. Scant years before, the notion of blasting a tunnel under the venerable Thames in order to unite the northern and southern parts of the city, and further linking them with an electric contrivance meant to run cars underground, struck any sane person as outlandish. I could remember my father grumbling as he read his newspaper, calling the scheme mad-ness. Yet humans had managed it. The small, cramped trains—so tightly fitted that the cars were referred to as "padded cells"—had been running ever since, to the general acclaim of the public. So great was their success that there was talk of extending the Tube throughout London and even into the suburbs beyond. Some utopians claimed that soon the streets above would be free of all traffic.

Marco did not hesitate but plunged downward, down and down and down until at last we came to a deserted platform. The air felt unnaturally cool and damp. There was scarcely any sound expect for the far-off whisper of the dynamos that main-tained the glowing yellow bulbs set in metal cages along the ceiling and the muted fans that made it possible to breathe. I shivered, not from cold for I was incapable of feeling that, but from the thought that this was how London would appear if we did not succeed—barren and empty.

"An hour ago," Marco said, "the trains were packed. Now they're scarcely running, but there should be one along fairly soon."

He was as good as his word. Before I had time to do more than glance around, an engine hauling three cars lumbered into view. A handful of latecomers hurried off and sped up the stairs. We jumped on in their place.

The rattle and clatter of the train was such that it was im-possible to speak. I was seated on the inside of a bench for two. With every sway along the tracks, I was pushed against Marco or away from him. The constant dance of our bodies distracted me from thoughts of what it meant to be passing under a vast river a few dozen yards above our heads. Before I could think overly long of it, the train slanted upward. Not too soon for my peace of mind, we slowed and shortly came to a station. Set in tile along the walls, I read the name Elephant and Castle.

We left the train—I admit to being very glad to do so—and ascended another long stairway. At last, we came within sight of natural light.

"We're at the top of the high street," Marco said as we emerged. "The foundry is that way." He gestured directly ahead but he needn't have bothered. The clang of metal upon metal combining with the heavy smell of molten iron left no doubt as to what lay ahead.

Even so, I was not entirely prepared for my first sight of the massive, dark monolith that rose above a neighborhood of far more modest shops and factories. The foundry dominated the skyline, its chimneys seeming to reach to the heavens while its vast brick walls scarcely contained the cacophony within.

Despite the general holiday declared in honor of Victoria, workers were streaming in and out of the massive, soot-darkened buildings. We appeared to have arrived just as a shift was changing. The men emerging through the high, iron-grated doors were covered with soot; only their eyes shone unnaturally white and bright. For the most part, they were big men, tall and broad shouldered, but more than a few stumbled as they fanned out into the neighboring streets. They kept their heads down and did not speak, seemingly intent on escaping the shadow of the foundry as quickly as they could. Those going toward it took no notice of them. They walked singly and in pairs, roughly clothed with tin lunch pails swinging from their hands. Few spoke and none smiled. They trudged on, appearing resigned to where they were going and what they must do.

"They look scarcely alive," I said. The privileged existence I had enjoyed as a human had not prepared me for the sight of these men. I was at once embarrassed by my own ignorance and appalled at what I was witnessing.

"The work drains them," Marco replied. "The heat is intense, men shovel tons of iron ore and pour vast amounts of molten metal until their bodies scream for relief. The air is foul, the light poor, accidents are frequent and often deadly. It is not a life anyone would seek."

"Yet they have no shortage of workers despite the strange things you told me are happening there?"

"People are desperate for jobs," Marco replied. "If a man falters, he knows two or three at the very least will be waiting to replace him. It concentrates the mind, I suppose, but it also grinds down the soul."

"Surely better provision could be made for them?" I asked.

He shot me a quick look. "We live in an age when better care is given to machines than to men. Ever more powerful machines have been replacing humans for decades now but of late, the speed with which they gain has increased. If it continues unabated, there will be nothing left for ordinary people in this world."

"Except to feed vampires." I regretted the words as soon as they were uttered. Marco truly did want to help me. It was the height of folly to remind him why his kind and mine were more naturally foe than friend.

"I doubt that humans will be content with that," he said. "They lack the strength of vampires but they are intelligent and they excel at being able to adapt to change. We should not rule them out just yet."

"Not to mention that there are so many of them," I

murmured. Despite the throngs crowding the route of the Jubilee procession, the streets around the foundry remained filled with people. Many were pockmarked, their faces pallid, their bodies stunted by lifetimes of too little food and too much labor, yet they appeared more vital than the foundry workers. Ragged boys, shoeless and dirty, hawked wares, some peddling newspapers, others carrying trays of cheap buns hung around their necks. Wagons trundled past, most so laden with every manner of barrel and crate that they looked likely to tip over. Along one side of the street, immense dray horses pulled trams up the incline of the high street hill, brakes shrieking as they made the trip back down again.

All this drew my eye but only briefly. Looming over all, the foundry commanded attention.

"Can we get inside?" I asked Marco.

"If we hurry. The doors are locked between shifts."

They were clanging shut even as we arrived, but Marco knew the guard on duty from his previous visits. A quick word, the exchange of several pound notes, and we were admitted.

"Good luck to you, sir," the man said, glancing around nervously. "And you, too, miss. Hope you know what you're doing."

Marco might but I was quite certain that I did not. Keeping that uppermost in mind, I stepped into the bowels of hell.

CHAPTER 12

A wall of sound slammed into us. Marco pushed against it as I followed, gripping his hand. His admonition to stay close no longer seemed foolish. Left to my own devices, I feared that I would be sent reeling back in defeat before taking more than a few steps. At length, we emerged onto a catwalk. Far below us, set deep below the ground, immense furnaces burned, their fiery red eyes like those of crouched beasts preparing to strike.

Open carts the height of a man and filled with raw ore entered one end of the foundry on narrow rail lines. The contents were spilled into the furnaces, from which a molten liquid emerged, flowing through elevated trenches into the casting vessels. Men with long grappling hooks swung blocks of metal toward immense rollers the size of small hillocks that flattened the blocks into thick sheets. From there they were pulled and dragged through razor-sharp cutters that turned them into metal plates and strips.

At every step, men stood perilously close to danger. If the flames of the furnaces and the heat of molten metal did not burn them, they were at risk of being pierced by the hooks, or falling beneath the crushing rollers, or losing a hand or worse to the cutters.

So intense was the roar of machines grinding against machines that conversation was impossible, not only for us but
also for the workers. The men who appeared tiny and shrunken
against the vast workings of the foundry were forced to communicate with hand gestures. Otherwise, each man was sealed off
within himself, performing his task over and over with numb-
ing repetition. After I had watched for a few minutes, it began
to seem that it was the machine that was alive rather than the
men themselves who were no more than cogs within it.

The heat was as intense as the noise, the air foul with the
stench of molten iron. Waves of acrid steam rose, shrouding
the workers as they labored. High above, behind a wall of glass,
light glittered in offices and a few faces could be glimpsed but
they seemed little more alive than those of the men on the
foundry floor.

Marco bent closer. I felt the warmth of his breath on my
neck as he shouted, "If you've seen enough, let's move on."

I nodded emphatically. A moment later we were through
a door and into the relative quiet of a stairwell. Rickety metal
steps stretched up the height of the building. I craned my
neck, trying to see to the top, but failed.

"Can you sense anything?" Marco asked.

"Besides the fact that this really does seem to be hell on
earth?" I shook my head. "The noise, the smells, it's all too much."

"Then perhaps we should leave?"

"No! I need more time, only a little. You will admit that
this place is a shock to body and mind alike."

"It is that," he agreed. "Come, let me show what I found
when I was here before."

He led me down stairs that swayed with our weight, the riv-
ets holding them to the walls easing in and out as though they

breathed. When we came at last to the bottom, I sagged a little with relief. But my respite was short. Marco started off down a long corridor that vanished into Stygian darkness.

"Where are we going?" I asked as I ran to keep up. He still had hold of my hand but it did not seem to occur to him to match his stride to mine. Not that it should matter. I was no wasp-waisted young lady perpetually short of breath. Indeed, I needed no breath at all. Reminding myself of that, I matched his pace.

"To a basement," he said, "below the lowest level of the foundry. It seems to have been part of the original manor."

I nodded even as I wondered how we were to find our way without light. As it turned out, I needn't have worried. A short distance down the corridor, Marco stopped near an alcove set into the wall. From it, he drew an oil lamp and a metal box of matches. Having struck a match against the wall, he set flame to wick. A small pool of light spilled from the lamp.

"This way." He stepped into the darkness. The stone floor slanted downward. After the heat of the foundry, the passage felt startlingly cool and wet. As the cacophony faded behind us, I became aware of other sounds—Marco's steady breathing, the murmur of air moving past us, and off in the distance, the faint gurgle of water.

"How much farther?" I asked.

"Just here," he said and held the lamp high. Ahead I could make out the entrance to a room. Beyond I saw rotting wainscoting along walls decorated with peeling murals of hunters giving chase. At the far end, an archway led deeper into the darkness.

Marco and I stepped into the room. I looked around slowly. "What is this place?"

He shrugged. "Your guess is as good as mine, but I think it may have been a reception area. Before Mordred purchased the manor, it belonged to a church prelate who either didn't know who he was selling to or didn't care. He had it in turn from the Duke of Suffolk, who was a great friend of Henry VIII's. That scene on the wall over there seems to show the king and the duke hunting together."

I stepped farther into the room and took a closer look. Two men, one with a trim beard framing his corpulent face, the other leaner and clean-shaven, were closing in on a stag. Trumpeters rode nearby, as did various lords and ladies of a long-vanished court.

"Would Mordred have kept this?" I asked.

"He might have found it amusing," Marco replied. "If you look closely, the artist has depicted all six of Henry's wives, including those he killed. They appear to be riding him down with blood in their eyes."

So they did. Anne Boleyn was in the lead, but Catherine Howard wasn't too far behind, and Henry's first queen, Catherine of Aragon, was wielding a lance that looked set to dispatch her erstwhile lord into the great beyond. I drew my eyes away and scanned the rest of the room. A few scattered bits of furniture remained. A table, the top covered by the powdery remnants of long-dead flowers fallen from a porcelain vase covered with a coat of dust. Alcoves painted with other scenes too obscure for me to recognize.

"No one has been here in a very long time," I said. Though I spoke softly, my voice echoed up to the domed ceiling high above.

"So it seems," Marco agreed. He stepped closer. I turned

toward his warmth, saw the golden glimmer of his eyes, and reached out a hand to—

The room shifted around me. One moment I was standing in the buried ruins beneath the foundry and in the next I heard music. The light of gleaming candles filled the chamber that looked as fresh and new as though it had been constructed that very day. Lords and ladies, all gloriously dressed, moved within it.

I moved away from them, toward a twisting stone staircase that coiled within the shell of a tower, climbing higher and higher until I came to . . . a library? The walls were lined with floor-to-ceiling shelves filled with leather-bound books. I glimpsed a copy of Dante's *La Divina Commedia* and another of Chaucer's *Canterbury Tales* before I was diverted by the view beyond the tall windows.

London lay before me on both sides of the gleaming silver ribbon that was the Thames. But it was a London I had never seen before. The tallest building in view was St. Paul's. East of it lay the Tower, looming heavy and threatening above the river. To the west, I could just make out the spires of Westminster Abbey. But the city between was . . . tiny? The buildings were low and huddled together. No Watchers moved among them, no turbines thrummed. It was a different age.

A man dressed in black stood near the windows. I walked deeper into the room, drawn to *him*. My own will was suspended; suddenly it was as if I was back on the moor, helpless to do anything other than his bidding. An eager accomplice to my own seduction.

He turned, saw me, and smiled. "Lucy . . . at last . . ."

A shiver of pleasure rippled through me. The drawing in Dee's book captured his features well enough but it could not do justice to the impact of his presence. The light that shone from within him dazzled my eyes. He was the being in the opera house, the singer who had drawn me from the grave, yet I now knew him to be so much more. Mordred, the son of Arthur and lover of Morgaine, who had sacrificed his humanity in a desperate bid to save his realm. How had the weight of centuries—and of power beyond the understanding of mere mortals—shaped him?

His hands clasped mine. I looked down, startled to see that while his were almost translucent my own appeared solid but wavering, as though caught in a blurred photograph where the subject is moving in and out of focus.

"You've left it rather late, dear girl." Sadness tinged his voice but so did relief. "Not that you are to blame. Damn Gladstone for his interference. If I'd any notion that he would learn of you and mistakenly think that you were a danger to the realm, I would have . . . But never mind, there is no time for that now. You are here and I am thankful for it."

As much as I would have liked to pursue the matter of the former prime minister's role in consigning me to the grave from which Mordred had drawn me, I agreed that this was not the moment to do so. My throat was very tight. I struggled to speak. "This place . . . how can you . . . ?"

"Memory and shadow, nothing more but enough for me to reach you. We have little time—"

"I know." Urgency gripped me. "Where are you really?" Not in a long-vanished tower above a modern foundry, that was for certain. I could believe that such was the power of his being that he could project the sense of himself into this place he must have known so well, and even draw me partway into it as he had drawn me from the grave. But his physical form had to be somewhere else entirely.

"A basement," Mordred said, "damp, moldy, and dark. I can hear the river. I think it is the Thames. There are boats along it, their horns hooting. I catch a whiff of sooty air now and again. In what I imagine is day, the ground above me vibrates with traffic. From time to time, I hear music. Occasionally, I hear people screaming."

What hell was he describing? Where the trapped screamed and music played while life above went on its frantic, turbulent way?

"Do you see anyone?" I asked.

"A man . . . human or a devil, I cannot say. Perhaps he is both. He comes to torment me but I never see his face. He is always masked."

I shivered at the vision he conjured. Who could have laid so great a king so low? How could I hope to save him? "What else do you see?"

"Nothing . . . only the masked man."

"There must be other clues to where you are. I beseech you, no detail is too small."

"I have told you all I can." His voice was fading; already he seemed to be slipping from me.

"Wait! If we cannot find you, human and vampire will fall on one another to the destruction of both our races. You must help us!"

He hesitated, his gaze sharpening even as darkness swirled around us both. In the distance, I heard the grunts and clangs of a strange beast, both alive and machine, grinding down all in its path.

"Us?" Mordred repeated. "Who is with you?"

"Marco di Orsini."

I waited, wondering what his reaction would be, but he did no more than ask, "What do you know of him?"

Belatedly, I realized how little Marco had told me of himself. "He says that he is not a Slayer."

Was that not the truth? Could he have befriended me only so I would lead him to Mordred? As a girl, I had skipped along the bright surface of life, rarely bothering to consider what lay below. Now I saw layers of motive and suspicion at every turn. If the conflicting sides of my nature had any chance of ever being reconciled, I had to hope that it would be on some surer middle ground.

To my great relief, Mordred said, "Indeed he is not. He is a Protector, scion of an ancient line sworn to safeguard humans from us. He is taking a risk allying himself with you. His kind will not approve."

The red pendant. The ease with which he had driven off the pair who had threatened me in front of the Bagatelle. His knowledge of all things vampire. He had been protecting me the night we met when I was a naïve, all-too-human girl. Was he still?

"Marco believes that only you can prevent war between humans and vampires," I said.

Mordred sighed. "Sadly, I suspect that he is right, but my strength is fading. If you would ask more of me, make haste."

"Wait!" I insisted. Loathe though I was to think it, I might fail in my quest to find Mordred. This could be my only chance to understand what had happened to me. "Why me? Why didn't you choose someone else?"

He hesitated. "How much do you know of your family history?"

"Enough, I suppose. My father—"

"The male line is inconsequential. I am speaking of your mother's people."

"My mother?" My kind, patient mother, who dreamed of seeing her daughters presented at court and was fiercely proud of her prize-winning camellias.

"Your mother is a descendant of the same bloodline as Morgaine. Do you know who she was?"

"If Dee is to be believed, you loved her—"

He winced. A look passed across his face that spoke such sorrow as mere words can never convey. "It is true, I loved her with all my heart when I possessed as much."

"But she was a Slayer."

"Indeed, and from that blood comes many things. Other Slayers, of course, but the next of those lies centuries in the future. Between comes the potential for something altogether different—neither vampire nor human but part of both."

"A halfling." I hardly dared to let my lips shape the word, but scarcely had I spoken than I saw the truth in his gaze.

"Ah, Lucy, you are far better informed than I imagined you would be, but perhaps that is for the best. Time is fleeting. *Find me. . . ."*

His last words were little more than a whisper. Mordred, the room, and the city beyond were dissolving. With his going so, too, did my own strength evaporate. My knees gave way. I touched a cold, hard floor only to be lifted from it by strong arms.

A deep, resonant voice spoke close against my ear. Breath—alive, vibrant—brushed my cheek. "It's all right, I've got you."

I clung to hard muscle and sinew, to warmth and life, to the thought of Marco and the reality, his face floating before me as I climbed up and up, out of time and memory until I came at last back to the place where I had begun.

"What happened?" my protector asked.

CHAPTER 13

M arco and I were standing on a narrow platform high above the foundry floor. Across the width of it, I saw blank-faced men moving behind a glass wall, men of the new technocrat class who kept such marvels as the foundry running without thought of the cost to others.

"I found him." Was that my voice, so thin and faint, like mist tangling in spectral branches?

"Mordred?"

I nodded. "The stories are true; he is here, as is the manor. But I only reached him for few moments. I couldn't hold on."

"It doesn't matter," Marco said. "At least we know now."

"It does matter," I insisted. "He couldn't tell me where he is."

"We'll find out, but come, we need to leave here."

He was right, of course, but that did not make the task easy. We staggered down the rickety metal steps until we came to the passage through which we had entered. Scarcely had we started along it than a rending shriek tore the air, drowning out even the cacophony of the machines. The walls shuddered all around us. I glanced over my shoulder in time to see the bolts holding the metal staircase in place snap as though they were made of tin rather than steel. The entire structure swayed loose from the wall and began to crumble.

"Run!" I yelled, and we did, thudding down through the passage out toward the gate, hurtling ourselves against the barrier.

Only to be reminded that it was locked. Beyond, I could see daylight, but it could have been a hundred miles away for all the chance we had of reaching it. Behind us, terrified workers had thrown down their tools and were racing for safety. In another moment, the least fortunate would be trampled underfoot and the rest trapped.

"You!" Marco shouted. "Unlock the gate!"

Startled, I saw the guard who had been bribed to let us in. The man looked pale and terrified, frozen in place. Marco grabbed hold of him and shoved him against the barrier. "Open it!"

In the grip of shock, the hapless fellow fumbled the key. It dropped clattering onto the floor. Marco swept it up and—as the panic-stricken workers closed in—shoved the key into the lock. With a twist, it opened. The gate swung, squeaking on its hinges. Around us, the walls of the foundry were giving way. I stretched out my arms, trying to keep my balance as the floor tilted. The screams of machines and men joined in an endless outcry of pain and horror. I looked back in the direction we had come just as an immense explosion rent the air. A ball of fire hurtled toward us down the passage.

"Go!" Marco shouted and shoved me out through the door. The ground rippled and quaked. We clung to each other as we ran. Men were pouring out behind us, many with their clothes on fire. They formed a vast wave that pushed us along. Debris was falling everywhere, striking down those trying to escape.

I saw an older man collapse, his skull split open by a brick. A younger man, lamed by a blow from a hurtling piece of steel, crumbled to the ground and was quickly lost beneath the rampaging mob.

A scream bubbled up in my throat. Before it could escape, Marco thrust us both into the doorway of a small shop. Sheltered there we turned in time to see the entire massive foundry give one last shudder before it surrendered to the inexorable pull of gravity. The hideous shriek of a dying beast filled the air. As it did, Marco pressed me against the wall, his body protecting mine.

Given who and what I was, our positions should have been reversed. My strength and stamina were greater, yet apparently I was still human enough to rouse his protective instincts. And to be glad of them.

Clinging to him, I stared over his shoulder, convinced that no one, not even a vampire, could survive the maelstrom of destruction about to consume us. Everything that had comprised the foundry—its massive walls and towering smokestacks, its huge furnaces and molds, casting vessels, rollers and cutters, all of it was cascading down upon the surrounding streets. A lucky few managed to evade the debris, but they were quickly covered in choking dust. Only those who, like Marco and me, were sheltered beneath deep overhangs, avoided the worst.

We remained unmoving until at last the dust began to settle. Slowly, Marco stepped away from the door. I did the same. Together, we stared at the ruins of the foundry, still shifting and settling like a creature in its death throes. All around us lay the dead and, in far smaller number, the dying, their piteous final moans filling the acrid air. Too quickly, unearthly quiet descended.

As from a distance, I heard my voice, flattened by shock. The horrible possibility rising in my mind could not be denied. "This can't be a coincidence, us being here, my seeing Mordred, just when this happened. Could what I did, crossing over the barriers that separate time and place, have caused this?"

Marco hesitated. Clearly, he wanted to reassure me that I had no role in what had happened, yet he was too intrinsically honest to lie. "We have no way of knowing and, at any rate, you did what you had to. If you want to blame someone, blame whoever took Mordred and set all this in motion." To forestall any further discussion, he added, "The authorities will arrive at any moment. We must go."

Already, the all-seeing dirigibles were moving overhead, the Watchers on board searching for anything that could explain the calamity that had just occurred. Quickly, I took Marco's arm. Together, we hurried up the hill to the train station only to discover what with hindsight we should have expected. Given the disaster at the foundry, the station was closed. A helmeted police officer stood out in front, directing everyone away. With great effort we retraced our steps and managed to reach the river, crossing at Blackfriar's Bridge. The statue of Her Imperial Majesty loomed over us. Victoria looked more than usually displeased, but perhaps that was only my imagination.

To the south on the opposite shore, vast clouds of smoke rose from the foundry site. As I watched, several more steam-powered fire wagons raced across the bridge. More dirigibles were moving into position above the wreckage.

Turning to me, Marco said, "We must get off the streets. Can you walk?"

Only then did I realize that I was sagging against him. The

encounter with Mordred had left me profoundly drained. My limbs shook and I felt scarcely able to hold my head up. Even so, I nodded.

Staying off the main thoroughfares, we made our way slowly through narrow, twisting lanes that I recognized as remnants of the London I had glimpsed from Mordred's tower now all but lost in the vastly greater metropolis reaching out in all directions to engulf everything in its path. But where a lane ended, a gate stood open, leading onward to sloping stone steps, a basement passage, and up again into the sunlight, the way made smooth by others who had gone before us, as intent as we were on avoiding notice. The ancient city seemed to be devising its own means of surviving in our harsh new age.

As we walked, I related to Marco some of what Mordred had managed to tell me. Of Gladstone's role, I said nothing. That could wait.

When I had finished, he said, "A subterranean room within hearing of the river. Traffic above. Screams and music. That is all?"

"I'm afraid so. Of course, there is the man . . . or devil. Mordred wasn't sure which he is."

"He is a man," Marco said flatly. "Mordred is all too familiar with dark spirits, devils, demons, and the like. He would have no trouble recognizing one of them no matter what disguise the creature came in."

I remained doubtful. "A man capable of capturing the king of the vampires and holding him against his will? What sort of man could that be?"

"I don't know," Marco admitted. "But I do know someone who might have an idea."

As he spoke, a pair of Watchers appeared at the end of the

lane. Seeing us, they paused. At once, Marco said loudly, "Dear heart, I know you are fond of what you insist on calling 'quaint old London,' but I must tell you that I have no desire to live anywhere other than Mayfair. What civilized man would?"

"But don't you see," I said, falling in with his ploy, "how artistic and interesting it all is?"

"What I see is mold and dry rot, nothing else. But if you must have an ancient pile somewhere, let it at least be in the country. We can go down to Kent next week. I've heard of several properties there that—"

Disinterested in our domestic conversation, the Watchers moved on. Marco and I waited until they were gone before we did the same. Through another close, down a shadowed alley, we came out into the narrow lane that ran alongside the Serjeant's Inn. A moment later, we entered the office of Barrister Nicolas di Orsini, who, once again, was not present.

"The bath is through there," Marco said. "If you'd like to clean up."

Catching a glimpse of myself in a framed mirror hanging on one wall, I flinched. Like Marco, I was covered from head to foot with ash and grit.

"I'll use another down the hall," he said.

The bath was well appointed including a large claw-footed tub that I looked at longingly. But with time so pressing and not wishing to presume upon the tolerance of my absent host, I washed my hands and face, then set about damp sponging my clothes. As I did, I found myself recalling how Marco and I had eluded the Watchers. An obviously mismatched couple arguing over where to live. Just the sort of nonsense that humans fell into and that I, when I was fully one of them, had observed with amusement. How fortunate I was to have escaped all that.

Yet Kent was pleasant at this time of year and Mayfair, where my family lived when they were in London, had much to recommend it. Such a couple might reach an accord after all. Perhaps even find that they could rub along congenially enough. Assuming one was willing to settle for a life of such petty concerns—love, children, a future destined to end in inevitable death. Death that lent such poignant flavor to life, shaping it and giving it meaning where otherwise there would be none. One night flowing into the next, lost in frivolous or worse, vicious pleasure.

How had Mordred endured the tedium of immortality for so long? How had he managed to find purpose in such an interminable existence? Did he find his strength in the realm whose king he surely would have been had his father only seen his worth? Or was it from Morgaine, the woman he had lost to remorseless fate, that he drew the will to go on?

Were vampires capable of such love? Could a cold, still heart hold fire within?

I caught myself rubbing far too hard at a stubborn bit of ash and stopped abruptly. My hair was a tangled mess. I set about rearranging it, pulling harder than I had to at the snarls. The last pin was scarcely in place when I heard the door to the street open and close.

Assuming that Nicolas di Orsini had returned, I gathered what strength I had left and stepped into the office. My intention was to introduce myself and explain my presence. If he was as knowledgeable as his brother, he was likely to recognize what I was. I had to hope that Marco would appear swiftly and put him at ease.

All this was in my mind when I caught sight of the man standing just inside the door. He was as tall and broad shouldered as his sibling, but where Marco's hair was brown, Nicolas' was black shot through with silver, the latter at odds with his obvious youthfulness. His eyes, when the light hit them, held an amber sheen. As I watched, his nostrils flared and he took a quick step toward me.

"What are you doing here?" he demanded.

A taste flitted across my tongue carrying with it a cascade of sensations—cold air, the rush of wind, flesh and blood, and the moon, low in the sky, beckoning. Fear gripped me but hard alongside it rode hatred and rage that threatened to be all con-suming.

My response to him stunned me. For a horrible moment, I felt myself plummeting into a chasm where reason did not exist and only bloodlust ruled.

"Your fangs are showing, Miss Weston."

His matter-of-fact tone was enough to draw me back. Em-barrassed, and not a little appalled with myself, I asked, "Do I know you?"

My question appeared to amuse him. He advanced farther into the room but did not come near me, circling around in-stead so that I was forced to turn to face him. I was shamefully relieved to notice that unlike his sibling, he did not wear any-thing resembling the red pendant.

"Of course not," he said. "How could you possibly? We've only just met." Shrugging out of his coat, he added, "I'll war-rant my brother has something to do with your being here."

"Guilty." Marco stepped into the room from the hall. Like me, he had managed to remove the worst of the ash and grit from his face and clothes. For the first time I saw that a gash several inches long ran down the left side of his brow. A little further and it would have reached his eye. Guilt stabbed me as I realized that he had likely acquired it while protecting me.

"What happened to you?" Nicolas asked, frowning.

Marco touched a finger to the wound as though he had only then remembered its existence. "This? It's nothing. You heard about the foundry?"

His brother nodded. "The authorities are wasting no time pointing the finger of blame at the anarchists."

"The truth is rather more complicated," Marco said. "I see you've met Miss Weston." As he spoke, he stepped between us. His manner toward his brother was entirely pleasant, yet I was struck by the odd sensation that he was once again intent on protecting me. At the foundry, the danger had been obvious. But here . . . ?

"Lucy, may I present my brother, Nicolas? He's not a bad sort, just a bit rough around the edges."

The younger di Orsini gave a quick, hard laugh, but at the same time he appeared to relax. More pleasantly, he said, "Pardon my manners, Miss Weston, or the lack of them. You should know that I am the black sheep of the family, rather ironically, since I'm not good with sheep at all." With a glance at Marco, he added, "But it seems that my brother is aspiring to take the title from me."

"Nicolas—" Marco looked disinclined to discuss the matter, but his sibling was not deterred.

"No, seriously, what are you thinking of, consorting with a vampire? I cannot begin to imagine how the family will respond. But I am sure that it will make what happened with me look like extreme tolerance."

"That isn't important now," Marco insisted. "Miss Weston

has been through an ordeal. She needs to rest. If you aren't prepared to help us—"

In truth, I was swaying on my feet. I had become so accustomed to the power of my new state that I was at a loss how to cope without it. The floor was rushing up toward me when I found myself lying on a leather couch. Marco loomed over me frowning. Just behind, his brother watched us both.

"Shall I call for tea?" Nicolas asked. "That is what one offers fainting females, isn't it? Or do you require something stronger, Miss Weston?"

"Leave her alone," Marco snapped. "She was able to find Mordred."

At once, Nicolas' manner changed. From his response, I gathered that he knew about the vampire king's disappearance and the urgent need to find him. "Why didn't you say so at once? If we know where he is—"

"We don't," I said. The weakness of my voice appalled me, but I struggled on despite it. "I've only managed to communicate with him. He was able to give us a few clues as to his whereabouts, nothing more."

"I don't understand—" Nicolas began.

"Lucy has a connection to him," Marco explained. "He incarnated her for a reason, but—"

Nicolas shrugged as though the answer was obvious. "Her mother is of Morgaine's bloodline."

"How could you possibly know that?" I asked. Indeed, how could he have known about me at all? Marco had not told him, that much was obvious from the exchanges between the brothers.

"I asked Stoker," Nicolas said. He was smiling as he spoke, clearly anticipating our reaction.

Marco straightened and stared at his brother. "You've talked with the Irishman?"

"Indeed. He's a font of information, shockingly little of which he included in his so-called novel. Perhaps he's saving it for a sequel."

I ignored the suggestion that Stoker could follow deceit with yet more deception and said, "I thought he was a pen for hire, nothing more." Surely that was the impression Mr. Stoker had gone to great lengths to create during our single meeting.

Nicolas looked surprised. "Stoker? Hardly. He's been one of Gladstone's operatives for years, mainly to do with the sorry Irish business. But he's had a hand in elsewhere, as well."

"Gladstone?" I repeated, mindful of what Mordred had revealed. "What has he to do with this?"

Former Prime Minister William Gladstone, the Lion of Parliament as he was still known, was a very old man who, having served his country for six decades, including no fewer than four terms as prime minister, should have been living in honorable retirement. But if the whispers were to be believed, he still had a firm hand on the British ship of state.

"If Stoker is so well informed," Marco said, "perhaps he is the man we should ask."

"Not a bad idea," Nicolas agreed. "Now about that tea—"

I declined. Hard on the sapping of my strength had come hunger I could not deny no matter how desperately I tried. As much as I wanted to challenge Marco about his nature as a Protector, it would have to wait. I stood, smoothing my skirts even as I observed how my hands trembled.

"I must go."

Marco rose, his face creased with concern. "Don't be absurd. You need to rest and we have much to discuss."

"Then discuss it with your brother. As for myself—" I could not bring myself to tell him the truth but no matter, Nicolas did it for me.

"She needs to feed."

Marco looked startled and then—just for a moment—appalled. He masked his disgust quickly but not before I saw it. Not that I could blame him. All that was still human within me shared his abhorrence of what I had to do in order to survive.

Even so, he tried. "We can find something. A calf . . . a stag . . ."

"I am beyond that." Felix had seen to that at Lady Blanche's behest. The taste of human blood that I had received had created an insatiable craving for more. Even so, I loathed the idea of returning to the Bagatelle in such a vulnerable state, certain as I was that Lady Blanche would not hesitate to take advantage of it.

As I turned toward the door, Marco moved to intercept me but Nicolas was quicker. Grasping his brother's arm, he said softly, "Let her go."

Marco started to resist until our eyes met. The remorseless need that gripped me must have been impossible to ignore. Even so, he shook off his brother angrily and moved toward me, but too late. I was gone between one instant and the next, in flight from my own dismay and regret.

Soot from the foundry hung heavy in the air, obscuring the sun. A pallor lay over all. My weariness fell away as I lifted my head, sniffing the air. Humans . . . frightened, distraught, uncertain of what to do or where to go.

Feed, my mind said.

CHAPTER 14

Mindful of the Watchers, I considered returning to the labyrinth of hidden byways, but as I was about to do so, a sudden impulse seized me. Tentatively, I touched the side of a building a short distance from the Serjeant's Inn. The pale stones were smooth beneath my fingers, but between them I felt depressions in the mortar just wide enough to offer a hand- or toehold.

While still a child at Whitby, I had gloried in climbing the gnarled old trees shaped by the wind that blew endlessly from the sea. On long summer afternoons, I would lurk in their sheltering branches, daydreaming or reading, waiting to startle hapless passersby. My mother had decried my hoydenish ways but never managed to reform them. My father had merely laughed.

I had thought my climbing days were over but I had been wrong. Slowly at first, then with growing confidence, I scaled the building. The ground fell away beneath me as gravity surrendered to my newfound powers. More quickly than I would have thought possible, I reached a roof covered with sooty tiles and dotted with chimneys. For a few minutes, I distracted myself from my hunger by watching the Watchers. In the

unnatural dusk settling rapidly over the city they took on
the appearance of black insects moving with the same blind
instinct that controls schools of fish or flocks of birds. Their
patterns were repetitious and predictable. Not once did any of
them look up.

Even so, had a dirigible passed just then, I would have been
seen. Fortunately, they were all occupied above Southwark.
After a few minutes, I continued on, leaping from roof to roof
with growing speed and agility. As I went, I saw reminders
of the hidden world. Little Alice was not alone in tending a
buried bridge. Another of her kind hovered near Walbrook
in the direction of the Tower where the resident ravens were
preparing to nest. It is said that as long as the birds remain,
the kingdom will not fall. Perhaps so, but ravens of a different
sort—larger, red-eyed, with curved beaks and glittering talons
that appeared sheathed in steel—kept watch on the ancient
ramparts. Nearby, the Thames was inhabited by hulking co-
lossi, their immense bodies so transparent that little was visible
save the vast columns of pale vertebra, flexing and arching
endlessly as though they were the spine of the great city itself.

When the light faded and darkness descended, I began to
catch glimpses of spectral figures, scarcely distinguishable from
the gathering fog. They drifted along the streets, never ventur-
ing very far before returning to particular buildings. The very
air seemed to shudder and moan with their grief. A shiver ran
down my back as I observed these ghosts, forever chained to
places that for whatever reason they could not leave.

The ghosts and all the forlorn hopes and regrets they represented were forgotten as I perched on the dome of St. Paul's,
looking out in every direction. London felt alive, a great beast

fed by history and ambition, stretching its powers far beyond the limits of the river that had nurtured it for millennia. In comparison, the puny humans who inhabited it were of no more significance than motes of dust blown on a puff of air.

What foolish weakness drove me to long for my lost humanity? I was stronger and swifter than I had ever been. My senses were far sharper and my mind as well. I was impervious to death by any usual means, gifted with eternal youth and beauty, freed from all the petty concerns that so weighed down hapless humans trapped in their mayfly lives. Feeding on them was really no different from sipping the nectar of a blossom that flowers for a day and is forgotten. They were of no more consequence than that.

Even as that thought passed through my mind, a young man emerged from a building across from the cathedral. Despite the gathering gloom, I could see that he was tall and fit, with a pleasant, open face. I noted the broad sweep of his shoulders, his ready smile, and the grace of his movements. My gaze fell on the strong column of his neck just visible above his collar where the thick curls of his golden hair brushed his nape. How easy it was to imagine the feel of his skin—smooth and warm, the pulse of his life beating just beneath it. His taste . . .

My fangs unsheathed, I slipped down the curve of the dome, no thought in my mind except to have him. I was about to leap into the street when the bells in the northwest tower of the cathedral began to toll the hour. The great, booming sound made the very air vibrate and brought me up short. In the space of silence between one peal and the next, revulsion swept over me. I was horrified by my intentions and by the ability of my mind to trick me into them. Gasping, I grabbed hold of a nearby drain spout, clinging to it with all my strength, refusing to let go until the young man moved on, heedless of the vile danger lurking above him.

With his departure, the hunger that gripped me raged unchecked. I had to feed and quickly or I would surely go mad. And then what might I do? Like it or not, I had no choice but to return to the Bagatelle.

By the time I reached the entrance to the club, an unending roar sounded in my ears, the scream of my stronger self demanding to be fed. The scent of blood clawed through the pores of my skin, a cruel torment that only served to heighten my hunger even further. In a world rippling with waves of black and gray, the red eyes of the snake glowed hellishly. His tongue flicked out. Glistening drops of venom shone on the tips of his fangs.

I pushed past the creature and through the door, moving as quickly as I could manage. Although it was still early, the club was crowded already. Several of the patrons noticed me as I entered. With what little control I had left, I struggled to appear as calm as possible even as I looked around anxiously for Felix. When I saw him, relief flooded me. I made my way to his side. He took one look at me and pulled me into an alcove.

"Where have you been?" Felix demanded. "I checked your room but you weren't there. The foundry . . ."

"Is gone, I know. Please, I can't speak of that now. I must feed." My voice sounded hoarse and far away, all but drowned out by the howl of hunger that threatened to swallow whatever remained of my sanity.

"Fine. Pick a supplicant and gorge yourself, but if you were there and Lady Blanche finds out—" He stopped abruptly and stared at me. "What's wrong?"

Not even the compulsion that Mordred had laid on me could stand against the struggle between the two conflicting sides of my nature. A dark abyss was opening before me. On the verge of falling into it, I could barely speak.

"Felix, please . . ."

He muttered something I did not catch and snapped his fingers at a thrall. When next I was aware, an empty crystal glass was on the table before me and I was filled with an exquisite sense of well-being.

"This business of refusing to feed properly has to stop," Felix said, but he looked more worried than condemning. "Seriously, Lucy, it will cause talk and you don't want that. Matters are too precarious. You have no idea—"

"I have some. You were right about the foundry. It does—or it did—coexist somehow with the manor. Mordred was able to communicate with me there but only up to a point. He is being held captive but there was little he could tell me about his prison. I still have no idea where he is."

"But you saw him, spoke with him?"

Felix's excitement was palpable. I was sorry to have to quash it. "Yes, but I doubt that I could do so again. Aside from the fact that the foundry was destroyed, Mordred is very weak. If we do not find him quickly, it will be too late."

"He must have told you something . . . some clue . . ."

"He is being held by a human, underground, near the river. That's all I know." I was taking a risk telling Felix even that much, but I believed him when he said that he feared war above all else.

With a quick glance over his shoulder to make sure we would not be overheard, he said, "A human? How is that possible?"

"I have no idea, but I do know that if you tell Lady Blanche this and she truly does not want Mordred to return, then—"

I broke off, interrupted by a sudden shout and the sound of glass shattering. Two males were squaring off against each another near the bar. Having seen enough altercations between young men wherein they poked each other's chests and growled threats before being separated by their friends, I was not alarmed initially. But the conflict quickly escalated out of all comparison to anything I had ever witnessed. In an instant, both males had unsheathed their fangs and rushed together, colliding with a bone-crunching thud. The tame humans cowered in fear but the other vampires screamed their approval. Tables and chairs tumbled to the floor as the club's guests jumped up in a rush to see what was happening. A ring of avid watchers formed around the combatants.

Locked in a savage embrace, the pair fell against the bar with such force that everything on it hurtled to the floor and the wood itself cracked. Staggering to their feet, both roaring, they went at each other again. The crowd's frenzied cheers rose to the ceiling and set the chandeliers to trembling.

Blood flew in all directions. The sight and smell of it maddened the other vampires, who began swiftly to turn on one another. I gaped in mingled horror and excitement as clothing and flesh alike were torn amid shouts of pain and rage. Only a very few maintained any semblance of control. Fortunately, one of those was Felix. He grabbed my hand and pulled me under the table. Moments before, the Bagatelle had been an exotic scene, sensual and bizarre yet not without its own appeal. Now it teetered on the edge of dark and writhing chaos such as one finds in the illustrations of Dante's *Inferno*, where the damned war endlessly against one another.

The sudden explosion of violence stunned me, but even more so was my sense that the madness I was seeing had been there all along, only lurking beneath the surface waiting for any opportunity to take control. Lurking, too, in me?

But if that were the case, how could the vampires or any beings who behaved in such a way survive for any length of time? Wouldn't they have long since devoured one another?

"Enough!"

Lady Blanche stood, sheathed in white, her hands on her slender hips, a look of fury on her exquisite face. The sight of her sent a bolt of visceral fear through me, but no one else seemed similarly affected. The struggle went on as though she had not spoken. With horror, I saw some licking their own blood even as they drew more from others.

I turned to Felix as we huddled under the table. Grasping his arm, I said, "Someone has to stop them!"

"Indeed, but who is insane enough to try?" he asked.

Lady Blanche, apparently. As it became clear that she was being ignored, she turned her rage on the crowd, seizing those in her path with stunning strength and throwing them against the nearest walls. Any who lingered too long in her grasp felt the thrust of her fangs. Blood sputtered, staining her face, her gown, and still she kept coming, advancing steadily toward the original combatants.

When she was almost upon them, she threw back her head and roared. "Cease!"

The very air shook with her fury, but incredibly, she still was not obeyed. One of the pair, having gained a momentary advantage, had his opponent on the floor. He looked up, directly at Lady Blanche, his bloodstained lips curled in a chilling smile. While his gaze held hers in defiance, he twisted the other's neck until it gave a sickening crack. The other vampires, subdued enough to break off fighting, roared approval.

I turned away as my stomach heaved. When I dared to look again, the sight I beheld sent a bolt of horror through me. The defeated vampire was sitting up. As I watched, his head turned entirely around, glaring in all directions. For a moment, I thought it would tear loose and fall to the floor but he steadied it between his hands and held it until it settled into place again. Having managed to stand, he pushed his way through the mob and limped from the club.

Lady Blanche turned on her heel and strode away. Felix crawled quickly from under the table and hurried after her. I was left alone in the midst of the bloodstained throng intent on celebrating the victor. My every instinct was to flee. Uncaring of the attention I might attract, I shoved my way through the bloodied crowd until I reached the door. Once outside, I stopped for a moment to get my bearings. Nothing stirred in the passage or beyond. The hour was very late, the silence absolute except for the whisper of freshening wind through the narrow streets and the faint lapping of water against the nearby quays.

With no destination in mind, I began to walk. As I increased the distance between myself and the ghastly scene I had just witnessed, my nerves calmed somewhat. The part of the city I was in was deserted at that hour. Nothing stirred save the dirigibles floating overhead. Even so, a few of the new electric lights shone here and there in scattered windows. Passing the offices of a banking firm, I heard a sudden burst of static that made me start. Someone was listening to a Faraday receiver, the means by which it was now possible to receive communications from all over the world. Or at least that part of it equipped to send them. So great was the excitement engendered by the new communications that my own father had spoken of acquiring a receiver for the house in Whitby. The notion had appalled my mother, who claimed we would all be electrified in our beds, whatever that entailed. I had found no such apparatus during my stay in the house, so presumably my father had been dissuaded. Or perhaps the disappearance of his daughter had driven out consideration of all else.

Lost in thought, I was startled when I turned a corner and found myself on the outskirts of Mayfair. A dog barked as I passed, but when I looked in its direction, the animal whimpered and fell silent. Instinct drove me on. Shortly, I came to a tree-lined street that was all too familiar. Halfway down it, I stood in front of my family's townhouse. A gracious residence three stories in height with a façade of dark stone ornamented with fluted pilasters, the house had been a gift from my mother's family upon her marriage to my father. He had been reluctant to accept such munificence, but in time he had come to love the house as much as my mother did. I had mixed feelings. The house reminded me of the far more restricted life I had known in London as both a child and a young woman. Whereas in Whitby I had contrived to run free, in the city I had been watched far more carefully. I had chaffed under the regimen of nannies and other minders, but now I marveled at how ignorant I had been of the dangers lurking just out of sight.

Now that I actually was one of those dangers, my perceptions were altogether different. I told myself that I should go, indeed that I should never have come. Yet I could not take a step away. To the contrary, I drew nearer. No lights shone on the ground floor where the parlor and dining room were located, and where my father had his office. Similarly, the windows tucked away under the sloping roof were dark. The household staff would not begin to rouse until shortly before dawn, when the race would begin to light the fires and prepare the breakfast trays before the family woke.

My parents' bedroom was in the front of the house, overlooking the street. It, too, was dark. I was beginning to think that they truly weren't there, having gone perhaps to the Continent. Nonetheless, I decided to visit the small garden in the back. Generally, the only access to the garden was through the house itself, but I had other means. A quick leap and I took the front wall easily, sped over the roof, and dropped onto a balcony that overlooked the garden. There I paused, looking down on the place where Amanda and I had played so often, where I had bedeviled her with my insistence on making mud pies and building twig forts when she wanted only to care for her dolls and sketch flowers. As sisters, we could scarcely have been more different, yet I could not help but remember how she had smoothed the way for me when I followed her into society, quietly insisting that her friends overlook my missteps and include me in their activities. So, too, she had given me confidence in my appearance, far removed from her own blond beauty, yet, she claimed, more interesting and compelling.

My hands tightened on the railing of the balcony as I admitted for the first time how much I missed her. Such was my yearning that I could have sworn I smelled the lavender perfume she always favored. A faint whiff of it seemed to reach beyond the closed balcony doors, perceptible to my heightened senses. I turned, only then realizing that I was standing directly outside my sister's room. A single light glowed within. By its illumination, I could just make out the figure in the bed.

Amanda slept, as she did everything else, gracefully. Not for her the open-mouthed gape with a hint of drool, far less the unladylike snore that even our mother was capable of producing on occasion. Instead, she looked as lovely as a princess needing only the kiss of her prince to awaken her to joyful life.

But that impression, born of memory and without concession to her more recent experiences, was mistaken. Even as I watched, her head tossed in agitation and she cried out. My hand was on the door, already pressing it open, when I stopped abruptly. Amanda sat up suddenly in the bed. Staring into the shadows, she called, "Lucy? Lucy, are you there?"

I froze, uncertain of what to do. She could not possibly have seen me, surrounded as I was by darkness. Yet she knew somehow that I was present. Indeed, she appeared to be so convinced that, to my dismay, she left the bed and stood beside it, a pale, slim figure in her white silk nightgown, her golden hair lying in a chaste braid over her shoulder.

Only then did I realize that Amanda not only still slept under our parents' roof but she slept alone. When she raised her hand to her brow, I saw that her betrothal ring was gone. I will not claim to feel even a flicker of regret at her continued freedom, but her obvious sorrow gripped me. As I hesitated, still uncertain what to do, she dropped her hand and murmured, "I must be going mad and why not? Night after night . . . these terrible dreams . . ."

A tear slipped down her pale cheek, followed swiftly by another. She wiped them away angrily and, to my horror, harshly pinched her arm, twisting the skin so cruelly that I was certain she would be bruised.

"She isn't here! She's gone! Wake up!"

Seeing her distress, I could not help myself. I moved just enough to draw her eye. At once, she stopped and stared. Breathlessly, she whispered, "Lucy . . . it is you! I know it! What has happened to you? For the love of God, tell me!"

She started toward the balcony door but I was swifter. Stepping into the room, I forced a smile to my lips. "Dearest sister, don't be afraid. I only wanted to see you but I shouldn't have come. I'm sorry—"

Amanda stretched out her arms to me. As she did, I could see how thin she had become. Between the two of us, she looked far more the wraith than I.

"Are you a ghost?" she entreated. "Only tell me that you are so that I can put that terrible book from my mind and know that it is not true."

Stoker, again. Had the Irishman appeared before me just then, I do not know quite what I would have done but surely nothing good. Worse yet, if his patrons, those who had inspired his lies, even Gladstone himself were to fall into my hands—

"Lucy—"

Anxious to soothe her suffering in any way I could, I said, "A ghost, yes, that is what I am. Whatever else you may have heard is tawdry fiction, the product of a weak and febrile mind."

"But it seemed so real. Everyone knows that we lived in Whitby when you disappeared, no one would tell me what had happened. And now that terrible book—"

"It is nonsense, Amanda, believe me." Without a flicker of remorse for so misleading her, I said, "Sweet sister, it is your grief that holds me earthbound. You must move beyond it, embrace your life and all that it is meant to be."

"I cannot!" She stepped closer, almost touching me. The moment she did so, she would realize that I was no spirit but as solid and real as she was, albeit a creature all too like what Stoker had revealed to the world. I could not risk that.

Holding up my arms to fend her off, I said, "You must. Marry, preferably someone more interesting than your previous choice but follow your heart. Have children—"

Abruptly, it occurred to me that among Amanda's descendants could be the next Slayer. Indeed, it was possible that only from her could one such come again. My mother had no sisters nor had I ever heard of her speak of female cousins. Alone in her family, she was the only female, or she had been until Amanda and I arrived. Perhaps there were others of Morgaine's bloodline in the world, tripping over daughters, but what if there were not? What if, now that I was no longer entirely human, there was only Amanda? Centuries hence, my sister's distant descendent would seek to cull my kind as Morgaine herself had done. We would fall before her as before a great scythe that might wipe us from the earth entirely.

How easily that could be changed . . . if Amanda had no children. If she died before she wed . . . from grief, despair, or by design. One frail human life so easily extinguished and the future changed utterly.

Thinking all that I was still only mildly surprised when I heard myself say again, "Have children, Amanda. You will be a wonderful mother. Have a bevy of little girls and boys who will delight you but do not waste your life in grief. Leave that to our queen empress."

My sister's smile was sad and fleeting. "Victoria holds séances, trying to summon the spirit of her lost Albert. Yet you appear to me so readily . . . seemingly so real." Again, she reached out. I jerked away but not before her fingers brushed my arm.

"You are real! I knew it! She told me that you lived still—"

"Who told you that? Who are you talking about?" In my confusion, I thought for a moment that she was speaking of Victoria, but that was impossible. With the exception of events surrounding her Jubilee celebration, Her Imperial Majesty rarely left the Crystal Palace, where she dwelled among the reminders of her lost youth and love. Even, it was said, to the extent of ordering that the tobacco her dead husband had favored be burned because she believed that it summoned his spirit.

"She did not tell me her name," Amanda said. "I met her several months ago when friends persuaded me to attend the theatre with them. It was a mistake, I could not tolerate it, so I stepped out of our box. That was when she approached me."

"She who?" Impatience gave my voice a sharp edge but Amanda did not seem to notice. She went on as though I had not spoken.

"She was all in white and wearing the most remarkable pearls. It was clear that she knew who I was. She said that all of us—Mother, Father, and myself—were in danger. She cautioned that the authorities were watching us and that if they had any hint that we were in contact with you, they would see us as a threat to the security of the realm and would respond accordingly."

Dread swept through me, swiftly overtaken by rage. I had not considered that Lady Blanche might know of my family, much less dare to approach any of them. Stoker's so-called novel must have alerted her to what had happened in Whitby. She must have been trying to find me, and trying to use Amanda to do so.

How else might she try to make use of my sister?

"I see. . . . What did she advise you to do if I contacted you?"

"To tell her at once. She said she could be reached at a club called—"

"—the Bagatelle. I know the place. Listen to me, Amanda. The woman in white is not to be trusted. You must promise me that you will have nothing whatsoever to do with her. If she approaches you again—"

What could I tell her to do? How could I protect her from Lady Blanche when I was scarcely able to protect myself?

My own helplessness threatened to choke me. Determined not to succumb to it, I said, "If she approaches you again, do not hesitate. Go to the Serjeant's Inn off Fleet Street and find Nicolas di Orsini. Tell him that you need his brother's help—"

"Marco's help? What does he have to do with this?"

I stared at her in surprise. "You know Marco di Orsini?"

She laughed and shook her head, as though my question was the height of foolishness.

"Of course, I know him, Lucy, how could I not? That last season we spent in London, you could scarcely speak of anyone else."

At my lack of response, her smile faded. Softly, she said, "Lucy, don't you remember? You were wildly in love with Marco di Orsini."

CHAPTER 15

Y ou met," Amanda said, "last spring at Lady Davenport's ball. Up until then, you had shown no interest in anyone, but that changed when Marco appeared. You and he began to go everywhere together. He scarcely left your side."

"I see. . . ." In fact, I was still reeling from my sister's revelation. We were sitting together on her bed, all pretense of my "ghostly" nature having been abandoned. It felt like old times, except that I had become a halfling who dwelled in the hidden world, drank blood, and might live forever, while Amanda was still . . . Amanda. Sweet, lovely, kind, and incredibly enough, sincerely overjoyed to see me, no matter who or what I was.

"Father liked him well enough," she went on. "But Mother didn't quite know what to make of it even though he comes from a very old and honored family that certainly doesn't seem to lack for wealth." My sister smiled wryly. "If he'd had an English surname, she would have been booking the church."

"What did you think of him?"

"I . . . also liked him, most important because he truly did seem to care about you."

"And yet . . . you had concerns, didn't you?" I could hear

them in her voice, so well did we still understand each other despite all that had happened.

She hesitated. "It's just that he seemed very mature. Not that the difference in your ages is all that great, it isn't, but you were still very young in so many ways and he . . . wasn't."

There had been a time when I would have hotly disputed being characterized in such a way, yet further evidence of how very young I truly had been. That I had learned better to my sorrow but not entirely to my regret was one more contradiction of my new state.

"But I was in love?"

"You certainly seemed to be. I don't think I'd ever seen you so happy."

I could just barely remember what human happiness felt like, that lightening of the spirit that comes when suddenly the world seems a better, finer place where all good things are possible. Had there been any foundation for such happiness apart from Marco's instinct to protect me as he was sworn to protect all humans from vampires. Any at all?

"Mother wanted you to spend some time apart from him. She believed it would help you to be surer of your feelings. Father agreed and we returned to Whitby."

"And Marco?"

"He stayed here in London. I don't know exactly why. To be honest, I thought he would follow you, but instead—"

Instead, fate had been waiting for me on a lonely moor. I could not blame Marco. Even hovering on the edge of extinction, Mordred was able to bend space and time to bring me to him in the dream memory of his manor house. The previous year, when he still possessed his full strength and power, how much easier it must have been for him to deceive Marco as to his intentions and make him believe that I was safe at Whitby when I was anything but.

At any rate, it was done. Nothing could be gained by tormenting myself with thoughts of what might have been. The future, however, was an entirely different matter.

"I must go." I stood and moved quickly toward the windows.

Startled, Amanda followed. "You can't leave! I've only just found you again. Mother and Father—"

I stopped abruptly. Seizing both her arms, I said, "You cannot tell them anything. Were any of you to show any sign of knowing that I had been here, you would draw attention that, believe me, you do not want."

"But you cannot expect me to pretend this did not happen! You are my sister and—"

"Have you read Stoker's book?"

"I wasn't supposed to, but Father had a copy of the typescript and I—"

"The way he described Dracula is a pale reflection of the reality. The truth is vastly worse. There are hundreds, perhaps thousands of such creatures. They exist in a hidden world but they can reach into your own whenever they wish."

Her face, already so pale, turned ashen. Shock turned her irises almost black. "What are you saying? It is a novel. He made it up. It isn't real!"

"Is that what you think, really? Then think of this." Without daring to consider what I was about to do, I unsheathed my fangs. Moonlight, pouring in through the windows, flowed over us both. At the sight of me, Amanda screamed and tried to pull away but I did not release her.

"We feed on humans, Amanda. *Feed*. We drain the blood

from you, taking your humanity and your lives. You are nothing to us except a means to an end."

My nostrils flared. I smelled the coppery fragrance of her blood and realized with a spurt of horror that although I had fed recently, my hunger was returning. Repelled beyond bearing by my own nature, I pushed her away so hard that she fell to the floor. While yet she lay there stiff with terror, I wrenched open the windows and fled. Behind me, I heard her call my name, but surely I was mistaken, for how could anyone, even the most loving sister, feel other than disgust for one such as me?

The night swallowed me. I raced on without thought, heedless of direction or purpose. Roofs flew beneath me until I realized that my feet had ceased to touch them. I moved through the air damp with rain that had just begun to fall, held aloft by a surging wind out of the west, no longer a creature of the earth but reborn instead in the sky. Under other circumstances, I would have been delighted, but my newfound power only served to emphasize how great the gulf between me and those I loved had become.

When I alighted finally, I saw that I was near the passage leading to the Bagatelle. The snake uncoiled and reared its head as I approached. Not slowing, I snarled and brushed past it. My only thought was to find Lady Blanche and impress upon her that she was never to approach my family again. How exactly I would persuade her not to do so or what risk I was taking in challenging her was of no significance. The anguish I felt at being forced to expose myself to Amanda drove out every other consideration.

Coming from the darkness, the light and noise momentarily knocked me off stride but I recovered quickly and looked around. In the aftermath of the brawl, the club was more crowded even than before. Some of those in attendance appeared to have arrived recently, windblown as they were and splattered with raindrops. No doubt they were drawn by news of what had happened at the foundry. The older among them would remember when it had been the site of Mordred's court, while the others would have heard of its connection to their kind. Speculation would be rampant as to what had caused the catastrophe.

Everywhere my gaze fell heads were bent together, eyes flitting, too-bright smiles appearing and disappearing with such speed that it seemed only a middling sharp knife would be needed to slice through the tension in the room. There was no sign of Lady Blanche, but Felix was at the bar. Although he appeared relaxed, I was not fooled. The moment he saw me, he hurried to my side and grasped my elbow urgently. "Finally! I'd just about despaired of you. Where have you been?"

"We can talk about that later," I said. "I must speak with Lady Blanche."

Felix shook his head. "Wild rumors are circulating. If they are even partly true, this isn't the time to approach her."

Determined though I was to confront her ladyship, his warning gave me pause. "What rumors?"

Bending closer, he ticked them off one by one. "That she is behind the destruction of the foundry. That she did it to prevent Mordred from ever returning. That she is moving now to claim power for herself."

I leaned back a little, the better to see him. His long face, so well constructed for melancholia, was strained. He appeared tired and deeply worried. "If that is true," I asked, "wouldn't you know?"

"I should but I don't." He shrugged, as though that was of no particular importance when we both knew what it truly meant. "It seems that I am no longer a part of the inner circle."

A stab of guilt darted through me. I had done what I had to do and would do the same again. My strange new existence left no room for self-recrimination. But by involving Felix, I had placed him in very real danger.

"I am sorry, truly, but—" I said.

He waved aside my feeble attempt at an apology. "It doesn't matter. The point is that neither of us should be thinking of anything other than surviving the next few hours."

I searched his face for some sign that he was exaggerating but saw none. "It's that bad?"

"I'm afraid so." He glanced around at the crowd. "No one here has the least concern about what the humans will do if all the restraints that Mordred imposed on us come off. They are so convinced of our superiority that they cannot believe there could be any reason to fear humans. The dirigibles keeping constant watch, the factories at work night and day, the steam contrivances of every sort, the Faraday transmitters that make distance irrelevant. Humans are changing everything, and we persist in ignoring it all. We are the fools, not them."

"There must be some others who believe as you do—"

"Don't count on that. I fear I am quite out of step with current thinking." He managed a faint smile. "But there is still hope. Half of them will betray Blanche at the first hint of weakness. The others will wait for a whisper of Mordred's return, then they'll line up to do the same."

"If they are so treacherous, why does she want to reign over them?" I asked. "It seems more trouble than it could possibly be worth."

"The lust for power is in her blood." He leaned a little closer. "Her human blood. All the way back to when her family rose against a king and earned only death for their pains."

"Do you think she remembers that?" It had been so long; centuries.

"I think she will still remember it when she has forgotten her own name."

I was considering that when the sensation of being watched crept over me. I turned to meet the gaze of a young male vampire standing nearby. With a start I realized that he was the golden-haired, blue-eyed male who had accosted me my first night at the Bagatelle.

"Who is that?" I asked Felix.

Following the direction of my gaze, he said, "Edward Delacorte. He's from one of the oldest families. Lady Blanche has been courting their support ever since Mordred disappeared."

Seeing our interest, Delacorte inclined his head and smiled. A moment later he had made his way through the crowd toward us.

"Miss Weston," he said with a bow. "May I say that you are lovelier than ever? And may I also beg your pardon for my atrocious behavior the other night? I cannot ask you to forgive me, that would be far too much. But I can entreat you to consider that I am not, all evidence to the contrary, quite the boor that I appeared."

From the corner of my eye, I saw Felix roll his eyes and resisted the urge to do the same. No doubt there were those who found Edward Delacorte charming in the extreme. I, however, thought he was worse than the boor he so disingenuously denied being. He was, in my regard, a bully who masked the ugliness of his nature behind a false gentility. I had known his kind as a human and I had no difficulty recognizing the species even when it came equipped with fangs.

Nonetheless, I smiled and offered my hand. "It is I who should apologize. I was quite lost and confused, but that is no excuse for my poor manners."

Felix frowned in surprise and would have spoken had not I continued quickly, "I am afraid that I am still very much in the same state. I have so many questions . . . so many concerns."

"Do you? Well, then, you must let me help." As though he had only just noticed that we were not alone, Delacorte added, "You don't mind, do you, Deschamps? I'm sure you have other matters to keep you occupied."

"You can't begin to imagine." As he spoke, Felix shot me a warning look that I had no difficulty interpreting. One wrong step with Delacorte and my position would be even more precarious than it was already. Even so, I did not see that I had a choice.

As I took his arm, my mind turned over and over, seeking a means to learn from him what I had to know. Was Lady Blanche really about to make her bid for power, quite possibly precipitating a war that no one could win, and was there anything that Marco and I could do to stop her?

That I thought of Marco at that moment should not have surprised me. I had, after all, only just learned that young, naïve, oh-so-human Lucy had loved him. Even as Morgaine's blood coursed in her veins and fate rushed toward her.

In my new incarnation, I was not capable of love, or so I wanted to believe. Love was a weakness, an impediment, and perhaps most important, a distraction that I could not afford and did not want. Yet it still existed in me rather like the dream-memory of Mordred's manor. Love for my sister, my parents, for the Lucy I had been in all her clumsy vulnerability. And for the man I had so briefly known when I was still only a young woman who walked in moonlight and gave no thought to what lurked in the darkness.

I knew what was there now, knew it all too well, for I was one of those beings who cause humans to cry out in the throes of nightmares from which they wake trembling and afraid, only to swiftly forget what it was that so troubled them. Not so for me. With each step I took at Delacorte's side, I knew that I was walking deeper and deeper into a nightmare that would never end for me until existence itself ceased.

I held my head high and I did not falter. That, and only that, I can say with pride.

CHAPTER 16

As we made our way through the crowd, Edward said, "Lady Blanche has told me something of your unorthodox origins. It is hardly any wonder that you feel confused. Please believe that I will help in any way I can." The smile he bestowed upon me should have made my heart flutter, had I still possessed an organ capable of such a response. Instead, it merely stiffened my suspicion of him.

No doubt Delacorte was popular with the female acolytes who would vie for his attention. No doubt as well that he found it easy to make use of human women when that urge was in him. But a halfling born of blood and desperation, incarnated by the great Mordred himself, risen from the grave to claim her place in the world of man and vampire alike—that was an entirely different matter.

With grim amusement, I girded myself to make use of his vanity and folly. Seeing him with such clarity as I did, I had no doubt that he was exactly what I had first thought him to be, a vicious, violent boy whose vanity blinded him to all reality.

It was almost too easy.

"Be honest with me," I said.

He frowned as though the idea was foreign to him, but then answered as though amused. "Of course."

"What do you think of Lady Blanche?"

He would have been wiser to answer at once, to swear his devotion and his loyalty, but instead he hesitated and I saw the calculation behind his eyes. Finally, he said, "She is magnificent, of course. You are most fortunate that she has taken you under her wing."

"I am indeed, yet I cannot help but worry . . ."

"About what?" He ducked his head a little, moved a little closer, inviting my confidence even as he plotted my seduction.

"She must have told you that Mordred incarnated me just before he disappeared."

"I believe something was mentioned to that effect. . . ."

"Did she tell you that I am linked to him?"

This was new indeed, vital news that he could carry to Lady Blanche. But first he had to know more. "Linked? How?"

"Don't ask me to explain it. I only know that he exists still and . . ." My voice trembled with feigned fear and excitement. "He is still incredibly powerful. I can *feel* it."

I leaned a little closer. He had fed recently; his breath smelled coppery. I only just managed not to recoil. "What if he comes back. Do you think he will be very upset?"

Edward lurched back a little as though I had stung him. "Comes back? Do you really think he could?"

"How could I possibly know? It is all so . . . strange. But if he did, wouldn't he be upset?"

"What do you mean, upset? Why would he?"

"You don't think Mordred would consider that Lady Blanche had . . . overstepped herself?"

His eyes darkened with alarm. "He might . . . it's possible. Do you think he would?"

"I'm far too inexperienced to know, and yet the brief time I spent with him . . . Let us just say that I am afraid."

"For Lady Blanche?"

"Of course! I owe her so much, but for all of us as well." Fighting the repugnance I felt, I bent closer still and laid my hand on his arm. "There are even times when I fear this is some terrible plot on his part to sniff out who is loyal and who is not." I sighed and offered him a wan smile. "No doubt I am wrong."

"No doubt," he repeated but he no longer appeared entirely aware of my presence. Instead, he seemed to be imagining the havoc that would follow if I was right. A vengeful Mordred let loose upon his kind, culling the disloyal. Truly, that was the stuff of nightmares.

Having gone as far as I dared to raise doubts about the likely success of Lady Blanche's plans, I turned away from the hapless Delacorte. For a time, I pretended an interest in cards. I enjoyed whist and could hold my own in quadrille, but the patrons of the Bagatelle played a game I had never seen before. It used not the deck to which I was accustomed, but a set of tarot cards.

When he had recovered himself sufficiently, Edward tried to explain the rules to me but I did not grasp them, most likely because I scarcely listened. My attention was diverted by the wages that were changing hands across the green felt tables. Gold coins, pearls, other precious gems flew back and forth as luck ebbed and waned. So, too, did acolytes who were exchanged as currency. I stood behind Edward, watching as he played, clumsily, for clearly he had other matters on his mind.

I was still trying to grasp the complexities of the game when Felix appeared at the entrance to the card room. Catching my eye, he gestured to me.

I edged away, not wishing to draw Edward's attention, but he was sufficiently distracted not to notice. When I reached Felix, he grasped my elbow and drew me into an alcove.

"Something is happening," he said, very low so only I could hear him.

A dozen or more thralls had just appeared. Moving in the odd, shuffling way they had, they drew back a pair of floor-to-ceiling curtains covering a wall. Behind stood large double doors. The thralls opened them, revealing a wide corridor lined with stone that I had not seen before. They stood aside, as though in invitation to enter.

At once, the mood in the club changed. Ripples of excitement spread out in all directions. Feral smiles and eager glances replaced the raucous conversation of a few minutes before. As one, the crowd moved toward the doors. Felix and I were carried along. I saw Delacorte nearby but he did not notice me, so absorbed was he in what was happening.

The corridor twisted downward. I smelled the river and was struck by a sudden possibility—did Lady Blanche have Mordred after all? Was she about to reveal him?

But what then of his conviction that a human held him?

Turning to Felix as best I could in the press of bodies, I murmured, "You don't think that she—?"

His eyes dark with apprehension, he said, "I fear we will wish that she did."

While I was still puzzling over that remark, the corridor ended in front of another pair of double doors. At the crowd's approach, thralls threw them open. Beyond lay darkness lit only by fires burning in iron lattice baskets set on high tripods.

"What is this place?" I murmured to Felix as we entered. Unlike elsewhere in the club, the air was warm, thick with the scent of burning coals.

Felix put an arm through mine, linking us together. He spoke in a low, urgent hiss. "Whatever you do, don't make a scene. It would mean the end of us both."

A sense of dread grew in me, deeper and darker than mere fear. Instinctively, I tried to step backward but the press of the crowd made that impossible. Instead, we were both pushed closer to the center where, I saw, a stone table had been placed. Before it stood Lady Blanche, garbed in white as always with her pearls draped around her slender neck. She had been beautiful before in her own glacial way, but now she glowed from within, incandescent with power and determination.

"Come," she called out, beckoning to us. "Let us celebrate together. The time of scarcity is over. The era of denying our true selves is past. Let us all rejoice in our strength, our cunning, our superiority above all others on this earth!"

As the crowd cheered, a door on the far side of the chamber opened. Two vampires entered—one male, the other female, both of whom I recognized from the club. Between them they supported a young man who appeared to be in his early twenties, clean-shaven, with thick auburn hair neatly trimmed. Unlike the acolytes I had seen, he was fully dressed in a gray riding coat, jodhpurs, and boots so well polished that the gleaming black leather flashed even in the dim light. Tall and broad shouldered, he appeared very fit yet he made no attempt to free himself from the vampires. He seemed dazed and unaware of his surroundings.

"What is this?" I asked Felix, but already in some sense I knew. Nothing could more clearly declare the beginning of a new reign than to openly violate Mordred's accord with the most powerful of earth's humans. The young man was clearly British and from the upper class. To take him captive and feed on him against his will amounted to a declaration that the vampires would no longer accept any limits on their behavior. If the likely consequences of that concerned anyone in the crowd other than Felix and myself, no one showed it. To the contrary, the vampires were shouting Blanche's name, praising her, and vying to declare their loyalty.

Even so, I tried to remain calm. For all her ambitions, surely Lady Blanche had been far too close to Mordred for too long not to understand that he had ruled as he had in order to prevent a war no one could win. She would make a gesture to win the vampires but she would know better than to go too far. Undoubtedly, this would be a terrible experience for the young man, but the supplicants were fed on all the time and they seemed to come to no harm. When she was done, she would let him go. Perhaps there was some means to keep him from re-membering what had happened. He would recover, go on with his life, and be none the wiser.

That was how it would be, wasn't it?

Lady Blanche flicked a hand. At once, the vampires seized the young man and tore off his clothing with such violence that they even shredded his boots. Through it all, he remained too dazed to offer any resistance. A part of me wanted to look away, if only to leave him some shred of dignity at least in my eyes. But the other, stronger part of me flicked the thought away. He was, after all, merely a human, albeit an attractive one. As I had guessed, he was very fit. Muscles rippled across his flat abdomen. His shoulders and arms were well defined, as were his thighs. He clearly was no idler.

"Very nice," Lady Blanche said. She approached him with a smile. He looked at her, blinked, and smiled in turn. A warm, open, innocent smile that would have wrung a groan from me had I not managed to press my lips together just in time.

"What is his name?" she asked.

The female vampire answered. "Lord Harley William Charles Langworthe, recently come up from Oxford, heir to an earldom in Essex. His mother was a Carlisle."

Her pale hand tipped in carmine painted nails traced a line along the young lord's chest. "Not a first-rank lineage, we would need a duke for that or a prince of the blood, but not bad either. I believe he will do."

At her nod of approval, the pair seized Lord Harley and lifted him onto the stone table. Even then, he showed no alarm.

"Why doesn't he resist?" I asked Felix. "Is he drugged?"

"Of course not. He's under some sort of compulsion."

Just as I was. I felt a sudden and most unwelcome kinship with young Lord Harley. Not that I should compare what Mordred had done in a desperate effort to save himself with what Lady Blanche was about to do. Not at all . . .

She stepped back a little and looked at him critically. "He isn't usually this passive, is he?"

"Not at all, milady," the female vampire said hastily. "The effects should be wearing off as we speak."

Lady Blanche nodded. "Then let us assure that our guest cannot harm himself."

I had failed to notice that shackles dangled from the sides of the stone table. As his lordship was secured at wrists and

ankles, the vampires pressed even closer. I had far too good a
view of his sweet smile that wrung what passed for my heart. A
moment later, a flicker of alarm darkened his gaze.

"I . . ." He attempted to rise, only to discover that he could
not. "Where . . . ?" His gaze fastened on Lady Blanche . . . her
lovely figure clad all in white, the silver sheen of her glorious
hair, the perfection of her features . . . her unsheathed fangs . . .

"Oh my God! You . . . what are you? Where am I?" Struggling against the shackles, Harley twisted in horror. "Let me
up! Let me go!"

I fought the instinct to try to help him, telling myself again
that he would be all right in the end. The acolytes vied to be
fed upon. I had seen with my own eyes the ecstasy they experienced. Yet there was a difference. They were willing and the
young lord was not. Nor did Lady Blanche seem to care.

Even as he strained, trying to break free, she raked both her
hands from his shoulders to his naval. So sharp were her nails
that they left a trail of bloody welts in their wake.

Laying her palm against his chest, she said, "So much
warmth . . . such life. I can feel his heart beating." She turned
and smiled at the crowd. "It feels like a trapped bird desperate
to escape."

"He is afraid," someone shouted. The others cheered.

"Fear is the essence of what it means to be human," Lady
Blanche said. "They come into the world screaming, as often
as not they leave it the same way and in between . . ." The cur-
tain of her hair fell across the young man as she bent over him.
"In between they live in terror of their own inevitable deaths.
Everything they do—their loves, their wars, their pretensions
to being something more than sacks of bile and blood—all of it

is just a means of distracting themselves from their inevitable fate."

She lifted her head and looked at the crowd again. "One could almost feel sorry for them, don't you think?"

Before anyone could respond, Lady Blanche turned back again. She spared a last smile for the young lord and then she struck. Her talons, as they appeared to my stunned gaze, grasped his shoulders as her fangs sank deep into his throat. At once, blood spurted across his chest, into her hair, and onto the stone table. His back arched and for an instant I saw a flash of the ecstasy that I had witnessed in the acolytes. But it was gone before he drew another breath. His mouth opened, screaming, as she rose and fell and rose again, sinking into him over and over, tearing at his throat, his arms, his chest.

Horrified, I tried to move forward, thinking to somehow stop her only to find that I could not move at all. Felix had a fierce grip on me, but the crowd itself prevented me from taking a step. I remained rooted in place as though my feet had been set in the slate beneath them. Helpless, all I could do was watch.

Even then she was not satisfied. She paused just long enough to caress him before sinking her fangs deep into the softer flesh below his belly and sucking hard. The young lord bucked wildly. His screams echoed off the walls of the chamber until there seemed nothing else left in the world save terror and blood and death.

He did die, of course. No one could have survived what she did to him. His lifeblood spurted out of him and what was not drunk thirstily ran across the floor, pooling in small depressions and sinking into the ground between the slabs of slate. When it was finally over, the stone table held only a drained husk, gray and empty where youth and life had been before.

Lady Blanche raised her head. Her face, so pale usually, was crimson. So, too, her hair, her neck, her once-white gown, all dyed the deadly hue of blood. She stretched her arms to the splattered ceiling and cried out, *"Sangra eterna! Forta eterna! Vampira eterna!"*

As though in a delirium, the vampires fell to their knees, crawling over the floor, licking up the trails of blood flowing across it. The boldest among them sucked at the sides of the stone table.

Abruptly, I was able to move again. I stumbled a step or two with no idea of where to go or what to do. I was sick with horror and more. Terror such as I had never known filled me, not in the least because some part of what I was wanted to join the others drinking Lady Blanche's leavings.

But another part wanted to launch myself at her and tear her limb from limb, destroying her in vengeance for what she had done to a human even as the vampire in me fed on her and took her power for my own.

At the touch of a hand on my arm, I whirled, fangs sliding free, ready to do whatever I must to defend myself. But it was only Felix—sad, brave Felix looked as ashen as I felt.

"Come," he said, no more but it was enough. I took his hand, cold as my own. Together, we fled.

CHAPTER 17

We got as far as the door to the club before I stopped and pulled Felix around to face me. I was trembling with shock and revulsion, yet I had to understand what had just happened and what it would mean for all of us.

"What madness is this? Why would she do such a thing?"

Felix's eyes were dark pools of horror. "Not madness, sound reason. It is one thing to feed on a willing acolyte, but the blood of an unwilling human, someone in the grip of terror fighting for his life, contains far more power."

Disgust welled up in me. I struggled not to think of the blood I had consumed. It had been given willingly, even eagerly, but out of a desire to become one of those who had crowded around the stone table, cheering the slaughter of a helpless human.

"Enough power to enable her to become queen in her own right, able to control all the others as Mordred did?"

"Not with one such feeding. She will need more."

"More?" Harley's fate to be repeated over and over? The prospect was revolting in the extreme, but young men and women of good birth could not begin vanishing without someone noticing and asking what was happening. The balance that had allowed vampires and humans to coexist for so long could not possibly hold up in the face of such monstrous crimes. Lady Blanche would be assuring that war was not only inevitable but also imminent.

"At first I really thought she wanted to use you to bring Mordred back because she still dreams of being his consort," Felix said. He looked inexpressibly sad, as though his romantic soul had been betrayed along with the dashing of all his hopes. "But after this, it is clear that she has decided she wants power for herself, more power even than Mordred has ever possessed, and she is determined to do whatever she must to obtain it."

As though it had just occurred to him, Felix added, "Which means that having set on this course, she cannot risk Mordred returning before she is strong enough to confront him. If she even begins to suspect what you are—" He broke off, as though the rest was too terrible to contemplate.

I could not afford to be so squeamish. "If she discovers that I am a halfling, what then?"

Reluctantly, he said, "Your human side would give her more of the power she has acquired from that poor young man, but in combination with your vampire side . . . Vampires share blood from time to time but only in small amounts as an act of intimacy. There is a reason why it is forbidden to feed on one another. It is widely believed that such a feeding would transfer the power of one vampire to another and more. It would give access to the power of the vampire who had transformed the one being fed upon. Given the duality of your nature and who incarnated you, feeding on you could make Lady Blanche the most powerful vampire the world has ever known."

How long, I wondered, would it be before that occurred to her? Presuming that it had not done so already.

"I cannot stay here, but what of you? Is there someplace of safety where you can—?"

Felix was shaking his head before I finished. "I've been a very good toady and with any luck I will be able to convince her that I tried to stop you. I will tell her that you have returned to Whitby."

"She won't believe you. She will go after my family—" The thought of Amanda on the stone table terrified me. But it was rage, not fear, that roared in my ears and threatened to erase all reason.

Felix's soft yet firm voice drew me back. "She will go after you, Lucy, and she'll have you if you don't leave now." As he spoke, he opened the door and pushed me through it. "Find Mordred. He is the only hope for any of us."

Before I could reply, the others began returning from the subterranean chamber. I heard their raucous, triumphant voices, harsh with the lust for blood that Blanche's exhibition had fed but far from satisfied. In another moment, they would see me. Try though I might, I could not hope to hide my revulsion from them or from Lady Blanche.

"Go," Felix said. He pulled the door shut as he turned to face them.

He had the best of intentions and I did not doubt his courage, but I could not count on him being able to deceive anyone for very long. With that uppermost in mind, I sped down the passage and out onto Fleet Street, only to come to a halt suddenly in the rain-darkened night. Sleek, feral shapes paced around the pedestal that held the griffin statue. *Wolves.* The same pack I had seen before. I recognized their leader—the largest of them all, golden-eyed, his body rippling with muscle. As I watched, he threw back his head and howled. The eerie

sound echoed down the narrow street, bouncing off the stone
walls before finally fading away into the darkness.

A frisson of fear moved down my spine. Driven by an entirely human instinct, I retreated step by step without taking
my eyes from him. Tendrils of fog drifted on the fetid air. Mist
rose from dank puddles that smelled of the acid sky. Behind
shuttered windows, I glimpsed a face peering through a crack,
gone as quickly as it appeared. A bolt fell across a door. A light
was snuffed out.

When I was a child, I had a book that fascinated me more
than any other. It consisted of semitransparent pages that
could be laid one over the other to show "the Progress of
Man," as it was called. Beginning with the image of humble
huts clustered beside a river, it advanced by seemingly inevitable steps to depict a thriving city. The book, as all good
children's books of the time, was intended to both inform and
encourage. But, of course, it could also be flipped backward,
creating a cautionary tale of mistaken assumptions and the
price of hubris.

All that flitted through my mind on the dark street as the
wolves howled and time itself seemed to peel away until nothing was left save a world in which fear ruled and hope was as
faint as the farthest star scarcely glimpsed above.

The alpha wolf and his pack made no attempt to go after
me, but remained standing vigil at the passage between the
Bagatelle and the outside world. They, at least, knew what
they were about, whereas I felt a little jolt of surprise when I
found that I had made my way to the front of the Serjeant's
Inn. Relief followed quickly and propelled me forward.

The black-robed barristers were likely snoring in their beds,
but a light still shone in the window beside the low, arched

door. As I approached, the door was flung open and a woman stepped out. She wore a beaded evening gown of shimmering taupe silk cut low to reveal her lovely shoulders and the curve of her breasts. A collar of diamonds adorned her throat with matching bands at each of her wrists. Her appearance on a dark London street in front of a shuttered inn was incongruous, to say the least. So was the battered lantern that she held in one hand. Lifting it, she gestured to me urgently.

"Hurry!"

Without pausing to wonder who she was or why she would be willing to help me, I did as she said. The moment I entered the inn, she slammed the door shut, thrusting an iron bar down to hold it secure. As the bar fell into place, she leaned over and extinguished the light in the window. Still holding the lantern, she said, "Follow me."

I had a quicksilver impression of a woman of mature years yet still remarkably beautiful with a cascade of ebony hair, vivid violet eyes, and skin that would have been pale as my own if not for the blush of life evident in her cheeks. She moved with swift grace and did not look back.

We left the great room smelling of ale, wood smoke, and sawdust and descended a narrow, winding stone staircase into a basement. As I hurried to keep up, I called after her, "I am looking for Nicolas di Orsini. I must get word to his brother, Marco."

I might as well not have spoken for the woman did not respond in any way. She continued until we were well within the interior of the inn. Stopping, she pointed to a spot on the slate floor.

"Stand there."

Perplexed, I complied. At once, she set the lantern down

and drew a small pouch from a pocket tucked away in her bodice. Having poured the contents into her palm, she began to sprinkle them out onto the floor.

"What are you doing?" I asked.

She ignored me and continued to trace the arc of a circle around where I stood, outlining it in what I saw was salt. When she was done, she straightened, returned the empty pouch to her bodice, and picked up the lantern. Without a glance at me, she turned to go. Apparently, I was to be left in the dark both figuratively and literally.

"Wait! Who are you? Why are you helping me?"

She hesitated, clearly still reluctant to engage me in any conversation. Finally, she said, "Are you truly so ignorant, Miss Weston?"

"You know who I am?"

In a tone that could have put frost on a fire, she said, "To my regret. I also know *what* you are. Stay within the circle. Someone will come for you when it is safe."

"I cannot stay here. I must find Marco—"

Abruptly, she turned and stared at me with such fury that I was taken aback. What could I possibly have done to earn her wrath?

"Haven't you harmed my son enough? Must you cause him yet more trouble?"

"Your son—?" I was surprised and yet as I looked more closely, I could see him in the shape of her mouth and the set of her chin. "You are Marco's mother." The discovery at once alarmed and fascinated me. Of course, he had a mother. I just hadn't expected to come face-to-face with her.

Pain lent a poignant edge to her pride as glared at me. "I am Cornelia di Orsini. Marco is my firstborn son, as Nicolas is my second. I should be able to protect them both but in-stead—"

My hands clenched at my sides. Fear for myself fell away as I considered what might have befallen others. "Where is Marco? What has happened to him?" When hunger drove me from Nicolas' office, I had not thought that either brother might be at immediate risk. Had I been terribly wrong?

"Do you pretend to care? You are using him—"

"Of course, I care. Marco is—" What was he? The man I had loved with a heart at once innocent and unaware. The man my body still recognized and yearned for more than I wanted to admit. The ally I was counting on to help me find Mordred.

"Marco is a Protector," his mother said over my stumbling silence. "That is what he was born to be and what he is. Our clan has stood between your kind and humans for centuries. That he should be associated with you in any way is a betrayal of all that we hold sacred."

I was no stranger to a mother's worry for her wayward child, nor did I mistake the love that inspired it. That gave me the confidence to say, "You don't really believe that he has be-trayed anyone, do you?"

She drew herself up to her full height, shorter than me in my new incarnation but tall nonetheless for a woman. The light from the lantern cast shadows across her face and form, but I could see the fierce will that sprang from deep within her.

"Who are you to say what I believe?"

I hesitated. For all that she was Marco's mother, I had no particular reason to trust her. True, she had let me into the inn, but was her intention to protect me or to hold me captive?

Determined to discover which it might be, I made to step out of the salt circle.

Cornelia stared at my foot, hovering in space just above the floor. She shrugged. "Do as you like but know this. If you leave the circle, any vampire hunting you will be better able to detect your presence." She waved a hand toward the stones that lined the passage on all side.

"The salt combined with the dolomite in these stones throws off the senses of vampires and confuses them." Looking at me closely, she frowned. "But you appear to be unaffected."

Slowly, I lowered my foot back inside the circle. Far off in the distance, muted by the walls of the inn, I heard the baying of wolves. No doubt Felix had tried to conceal my absence or at least pretend that there was an innocent explanation for it. But Lady Blanche was far too old and wily to be fooled for long. After her blood-drenched display of power, the others would be eager to do her bidding, whether that meant bringing me back to her or destroying me, as she willed. Either would doom Mordred and all of us.

But it seemed that I had unexpected allies, including the four-legged variety.

Cornelia stared at me, her expression guarded. "Marco thinks that you may be . . ." She could not bring herself to speak of a possibility that would challenge everything she thought she knew about me and the struggle threatening us all. "But that cannot be true. There has never been such a being. No vampire would take the risk of creating a . . . halfling."

"Mordred did." Best she know that she was not the only female of proud ancestry and a long tradition of service to humankind. Indeed, when it came to such measures, I outranked her. Best she know that, too.

"I am of Morgaine's blood, the blood of the Slayer. Mordred must have understood the risk when he incarnated me but he needed the connection that could exist only between us."

Her shock was unmistakable but so was her skepticism. "Needed it why? Surely he would have understood the danger to his own kind from one such as you claim to be."

"I agree, he must have, which tells us how desperate the situation is. Only the greatest duress could have driven the vampire king to bring into being the very creature that legend says can destroy the entire vampire species."

Although she still appeared reluctant to believe me, neither could she dismiss what I was saying. Instead, she probed more deeply. I was beginning to understand the source of her sons' intelligence and their tenacity. If their father was as formidable as their mother, the di Orsini brothers would be a force to be reckoned with under any circumstances.

"How can you help Mordred?" she demanded.

"I can find him, but time is running out. If I do not discover his whereabouts quickly, it will be too late."

"For whom, Miss Weston?" Before I could respond, she said, "There are those who say that humans have grown too powerful to have to share the world any longer with those who prey on us."

"And there are those who say that humans and vampires cannot survive without each other," I countered. "Our need is the more obvious but yours may be the greater. Without us, you would have destroyed yourselves in wars and conquests long ago."

"Are you seriously claiming that vampires protect humans?"

"On occasion. Mordred has certainly done so, and every British government for centuries has had the sense to appreciate it."

"The privileged few have appreciated it," she corrected. "But what of the common people who are too often sacrificed? Only the Protectors have stood for them, and at great cost." Her face tightened. She looked away. "And now my own son has been called by our ruling Council of Protectors to account for his failure to abide by our ways. Because of you, he could be cast out, left alone without the support of the other Protectors, to survive as best he can in a war with your kind. How long do you think he will live under those circumstances? Hours, days?" Tears shone in her eyes. She blinked them away furiously. "I have lost one son already, but at least that was to the cruel vagaries of nature itself. How am I to bear losing another?"

What son had she lost? To what cruel vagaries? Reluctant though I was to admit it, I truly did not understand. Nor was I about to be enlightened. Without another word, Cornelia turned on her heel and left me alone in the stone corridor, held fast within the circle of salt. A prisoner of my own thoughts and fears.

CHAPTER 18

As my eyes adjusted to the absence of light, the darkness that had seized my soul eased, if only a little. Slowly, a measure of calm returned. I could not blame Cornelia di Orsini for holding me responsible for putting her son in danger. Indeed, I was none too happy with myself just then. But nothing could be allowed to distract from the urgent necessity of finding Mordred. To that end, I was torn between the urge to set out in search of him at once and the certain knowledge that to do so while a hunting pack of vampires was nearby would be the height of folly.

Even so, waiting was very hard. Moment to moment, time did not so much pass as stretch like taffy being pulled, folded in on itself, and pulled again, a process that, I recalled just then, had fascinated me as a child. During our family jaunts to the seaside, I was content to watch apple-cheeked women in crisp white aprons maneuvering the wooden frames on which the taffy was made. But Amanda always had to have a paper cone of the gooey stuff, which she would savor with such patience that much of it made its way back home to lie dried out and lint covered in a drawer until finally being disposed of by a conscientious maid.

I, on the other hand, preferred rock candy and would de-
vour every scrap of it with greedy haste that left me wanting
more. The little chunks of crystal were sharp on my tongue
and hard on my teeth but that made them all the sweeter. I
could almost taste them now.

Marvelous though they were, the candy crystals did not
glow, not like the shards of dolomite in the walls, floor, and
ceiling of the basement. Had they been that bright all along
or had I become more sensitive to them? Belatedly, a third
possibility occurred to me. Could they be reacting to my
presence?

As I watched, the stones began to shine even more brightly.
Warmth spread through me, made all the more disconcerting
because coldness had come to seem my natural state. But this
was not the heat of life as I had known it, the product of the
processes needed to sustain a human existence. This was something else entirely, a power that long predated the appearance
of mere mortals on this planet.

From ancient stone melted in the fires of the first volcanoes
that took their substance from the living sun, the heat spread
through me. I felt its tingling in my hands and feet, along the
column of my spine, until finally in a piercing lance it pen-
etrated up through the stem of my brain and into every aspect
of my consciousness.

The world exploded. Stone, light, air, and earth all flew
apart as though they had been held together only by a feeble
web spun by the limitations of my own mind. I gasped and the
sound reverberated through endless chambers of eternity. I
reached out and found . . . nothing.

Everything.

"Lucy, is that you?"

A voice in the void . . . a hint of hope but also of desperation.

"Mordred?"

"Thank God!"

Let us leave aside for the moment the inappropriateness of that remark. Let us ignore those credos that claim vampires are the spawns and servants of the Devil, barred forever from the deity's loving presence. Let us take it as a conversational convention.

"Where are you?" he demanded. Kings, even or especially those in duress, are not noted for their patience.

"Rather more to the point," I replied. "Where are you?"

"I wish I knew. "

"Forgive me, but that isn't very helpful."

"Yet you are here." He sounded weak but doing his best to conceal it and equally determined to find the silver lining in our unexpected encounter. "After the foundry, I thought any hope of reaching you was finished."

"What happened there?" I asked. "People are saying it was anarchists."

"People are idiots. Where are you?"

I hesitated to tell him lest I sound craven but deception would help neither of us. "In the basement of the Serjeant's Inn, standing in a circle of salt."

"Is Marco there?" Of course, he would not be surprised by my circumstances.

"He's been called away, something about answering to his clan for allying with me. But his mother was here."

"Cornelia?" I thought I heard a faint chuckle but surely I

was mistaken. "What of Blanche . . . up to no good, I assume?"

"Worse. She has killed an unwilling human, made a sacrifice of him."

"Bloody hell . . ." The curse was little more than an exhausted wheeze, yet beneath it I heard an echo of the power he had possessed for so long and was looking forward to claiming as his own once again. With full vengeance against those who had betrayed him to follow promptly.

"River." He said, his voice fading. "Bridge but not close. Screaming. Humans. Come quickly."

"I will try." That was all I could do, but there was a very real possibility that it would not be enough.

"Lucy . . ."

He was gone. I drifted again in the formless darkness, content for a moment of folded time to do nothing other than consider my dual identities and the contradiction to which they had brought me. The truth is that I would not have gone back to being naïve innocent Lucy for all the warm, coppery blood in London or anywhere else. Granted, I had a lingering affection for her but she was not . . . me, not anymore. I had outgrown her.

Yet neither could I imagine myself moving beyond what I had become, whatever that might be. Half one thing, half the other, precariously balanced with each foot on either side of what felt like an ever-widening chasm. Such is life in all its foolish glory.

Christmas around the family table. The goose picked almost clean. Amanda and I holding between us the gleaming wishbone, that fragile stirrup upon which hopes and dreams so improbably ride.

"Close your eyes, dears," Mother said. "And listen to your heart's desire."

"Lucy!"

Stones pressed against my back. Mordred and the glowing stones were gone. Only their memory lingered. I was fiercely cold, robbed of all warmth, but filled with a shattering clarity. My heart did not beat, my lungs did not move and yet . . . I was alive. Utterly, stubbornly, and it must be said, triumphantly alive, and never mind whoever thought me anything less.

"Damn it, don't just lie there! Wake up!"

"Marco . . ."

"What happened to you?" he demanded. "Where did all this salt come from?"

I sat up, leaning on my elbows, and endeavored to collect yourself. "Your mother . . ."

I was on my feet by the simple expediency of Marco hoisting me up. Still holding me, he looked down at the circle. Rather incredibly given the circumstances, he laughed.

"Salt, seriously? That's an old wife's tale, no one really believes it. The dolomite in the walls is enough to keep you safe."

I could have been sitting in comfort in a nice chair with a snifter of something good and a book to pass the time, not standing like a fool in the dark. Cornelia had made her point. I was a very unwelcomed intruder into her life and the life of her son. Yet I had to thank her all the same.

"It does more than that. I reached Mordred again. Wherever he is, he can hear humans screaming."

Marco frowned. "Not very reassuring but it might help."

"I hope so. I have to tell you—" As quickly and succinctly as I could, I related what had happened at the Bagatelle. The horror I felt at what I had witnessed was equaled only by my shame that those with whom I was associated, however unwillingly, had committed such a heinous crime. Most of all, I feared that Marco would see me in the same light and turn away in disgust.

Instead, he took a deep breath, let it out slowly, and said, "It is as well that you got away. Vampires are out hunting throughout the city. The wolves are after them but we will have to go carefully."

"Go where?" I asked.

"Where we must," he said and took my arm.

CHAPTER 19

B ut first there was Cornelia again. She was the very picture
of courtesy as she descended to the basement, waylaying
us with tea. Earl Grey for Marco, some combination of bergamot, anise, and fennel for me. The brew was vile but I sipped
it all the same.

"It will help with your . . . cravings," she said delicately
as she hovered over me, pouring from a porcelain teapot. No
doubt she was far more accustomed to silver. I appreciated her
restraint even as I struggled to keep down the tea.

We were seated in a chamber in the inn's basement, surrounded by tall bookcases that held tomes devoted to all
manner of subjects related to the occult. At a glance, I noted
treatises on astrology, divination, demonology, and the like.
Aware as I was of Marco's involvement with the Golden
Dawn, I wondered if the books were his, but when I suggested
as much, I was corrected.

"This is Nicolas' library," Cornelia said. "That is everything
except the part of it pertaining to the law. Those books are in
his office above." She grimaced. "I cannot understand why he
insists on living in such a place."

"He likes it here," Marco said. "The inn is close to the

courts. All sorts of information flows with the ale. And his . . . eccentricities are respected."

"Is he here now?" I asked. I was curious as to the other di Orsini brother's whereabouts, but my attention was still diverted by the books. Looking more closely, I also saw Mr. Darwin's work along with titles by Sebastian de Vere, not the same ones that I had noticed in the library at the Bagatelle but others with such titles as *Speciation Among Hominids* and *Devolution: A Morphological Perspective*.

Mother and son exchanged a glance. Marco said, "Nicolas will be here shortly." To Cornelia, he added, "It will be dawn soon. Lucy and I must leave then."

She set her cup down with care, yet the china clattered slightly all the same. Sitting so erectly that her spine did not touch the back of the chair, she said, "You are still determined to associate yourself with the enemy?"

Marco winced slightly. "Lucy is not our enemy, but even if she were, I have no choice. Without Mordred's return, war is inevitable. And without her, I cannot find him."

As though I were not present, Cornelia replied, "You know what she is?"

He nodded. His dark eyes moved to me. "I had trouble believing it at first, but nothing else fits. We have always suspected that a halfling could come only from the Slayer's line. Now we know that is true."

"Is that why you . . . took an interest in me when I was still human?" It was as close as I could come to mentioning the relationship that had existed between us, especially in front of his mother.

As it was, Cornelia clearly disapproved of the subject. Abruptly, she stood and said, "I will be upstairs. When you can tear yourself away, Marco, I would like a private word with you."

Refusing to be baited, he responded mildly. "As you wish, Mother. I will be with you shortly."

When she was gone, leaving a trail of ice behind her, he sighed. "She means well."

Not where I was concerned, but I could hardly expect otherwise. "She is very worried about you." As was I. "This Council of Protectors you were called before . . . how much of a problem are they?"

"If we fail, none at all. They will be too busy trying to defend humans in the war that will follow. On the other hand, if we succeed and war is averted, I will be held to account. But there is no point worrying about that now."

Standing, he clasped his hands behind his back and paced a short distance in one direction, then another. Finally, he said, "You asked what drew me to you . . . before."

Already I regretted my ill-timed words but I could hardly take them back. "I did, yes."

He nodded, as though having come to terms with the necessity of providing me with an explanation. "Last year," he began, "the Council of Protectors charged me with discovering whether a secret cabal operating within the government, known as the Star Committee, had authorized the development of a weapon of such power that it could be used against vampires. You will understand that we wanted to determine if any such weapon existed because if it did and vampires learned of it, the inevitable result would be more attacks on humans."

I noted that he did not say that the Protectors opposed the creation of any such weapon, merely that they wanted warning of its existence. But I said only, "Surely the members of this Star Committee would realize the risk to humans, too, wouldn't they?"

"No doubt, but that doesn't mean that they were deterred by it. I made enough progress to suspect that the rumors had some substance but I couldn't get to the bottom of them. Finally, it occurred to me that no one would be more interested in discovering the existence of such a weapon than would Mordred himself. Without any other options, I decided to watch him, thinking that he might lead me to members of the cabal. To my surprise, I discovered that far from investigating the matter, he seemed entirely occupied in watching you."

The notion that I had been under the surveillance of the vampire king for some time before the events at Whitby was unsettling in the extreme. "You had no idea why he would do such a thing?"

"Not at the time, but I did know that it was out of character for him to take an interest in a seemingly ordinary young woman."

I raised a brow in mocking reprimand. Half mocking, at any rate. "Ordinary?"

He had the good grace to look abashed. "Forgive me, I didn't know you then. When we did become acquainted, I was even more puzzled. You were . . . a surprise."

"How so?"

He hesitated long enough for me to wonder if he would answer at all. Finally, without taking his eyes from me, he said, "A Protector's life tends to be solitary. When we do form relationships, they are within the bounds of our clan. I would never have set out to draw a young, innocent woman into an existence that of necessity encompasses considerable darkness and danger. But there I was suddenly drawn into yours and you were . . ." His smile was real for all that held a note of sadness. "You saw the world in all its amazing beauty and possibilities, and you embraced it. I couldn't help but be affected by your enthusiasm and your genuineness."

"But you still didn't believe there could be a future for us," I reminded him.

"I knew that there shouldn't be for your sake. But I would be lying if I said that I wasn't very tempted. For the first time, I began to question what I had simply accepted before." He gestured at the red pendant above his heart. "I was entrusted with this on my twentieth birthday. I had worked, trained, and studied since early childhood for the moment that I would ful-fill my destiny and become a Protector. Never had it occurred to me that I might want something else."

Whereas I had challenged from the beginning the path laid out before me. Was that part of what had drawn Marco and me together . . . and then torn us apart?

"Is that why you let me go back to Whitby? Because I made you question what you thought you should not?"

The flash of pain that crossed his face caught me by sur-prise. Until that moment, I had not realized how deeply he regretted all that had happened.

"Mordred seemed to have lost interest in you and the rumors of the cabal's activities were growing stronger. I told myself that my duty lay in London." He spread his hands in a plea for my understanding. "I believed that you would be safer away from me."

I could not cry, at least I did not think I could do so, but just then I came very close. Rising, I went to him and took both his hands in mine. The warmth of his skin threatened to melt the coldness that encased me. I felt his strength and will honed from childhood to stand between humanity and the evolutionary rival whose natural superiority could condemn all humans to being little more than cattle kept to be fed upon. Felt, too, the harsh discipline of duty that had taken him so far from any semblance of normal life. Almost as far as Mordred had taken me.

"It wasn't your fault," I said. "You couldn't have known what he intended."

His eyes were filled with sadness. "You absolve me too readily. Instead of just accepting that you were an enchanting young woman, I should have looked more closely. Had I understood the importance of your mother's bloodline . . ."

"What would you have done then, tried to stop Mordred?" Deliberately, I stared at the red pendant. "With that?"

His fingers brushed the heavy gold chain but did not touch the stone itself. "Do you know what this is?"

"It looks like a ruby, but surely it is too large."

"Indeed. It is something far rarer and vastly more precious. The heart of a vampire, found centuries ago in a cave on Crete and brought to Britain by one of the first Protectors."

I heard him clearly enough yet my mind could not grasp what he was telling me. "That isn't possible . . . it is beautiful."

Gently, he asked, "What do you think your heart looks like now, Lucy? Do you imagine that it is some poor shriveled thing?"

"How could it be otherwise? It no longer beats."

"It doesn't have to. We are only just beginning to understand the cellular changes that come with incarnation, but we do know that they are profound. A heart that does not beat but generates seemingly unlimited energy is only the beginning."

I stared more closely at the pendant, trying to understand its purpose. "What are you saying? That this energy still exists when the vampire no longer does?"

He nodded. "In the hands of a human who has been trained to use it, a vampire heart is a weapon. The energy in it can be directed to overload the cellular processes that enable vampires to exist. Essential functions are disrupted and the integrity of the body quickly disintegrates."

That something so beautiful and powerful could also be so destructive filled me with horror. I could barely comprehend it. "What are you saying . . . we just fall apart?"

He looked uncomfortable. "It's more like a shower of stars."

So evocative a description made me wonder how many times he had witnessed it for himself. Rather than think of that, I asked, "Are all the Protectors armed as you are?"

"The fighters among us are."

"All with vampire hearts? You have found so many?"

He did not flinch but met my gaze directly. "Mine is the oldest; it was found. The others were taken."

I did not have to ask how—the answer was starkly obvious. Armed with the first heart, the Protectors had hunted vampires to acquire as many more hearts as they needed. Their strength was limited only by however many fighters they could breed.

How close had my species, as much as a halfling could claim it as her own, come to extinction at their hands?

"You, too, want the destruction of vampires."

He was shaking his head before I finished speaking. "Not all of us. Not even most. Not anymore. We realize as Mordred did that we have to find a way to share this planet."

I wanted to believe him, truly I did. But what I had seen

since coming to London weighed heavily against him. "What has happened to the trolls, the gnomes, all the rest of them? Only a few remnants still exist."

"I have no idea," he said. "You can't hold me responsible—"

"You are human! You claim control over all the earth. And you . . . your kind is trained, as you yourself said, from childhood to kill vampires. Don't tell me you have suddenly discovered tolerance."

"I claim no such thing," he insisted. "But we have a right to preserve our own existence. Surely you would not argue otherwise?"

"Have you read Darwin?" I demanded. "Nature favors the fittest. You can't believe that a species that lives forever is not more fit than your own and therefore a threat to your very existence."

"And you cannot argue that a species incapable of emotion, creativity, and all the rest deserves to inherit the earth!"

There we were, faced off against each other in the subterranean refuge surrounded by the dolomite walls. A halfling and a human. Somewhere the gods were cheering and laying bets.

"I am incapable of emotion? Let us not forget that you left me because you could not deal with the emotions I provoked in you. Mordred judged you perfectly. You were his foil."

It was cruel, I admit, but it was also accurate. As Marco surely knew full well.

I waited, daring him to respond, and perhaps he would have done so. But just then Cornelia screamed. A long, drawn-out sound of agony and fright that came down to a single word.

"Nicolas!"

CHAPTER 20

I scarcely recognized the man who lay bloodied and battered on the office couch. He was covered by a blanket but
otherwise appeared to be naked. His powerful arms and broad
shoulders were bare, as were his feet. All were dark with dirt
and gore. At a glance, I made out several deep wounds in the
vicinity of his neck that looked severe enough to have killed
him. Yet he was still breathing, if only barely.

Marco hurried to his side, joining his mother who was
kneeling beside the couch grasping the man's hands and visibly
struggling not to weep. I approached cautiously and looked
more closely. Only then was I able to acknowledge that he
really was Nicolas. My first thought was that he had run afoul
of footpads in the dark streets, desperate men who were known
to slit a throat for a fat enough purse or sometimes for no purse
at all. But in such duress, I was reverting to memories of the
London of my childhood before the Watchers and the dirigibles. In our new times, crime, at least the sort that can be seen,
had been stamped almost out of existence.

"What happened—?" The moment I spoke, his eyes flew
open. He stared directly at me. His teeth barred in a snarl

before he seemed to recollect himself. With a low groan, he fell back against the couch.

Turning, Cornelia shouted at me. "Get out! How dare you be here? Get out!"

Marco laid a hand on her arm gently. "Easy, Mother, this isn't her fault." To me, he said, "There are bandages under the sink in the bathroom. Also a basin, if you could fill that with warm water and bring soap as well."

Cornelia started to object but I did not wait, hurrying instead to help as best I could. My hands were shaking as I filled the basin. Coming on top of the horrific events at the stone table, the violence done to Nicolas by unknown agents shattered any sense I still had of safety or stability. I felt myself spiraling into depths from which there could not be even the hope of escape. In my duress, I clung to the certainty that a person of character does not fall apart in even the most difficult circumstances. To the contrary, adversity should bring out the best in us. So I had been taught as a child and to that teaching I clung with all the strength I could muster.

With the bandages and a bar of soap tucked under my arm, I returned to the office. The smell of blood was beginning to affect me. As Marco went to work cleaning his brother's wounds, I backed away a little but did not think of leaving. Whatever had happened, I had a part in it.

"It is her fault," Cornelia insisted, throwing me a look of rage. Tears that she could not hold back coursed down her cheeks. "You cannot deny that they were after her."

Marco made no attempt to do so but he did say, "You know that Nicolas would never allow a pack of vampires to rampage through the streets of London without doing his utmost to stop them whatever their reason."

Cornelia's mouth worked in anger but she did not contradict him. To her credit, she gave all her attention to caring for her son. Swiftly but carefully, Nicolas' wounds were cleaned and bandaged. They were even more extensive than I had realized. Deep gashes scored his chest and back. One in particular reached almost to his abdomen, where it could have ripped out his intestines.

Through it all, Nicolas did not make a sound, but I saw the muscles of his jaw clenching. When he was finished, Marco turned to me. He was very pale, his eyes dark pools of anguish, yet he spoke calmly. "There's a bottle of whiskey in the desk."

I fetched it quickly along with several glasses. Marco filled one almost to the top and pressed it to his brother's lips. "Drink."

Nicolas emptied half the glass in a single swallow. When he was done, he sighed deeply, opened his eyes again, and said faintly but unmistakably, "It isn't as bad as it looks."

Cornelia murmured something under her breath that I did not catch. More clearly, she said, "What a fool you are." The harsh words were at odds with her gentle, loving tone. She brushed her son's hair back from his forehead and managed a weak smile. "Rest. The more you do so, the sooner you will heal."

Even as she spoke, his head sagged against her shoulder. In the next moment, he was asleep. Marco stood up slowly. He filled the three remaining glasses, passing two of them to his mother and me before drinking deeply from his own. Cornelia took only a few sips. I did better after discovering that the liquid not only tasted of peat smoke and heather but also had the ability to steady the nerves. No wonder my father had kept it on hand.

"I will bar the door inside and out when you have gone," Cornelia said. She had pulled a chair from behind the desk so that she could sit next to her sleeping son. "No one can see him like this."

"You know that his strength and stamina are unequaled," Marco said. "He will recover in a few hours."

Cornelia leaned a little closer, gazing at her son. She seemed to have forgotten the other momentarily but I was not misled. "He is lucky to recover at all," she said. "I had thought to be spared this with him at least but now it seems not."

Marco crossed the room and knelt again beside the couch. He spoke gently to his mother. "He has your courage, as do I. It will serve us well."

Her violet eyes swam with tears as she cupped his face in the palm of her hand. "We pay a heavy price for what we are. I hope that it will prove to be worth the cost."

He nodded, kissed her fingers lightly, and rose. With a glance at the clock, he said, "It is almost dawn. We must go."

Before we did, I took a long look around the office—the sleeping man, the mother keeping watch, the bloodied bandages disposed of neatly, all seemed to speak of a crisis successfully surmounted. Yet the more I looked, the more I realized that what was not present was far more telling than what was.

I saw only one pendant—that around Marco's neck. And no clothing such as would be removed from an injured man prior to treating his wounds. But on the front of the door leading to the lane beside the Serjeant's Inn, I noted freshly made scratches, as though the wood had been clawed by something in a rush to enter. Someone?

Outside, I paused for a moment to clear my senses. The

smell of blood had been very strong and with it had come hunger. I did my utmost to push that aside as together Marco and I started toward Fleet Street. At that early hour, only a few peddlers were about making their way under a dank yellow sky carrying the threat of rain. They stepped around the ample evidence of disorder without giving any sign of noticing it. I, on the other hand, was aware of everything that was out of place and seemed to shriek of what had happened in the dark hours of the night.

A wooden cart left chained beside a building had been wrenched loose and thrown into the street. Clumps of rough, gray fur were snagged around a lamppost. Nearby what looked like blood stained the pavement. A fragment of red silk caught my eye. It hung from a creaking iron sign outside a newsstand. Not far away were the torn and crumbled remains of an eve-ning jacket. Both were the sort of apparel commonly worn at the Bagatelle. Where the owners of those garments had gone I could not say.

"There was a battle," I observed, rather unnecessarily.

"If there hadn't been, there would have been even more carnage," Marco replied. "Lady Blanche's decision to set vampires upon London amounts to a declaration of war." His manner could scarcely have been more somber. I hesitated to worsen it but the conviction that under the present circum-stances we could not afford to have any secrets between us overrode all else.

"How long has Nicolas been a werewolf?"

A hiss of surprise escaped him. He gripped my arm. "What are you talking about?"

I ignored the instinct to wrench free and spoke matter-of-factly. "Do you really mean to deny it? It's not as though I'm going to run off shrieking in fright or worse yet not believe you if you tell me the truth."

When he remained silent, I ticked off the evidence. "Nicolas' wounds appear to be largely from fangs. The absence of any pendant like yours suggests that he was not injured while performing his duties as a Protector. There was no evidence of damaged clothing. But most important, I had the sense from the moment I met him that we had crossed paths before and I finally realized where. I encountered the wolf pack the first night I came to the Bagatelle and they were there again last night when I fled."

He let go of me and pushed both his hands through his thick hair in a gesture of pure frustration. "You don't understand what you're saying."

"Then explain it to me."

Marco sighed deeply. "Nothing is ever simple with my brother."

Amanda could have said the same of me but I never had any reason to doubt her feelings. Nor did I doubt Marco's.

"Yet you love him."

He shot me a look in which caution mingled with gratitude that someone, however unlikely, understood how he felt. "How can I do otherwise? He was my best friend when we were growing up. We made all sorts of plans to travel the world together as Protectors, keeping humans safe. And then . . ."

Gently, I asked, "What happened?"

"What we always knew might but still hoped would not. He . . . turned."

I frowned, not understanding. "People can't just spontaneously become werewolves, can they? Surely there must be some catalyst involved as with vampires."

"There is, but it is of a particularly insidious type. Are you familiar with the work of Gregor Mendel?"

I had not been until the weeks spent in the library at Whitby when I had come across references to the Austrian scientist who had died a few years before. Belatedly, I wondered about my father's interest in such matters. Did it perhaps have to do with his awareness of my mother's background and what she might have passed to their children?

"Mendel studied inheritance patterns in plants," I said. "His findings convinced him that in many cases the chances of inheriting a particular trait can be computed by reference to basic mathematics and rules of probability."

Marco nodded. "His work was largely ignored until recently when it began attracting attention from a variety of sources. Unfortunately, not all of them are benign. There is talk of using Mendelian genetics to breed a super race of humans better adapted to the new world that is being shaped by advances in science and technology."

I needed a moment to grasp what he was saying, so extraordinary was the idea. The course of natural selection was incredibly complex, involving as it did millions of species developing over vast stretches of time. Until Darwin had come along a few decades before to explain it, humans had been completely ignorant of how life changed and advanced. Yet some among them imagined that they were capable of taking charge of the process?

"The proponents of this idea," Marco said, "argue that the first nation to come to grips with it and make it work will achieve an insurmountable advantage over everyone else."

"Then what happens to all the rest?" I asked. "There will still be hundreds of millions of ordinary humans."

"I suppose some use will be found for them until they die out in the natural course of events," Marco replied. He left it at that and went on, "At any rate, werewolves have their own bloodlines dating back thousands of years. Several centuries ago, one of those lines crossed with that of the Protectors. For most of us since, the only effect has been to endow us with greater strength and stamina. But for one in four, the result is far more profound. That is, as my mother said, the price we pay for being what we are."

The price Nicolas paid when random chance transformed his existence. How had he managed to cope as well as he had done?

"There is no way of knowing who is affected or doing anything about it until it is too late?" I asked.

"None. Efforts have been made over the years to predict the condition, but they have all failed. No one is ever prepared when it happens. Nicolas turned for the first time when he was sixteen. He barely survived the ordeal."

"But he has survived despite everything." I thought of him standing rugged and proud at the head of his pack. "He is the alpha wolf, isn't he?"

Marco nodded with a faint smile. "He was never one to take second place. There have always been werewolves in London, but I don't believe they have ever had a leader such as Nicolas."

"After what happened last night, can we still hope for much help from them?" I hated even to ask, but neither could I underestimate the danger we would all face if we failed to find Mordred.

"Werewolves fight to the death, they never surrender. It is not in their nature."

Something for all of us to remember, I thought, as Marco stepped out into the street and hailed a passing hackney. Several Watchers were nearby but their attention was diverted by the evidence of the battle that had occurred.

"Where are we going?" I asked as he handed me up.

After a quick word with the driver, Marco took the seat next to me. "It is time to beard the lion in his den," he said. "But first we have a stop to make."

CHAPTER 21

At that early hour, the streets around the Lyceum Theatre were empty but for the harried office workers on their way to the nearby banks and trading houses. Their presence well in advance of what had been normal business hours was made necessary by the new high-capacity transoceanic telegraph cables that had begun operating between New York and London a few months before. The world was becoming smaller, which some termed progress. Others complained that men were being made slaves to machines. And now this business about breeding a super race. Truly, we lived in unfathomable times.

The placards I had seen before in front of the theatre were gone, replaced by advertisements for the stage version of *Dracula,* now apparently to be a play as well as a novel. I bit back a sharp remark as Marco and I walked around the back to the stage door. To my surprise, the entrance stood slightly ajar.

"Wait here," Marco said. Rather inexplicably given that he had every reason to know me better, he took my obedience for granted. Naturally, I ignored him and followed on his heels. If something was amiss, he would do far better with a vampire, even of the halfling variety, fighting at his side than he would alone, whether he cared to admit that or not.

The passage across the back of the theatre was as I remembered—crowded with trunks and baskets, backdrops, and bits of scenery stacked along the walls. But whereas before I had seen it in near total darkness, now it was faintly illumi- nated by the pale yellow light filtering in through narrow win- dows set high under the building's eaves.

No sound came from the office at the far end but there, too, the door stood open. Marco and I approached cautiously. The large rolltop desk at which the Irishman labored was thrown onto its side, the overstuffed leather chair lying some distance away. A tall bookshelf also lay on the floor. The worn Oriental rug had been torn up and left in a heap in one corner. A lamp was broken, a table shattered. . . . There was no sign of Stoker.

My nostrils flexed. "There is no blood. Nor is there a body. We should visit his home, make sure that everyone there is all right." As disagreeable as I found Stoker's "novel," I wished no ill on his family. If memory served, he had a wife and children. I had to hope that he had gotten them to safety.

"Give me a moment." To my surprise, Marco began a slow circuit of the room, tapping lightly on the walls. He was half- way between the door and a window when the sound suddenly rang hollow.

With a smile, Marco called, "It just us, Bram. You can come out." When there was no immediate response, he rapped again. His effort was rewarded by the creaking of wood and metal, fol- lowed by the emergence of a mussed and bleary-eyed Irishman from what looked like a comfortable little hidey-hole.

Hoisting himself to his feet, he said, "I must have fallen asleep in there. Hell of a thing here last night—" Seeing me, he flinched but recovered quickly. "Miss Weston, what a sur- prise." His tone left no doubt that I did not fall within the category of surprises commonly termed "delightful," but instead was considerably more in the direction of "to be avoided at all costs."

Nonetheless, he plunged on with admirable eloquence. "May I just say that I truly regret being less than forthcoming with you at our previous encounter? Not to mention my unfortunate role in perpetrating certain falsehoods regarding the appalling events to which you fell victim?"

For a speech hastily conceived in a spasm of fear, it went over well enough. I nodded. "May I say, Mr. Stoker, for my part that I regret choking you the last time we met?" I tried to remember if I had done anything else to him, other than leave him thoroughly terrified, but nothing came to mind.

Under other circumstances, his look of relief would have been comical. "Water under the bridge, Miss Weston. Marco, good to see you. I take it you're aware of what happened last night?"

"We've just come from Nicolas' side. He is rather the worse for wear. But what of your family, are they safe?"

Stoker's face darkened. "I am sorry to hear about your brother. My wife and children are with friends in the country. I was working late when I happened to glance out the window in time to see the most extraordinary creatures approaching the theatre. Thralls, I think they are called? At any rate, I only just had time to slip into my little bolt hole before they burst in."

"You just happened to have a hiding place here?" I asked.

"Have you ever heard of Samuel Beazley?" he inquired. "He's the fellow who designed this theatre and several others. When he wasn't doing that, he was a novelist and playwright. Despised actors, felt anyone who had to deal with them ought to have a means of escape. Must say, I'm very grateful to him."

On that note, he put a handkerchief to his nose, gave it a prodigious blow, stuffed the results into his pocket, and said, "I have been making inquiries along the lines that you suggested, Marco. Seems as though this all runs a bit deeper than we wanted to think. There was a meeting last year of the Star Committee that I've only just found out about. Strictly off the record, the topic of discussion was whether it is still necessary or beneficial for humans to coexist with vampires."

Marco's face tightened. Quietly, he asked, "The alternative being what?"

With an apologetic glance at me, Stoker replied, "That a means be found to destroy them. Research to that end was authorized."

"Authorized by whom?" I asked.

"I don't know," Stoker admitted. "The members of the Star Committee are never identified, not even by those willing to speculate about their activities. Officially, they do not exist. However, they are generally assumed to be among the most powerful men in the realm."

"I can name one likely candidate," Marco said. "Your patron, Gladstone. As it happens, we are on our way to see him. Would you care to come along?"

"Truthfully, I'd rather not, but with the stakes as high as they appear to be, I don't think that I have a choice. Gladstone has had my loyalty for well on twenty years. It's time he prove that he deserves it."

So stolid a declaration of principle almost made me regret my harsh opinion of Stoker. Truly, if he had been as good a novelist as he was a man he might have found something better to write about. At any rate, he was willing to put himself in the path of danger for the sake of a higher good, and for that I was duly grateful. There are times when the solitude of the night, filled as it is with the music of the spheres that the earthbound can never appreciate, is all that a creature such as myself needs. But in the dank light of a London morning, with ominous clouds hovering on the near horizon, there was much to be said for the simple comfort of companionship and the knowledge that one did not face the gathering storm alone.

Although former Prime Minister William Gladstone no longer resided at Number 10 Downing Street, he had not gone any great distance from it. The Lion of Parliament had taken up unofficial residence only a few doors down in an elegant townhouse a short walk from Buckingham Palace, the residence of the Prince of Wales and heir presumptive whose ear, it was said, Gladstone had. He was far less welcome at the Crystal Palace, his relations with the Queen Empress being as frosty as the glass-enclosed interiors where she dwelled, swaddled forever in her mourning clothes.

All this Stoker explained to me as we made our way to the lion's den. With the Jubilee celebrations completed save for a final gala event to be held two nights hence, the streets were passable once again. I had only a little time to worry about meeting such an august personage.

"Admittedly, he is not the man he was," the Irishman concluded. "His health is poor and since he left office, he has been prey to melancholia. However, all that means is that he is only ten times as formidable as other men."

"Is that why you still do his bidding?" Marco asked. He and I were seated side by side facing Stoker. When the carriage stopped abruptly to give way to a passing police wagon, the sudden lurch sent us swaying toward one another. I straightened with alacrity but, I will admit, also with regret. Since he had confided in me about Nicolas' true nature, I felt closer to Marco than ever before. This despite what he had revealed about the fate of vampires' hearts. Truly, if I had any sense at all, I would have kept a closer guard on my own.

"How could I not?" Stoker countered. "Gladstone's Irish policy was far from perfect, but it was considerably better than anyone else's. At least he believes that the Irish are human."

I recalled the sorry history of the famine that had ravaged the Emerald Isle a few decades past, when food grown in Ireland continued to be exported to England while a million men, women, and children lay dead and dying in the streets and beside the hedgerows. Those who claimed to be philanthropists sent aid in the form of cattle feed, sadly indigestible by the starving masses.

Still, a man who is principled in one regard may not be in another. What had I represented to Gladstone when he sent men to drive a stake into my heart and hide me away in a rude grave? A tragedy, perhaps, involving the destruction of a young girl. But in his ignorance of Mordred's true intent, he had also seen me as a danger that had to be eliminated at all costs. The instinct to destroy what it did not understand might yet condemn humanity to extinction.

Stoker continued, "In his defense, only a very small group has ever known about the presence of vampires in Britain. Gladstone thought it should stay that way lest there by widespread panic."

I thought of the Watchers appearing everywhere on their Teslaways and the dirigibles that darkened the skies. Rumor had it that the new telegraph cable was designed so that messages could be intercepted. The same was being said of the new telephones that government subsidies were helping to put in the better class of homes and business. "He still believes there is such a thing as secrets?"

"He is an old man," Stoker said bluntly. "The world is moving beyond him. But he asked for my help and I gave it. Now I feel entirely justified in asking for his."

"It won't be easy," Marco said. Yet he did not appear unduly alarmed. To the contrary, he seemed to be relishing what was to come.

Speculation about what we might encounter once we met the aging lion occupied me as the carriage turned onto Downing Street. We passed Number 10 and continued on toward what some said was still the true seat of power in the British Empire.

A butler—young for his post, square shouldered and straight backed with a soldier's manner—admitted us. "The prime minister is expecting you," he said.

The title might be honorary now, but the security surrounding Gladstone was anything but. In addition to the butler's martial bearing, we passed several men in civilian clothing with bulges beneath their jackets that suggested they were carrying sidearms.

As we followed the butler, I murmured to Marco, "Gladstone knows about the foundry? And the manor?"

"We must assume that he knows all. Never make the mistake of underestimating him."

With that bit of advice uppermost in mind, I stepped into a room that looked not like the refuge of a retired gentleman but rather the hub of an imperial venture. Maps of every part of the world covered the walls. Teleprinters clattered with incoming messages. I even recognized a Babbage difference engine capable of executing computations far swifter than any human. Increasingly, they were being used to correlate reports on activity throughout the realm.

Several male secretaries were in attendance, but they departed speedily when the man behind the desk waved them out. I saw in a glance that Gladstone was very old. His large head was sparsely covered with white hair, but his muttonchop whiskers were still impressive. He had a square face with a strong jaw and large eyes surrounded by a web of lines. Despite Stoker's warnings about his health, his back was still straight and his shoulders well set.

At the sight of us, he rose and came out from behind his desk. He moved a little stiffly but no more so than many men decades his junior.

"Marco, good to see you." His voice was deep, steady, and resonant, the voice of an orator who had held Parliament spellbound. "Bram . . . and this is—"

His gaze, still penetrating despite his years, shifted to me. In a glance, he seemed to see all that I was or could be. But that was a trick, I told myself, the stratagem of a man for whom politicking and manipulation were second nature. "Miss Weston, is it? I thought our paths would cross before too long."

I knew what I was supposed to say, something about the pleasure of meeting him, perhaps even what an honor it was. But such niceties were beyond me.

"They might have crossed sooner had you attempted to help me rather than drive a stake through my heart and consign me to the grave."

Stoker made a choking sound. Marco's reaction was more interesting, confined as it was to a faint smile. He showed neither shock not disapproval at my accusation, which I took to mean that he had already figured out for himself what must have happened.

"Your operatives followed Mordred to Whitby," I said. "When they realized what he had done, they notified you immediately." I gestured at the clattering teleprinters. "It would not have been difficult. With no thought as to why Mordred had acted as he had, you ordered that I be destroyed. Had I been fully a vampire instead of what I am, I would have been."

I expected Gladstone to deny the charge, but the Lion of Parliament was beyond any such consideration. To the contrary, he appeared entirely unapologetic.

Regarding me with the interest he might give to a particularly exotic creature, he said, "It's true, then, you're a halfling. I must say that's a surprise. Those who are expert in such matters have always said that any such hybrid is impossible. Too many contradictions in cell structure or something to that effect."

"Apparently, they were wrong."

"Indeed. At any rate, you are correct that my instinct was to have you disposed of quickly. Mordred seemed to have lost control of himself, violating the pact that had existed between us for centuries. No unwilling human was to ever be taken by a vampire. And only very small numbers of those who were willing were ever to be incarnated. In this manner, we have preserved social order and stability. What do you imagine would have happened had we failed to do so?"

"People would have realized that the world is far more richly varied than they have imagined," I said. "They would have adapted accordingly."

Gladstone snorted. "That sort of dangerous naiveté will doom us all. If ordinary people ever wake up to the fact that they share this realm with a race of beings possessed of vastly greater strength and stamina who regard them as *food*, devastation will follow. Blood will run in the streets, anarchy will rule, and we will descend into a new dark age. To prevent such calamity, honorable men may be compelled to take measures repellant to their finer natures, but—"

Before he could lapse into an oration better suited to the floor of the Commons, I said, "They are closer to being awakened than you know. A young man named Harley Langworthe was slaughtered last night by vampires at the Bagatelle. Afterward, they went on a rampage through the city that was stopped only by the efforts of other nonhuman creatures, all that stood between humanity and mass destruction."

The color fled from Gladstone's face. He staggered and had to put out a hand to steady himself. I had a moment's concern that I might have gone too far but he recovered quickly. "I knew about the trouble last night, but Langworthe . . . for God's sake, he was little more than a boy."

"He is only the beginning," I said. "If Mordred isn't found and restored to power, the secret you and others like you have kept for so long will be secret no more. The anarchy you fear will be upon us. Everything you have worked for, everything you love will fall into ruin."

"Lucy . . ." Marco spoke softly but his meaning was clear. He thought I should stop, but I had no intention of doing so. Creature of the dark though I was, I was determined to shine a light into the abyss that we were all approaching at terrifying speed.

"No," Gladstone said. In place of his earlier confidence, he sounded suddenly weary. "It's all right. Miss Weston is correct. We have no time to waste. Come, let us sit down."

We took chairs before the large fireplace, swept clean and

filled with flowers. As though feeling the need to remind him-self, our host said, "For almost three hundred and fifty years, there has been a pact between the British government and the vampires ruled by Mordred. We have accepted their pres-ence in Britain, and in return, they have helped to protect the realm. It has worked out to all our benefit."

Leaving aside that humans had been fed on regularly. Pre-sumably, they were not typically from Harley Langworthe's class.

I looked around at the three men assembled there—Gladstone of the ruling class, Stoker the loyal subject who nonetheless was showing signs of being able to think for him-self, and Marco, whose clan of Protectors had challenged the agreement with the vampires by defending humans even in the face of it. For all the differences they represented, a balance of sorts had existed.

"What changed?" I asked.

"We did," Marco replied, preempting whatever the prime minister had been about to say. "Humans changed. The more control we have gained over nature, the more we have sought. Little regard has been given to how fundamentally we are al-tering ourselves in the process."

Gladstone snorted. He appeared to have recovered from his shock over Langworthe. "Nonsense. Human nature is eternal. Cain is still very much with us, as is Abel. Judas walks our streets but, it is to be hoped, so do Peter and Paul." With a nod in my direction, he added, "Not to forget the female, we still have faithful Ruths and perfidious Delilahs."

I remembered that Gladstone had been an evangelical in his youth, of the unyielding Scottish variety. Later, as his political stature grew, he had adopted a more High Anglican view of the world, but in his twilight years the teachings of his childhood seemed to have overtaken him once again.

"Human nature," I countered, "can be changed beyond all recognition in the blink of an eye. If you doubt it, consider what happened to me."

"Well . . . yes, but," he said, "that was a highly unusual case. We had no idea what Mordred intended, none whatsoever. It was completely out of keeping with all his previous behavior." He looked at me closely. "Did he not realize what he was creating, or did he have some particular purpose for doing so?"

With a note of pride, I said, "I am a descendant of Morgaine le Fey. The blood of the Slayer runs in my veins. Mordred knew that when he incarnated me. He understood what I would become. Whether because I am a halfling or because of Mordred's own connection to Morgaine, I am able to communicate with him. He chose me for that purpose."

At once, Gladstone sat up in his chair. His prodigious brows drew together in a fierce stare. "Has he told you his whereabouts?"

Reluctant as I was to trust him, I replied noncommittally. "Not precisely. What do you know of them?"

"If I knew anything at all, do you imagine that I would have kept it to myself?"

I was about to answer when Marco forestalled me. Quietly but with unmistakable command, he said, "Prime Minister, you were present at the meeting of the Star Committee last year when the decision was taken to seek a means of destroying the vampires, were you not?"

Gladstone shook his head in dismay. "I will not ask how you come by such knowledge as no doubt you would not tell me. But you have it wrong. The only decision was to authorize research, nothing more, and that strictly as a contingency should it ever be needed."

"I see," Marco said slowly. "So the idea was that a means of destroying vampires would be found but not necessarily used. Kept in the back pocket, as it were?"

"It is the responsibility of those in power to plan for all sorts of contingencies," Gladstone insisted. "Our pact was with Mordred, but we were aware that there was opposition to him among some of the vampires. We had to ask ourselves what would happen if he was deposed as their king."

"Deposed by Lady Blanche?" I suggested.

The lion nodded. "She seemed the likeliest candidate and now she has made her intentions clear." Speaking to all of us, he said, "She must be stopped."

"We cannot do that without Mordred," I said. "Where is he?"

"I don't know. . . ."

"But you do know who may be responsible for his disappearance." Stoker had not spoken until that moment. I had thought him still too overawed by Gladstone or to loyal to pressure him in any way, but apparently I was mistaken.

"I can scarcely believe that what happened at that Star Committee meeting has anything to do with Mordred's disappearance," the prime minister insisted.

Stoker was having none of that. Firmly, he said, "How could it not? Anyone serious about researching a means of destroying vampires would, first and foremost, require a vampire to study. Isn't that so?"

"Yes, of course, but it was supposed to be someone very junior . . . perhaps one newly incarnated and still not certain how to get about. Someone like that would be vulnerable, but not Mordred, never him. None of us ever imagined that he would be the target."

"Whose target?" I demanded. "Give us a name."

Gladstone stared off into space. He appeared to be reliving the actions that had brought us to our present dire circumstances, trying to understand how he could have made such a terrible miscalculation.

"Dr. Sebastian de Vere presented a very reasonable proposal," he said at length. "Natural outgrowth of his earlier research . . . prudent thing to do . . . our responsibility . . ." Abruptly, he pounded his fist in the palm of his hand. "He virtually guaranteed success! Said we were on the verge of a new world order in which humanity would finally assume its rightful place above all others. It was up to us to make sure that happened or someone else would."

At mention of the name, I froze, so much so that I almost missed what followed immediately thereafter. Not that it mattered. Stoker summed it up perfectly.

"In all candor, Prime Minister, whoever you're talking about sounds insane. You cited Scripture earlier, but even before then men knew that we are not meant to be gods. Look what happened to Prometheus when he brought fire to earth or to Icarus when he flew too close to the sun."

"Sebastian de Vere may be insane," Marco interjected. He looked deeply concerned but not particularly surprised. "What we can be certain of is that he is brilliant. His research into human evolution and cellular change is unparalleled."

I recovered myself enough to ask, "De Vere is a member of the Golden Dawn, is he not? Didn't you tell me that his research has skirted too close to the wind on more than one occasion?"

Marco nodded. "He has a reputation as a man who believes that the ends always justify the means."

"That's well and good," Stoker said, "but I fail to see how any human, no matter how determined, could have captured Mordred."

The prime minister made to rise only to fall back in his chair when he heard Marco's reply.

"De Vere is no ordinary human; he is a renegade Protector. He was born into my clan and trained for that role. The night before he was to be inducted, the heart he was about to receive disappeared. De Vere claimed to have no idea what happened to it. Before another could be found for him, he declared that he was no longer interested in being a Protector but intended to devote himself to his scientific studies."

"Was the heart ever found?" I asked, even though I was already certain of the answer.

"It was not," Marco replied. "Suspicion remains to this day that de Vere stole it so that he could use it for his own purposes outside the scrutiny of our council. I would say that we now have confirmation of that."

"Bloody hell," Gladstone muttered. He slumped in his chair, suddenly looking his age and more.

"He has to be stopped," Stoker said, rather more resolutely. The Irishman had pluck, I gave him that. "Where is de Vere likely to be?" he demanded.

The prime minister shook his head as though by that action he could drive out the miasma of dread that threatened to overwhelm reason. Thinking aloud, he said, "His residence is in Belgrave. He belongs to various clubs. He is a Fellow of the Royal Society. He has privileges at the Royal London Hospital, St. Bartholomew's, Bethlem—"

"Bethlem?" Marco and I spoke as one. Bethlem hospital—or Bedlam, as it was more commonly known—had a particularly dark reputation that all the recent efforts at reform had scarcely managed to lessen. For centuries, it had housed those unfortunates deemed to be mentally unstable—or cursed, depending on the prevailing view of the time. While treatment was said to have improved of late, it was not a place where anyone would want to be.

Softly, Marco said, "People screaming."

Perplexed, Gladstone looked at us. "What's that you say?"

"Mordred doesn't know where he is," I explained. "But he says that he can hear people screaming."

I got to my feet. Marco rose as well, as did Stoker. Together, we headed for the door.

Behind us, Gladstone murmured, "Extraordinary . . . he seemed like such a rational chap . . ."

I hardly heard him. Even as I wanted to believe that we had discovered Mordred's location at last, I sensed that the connection between us was growing weaker by the moment. Hastening down the stairs and back out into the leaden London day, I could only hope that we were not too late.

CHAPTER 22

S moke from the still unextinguished fires at the foundry stained the sky to the west as we crossed Blackfriar's Bridge. A little farther on through streets where Watchers lurked at every corner our hackney drew up in front of the sprawling three-story stone building that housed the Bethlem Royal Hospital. Since its founding in the thirteenth century, the hospital had occupied several locations around London, but none as large or grandiose as its current residence in St. George's Fields near Southwark. A stranger to the place could be pardoned for assuming that it was the home of a wealthy duke or, even more likely, one of the new men of business and technology who were remaking our world.

Passersby strolling by the wide wrought iron gates paused to glance into grounds where chestnut trees were in full leaf. Here and there, inmates in the company of their custodians could be seen availing themselves of the relatively fresh air. The setting appeared as close to idyllic as it was possible to come within the city. Until, that is, I noticed the high stone wall that began on either side of the gate and continued around the entire expanse of several acres. Iron spikes were

planted at intervals along the top of the wall, but they were
not as ominous as the signs facing outward that read Warning:
Electrified Barrier.

"How are we to get in?" I asked as we descended from the
hackney. In the previous century, a penny had bought admis-
sion for the purpose of viewing the inmates and their "antics,"
but such callous practices were frowned upon in our more enlightened age.

"Leave that to me," Stoker replied. Visiting hours had
begun and people were walking alone, in couples, or in small
groups up the cobblestone drive to the columned main entrance. We joined them. I had just begun to hope that my
concerns might be unfounded when we stepped into the cavernous central hall adorned with murals depicting the progress
of medicine through the ages. A line was forming up in front of
the admitting desk, where names were being checked against a
list of those approved for entrance.

As Marco and I waited at a discreet distance, Stoker joined
the queue. When his turn came, he had a few quick words with
the attendant at the desk. The man, whose frown appeared so
habitual as to be etched into his mouth, suddenly smiled. Several moments of voluble conversation followed at the conclusion of which Stoker waved us forward.

We made haste past the desk as the Irishman explained,
"I told him I was here to research a new book. He thinks it a
splendid place to set a story."

"That easily he let you in?" Stoker had achieved a kind
of celebrity since the publication of *Dracula*, but even so the
readiness with which we were admitted surprised me.

"He's writing a novel. But then, apparently, so are most

people, if only in their own minds. Unfortunately, that fellow has actually committed some of his to paper." With a grimace, he added, "I believe I agreed to take a look at his efforts."

Marco stifled a laugh that would have been out of keeping with our surroundings. I took a closer look around. Having never been in a hospital of any sort before, my curiosity was natural. Bethlem's peculiar history only served to accentuate it. Yet I had to admit nothing in the appearance of the building inside or out hinted at the tormented state of the patients there. To the contrary, my first impression was of an almost sanctified air of calm. Having turned its back on its brutal past—or so was the claim—Bethlem appeared to be nothing less than a temple of healing.

A man of middle years with the air of a busy professional walked briskly across the hall trailed by an eager group of students. An unbuttoned white lab coat flapped behind him. He was lecturing as he went. At first glance, I thought he might be Sebastian de Vere, but he was inches shorter and of far less formidable appearance. I wondered what he thought of the admittedly shocking theories coming out of Austria, the results of work done by a certain Sigmund Freud who was developing something he called "psychoanalysis." Could the human psyche be subjected to the same sort of rigorous scientific investigation as, for example, the genetics of a plant? Perhaps the new, improved variety of the species that Marco said some wanted to create would be susceptible to such efforts, but I doubted it. Certainly, the current, more primitive form could never be so neatly catalogued.

From the main hall, corridors lined by oak and glass doors led off to both the left and the right. Brass plaques gave directions to various offices, examining rooms, laboratories, libraries, and an auditorium. I surmised that patients were housed on the upper two stories, and indeed, visitors were streaming up a broad staircase. Mordred had said that he was underground.

"We must find a way to the basement," I said. A small door behind a pillar appeared promising but when we approached, it turned out to lead to nothing more than a supply closet. Frustrated, I was looking around again when Marco touched my arm.

"We are attracting attention."

At a glance, I saw that he was right. A burly attendant with the face of a footballer who has led too often with his head was moving in our direction. His intent may have been to offer help to visitors who appeared uncertain as to where to go, or he may have meant to question our purpose in being there and perhaps even summon help to evict us. I was not interested in finding out which it was, nor was Marco or Stoker. Together, we mounted the staircase with the rest of the civilians and climbed swiftly. I had no real idea of what to expect when we reached the first upper floor, but even so, the scene we walked into took me by surprise.

The stairs gave way directly onto a broad landing beneath a high dome. Tall windows looked out over the chestnut trees. The wicker furniture, potted palms, and gently revolving wooden ceiling fans were reminiscent of an elegant seaside resort. Several dozen well-dressed men and women were taking tea.

A violinist strolled among the potted palms while playing Debussy's "Clair de Lune." Waiters in white jackets offered trays of finger sandwiches and pastries. The air carried the scents of tuberose and honeysuckle blooming on trellises near the windows. The only discordant note was the presence of several attendants keeping watch along the edges of the room, but they could be easily overlooked in such pleasant surroundings.

Everyone, whether visitor or patient, seemed to be if not happy at least content. Whatever torments they suffered—and I did not presume that only the patients themselves were so afflicted—they showed no sign of them. Their behavior was of such unblemished banality that a mad notion occurred to me: Perhaps Bethlem was no more than a sham, an elaborate hoax to conceal its true purpose, whatever that might be.

Stoker may have sensed the direction of my thoughts. Leaning close enough so that he could not be overheard, he said, "These are among the 'Curables,' as they have been declared by their esteemed physicians. People of good breeding in need of a little rest, a bit of bucking up, an electric shock or two, nothing more."

"Is that really enough to cure them?" I asked. Beneath the smiling civility, I began to notice the odd twitch here and there, the strain around the eyes, the nervous laughter. It struck me that more than a few found the pretense of normality to be an ordeal.

He shrugged. "Some perhaps, as for the rest, if they act out, opium works well enough to quiet them. And there are other measures. Ice baths are effective, I hear. Sensory isolation chambers are even more so."

I wondered how he was so well informed but did not ask. It was beginning to sound as though Bethlem had not changed that much after all.

"This hospital is supposed to serve everyone in London who has need of it," Marco said. "They can't possibly all be as well off as these people appear."

"They aren't," Stoker said. He inclined his head toward the second floor. "It's rather like first and second class on an ocean liner. Upstairs the rooms are smaller, the tea plainer, and there is no violinist, but the patients there are still considered curable."

Marco and I exchanged a glance. "In that case," he said, "we must be looking for steerage."

Somewhere there had to be a staircase used by servants to transit the various floors, including into the basement. I was glancing around, trying to find it, when I noticed a slender young woman looking at me. She wore a day dress in creamy silk trimmed with lace. Her dark hair was swept up in a chignon with soft wisps framing her face. A pearl choker adorned her throat. At a guess, I would have said that she was about the same age as myself, twenty years, and that she was a visitor, not a patient. But on that last score, I was quickly proven wrong.

The moment our eyes met she wrenched hers away, only to turn back again with so fierce a stare that her face, placid moments before, was transformed into a mask of fear and loathing. Abruptly, she screamed, "Monster! Monster!" Rising from the chair in which she sat, she stretched out a slim arm and pointed a trembling finger at me. "Monster!"

Several attendants pushed away from the wall and started for her. Some of the people closest to where she sat tried to soothe her while others shrank back, hiding their faces in their hands. One or two others began to wail. In an instant, the ordered scene was shattered.

"Damn," Marco muttered under his breath. "A sensitive." He grabbed my arm and half dragged, half propelled me around to the other side of the stairs. Stoker kept pace as we hurried down a corridor that led to a small service kitchen at the back of the building. Behind us, I could still hear screaming.

"What happened?" I asked when we finally stopped next to a dumbwaiter used for hoisting supplies up from below. I was more shaken that I wanted to admit. Even as I told myself that the young woman was ill and could have behaved the same way toward anyone, I sensed otherwise.

"The girl is a sensitive," Marco said. When I looked at him without comprehending, he explained. "People like her can recognize vampires, werewolves, and others of the hidden world even when they look human."

I thought of what she had called me. "She sees monsters."

"She doesn't know what she's seeing," he insisted. "Or understand it in the least. In all likelihood, she really thinks that she is mad as does everyone around her."

The girl had been condemned to a mental hospital because she saw the world as it really was, not as those less gifted than herself believed it to be. I wondered if Gladstone or any other of the powerful men who had kept the truth hidden for so long considered the cost to people like her. Or if they were regarded as no more than unfortunate casualties of the need to preserve what passed for peace.

"How terrible," I murmured. Fully aware as I was that had anyone believed the girl, our efforts to find Mordred might have ended there and then, I could not help but pity her. To be condemned to believe that reality is a phantasm of one's own disordered mind seemed a cruelly refined torture.

As I was struggling to come to grips with the existence of such poor souls, Stoker had been occupied more productively. He turned to us. "Over here. I've found a staircase."

He had indeed, half hidden behind a pantry. In the great

houses, staff went unseen through concealed passages and up and down hidden steps. Apparently, the same was true in Bethlem.

Electric lights attached to the wall illuminated a metal staircase built for practicality without the least evidence of the grace and effort put into the public aspects of the building. A dank odor rose from below, floating upward on currents of cool, damp air. I smelled stone, soil, and . . . the river. Just as Mordred had described.

"Quickly," I said. The heels of our boots clattered on the steps as we began our descent. Left to my own devices, I would have covered the distance in several long leaps. Marco no doubt would have been right behind me, but Stoker was not a young man and the years spent laboring behind a desk had not prepared him to keep pace with a halfling and a Protector. Though he strove to do so manfully, it was clear that the exertions of the day were catching up with him.

Finally at the bottom, Marco called a halt on the not very believable grounds that he needed a brief rest. As the Irishman took the opportunity to regain his breath, I closed my eyes and reached out to Mordred.

For an instant, I thought that I sensed him, but the impression was so fleeting that I could not be sure. Either we were in the wrong place after all or Mordred could not respond. He might be too weak to do so or he might no longer exist. Yet if he was gone, surely I would sense that. So great an alteration in the fabric of reality could not go unnoticed, could it?

"Anything?" Marco asked.

Grimly, I shook my head. We proceeded with care through the steel door at the bottom of the stairs and into the narrow corridor on the other side. Unlike the sunlit floors above, the only illumination came from electric lights in cone-shaped metal shades dangling from the ceiling. They swayed on currents of the dank, clammy air.

Barred doors with small mesh-covered windows lined both sides of the corridor. I peered into one, saw a figure huddled on the floor in a corner, and looked away hastily. Judging by the neatly scripted white name cards set in slots beside most of the doors, what Marco had referred to as the "steerage" section of Bethlem was well occupied. I did not expect to come across one helpfully labeled Mordred, King of the Vampires, but I will not deny that I kept an eye out just in case.

A little further on we came to the laboratories.

If I had possessed any preconceived idea of what such facilities looked like, it fell far short of the reality. What shall I say of those chambers of scientific advancement wherein the most rational labored to uncover the secrets of the human mind? Shall I describe the gleaming equipment with which they were furnished? The surgical tables equipped with restraints and set under banks of lights? The carts laid out with scalpels, forceps, clamps, drills, and an array of other instruments the purpose of which I did not care to guess? Shall I extol the impeccable cleanliness and order of the slate-topped workbenches and glass cabinets filled with neatly labeled supplies? Saline. Hydrochloric acid. Albumin. Ether.

Or perhaps I should describe the smell. The air was filtered. Looking up, I saw that it blew from vents near the ceiling. All hints of the river were gone. The only aroma was chemical, with formaldehyde the overriding note. That was easily explainable by the shelves of specimens floating in liquid—entire brains or parts of them, spinal columns, eyes with the nerves still attached.

"What in the name of God are they doing here?" Stoker said.

Marco turned away from the preserved remains of an embryo that appeared almost but not quite human. He looked particularly grim. "I rather doubt that God has any part in whatever goes on here."

"God may not," I observed, "but Sebastian de Vere does." I gestured to the rows of books, most bearing his name. This was his doing, I was certain of it.

However unclear it was what contribution, if any, such laboratories could make to the study of human sanity, it was odd that they were not in use in the midmorning of a workday. Nor, now that I thought of it, did I hear any of the screaming that Mordred had mentioned.

It fell to Marco to provide the answer. "Visiting hours. They aren't taking any chances."

When we entered the next lab, I saw exactly what he meant. This one was filled with cages stacked along two walls and occupied exclusively by primates of various descriptions. I cannot claim to be able to identify them all, but I saw monkeys, chimpanzees, and several species of larger apes, all remarkably docile as though they had been drugged.

"Mordred was certain that he was hearing humans screaming, was he?" Stoker asked. He was pale and sweating as he looked at the caged animals. I did not have to wonder why. The size of the cages allowed for almost no movement. All the primates were hunched over, similar to the patient I had seen. Many had scratched and otherwise worried their fur so they were bald over much of their bodies. Despite being drugged, or perhaps because of it, all looked wracked by suffering.

"I believe so." My voice seemed to come from far away.

I was caught by the poignant gaze of a gorilla that curled its hands around the bars of its cage as it stared at me. Electrodes protruded from its skull. I had to wonder if we would find humans in a similar condition.

The Irishman was still muttering about the need for laws against such things when we returned to the corridor. A pulse beat in Marco's jaw but his eyes spoke fury. It was left to me to say what we all knew.

"We are wasting time."

It was callous, I know. But there was nothing to be done for the animals, not then. Their only hope lay in our getting to the bottom of whatever it was that de Vere was doing and making sure that it was stopped for good.

But first we had to find Mordred, and to that end I had no idea what to do. The basements were cavernous, fading off in both directions under the vast reaches of Bethlem. Hundreds of people might easily be confined in them.

With no idea of how to proceed, I asked, "What was here before the hospital?" London was a very old city. It was a rare scrap of ground that hadn't been occupied by a parade of hovels, markets, townhouses, churches, and the like through the centuries.

After a few moments' thought, Marco said, "There was a Priory of St. George in this area, hence St. George's Fields, but it was destroyed centuries ago during the Reformation. Why do you ask?"

I reached out a hand and ran the tips of my fingers over the nearby wall. The building we were standing in had been built decades before, but it was still young by London standards. And like the foundry that had stood until so recently where Mordred's manor had been, something had been there before it.

Slowly, I said, "Where there was a priory, there would have been a vault. Isn't that so?"

The two men exchanged a glance. "If there was," Marco replied, "then it was likely left intact when this building was constructed. Doing anything else would have risked an outcry about the desecration of bones."

"You think Mordred could be in such a place?" Stoker asked. His distaste for the possibility was clear, but I could not relieve him of it.

"I think de Vere would want to conceal him as thoroughly as possible, not only from prying human eyes but also from others as well. How better than in a forgotten tomb?"

By then, I was at least half convinced myself that such a place existed even though as yet I had no real evidence of it. I was that desperate to find Mordred. In running my fingers over the wall, I had felt again the brief flicker of awareness that I had experienced earlier. But, like the fading coda that brings a musical composition to its end, the final notes were sounding. Soon they would be extinguished forever.

"We should split up," I said. "That way, we'll be able to search farther before visiting hours end and staff members return."

Stoker looked less than taken with the idea of being on his own in such a place, but he straightened his shoulders and nodded. "Perfectly right."

Marco, whose first instinct was to protect even the half-vampire hybrid he still remembered as a human young woman, was less enthusiastic. But I didn't give him time to object.

"Good. Mr. Stoker, you and Marco can take the north wing. I'll take the south. Whoever finds anything should call out."

I had no intention of leaving the Irishman to his own devices, but neither did I want his company. The mere possibility
that he might write another book—or worse yet already be
working on one—made me reluctant to risk supplying him
with any new material.

Marco took a bit more convincing before he agreed. I cut
that short by the simple expediency of heading off on my own.
Over my shoulder, I said, "If you find anything, don't try to approach Mordred on your own. There's no telling how he would
react."

The thought had occurred to me that if the vampire king
still existed, after so long and arduous a confinement he was
likely to be very hungry.

CHAPTER 23

I started down the corridor extending away to the south as I tried to decide where to begin. If the vault existed and de Vere was using it, there would have to be an entrance that was relatively convenient but also easily concealed. Surely that ruled out the labs, as they were obviously designed to accommodate dozens of scientists and technicians. The labs suggested that de Vere enjoyed far more than mere privileges at Bethlem. He had sufficient power to do as he liked within its walls.

Which meant . . . what, exactly? Since my incarnation, I had experienced a heightening in physical strength and stamina, as well as of all my senses. But I cannot claim that any of that translated into enhanced intellectual ability. I was no smarter than I had been as a young human woman. Insights did not come to me with blinding clarity; I had to work for them.

And so I did, standing there in the dismal corridor, until after what seemed far too long but was no more than a few moments, it occurred to me that the answer was directly in front of me. There were hundreds of cells, all appearing from the outside to be virtually identical. If an entrance to the vault was

concealed within one of the cells, no patient would be present
to discover it accidentally or to interfere with de Vere's own
comings and goings. This heartened me briefly until I recalled
that although the majority of cells were occupied, even to
search those that were empty would take more time than I was
likely to have.

That left only a few other possibilities. Halfway down the
south wing, set between rows of cells, I came across a series of
chambers each innocuously labeled Treatment Room. There
were a dozen in all and at first glance they appeared to be similarly outfitted with large steel tubs and chairs equipped with
electrical prods to administer shock therapy. The pity I felt for
the young sensitive returned even more forcefully as I considered what helpless patients were made to suffer.

But I had not yet seen all the torments inflicted on them.
The last room on one side was different from the others, being
smaller and bare of any furnishing or equipment other than a
large tank positioned in the center of the floor. A lid on the
front of the tank could be opened to allow a person to enter
and lie down. Once the lid was closed, the interior would be
entirely dark. No chink of light would show through the carefully welded seams and the metal framework around the lid. A
drain at the bottom indicated that the tank was meant to be
filled with water. There was even a heater to maintain a steady
temperature. The dial was set at thirty-seven degrees Celsius,
the normal temperature of the human body. I looked more
closely, noting that the tank itself was constructed of heavy
steel. Not only would there be no light inside, or sensation of
heat or cold, there would be no sound.

I had found the "sensory isolation chamber" Stoker had
mentioned. Straightening, I stared at it in dismay. How long

could a human mind remain intact while being denied all contact with the world? How soon before sanity dissolved and consciousness was driven inward to a landscape where madness reigned? More to the point, what possible benefit could come from such "treatment"?

Unless, of course, none was expected and the whole effort was nothing more than a ploy to conceal the room's true purpose. A patient confined within the tank would be unaware of anything happening outside. A person of sufficient authority to conduct such an experiment—de Vere again—could come and go with impunity. And keep everyone else away.

I was about to continue searching the room when a low knocking stopped me. At first, I thought that I had imagined it but the sound came again. It was so faint that had I not been possessed of acute hearing, I would never have noticed it. But there it was once more. Coming from the direction of the tank.

No, from inside it.

Horror filled me. It was all well and good to theorize about how the tank was used, but to confront the reality of someone actually being trapped inside it was considerably different. Without pausing to think, I grasped the handle of the lid and tried to open it, only to discover that it was locked. For reasons I did not pause to consider, that infuriated me. I tightened my grip, pulled my arm back, and wrenched the lid completely off its hinges. It flew from my hand and slammed into the far wall.

At first, I could only make out a shape slightly paler than the darkness of the surrounding water. Then it moved and I realized that I was looking at a . . . person? A hoarse voice whispered, "Please . . . let me out."

For an instant, I wondered if I could possibly have found Mordred, but I had no sense of him at all. I made to reach into the tank to help whoever was in there when a face swam into view. I stared into the red-rimmed and bleary eyes of an unshaven young man who appeared as shocked to see me as I was to see him. He was naked, his skin as pale as that of a cave-dwelling worm with the unhealthy puffiness that comes from being too long exposed to water. His gaze appeared feverish with inner demons.

Dreading that I might have come upon another sensitive, I was actually relieved when he chortled suddenly and in a high-pitched voice said, "My best hallucination yet! Won't the doctor be pleased? I must remember exactly what you look like so that I can tell him. La-la-da-tra-la such a good boy is Jack!"

Was Jack his name? Was he truly mad or had he been made so? The water was deep enough to come to his shoulders when he was lying down, as he promptly did again, folding his hands over his chest in the pose of one already dead. And still he continued to sing after a fashion in the voice of a child.

"La-la-da-tra-la Jack shall eat beans and mutton. La-la-da-tra-la a fine pudding there'll be for Jack. La-la-da-tra-la . . ."

"Stop!" The discordant sound was unbearable. I reached into the tank and tried to grasp hold of him. "Don't be afraid. I'll help you out. You'll be safe now—"

"No!" Without warning, he began to struggle, trying at once to fend me off even as he squirmed as far back in the tank as he could get. "Jack is a good boy!" He curled his hands into fists and began to beat them against his head hard enough to damage himself. "Get out! Get out!"

Fearful that he would be harmed, I stepped away. As with the caged animals, there was nothing more I could do, at least not then. A sense of helplessness swept over me, followed hard by fury.

I might not be able to help poor Jack, but I knew the best possible way to stop de Vere. Find Mordred.

As the young man continued his fractured song, I made a circuit of the isolation room. Remembering what I had seen Marco do in Stoker's office, I tried rapping on the walls, but with no results. They gave every evidence of being solid stone. The floor was slate, and though I looked for signs of a hidden entrance to a lower level, I found none. Finally, with no other possibility left, I returned to the tank.

I could still hear Jack as I bent over, peering at the space between the bottom of the tank and the floor. That there was a space at all surprised me. Straightening, I laid a hand tentatively against the end of the tank farthest from the drain and pushed very lightly.

At first, nothing happened. I had to try again a little more firmly before I felt a slight motion. Convinced that I was on to something, I pushed again, only to gasp as the entire tank moved readily, pivoting on the end toward the drain. With very little effort, I rotated it ninety degrees from its original position.

Beneath where the tank had been was a trapdoor. I opened it to reveal worn stone steps leading down into utter darkness.

Now was the time to summon Marco and Stoker. But that would take precious minutes that I might not have. With only the briefest hesitation, I lowered myself into the bowels of the earth beneath Bethlem.

Keen as my eyes were, I needed time to adjust to the almost complete absence of light before I was able to make out a passage just barely tall enough to stand in. It must have been created centuries ago when the priory stood on the spot, yet the walls were lined with stones that showed no sign of wear.

When I examined them more closely, I realized that they contained the same flecks of dolomite found in the basement beneath the Serjeant's Inn.

Someone had gone to a great deal of trouble to block the ability of vampires to sense one another. More convinced than ever that Mordred had to be nearby, I proceeded quickly. As the last glimmers of light from above faded away, I regretted not having the foresight to bring one of the new electrical torches or even an old-fashioned kerosene lantern. As it was, I would have been hard-pressed to continue had I not become aware of a pale luminescence coming from the stones themselves. With that assistance, I was able to locate a metal door at the far end of the passage. It was locked.

Girding myself for whatever lay on the other side, I took hold of it as I had the lid of the tank and attempted to wrench it free. This proved more difficult than I had expected, the door being unusually thick and heavy. I had to assume the quite undignified posture of one foot pressed high against the adjacent wall while the other remained planted firmly on the floor. With both hands, I simultaneously pulled and twisted. At first, my only reward was a slight creaking. I persisted as my palms burned and pain shot up through my arms to my back. The handle itself began to fold under my grip, making it all the harder to hold on. But finally, just when I thought I might truly be thwarted, one hinge popped loose. The other followed swiftly. I barely managed to jump out of the way as the door crashed to the ground.

Stepping over it, I looked ahead anxiously. Not far from the door was a long, low table similar to those I had seen in the labs above. A bank of electric lights was positioned above it. I was about to try to turn them on when a low moan from the far end of the room froze my hand. Something stirred in the darkness. The movement was so slight that I could scarcely credit it as real. When it happened again, I approached, but cautiously, uncertain of what I was about to confront.

At the first sight of the being chained upright to a rack against the far wall, a scream bubbled up in my throat. Not of fear, for the wretched creature was far beyond being able to harm anyone, but rather of horror that anyone, regardless of who or what, could be subjected to such torment. Only with the greatest effort did I manage to remain silent.

He was taller even than myself but severely emaciated. His head hung forward onto his chest. A mass of dark, thick hair hid his features. He wore the remains of what must have once been elegant evening garb, but it had been sliced to tatters, exposing his arms and chest. His skin was crusted over with dozens of wounds. I shuddered at the thought of what had caused them.

Hardly daring to speak, I mouthed his name. "Mordred?

When there was no response, I tried again, even going so far as to touch his shoulder lightly. "Mordred?"

Slowly, the head lifted. I steeled myself, waiting. . . . A high, pale forehead . . . the dark slash of brows . . . eyes . . .

I took a quick step back, staring into eyes that glowed red in the darkness. Eyes filled with pain and rage inhuman in their intensity. His nostrils flared, taking in my scent. Parched, cracked lips moved, emitting little more than a hiss.

"Lucy?"

I had to bend a little closer to hear him but there was no mistaking my name. Nor could there be any lingering doubt as to his identity. Relief flooded me.

"We have to get you out of here."

He tried to respond but the effort proved too much. His

head slumped forward again as he sagged in his chains, insensible. I struggled to decide what to do—go for help or try to deal with the situation alone—before remembering that de Vere might appear at any moment. Under ordinary circumstances, I could defeat him or any other mortal easily. But I dared not forget that he possessed a vampire's heart.

Without a key, I had no hope of freeing Mordred from the chains quickly. The only possibility was to work him loose from the rack, but the moment I attempted to do so, I realized how de Vere had managed to hold the vampire king for so long. The rack and the chains were crafted of silver. The moment I touched them, I felt the searing heat they inflicted. Even standing close to them drained my strength.

With a cry of frustration, I jumped back. No choice remained but to seek help. As quickly as I could manage, I returned to the isolation room and stepped out into the corridor. To my great relief, Marco and Stoker were approaching already.

"Hurry! I've found him." Without waiting for them, I hurried back to the trapdoor. Over my shoulder, I said, "He is held by silver chains. I can do nothing with them."

Marco understood at once. He stared at the lid of the tank that I had wrenched off. Nearby lay the handle itself. Scooping it up, he followed us into the passage.

I remained outside the cell while Marco and Stoker worked to free Mordred, so I cannot attest to their reaction at finding him. I did hear several grunts as they labored, but it was done quickly enough. Silver is not quite as soft a metal as gold, but it is malleable enough to bend and snap with the proper application of force.

Marco emerged carrying Mordred across his shoulders.

Stoker followed. Together, we made our way back up the steps. While we waited, the Irishman stuck his head out the door of the isolation room.

"The corridor is clear," he reported. "However, I cannot think where we go beyond that. We can hardly stroll through the central hall and out the door in the company of the vampire king. Even if no one other than de Vere has an inkling who Mordred is, his obvious distress will attract immediate notice."

He was right, of course, and I should have thought of it, but with all my attention focused on finding Mordred, I had given no consideration to how we would escape from Bethlem with him. Fortunately, a solution was at hand.

As the three of us—I cannot count Mordred as he was unconscious—stood about considering what to do, Jack leaped from the tank and ran past us. I had only an instant to perceive that he was completely naked before he was gone down the corridor in the direction of the stairs. A moment later, I heard him clattering up them.

Stoker, whose eyes had widened considerably, said, "We should go after him." Even as I considered that the Irishman's instinct for human compassion was to his credit, he added, "His presence above will cause an uproar. We can use it to slip out."

His assessment proved correct. By the time we reached the central hall, pandemonium reigned. Jack was dashing back and forth, still entirely in a state of nature, while pursued by attendants, all trying to get an arm around him or, failing that, throw a sheet over his nakedness. Meanwhile, visitors descending from the upper floors were riveted by the spectacle. Some shouted in dismay, while several ladies made a convincing show of fainting. For however brief a time, Bedlam showed its older, darker side.

I was not without sympathy for the poor young man. What-ever his mental state had been originally, the "treatment" to which he had been subjected would drive anyone to madness. I could only hope that the attention being drawn by his plight would result in better care, but until de Vere was exposed for the monster he was, that could not be guaranteed.

Marco wasted no time but made haste across the hall and past the admittance desk. He had almost reached the doors when one of the attendants noticed us.

"Hey, you there, stop!"

In the Jack-induced chaos, few eyes turned in our direction. Nonetheless, the attendant hurried to block our exit. In an instant, I stepped between Marco and the man. "Leave this to me."

He hesitated but Stoker did not. Gripping Marco's arm, he drew him out the door. The attendant made to go around me only to stop abruptly when I took hold of him with both hands and lifted him off the floor. I smelled his fear but beneath it was the hot, coppery tang of blood. Hunger stirred. My fangs slipped free. Confusion turned to terror. The man screamed and struggled to escape.

I held him long enough to be sure that Marco had gotten Mordred out, then tossed him against a nearby wall. My last sight of Bedlam was of Jack still cavorting with the attendants in pursuit as visitors and staff alike milled about in disarray. De Vere was nowhere in evidence, but I was certain that he was close by or would be shortly, as soon as he received word of what had happened. He would pursue Mordred with all means possible. The Watchers, the dirigibles, the omnipresent

cameras, all would be searching for us. Nor could I forget Lady
Blanche. Word of what had taken place would reach her as
well. When she realized that a halfling, a Protector, and the
author of *Dracula* had freed an unknown personage from the
bowels of Bedlam, she would reach the only possible conclusion. We had to find a place of safety, and quickly.

CHAPTER 24

Marco was a step ahead of me, having already determined the one location where we could hope to hold out against the attack that was bound to come.

"The members were up in arms after the Watchers' intrusion the other day," he explained as we made haste in the hackney toward the headquarters of the Golden Dawn. "Steps have been taken to assure that nothing of the sort can ever happen again."

I did not ask what sort of measures were available to a group that had, as Marco mentioned earlier, a bit of a problem with demons but nothing that couldn't be handled. We reached the society's townhouse in Mayfair to find the front door barred. A dour-faced fellow with a steely glint in his eye answered the pealing bell. Recognizing Marco and Stoker, he stood aside at once to allow us to enter. Apparently, not even the presence of an unconscious form in exceedingly tattered evening clothes and a young woman of dubious lineage could impinge on the privileges of membership.

"Make haste," he directed. "All sorts of riffraff in the streets this morning."

We had seen that for ourselves during the drive from

Bethlem. The Watchers were out in even greater force than usual, but they were the least of it. From the nooks and crannies of the less reputable parts of London, a new force had emerged. Hale and hearty young men all dressed alike in brown shirts and trousers, sporting armbands emblazoned with the crest of St. George, the patron saint of England, were armed with truncheons that they swung at arm's length as they marched. We had encountered them as we crossed Blackfriar's Bridge and then again along the Embankment. They appeared to be con-centrating toward the Houses of Parliament near Westminster.

"Any idea who that lot are?" Marco asked the man as to-gether they carried Mordred into the library.

"The Brownshirts? Hard to say, they seem to have come out of nowhere, but they're obviously organized. Likely as not one faction or another in the government is behind them." Glanc-ing down at his burden, he added, "I say, is this—?"

Marco nodded curtly. "If you would be so kind as to alert the members who are here. Obviously, precautions will have to be taken while he is in residence."

I had hurried ahead to clear off the large table in the library not far from the portrait of Dr. Dee. Once Mordred was laid upon it, the man hurried off to inform the others.

"I don't imagine that we'll be thanked for coming here," I said.

Stoker gave a low snort. His color was high and he ap-peared agitated, as well he might given the circumstances, but he spoke calmly enough. "This is the most exciting thing that's happened to the society since Flinders Petrie's unfortunate run-in with the Great Sphinx. Besides, no one is more aware of the role Mordred has played in the history of our realm than our own members. They have great respect for him."

His words were shortly proven true as a procession of gentlemen of varying ages and dress, some considerably more exotic than the rest, appeared offering casks of esoteric medicines and other items they hoped would be useful. Marco greeted them all at the entrance to the library and relieved them of their burdens with thanks but admitted no one. Several craned their necks trying to observe the figure stretched out on the table, only to withdraw grudgingly as Marco shut the door on them.

Meanwhile, I went to work on Mordred. Having cut away most of his clothing, I perceived that his injuries were even more extensive than I had realized. Given their severity, it was amazing that even a vampire capable of immortal life had survived them. His abused flesh was pulled tautly over his bones, giving him an almost skeletal appearance. Under normal conditions, he would have been pale, but the intensity of his pallor made him appear as though carved from a thin layer of delicate stone that could dissolve into dust at any moment. His eyes were closed, sparing me their intensity, but as I watched, I saw movement beneath the lids.

Mordred, it seemed, was dreaming. I could only hope that his mind had escaped to some far more pleasant realm and that it would remain there while I did what was necessary.

Having secured the shutters across the library windows and drawn the draperies closed, Stoker came to assist me. He shook his head in dismay. "Sections of his skin have been cut away down to the underlying muscle. What possible purpose could that have served?"

Marco had paused at the door for a quiet discussion with several of the members, all notable for their military bearing. From what little I was able to overhear, the defense of the

Golden Dawn headquarters was well in hand. Now he joined us and stared down at Mordred grimly.

"De Vere claims to be a scientist. He regards the collection and analysis of specimens as essential to his studies on cellular structure."

"Is this what you were referring to when you suggested that he went too far in his methods?" I was well aware that scientists commonly used dissection as a means of collecting specimens, but not, as far as I knew, from living subjects. That the argument can be made that Mordred was not strictly speaking "alive" struck me then and still does as moot. We are all of us—vampires and humans alike—sentient, self-aware beings. We hope, dream, regret, yearn, and engage in all sorts of behavior good and bad that reveals the inner workings of our spirits. Nothing more than that should be needed to qualify as alive. I was never more convinced of that than in the presence of de Vere's handiwork.

"He is a sadist," Marco said bluntly. "It is astonishing that Mordred managed to survive such captivity."

"His survival is not yet assured," I said. "If he were stronger, I would be more confident of his ability to heal himself, but in his present state—" I broke off as Marco opened one of the casks and drew a small vial from it.

"Try this. It contains some of the same ingredients as the tea you sipped but in considerably more potent form. From what I understand, vampires use it on those rare occasions when they suffer injury severe enough to concern them."

"As from Protectors?" I asked. The glowing heart of a vampire was tucked discreetly beneath his shirt but I was well aware of its presence all the same.

Marco shrugged. "It happens. At any rate, we have nothing

else that is likely to help." To my surprise, he touched my hand lightly. For a moment, our eyes met. "I'm sorry."

I nodded even though I was not at all certain what he was apologizing for. The lack of other medicines, the situation itself, or the gulf between us that had never seemed so large as at that moment when we both stood beside the vampire king struggling to preserve his existence.

The moment passed. I resumed my task, hoping against hope that the balm fragrant with bergamot, anise, fennel, and other substances that I could not identify would be of some actual help. When I was done, I drew a blanket over Mordred and sat down to wait. There was nothing else that I or any of us could do. Marco left briefly and returned with a tray of sandwiches, as well as tea for himself and Stoker. I had rejected any sustenance, my appetite having fled entirely.

A short time later, we heard banging at the front door and a shouted demand for admittance. Stoker peered out through a chink in the shutters and reported that the Watchers had arrived in force. A member of the society shouted down from his post on the roof that they would withdraw at once or the consequences be on their heads. I expected them to storm the building and perhaps they would have done so if not for the sudden, acrid smoke that appeared at their feet and billowed upward to engulf them. Hacking coughs and cries of pain replaced threats as the Watchers quickly withdrew.

The Brownshirts were next. They came—again according to Stoker—with goggles over their eyes and bandanas tied around their noses and mouths but to no avail. They were shortly on the run from the acrid smoke that made eyes tear and breathing next to impossible.

"They'll be back," Marco said. "The military has been producing gas masks for just this sort of contingency."

I suppose it was a measure of my lingering innocence that I had difficulty understanding what he meant. Gas was to be a weapon and people would have to wear masks to protect themselves from it? Truly, man's genius for new and ever more creative ways to kill one another knows no bounds.

"Perhaps we should think about getting Mordred out of here before then," Stoker suggested.

I shook my head. "He is far too weak and besides, where would we go? Our only real hope is for him to recover quickly. Once he has regained at least some semblance of his power, those who are so eager for war will have to think twice."

"That is to be hoped," Marco agreed. We were seated next to each other on a settee near the table where we could both keep watch over Mordred. Once again, he reached over and took my hand in his. His skin was warm, his touch undeniably arousing yet also with an element of comfort that I could not help but embrace. Neither of us spoke but words were unnecessary. We both knew that the chances of Mordred being restored to himself anytime soon—or at all—remained slim.

Moreover, in a few hours it would be dark. The threats we had faced from the Watchers and the Brownshirts would be as nothing once Lady Blanche and her legions began to stir.

"We have to do something," Stoker protested.

I agreed with him but I had no idea how to proceed until suddenly a thought came to me. Rising, I walked to the table where Mordred lay. Perhaps it was my imagination, but his color appeared a little more naturally pale and less like the pallor of extinction. Moreover, he appeared to no longer be in pain but instead seemed to be resting peacefully.

Given enough time, he might recover. Unfortunately, we could not wait. Time was of the essence, even as it had been when I lingered in the grave from which Mordred had called me.

Despite my love of opera, I had no particular talent for music. Amanda was the gifted one. But I could still try. Hesitantly at first but with swiftly growing certainty, I began to sing.

Wouldst die then? ah me! consent to live.
Live, of all my love assured;
The keenest pangs that death can give
For thee have I endured.

The first notes were faint and uncertain but I steeled my resolve and tried again with somewhat better results, well enough at least not to set dogs howling. All the same, Stoker started in surprise. He moved toward me, but Marco held out a hand to stop him. I closed my eyes, willing the library to fall away and saw before me once again the stage at the Royal Opera House. It was a trick of memory, of course, nothing more, but just then it was as real as it had been when Mordred used the same artifice to draw me from the grave. He was not there yet but he would be soon if I could not draw him forth, too.

From my hand, thou warrior glorious,
Take thy standard aye victorious,
Let it ever lead the way
For thy opponent's overthrow.

My familiarity with the libretto was spotty, consisting mainly of the passages I found the most moving. As for my vocal range . . . the less said the better. But just when I thought the whole exercise was folly, a finger on Mordred's right hand twitched. Only that, a finger and nothing more, yet it was enough. I pressed on, ready to sing the whole damn opera if that was what it took. And when I finished with Verdi's *Aïda*, I was prepared to launch full bore into Wagner's *Götterdämmerung*. If it took Ragnarök and the final battle of the Norse gods to rally Mordred to his duty, so be it.

Fortunately, I was spared any such extreme measures. Hard on the twitch of his finger, the king of the vampires opened first one eye and then the other. Looking into mine, he said, "Who . . . ?"

I leaned forward, eager to tell him whatever he wanted to know. Who had rescued him from de Vere. Who would stand by his side as he reclaimed his throne. After that, we could talk about what he had done to me and why but for the moment, nothing mattered except—

"Who gave you the idea that you could sing?"

A short, surprised laugh broke from Marco. To give him credit, he cut it off quickly, but not before I had to press my lips together to keep from laughing in turn. For his part, Stoker stared at us all in bewilderment, as well he might have for we were far from any laughing matter. Yet there was relief in levity, however brief.

"My sister," I said, "but she loves me so I believe her opinion is less than impartial."

A low sigh escaped him. He struggled to sit up. At once, Marco moved to assist him. At the sight of a Protector being so helpful, Mordred raised a brow. "Truly, this is a night of miracles." He glanced toward the drawn curtains. "It is night, isn't it? Or close to?"

"It will be dark in an hour to so, sir," Stoker replied. His deference surprised me until I remembered that he was one of Gladstone's men. Whatever mistakes the Lion of Parliament had made, he at least understood Mordred's role in protecting the realm from both human foes and the vampires themselves. A role he was about to be called on to play yet again.

"Lady Blanche will be here soon," I said. "She aspires to take your place, therefore is unlikely to welcome your return."

Mordred cast me an amused glance. "You think not? Ah, love, so frail as to shatter on the altar of ambition." Shrewdly, he added, "How far has she gone?"

"She has used the stone table," Marco said.

Mordred stiffened. He was sitting up by then, having swung his legs over the side of the table. Though the blanket still covered most of him, I could see that his condition was somewhat improved. His healing powers were astounding, but perhaps I should not have been surprised. The ability to regenerate tissue and organs, and to fight off illness or infection of all kind, is fundamental to the longevity of my kind.

"I possess no such thing," he said. "Nor would I ever allow one in this realm."

"Nonetheless, she installed one at the Bagatelle," Marco replied, "no doubt drawing on legends of vampires in other parts of the world. Harley Langworthe was her first victim, but he is not likely to be the last unless she can be stopped."

"Then we had best do so," Mordred said. To me, he added, "We will talk later, Lucy. No doubt you have many questions. I will endeavor to provide the answers, but first—" He held out a long, slender hand to Marco, who helped him rise. With a faint smile, the king of the vampires said, "If it's all the same to you, I would prefer not to meet my rebellious subjects while wrapped in a blanket."

Such were the resources available at the Golden Dawn that when Mordred returned to the library a short time later—having left in the company of Marco and Stoker, leaving me alternately to pace back and forth or slump disconsolately in a chair—he was garbed far more fittingly. Although the trousers, waistcoat, shirt, and cutaway frock coat that had been found for him were all a trifle large for his shrunken frame, he looked remarkably better than the being who had emerged from Bedlam only a short time before.

Gratified though I was to see that, I was not entirely fooled. The connection between us made me aware of how weak he was still and of how determined he was to hide it. There was really only one remedy. I was girding myself to mention it when a shout of alarm stopped me.

A dozen or so vampires were at the threshold, led by a woman in white, the sentinels on the roof had reported. Unlike the Watchers and the Brownshirts, beings who did not breathe would not be deterred by an application of gas no matter how potent. Other measures would be needed, but before they could be attempted Mordred strode into the entry hall. He brushed past the startled members of the society, flung open the door, and stepped outside.

The street beyond was empty except for the delegation of vampires. Not a single light shone in any of the nearby houses. The inhabitants had likely fled or were huddled in the basements. But just out of sight, I could hear a low, constant rumbling, the combined sounds of many vehicles and masses of men only waiting for the order to advance. Dirigibles floated overhead, and off toward the river I heard the clatter of the new armored diesel boats. London had the feeling of a city under siege, bereft of all normal life, hanging poised on the edge of a war that could bring only destruction and defeat to all those foolish enough to take up arms in its misguided cause.

At Mordred's appearance, the others behind Lady Blanche fell silent. Felix was not in evidence, but I did see several that I recognized from the Bagatelle, including those who had clustered most avidly around the stone table. They were less eager to press forward now, instead leaving it to Lady Blanche to do so. To her credit, the flash of shock that flitted across her face was quickly masked. She held out her arms in apparent joy. Her features, admittedly quite beautiful, seemed to glow with the same opalescence as the pearls around her neck.

"My lord, at last! How we have all yearned for your return! Your absence has left us bereft. To find you again is more than we have dared to hope."

It was a graceful speech and prettily made, but I was not fooled. She had come expecting to find the pitiful figure taken from Bedlam. Instead, she confronted the king who had held sway over her and all her kind for centuries. The sovereign she had dared to imagine that she could replace, and who had now returned to claim what was his and his alone.

Mordred smiled. He lifted a hand in gracious acknowledgment of his subjects. "Yet here I am, dear Blanche, whole and intact. How could you have feared otherwise? You—all of you—know my power. I made each of you, and to me you owe your absolute loyalty."

Blanche's mouth worked with the effort to swallow her dismay. But she was not to be so easily discouraged. "Come with us, lord. Let us welcome you properly in more fitting circumstances. Surely you do not wish to tarry among these humans when your own kind wait to serve you?"

At once, the others took up the idea, calling out to him to come with them. For a moment, I feared that he might agree, but instead he shook his head.

"In time, but for now I will linger here among my friends—" He turned to where Marco, Stoker, and I stood directly behind him in the open door. "My *friends*"—he stressed the word—"who recovered me from where I had been hidden and brought me here safely."

As he spoke, Lady Blanche turned her gaze on me. For a moment, the mask dropped. I saw the full fury of her malevolence but I did not flinch. Since witnessing her savagery at the stone table, I understood that she would go to any lengths to supplant Mordred. I stood in her way, and for that she would have her vengeance, or not. Only one of us was likely to survive what was coming. I accepted that it might not be me but that would not be for lack of effort. I would do everything possible to stop her once and for all regardless of how that fit with Mordred's own plans.

In realizing that, I realized something else as well. The compulsion that Mordred had placed on me had run its course. In freeing him, I had freed myself. As we stepped back inside the Golden Dawn, I could not help but wonder where my newfound liberty would lead me.

Tantalizing though that prospect was, there were more immediate concerns. Barely had we reached the library that Mordred slumped and would have fallen had not Marco caught him. Helped to a chair, the vampire king was unable to speak for several moments.

"You've overdone," Stoker said. "Best you rest for now."

Mordred lifted his head and looked at him. The red light flashed in his eyes. "Rest won't help." His gaze shifted to me. "I need to feed."

CHAPTER 25

Felix had told me that vampires sometimes shared blood in small amounts as an act of intimacy. But he had also said that it was forbidden to feed on our own kind because doing so would give access to the power of the vampire who had turned the one being fed upon.

As I met Mordred's gaze, an unpleasant thought occurred to me. I had been incarnated as his ultimate defense against de Vere. If everything else went wrong and he was captured, I would be compelled to find and free him, exactly as I had done. To that end, he had been willing to create a halfling, the very creature who, if legend was to be believed, was a threat to all vampires. But was that the extent of Mordred's plans for me? Was I in effect a repository for the power he now intended to reclaim?

All this passed through my mind in far less time than needed to recount it. Mere seconds elapsed before I became aware that Marco's hand was drifting toward the vampire heart concealed beneath his shirtfront.

Mordred gleaned his intent at the same time that I did. With a faint smile, he said, "Be easy, Protector, I mean her no harm."

"Perhaps you mean her no more," Marco corrected. "Surely, you have inflicted enough."

In the glow of the few lamps we had lit, Mordred sat half revealed in shadows. His long, pale face had the purity found in medieval statues of saints, a comparison that no doubt would have amused him greatly.

"We can debate the morality of what I did at another time, assuming that we are all still here to do so. For now, I have to hope that none of you believe that Lady Blanche has gone meekly away and will give us no more trouble. She is primed to act, and when she does, the forces that de Vere and his allies have assembled—the Watchers, the Brownshirts, and the like—will be unleashed. The war between humans and vampires will have begun. It will not end until civilization itself is destroyed."

Marco did not disagree, but he did say, "I will spare you the trouble of arguing that the good of the individual must be sacrificed for the good of the many or anything of that sort. Even so, you do need to feed. Therefore—"

"No!" I was not absolutely certain what Marco intended, but I feared that he meant to offer himself. Such was the nature of my feelings for him that I could not bear the thought of him doing so.

"We need your strength as much as we need Mordred's," I insisted. "And if we fail, if war does come, humans will have to depend on Protectors more than ever."

We stood, armored in our determination that no harm should come to the other, until Mordred said, "Very touching, children, and I do hope that you have an opportunity to explore all that passion seething under the surface, but neither of you is a solution to my problem."

His gaze shifted to Stoker, who had taken up a position near the windows and was observing us with the bright-eyed interest that writers display as they experience life vicariously, sopping up bits of it for later use. More than ever, I feared he was planning another book.

"I've read your magnum opus," Mordred said.

In the midst of stroking his beard, Stoker froze. "Have you really? Well . . . imagine that. . . . Never occurred to me actually." He straightened, took a breath, and asked, "What did you think of it?"

"It was . . . amusing. A tad disjointed here and there but I liked the bit with the dog."

At once, Stoker brightened. "Did you? I rather liked that myself. It was my idea, you know, not suggested by anyone."

"I thought it might be. Rather difficult, I imagine, writing to order as it were. Was Gladstone a very demanding editor?"

"Actually, I don't think he read any of it, but certain of his staff were . . . well, let's just say they showed little sensibility for the novelist's art."

"How tiresome of them. If you wouldn't mind a suggestion—"

"I'd be delighted. Quite stuck at the moment, if I may say, for what to do next. Bit of pressure from the publisher and all that."

Mordred's nod communicated both sympathy and understanding. Anyone would have thought that he had labored to bring forth an opus of his own, and for all I know he had. "What you need is the personal touch. I think we can agree that nothing replaces actual experience."

Stoker opened his mouth to reply, no doubt in ringing affirmation, only to shut it abruptly when he perceived—rather belatedly, I thought—the direction in which the conversation was going.

"Oh, I say . . . you don't mean—"

"It's entirely up to you," Mordred assured him swiftly. "On the one hand, you can gain invaluable insights into the entire vampire-human relationship while doing a great service for the realm, or on the other . . . I've already mentioned the destruction of civilization, haven't I? I'd just as soon not belabor it."

"How much would you take?" Marco asked that, not Stoker. The Irishman was too busy opening and closing his mouth rather like a fish to say anything at all.

Aware as I was that Marco and Stoker were both members of the Golden Dawn and, if not friends, at least amicable associates, and moreover that Marco was a Protector, his willingness to entertain even the idea of what Mordred wanted surprised me. Yet with the benefit of a few moments' thought, I realized that there was no better option. In a sense, Stoker's presence in the library that night had already decided the matter. Only the details remained to be worked out.

Mordred leaned back against the settee, crossed one leg over the other, and appeared thoughtful. "Well, I certainly wouldn't kill him, if that's what you're asking. A few days and he'll be right as rain." As though to confirm this, he turned to the Irishman. "You don't have any sort of liver condition, do you? I only ask because that could delay your recovery."

Stoker only just managed to shake his head. "Uh . . . no . . . not that I know of, but—"

Mordred stood. He put his hands together with the air of a man who has done a satisfying bit of business. "Good, then it's settled. Just think of it as fodder for the creative mind. Your competitors—and don't fool yourself, they're already scribbling away aiming to outdo you—will be awestruck, and your publisher—I hesitate to imagine the paroxysm of delight that will afflict that happy man when he sees your next creation."

Far more gently, Marco said, "It's really up to you, Bram. If you say no, we'll find an alternative."

Unhappily, but with more courage than most could have mustered, the Irishman said, "No, we won't, there isn't any time. Like it or not, it's up to me." As that sunk in, he added, "I've spent most of my life studying the hidden world. I've had plenty of fantasies about experiencing it but never dared to take a step off the straight and narrow. I'd say this is my chance."

Even Mordred appeared affected by this testament to humility and self-sacrifice. A bit awkwardly, he said, "It doesn't actually hurt, you know. At least not after the fangs are in. They emit a neuropathic compound that increases blood flow. Quickens the process, as it were, and it will all be over in a matter of minutes."

I thought of what I had witnessed with the supplicants and what I had experienced myself. Apparently, there was more than one way for a vampire to feed, some far less stimulating and intimate than others.

Stoker seemed as reassured as it was possible for a man to be under those circumstances. He fumbled to loosen his shirt collar, then looked around uncertain of what to do next.

"Just stand right there," Mordred said. "Keep your attention on that splendid portrait of Dr. Dee. He had an extraordinary mind, you know. In another age, he truly would have been a magus, but he'd gotten a whiff of the new rationality and it affected him greatly. Elizabeth thought the world of him. She was always seeking his advice—"

Stoker did as he said, staring rather desperately at the portrait, which I fancied had taken on something of a look of dismay. Mordred moved behind him, bent his head, and—

What shall I say of what followed? It was quick, as Mordred had promised. But even a minute or two is an eternity when the lifeblood is being drained from one's body by an immortal being of the netherworld. Stoker stiffened as the fangs went in, his eyes wide and stunned. Instinctively, he tried to raise a hand to his throat, but Mordred pushed it away easily. In a gesture I can only think of as intended to reassure, his fingers intertwined with Stoker's, steadying him. A few carmine drops appeared on the collar of the Irishman's shirt. I heard a sucking sound . . .

The rest I would rather not think of. Compared to what I had seen at the Bagatelle, it was nothing at all, but it stirred memories of the far more intense encounter I had experienced. Reliving that, especially in Marco's presence, was strangely disturbing.

When it was over, Mordred helped Stoker to the settee and sat him down gently. I was prepared with ointment and a bandage, but the latter was not needed, the bite marks were that contained. Elegant really, although I admit that is an odd word for them.

Marco brought Stoker a tumbler of whiskey and stood close to hand as the Irishman managed a few tentative sips. His color revived but only a little and he still seemed disoriented.

"I'm taking him upstairs," Marco said. "He can rest in one of the bedrooms."

At the library door, he hesitated, clearly uncertain about leaving me alone with Mordred, but I mustered a confident smile and sent him on his way.

When we was gone, I turned to the being who had ripped me from my human existence and plunged me into a maelstrom of deadly danger. Mordred was far from fully restored but he looked considerably better. Moreover, his mood appeared to be excellent.

"I shouldn't feel quite this jubilant," he said, "not given what we're still facing. But my relief at getting out of that hellhole has made a huge difference in my outlook. Not even Blanche's misbehavior changes that."

As he spoke, he glanced at the books on a nearby shelf. I thought his eye lingered on the work by Dr. Dee that Marco had shown me, but he passed by without touching it. Still, it was enough to recall for me what Dee had written about him.

"Thus did he who I fear above all the rest explain the coming of his kind and the terrible bargain he made for what he claimed was his love of this realm . . ."

Was it that terrible bargain that had so inured Mordred to suffering, even his own? Or was such seeming callousness simply the result of a too-long life in which all experience, even the most profound, becomes mere repetition?

"Misbehavior? Is that how you characterize her murder of Harley Langworthe, not to mention the war she's about to start?"

He waved a hand negligently. "I forget how human you still are. It's extraordinary really. Do you know only a Slayer's bloodline can produce a halfling? The compromises that have to be made at the most fundamental cellular level shouldn't even be possible."

Nor should the compromises made by the mind and the spirit, but I saw no point in mentioning that to him. Even so, his detachment provoked me.

"You sound as though you share de Vere's interests. Is that how he was able to capture you? Did he play on your curiosity? Or perhaps it was to your vanity that he appealed."

Mordred had stiffened at his captor's name. With what I can only describe as a kingly look of disdain, he said, "Do not mention that man to me."

"Why? We have to talk about him at some point and this may be our best opportunity. Or would you prefer that Marco be present?"

I knew the answer before I asked. Vampire he was and a ruler as well, one rapidly returning to himself, but he was not about to discuss what had happened with de Vere in front of a man who was in some way his rival.

My encounters with Mordred on the moor at Whitby and later when he drew me from the grave had awakened me to passion in a way that not all my young girl's dreams could have done. By comparison, the feelings I had nurtured for Marco were innocent and unformed. But no more. Now I looked upon him with full awareness of what such yearning meant and where it could—even should—lead.

"De Vere," Mordred said, "is more of a monster than I could ever aspire to be. Moreover, he is extremely clever. He knows how to hunt his prey, how to bide his time patiently, and how to find the weakness that will give him the opportunity he needs."

"What weakness did he find in you?" Try though I did, I could not imagine how a human, even one equipped with a vampire's heart, could have overcome a being of Mordred's experience and power.

He hesitated long enough that I thought he did not intend

to answer before he said, "The same to which so many fall prey. I loved not wisely but too well."

I remembered what else was written in Dee's book and felt a surge of sympathy for him. "You still think of Morgaine."

"Most surely, but it is not of her I speak. In an existence as long as my own, there was always bound to be another." He smiled faintly. "If nothing else, I am consistent." At my puzzled look, he said, "I had gone to her tomb in Westminster. De Vere found me there. Do you know, they put her in next to Mary? Not her sister, the Scots queen. Elizabeth loathed that stupid woman, absolutely despised her, not in the least for being forced to order her execution. Now they lie there side by side in their separate tombs, Elizabeth and her headless foe. Although, come to think of it, they would have put Mary's head in with her, wouldn't they?"

"I suppose . . ." Queen Elizabeth, the Virgin Queen, she who never married but who had ruled her realm with skill and wisdom, guiding its first infant steps from a bankrupt backwater country to the empire it would become.

"You loved Elizabeth Tudor?" Was such a thing even possible and if it was, had she known? Could she have returned his affections? What dealings had the two of them had? My mind reeled at the implications.

Mordred stared at the far wall where Dee's portrait hung, but I was certain that he did not see the good doctor. Rather he appeared to gaze upon a landscape far removed in time, if not in space.

"I think that at first I loved the idea of her, but as I came to know the actual woman . . . Let us just say that the greatest sorrow of my life has been having to stand by while she aged and died, knowing that I could have saved her so easily."

"You would have incarnated her?" The idea was shocking in some ways—a vampire queen of England? Yet surely it had been within his power.

His emphatic nod left no doubt. "In an instant, if she had agreed. But she refused again and again. Something about having to live out her own destiny. The particulars fail me, nor do they matter. What does is that my feelings for her lingered long after her death. I fell into the habit of visiting her from time to time. When the abbey isn't thronged with tourists, it's a very restful place to sit and think. Unfortunately, de Vere must have used that to predict where and when I would be at her tomb. Such was the extent of my preoccupation that he was able to take me unawares."

"I see. . . ."

He raised a brow. "Do you really? I certainly didn't until I was in that disgusting cell with all the time in the world to contemplate my folly. But no doubt your tame protector told you everything. You know, of course, that Elizabeth was the second Slayer after Morgaine and that her blood, too, is in you?"

My mother had claimed a connection to the family of Anne Boleyn but I had never paid it any mind, being little impressed with such things. However, Mordred had, wittingly or not, raised a possibility that interested me a great deal.

"The next Slayer will come of the same line?"

"Eventually, centuries hence." He cast me a sharp look. "But the line is running rather thin, dear girl. If your sweet sister doesn't marry and have children . . ." He paused, then added, "Or if you don't."

It was not that I had failed to think of Amanda since

leaving her. Her safety and that of all my family remained a great concern. But what was that Mordred had added?

"Me?" Cautiously, I said, "I had the impression that vampires do not have progeny in the conventional fashion." Not that I had inquired into the process, but hadn't Felix said that all the vampires in Britain had been created by Mordred?

"We don't, which is probably another reason why we don't age. Children seem terribly wearying. However, you aren't precisely a vampire, are you?"

"Apparently not, but you would know far more about that than I."

He peered into one of the casks the society members had brought, lifted out a vial, sniffed the contents, and made a face. Putting it back, he said, "Indeed. Your link to Morgaine and Elizabeth gave me reasonable assurances that you would be able to find me, for no one is so well equipped to hunt down a vampire as is a Slayer or the next best thing to. You stand between two worlds, two species, and if the legends are to be believed, you can bring ruin to one or the other."

"I thought only vampires are at risk from a halfling."

"That's not entirely clear, it could go either way. But destruction is mentioned prominently."

I understood the desperation that had driven him to such a fateful course of action, but I still had to hope that nothing was predestined. "You made it possible for humans and vampires to coexist all this time. Why can't we just go back to that?"

"It is my hope that we can, but the threat of a halfling hanging over us may make that difficult for some."

What was he saying? That my usefulness was swiftly coming to an end and that for the greater good I would need to be destroyed. Or—

"Are you suggesting that it is possible for me to become entirely human again?" Until that moment, I had not considered that there was any chance of regaining what he had taken from me. But his talk of children—my children—made me dare to think otherwise.

His gaze narrowed. "Would you go back, if you could? Become again what you once were?"

I had no answer for him, not then, but I did have an overwhelming need to be certain of what I thought I understood. "Are you saying that what you did to me is reversible?"

"Theoretically. I don't claim to know the particulars of how it could be done, but if that was your choice, I would do what I could to help you achieve it."

In the back of my mind, I realized that in offering his assistance he was coming as close as he could to apologizing for what he had done. But that made little impression on me. I was filled with sudden confusion and, it must be said, resentment.

"You would do that once I've served my purpose?"

He frowned but did not deny it. "One doesn't rule as a king for centuries without using anything or anyone that comes to hand. I am no more guilty of that than was Elizabeth or for that matter, Arthur."

The father who had spurned him for the choice Mordred himself made to save England.

"There is one thing that I don't understand. Why would you want to preserve the Slayer line?"

He glanced at Dee, looked away, and said, "Because like it or not—and I don't—the periodic culling of vampires by a Slayer is part of the natural order. Left to their own devices, humans and vampires both are capable of destroying this world on their own. For humans, the problem is a conviction that the next conquest, the next weapon, the next advancement of science or technology will finally make them feel safe when nothing of the sort can ever occur. As long as death is inevitable, safety is an illusion. They need to reconcile themselves to that, but they show no ability to do so. As for vampires . . . we have many admirable qualities, not the least is the ability to take the long view and plan for the future in a way that eludes humans. But as you saw with Lady Blanche, we also possess voracious appetites that, when not properly controlled, lead us to commit acts of unspeakable violence. Without restraint, we could easily depopulate the earth of all humans even though that meant our own inevitable extinction."

As much as I longed to be able to refute at least part of what he said, I could not. Mordred had summed up the failings of humans and vampires all too accurately. That left only one possible conclusion.

"You are saying that we need each other."

"Exactly." He waved a hand toward an as-yet-undefined future. "Who knows, perhaps someday nature will meld humans and vampires together to craft a species that can live in harmony with the earth and with each other. But it should be left to nature to do so, not to the likes of de Vere."

I took it as a measure of Mordred's returning strength that he could bring himself to speak of his captor even if I was not entirely clear what he meant.

"De Vere told Gladstone and the others on the Star Committee that he was seeking a means of destroying vampires," I said, "not combining them with humans into some new species."

"He lied," Mordred said flatly. "In the course of conducting his foul experiments on me, he revealed his true intent. He wants to create a 'new man'—stronger, longer lived, and, in his view, better suited to the world of technological marvels that is just beginning to unfold before us. He envisions such a man achieving ready dominance over the earth but sees no reason for him to stop there. Our destiny, according to him, truly is in the stars and de Vere wants to be the one to write it."

"He is insane."

Mordred nodded. "His supreme belief in the rightness of his cause is the key to his ability to persuade others to it, as he did with the Star Committee. Never mind that he misled them as to his true intent, they were ready to follow him because he is a man of certainty while they are plagued by doubts and fears."

I suspected that Mordred had just defined the characteristics of every successful dictator past and future, but I was determined that de Vere would not be among them.

"He must be stopped." I had known that since first learning of the mad doctor's role in what was happening, but never had I understood it more clearly.

"Precisely, dear Lucy, but there is one thing you should keep in mind. He is seeking a way to create a human-vampire hybrid, but such a being already exists: you. If he realizes what you are—and he may already suspect—he will want nothing so much as to have you at his mercy."

The mercy of a madman who had none. Forewarned, they say, is forearmed, but I could muster little thought for my own safety. However the human and vampire sides of me might clash, both were in agreement on one score—I would not rest until de Vere was brought down and made to pay for his crimes no matter what the cost.

I was contemplating the swiftest means of accomplishing that when Marco returned. As he entered the library, he gave us a quick, searching look. Whatever he saw must have reassured him that we were both still intact.

"How is our novelist?" Mordred asked. "No ill effects, I trust."

"Bram is sleeping," Marco replied. "I've sent word to his family that he is well. Obviously, they can't be told anything else." After a moment, he added, "I have had a message from my brother."

Mordred brightened. Clearly, he was familiar with the di Orsinis. "How is Nicolas? And your mother, is Cornelia well?"

"She is fine. Nicolas is recovering from injuries he received while fending off the vampires who Lady Blanche let loose on the city."

"I regret that he was hurt. As to the lady . . ." A shadow moved behind his eyes, nothing more, but I would not have wanted to be Blanche just then. "She will have to be dealt with. Word of my return will spread quickly. In a few hours, I should have an idea of who will support her and who will not."

"How do you intend to determine that?" I asked.

Instead of answering directly, he said, "When Elizabeth was dying, those most faithful to her clustered close around, taking comfort from one another's presence. But there were also those who preferred a swift horse and the high road to Edinburgh, where they wasted no time falling on their knees before her successor."

I needed a moment to grasp what he was saying. "You think some of the vampires will desert Blanche and come here to you. You want to give them time to do that."

"I see no reason not to. It will be dawn in a few hours. By then, we will have a much better idea of where we stand."

While Marco grudgingly agreed to get some rest himself, I remained at Mordred's side. An hour passed and another without anything happening. But in the deepest dark of night, just before dawn broke, singly and in twos and threes, vampires made their way to the headquarters of the Golden Dawn and the side of their king. Not all, not even most, but enough to make me hope that the balance was shifting in our favor.

Among the last to arrive even as the first gray light of morning tinged the sky was Felix. So relieved was I to see him safe and well that I threw my arms around him heedless of who was watching.

"I am so glad that you are here!"

He managed a faint smile, but I could see that he was sorely tried. "So am I, believe me, but I doubt you're going to like what I have to say."

Just then he saw Mordred through the crowd. Leaving me, Felix went to him. With a quick bow, he said, "My lord, I bring news. Lady Blanche has promised a great sacrifice on the stone table this coming night. She says that the flower of England will perish there, its strength flowing into those who follow her." He glanced back at me, then said, "With that strength, she swears to defeat you, end the pact with humans, and make our kind supreme over all."

A quick murmur broke out among the impromptu court but it died away quickly when Mordred spoke. "I would hardly expect anything less of her. Blanche has been planning her revenge since her family rose in rebellion against the throne centuries ago and was wiped out virtually to the last man, woman, and child. She was the only survivor and for that I must take full responsibility." He thought for a moment, then asked, "Would you happen to know where she intends to acquire this 'flower of England'?"

Felix did not but I did. With sudden clarity born of desperate calculation, I knew exactly where the thirst for revenge that had haunted Blanche for so long would find its final culmination. What better place for mass death than a palace of mourning?

CHAPTER 26

The final event of Queen Victoria's Jubilee was scheduled to be held that coming night at the Crystal Palace. The cream of British society would attend. And so, I was sure, would Blanche. Nothing else would satisfy her craving for revenge or her instinct for display. She would make a grand show of it, publicly declaring war on humans at the same time she struck terror into every heart.

Having told Mordred what I believed, I made haste to wake Marco. He was stretched out on top of the bed in a room next to where Stoker was sleeping. His boots were on the floor nearby and he had removed his jacket, but otherwise he remained fully dressed. At the sight of me, he sat up quickly, a certain indication that he had been doing no more than dozing lightly. A lock of dark brown hair fell into his eyes. He brushed it back impatiently.

"Are you all right?" he asked.

That his first thought should be of me touched me deeply. Determined to conceal my too human response, I said, "Felix Deschamps has brought word that Lady Blanche intends an attack tonight to seize victims for the stone table. I think it's going to happen at the Crystal Palace."

He nodded slowly. "The final Jubilee celebration . . . yes, that makes sense." He held out a hand. "You look tired. Sit down."

I did so on the side of the bed, a bit gingerly. A wave of self-consciousness such as I had not known since my incarnation washed over me but was as quickly gone. There was something undeniably right about being alone with Marco in such a setting.

"What else is happening?" he asked.

"Sixty or so vampires have come over to Mordred. They are downstairs right now." Incongruously, I felt a sudden urge to laugh. "I can't imagine what the members of the society are making of all this."

He smiled fleetingly. "Don't worry about them. They're having the time of their lives. Does Mordred have a plan?"

"He's drawing that up right now. Do you want to help him?"

"I doubt he needs my assistance but I'll offer it. Just not quite yet." He sat up further, looking at me. "Lucy . . . there's something I want you to know."

Hardly aware of what I was doing, I leaned toward him, needing his nearness as I had once needed sunlight and air. Fragmentary memories—still all I had—darted through my mind, snatches of conversations, moments of laughter.

"Limericks," I said.

He looked taken aback. "Beg pardon?"

"You like limericks. It's not something you tell everyone but you have a definite fondness for them. I wondered if that included the bawdy ones but you would never tell me."

"Of course I wouldn't. You were a sheltered young girl."

"I didn't want to be, you know. I had a great yearning for the wider world."

Softly, he said, "I wanted to take you there."

My throat was thick. His heat, his blood, my own stirring hunger, I was aware of it all but none of that mattered, not just then. I wanted . . .

Too much, everything, all that was utterly beyond my reach unless . . .

"Mordred has hinted that I could become human again."

I heard the sharp intake of his breath in the moment before he went very still. "What are you saying?"

With far greater calmness than I felt, I replied, "It may be possible to undo what happened to me."

He took hold of my chin and turned me so we faced each other directly. "Would you want to undo it?"

I answered instantly, without thought. "Yes, of course, how could I not? To be human again . . ." To never again soar into the night free from the constraints of gravity. To lose the keener senses, the strength and stamina, the awareness of the hidden world all around me. To age and ultimately to die. More honestly, I said, "I don't know."

Truly, I didn't. By all rights, I should want to be human again, but knowing that I should want something and actually wanting it were not at all the same. Marco's closeness only added to my confusion. If I could be restored to what I had been—

"You wanted to tell me something?"

"What?" He was staring at my lips, watching as they moved. I found that strangely arousing and had to resist the impulse to moisten them.

"Something . . . ?" I said.

"What you said about the wider world. I used to lie awake at night after I had left you thinking about the places we might go. You'd told me how much you enjoyed Paris and I knew that you'd tried skiing and liked it. I imagined us together, free of everything else." He shrugged. "A foolish dream, I know. We are neither of us the sort to walk away from our responsibilities. But I truly did want to be a part of your life." His gaze met mine. "I still do."

His declaration could have been made under more proper circumstances, but I knew it to be no less sincere for that. Nor did I mistake the depth of my own response. Tentative hope, even a kind of fragile happiness, filled me, but so did a cautionary note.

"If I can become human again—?"

He shook his head emphatically. "That has nothing to do with it. I didn't know such a thing was even possible until you told me. What I mean is just as you are . . . however you are." He moved a little closer so that I felt the warm caress of his breath on my cheek. My hand slipped to his chest. The vampire's heart was hard and cold under his shirt yet I remembered how beautiful it was. And how dangerous.

"Are you certain?" I asked. "Your clan is already upset by our alliance."

"My clan, my family, all of them will have to accept how it is between us. But, as we are speaking honestly, what of Mordred? How accepting do you think he will be?"

I did not pretend to misunderstand him. Although the compulsion Mordred had laid upon me was gone, an undeniable connection remained between us. I had no reason to believe that would change even if I regained my humanity, especially not given that I was of the same bloodline as the two women he had loved.

"I don't know, but I will not be swayed by him. It is you

I want, only you." On this the conflicting sides of my nature were in full accord. I wanted Marco with a passion that would not be denied. If I remained as I was, I would have to watch him age and die as Mordred had watched Elizabeth do. And if I became human again, the time we would have together would be so short, a mayfly's breath in the vastness of eternity.

So do I excuse why I pressed him gently back down onto the bed. Our lips met, our limbs entwined, the strictures of propriety burned away as though they had never been. There was a moment when, wrapped in his arms, I gazed at the fine blue tracing of his lifeblood in his throat and felt an urge to taste him, but it passed swiftly as I discovered the many other ways that hunger can be assuaged.

We had little time, as I think we both knew, but never has time been better spent. Moment to moment, touch to touch, we laid claim to a future of our own making even as we knew that it might remain forever beyond our grasp. Together, we forged a private world far from the conflicts that raged outside the walls of the Golden Dawn.

But inevitably, those conflicts were bound to intrude. When the knock came at the door, neither of us were surprised.

Felix stood in the hall. He cast a glance at Marco hastily tucking his shirt into his trousers, and at me struggling to confine my hair into some semblance of order, and sighed. His eyes spoke volumes but he said only, "It's dawn. The others are asleep. Even Mordred is getting some much-needed rest. He's vetoed a plan to attack the Bagatelle directly. Instead, he wants to draw Blanche out into the open."

"Tonight," Marco said, "at the Crystal Palace?"

Felix nodded. "So I gather. It's risky, of course, and far too public but it may be the best option. If they were to clash in the streets of London"—he shuddered—"the fighting would be horrific. He thinks this way will be quicker and cleaner."

I understood why Mordred wanted to act without delay. After his months in captivity, whatever patience he had possessed must be long gone. Moreover, he was likely concerned about his ability to retain the support of those who had been willing enough to abandon him a short while before. He would want to dispose of Blanche, then move on de Vere in short order. All that made perfect sense, but I still feared that he had not given himself the opportunity to think the matter through.

"A better possibility," I said, "would be to cancel the event altogether. Deny Blanche the opportunity to seize any more victims or trigger a war, at least for the moment." Nothing would really be solved by doing so, but having more time could only work in our favor. Mordred would be able to better recover his strength, others might come over to his side, it was even possible that Blanche could begin to see the folly of her ambitions. I turned to Marco. "There is still time to cancel it, isn't there, if the right people could be convinced to do so?"

"There is only one person who would have to be convinced," he said. "Her Imperial Majesty, Queen Victoria. The problem is that she sees almost no one."

He was right, of course. The enormity of trying to reach the reclusive queen empress and persuade her to alter her plans for the evening seemed overwhelming, until a possibility occurred to me.

"I know someone she will see. Her old adversary, the prime minister who plagued her for so many years. If he bends his knee and begs an audience, she will not turn him away."

To me, it seemed like a starkly logical plan. Marco also claimed to see good sense in it. Even Felix managed a hint of enthusiasm.

Only one party to the scheme was adamantly opposed.

"You want me to do what?" the Lion of Parliament roared. "Beg that woman to grant me a few moments of her time so that I might—yet again—preserve her realm? Do you have any idea how she and I clashed? Or how gleeful she was when I left office for the last time? I wouldn't have been invited to this event tonight at all if she didn't want to sit on her throne and stare me down. *I'm still here*, she'll be thinking, *and you're nothing but an old man who's been put out to pasture*."

Marco and I were standing in Gladstone's office on Downing Street, but this time we were not alone. Several stricken aides were present, all looking as though they most fervently wished they could be anywhere else.

Marco cleared his throat. "Hardly that, sir. If anything, your authority has only increased since you cast off the fetters of public service. Her Imperial Majesty may not be eager to admit that, but she undoubtedly knows it, just as she knows that however much she disagreed with you in the past, you never gave her any but good counsel. I wouldn't be at all surprised if she doesn't regret not taking more of it."

Gladstone's brows worked mightily. Grimacing, he said, "Tell me, Marco, what exactly were you doing over in Ireland when you found time to kiss the Blarney Stone? For kiss it you have obviously done, given the nonsense you're spouting. Our queen empress is unburdened by any regrets, apart from the loss of her dear Albert. In her eyes, she has lived a life of unblemished correctness."

"Then surely she wants to continue doing so," I suggested. "Now in the winter of that life is not the time for her to make a single fatal mistake that will plunge her realm into a war that cannot be won." When he still hesitated, I added, "Has she not had enough of these Jubilee celebrations? What a burden they must have been on her, dragging her from her life of solitude. Surely she would welcome a reason not to have to endure yet another."

"She is a stickler for duty," Gladstone said, but I could see that his mind was working. "Yet there is something to your point. The events of the past few days undoubtedly have exhausted her. However disappointed people were, they would have to understand if she declined any more such activity."

"Then she must be persuaded to do so," Marco said. Pointedly, he added, "You are the only man who can make her see reason, Prime Minister. We will help, of course, but everything depends on you."

The lion smoothed a hand over the thick white mane of his hair in a gesture at once anxious and pensive. Old as Victoria was, he was older still and his life had not been easy. Together they had borne the weight of keeping the realm safe through turbulent decades. Foes though they were, I could only hope that they still had within them the strength to bear that burden just a little longer.

"All right," he said at last. "I will request an audience but I will not go alone. The two of you are coming with me. She'll have questions, likely not many because she's never been one to rattle on, but they'll be sharp and to the point. Not much gets past her even now. Answer her honestly and we should be all right."

Marco appeared completely unfazed by this but I could not say the same for myself. My mother had dreamed of seeing her daughters presented at court. Her wish was about to become reality for one of them, if only in the most unorthodox fashion.

CHAPTER 27

The Crystal Palace had been built at the direction of Her Imperial Majesty's consort, Prince Albert of Saxe-Coburg and Gotha, to house the Great Exhibition of 1851 in which scientists, engineers, and entrepreneurs from all over the world came together to celebrate the achievements of the new industrial age. With the conclusion of the exhibition, there had been talk of removing the massive iron and glass structure from its site in Hyde Park, but for one reason or another this was not done. After the prince's sudden death in 1861, his widow insisted on preserving the magnificent building she regarded as a symbol of his service to the realm and to her.

Going one step further, she moved into it, abandoning Buckingham Palace and dragging most of the royal court along with her.

"You can imagine the scramble that set off," Gladstone said as our carriage turned into the park. "It had never been intended to be used for more than a few months. There were no rooms to speak of, just vast exhibition spaces. Come winter, it was colder than a witch's—" He broke off, glancing at me. "Let's just say that it was very cold. If that fellow Faraday hadn't perfected his electromagnetic rotary much sooner than anyone thought possible, providing central heating to a place that size, not to mention lighting it, would have been just a pipe dream."

"Has Her Imperial Majesty ever considered leaving?" I asked.

Gladstone shook his head. "Not as far as I know. She's a tough old girl, I'll give her that. But security was a nightmare from the beginning. The walls are glass, for heaven's sake! Anyone could stroll up and have a peek inside, and plenty did. It was all well and good for her—she had private rooms constructed for herself—but the rest of the court was left feeling like players in a pantomime."

"That's why the outer walls were built?" Marco asked. We came up on them as he spoke. Taller even than the walls around Bethlem, the massive stone structures enclosed all of what had been first a royal hunting ground beginning in Tudor times and later a park open to the people of London. Very few ordinary men and women had been allowed within the precincts since shortly after the queen took up residence. The 350 acres that comprised Hyde Park were closed off to all but the chosen few.

Impressive as those walls were, I knew that they would present no impediment to Blanche and her followers. The vampires would go right over them as though they did not even exist. We, on the other hand, drove through the heavy wrought iron gates after being cleared by the royal grenadiers standing watch in their massive bearskin hats and red jacketed uniforms. They were a reassuring reminder of how things had been in a gentler time, but they were not alone. Watchers hovered close and there were even a few Brownshirts in evidence.

"Who are that lot?" Marco asked as we drove past a cluster

standing about looking at once nervously pleased with themselves and ill-at-ease in their exalted surroundings. "They seemed to appear last night out of nowhere."

Gladstone looked grim. "They've been recruited from the slums, promised a few quid a week and the chance to march about making fools of themselves. In return, they're not to question where they're sent or what they're told to do."

"Who's behind them?" I asked.

"No one, if you can believe it. The current PM claims to know nothing nor does any cabinet minister. They're lying, of course. The government's only concern these days is how to maintain public order as people wake up to the fact that the world they've known is being engineered out of existence."

I looked ahead toward the walls of the Crystal Palace glittering in the morning sunlight. Prince Albert's creation was still beautiful despite having long outlived its natural life. But it had about it an air of brittleness that I could not ignore.

"The whole thing could come tumbling down in a moment," I murmured.

"Are you talking about the building," Gladstone asked, "or Britain itself?" Without waiting for an answer, he rapped on the roof of the carriage. "Faster, by God! Faster! Think we have all day, man?"

Gravel sprayed under the wheels as we drew rein in front of the entrance jutting out from the center of a three-story structure that resembled nothing so much as an elaborately tiered cake. Seeing it so near, I could only marvel that a building made almost entirely from glass could stand that tall. Graceful iron girders secured the immense panes that made up most of the exterior, but the overall impression was of unimpeded light and air. If her critics were right when they said that Victoria

had immured herself in a living tomb, she had chosen one remarkably free of darkness.

Gladstone was recognized at once and we were allowed to
proceed without hindrance. We stepped into a vast hall that
ran the width of the building, almost five hundred feet deep
by my estimate. Living trees filled the space including many
elms that had likely been in the park long before the palace
was built. Birds darted between them and a large fountain that
stood beneath the central dome. Water cascading over terraces
into deep basins threw off fine mists in which miniature rainbows danced.

"How extraordinary," I said. My view of the queen empress
was changing rapidly. Had I the opportunity to live in such a
place, I would have taken it, too.

"This way," Gladstone said. He led us toward the wing
that housed Her Imperial Majesty's receiving rooms, staff offices, and private chambers. The opposite wing, he told us,
was reserved for the public reception areas including those in
which the final Jubilee celebration was due to take place. I was
fascinated to see that given the opportunity to build interior
walls, Victoria had chosen to make those, too, mostly of glass.
Through them, officers of her court could be seen going about
their business at their desks or around meeting tables. Others
hurried to and fro bearing red boxes of government docu-
ments. It was not until we reached Her Imperial Majesty's own
chambers that the walls became concealing.

A lady-in-waiting greeted us at the door to the inner sanctum. She peered down the long beak of her nose, sniffed, and
said, "Fifteen minutes, no more. Her Imperial Majesty must
rest before this evening's activities."

The Lion of Parliament brushed past her without comment.

Marco and I followed. We found ourselves in a parlor that appeared to have been lifted whole from a more refined time. Victoria's taste apparently had been frozen in the early years of her marriage, that is to say in the elegant neoclassical style. A graceful desk with an inlaid wood surface in the design of a sunburst sat at the center of a gently worn Persian rug. Nearby a grouping of high-backed couches and chairs faced out toward the grounds.

Everywhere I looked, my eye fell upon some small but pleasing detail—family photographs on a circular table the base of which was a tripod of carved winged griffins, several Chinese vases likely of great antiquity filled with peonies, and a chinoiserie cabinet displaying porcelain so thin as to be almost transparent. The only jarring note was the large portrait of the late Prince Albert propped against an easel. The prince was portrayed as he must have appeared on his wedding day. A black mourning swag was draped over the frame.

"She talks to him," Gladstone muttered. "Morning, noon, and night. Tells him everything and asks his advice."

The prince had been dead for more than thirty-five years. For the first time, I began to fear that Her Imperial Majesty might not be entirely sane. But the moment she appeared, garbed in black as always and leaning heavily on a cane, I knew otherwise. In the face of that small, plump woman— little more than the height of a child and swaddled in so many garments as to be almost round—I saw a keen intelligence that not even the loss of her only love could diminish.

However much he resented her for thwarting so many of his political initiatives, Gladstone clearly respected the queen empress. He approached, bowed low before her, and said, "Your Imperial Majesty, thank you for seeing us. I assure you that we would not intrude upon you in such a way without good cause."

"I'll decide that, William," she replied. Peering through her lorgnette, she said, "Mr. di Orsini. Any news of your father?"

Marco bowed before he replied. "I'm afraid not, Your Imperial Majesty. But we have not given up hope."

I knew nothing of Marco and Nicolas' father, Cornelia's husband, and wondered what had happened to him, but that would have to wait for another time.

"And this," Her Imperial Majesty said, "must be the subject of Mr. Stoker's very odd novel. Where is the Irishman, by the way?"

"He's a bit indisposed, ma'am," Gladstone said quickly. "May I present Miss Lucy Weston. It is through her efforts and Mr. di Orsini's that we have gained the information that brings us here."

The queen empress fixed her gaze on me. I stared back, caught by the gimlet brightness of her eyes. She reminded me of nothing as much as a crow that would sit on a branch outside my window at Whitby and caw whenever it wanted to be fed. After a time, I came to realize that it had trained me to respond.

I curtsied, not particularly well or gracefully and certainly not to a standard that would have pleased my mother, but Her Imperial Majesty appeared satisfied. When she had taken her seat, she flicked a finger in permission for us to do the same.

"Well, then, William, what brings you here? Your message said something about the greatest urgency?"

The former prime minister nodded. "I am not certain how much of recent events you are aware of, ma'am, but—"

"I know that Mr. di Orsini and Miss Weston in company with Mr. Stoker removed a patient from Bethlem Hospital yesterday. Should I conclude that Mordred has been found at last?"

Her awareness of Mordred's existence was not surprising. Although her family line had only the most tenuous connection to that of the Tudors, if any at all, she had been crowned and anointed on the same throne as had Elizabeth. She was in every sense her successor. That she knew about the presence of vampires in her realm and their role in its history was only to be expected.

But I was surprised that she knew Mordred had been missing. Did that mean she also understood how close the pact between humans and vampires was to being undone altogether?

"He has been found, Your Imperial Majesty," I said. "Unfortunately, during his absence, a challenger to his rule emerged. She is—"

"Lady Blanche, I assume? I warned him about her. Vampire or not, a jealous female too long denied what she regards as her rightful place is not to be trusted. What is she planning?"

"Something quite dreadful, ma'am," Gladstone said. As gently as he could, he told her what had happened to Harley Langworthe and how Blanche intended to acquire more victims for the stone table. Concluding, he said, "The simplest way to prevent the attack tonight is to cancel the event. We can give it out that you are fatigued by all the celebrations. Everyone will understand and—"

A wave of color swept across the queen empress' face. She suddenly looked a much younger woman. "Poppycock! I will do no such thing. Do you imagine that I, Victoria, by the

Grace of God, of the United Kingdom of Great Britain and Ireland Queen, Defender of the Faith, and Empress of India, will quail before an upstart vampire with delusions of grandeur? Let her come, I say. By God, we will give her a fight!"

I was beginning to understand why the sun never set on the empire ruled by this woman. Tiny, aged, the embodiment of loss, she still had an indomitable will and the presence of a force of nature.

"But ma'am—" Gladstone began.

Before he could continue, Marco stood, inclined his head to his queen, and said, "As you say, ma'am. We'll give them a fight they will never forget."

I looked at him in dismay. If the gala went ahead as planned, the illustrious guests attending it would be little more than bait to draw Blanche into battle. Surely, I could not be the only one who thought that it was wrong to use people thusly?

Victoria appeared to harbor no such concern. She bestowed a smile on him. "Well said, Mr. di Orsini. I have always been able to count on you, and your brother as well, I hope?"

"I'm sure that Nicolas would have it no other way, ma'am."

"Good, then it is settled." With a glance at Gladstone, Her Imperial Majesty said, "Shall I ring for tea, William? You look a bit peaked."

The lion began to reply, thought better of it, and said, "If you would be so kind."

Servants came and went, silent and efficient. Tea appeared in a golden pot on matching tray. I inclined my head in thanks for this act of courtesy even as I took note that I apparently was not the first vampire the queen empress had entertained.

How often had she and Mordred met? What had they talked about? Had he charmed her with tales of her predecessors? Or had he warned her of the trials they had faced?

Beyond the high walls, the life of London went on, ordinary people going about their day with no awareness that they stood on the edge of an abyss. But others did know—de Vere, wherever he was; the members of the Star Committee; Mordred and all the rest. In a matter of hours, a decisive battle would begin. Out of it would come a world in which humans and vampires could still exist, or one in which neither species survived.

What would come after us, I wondered, if the worst happened? What would rise in our place? Apes, perhaps, such as the one I had seen in de Vere's lab. Would they remember their tormentors and be glad that we were gone?

Or perhaps the denizens of the hidden world would emerge again to reclaim the land that had been theirs long before the coming of either humans or vampires. Little Alice and the others like her would stand guard once more beside the rivers and streams. Water sprites would return to the Thames and fairies would dance in whatever was left of Kew Gardens. In time, the air would clear of both soot and dirigibles. The machines would fall silent. The clamorous struggle to give meaning to life—whether mortal or immortal—would be over. And the world would be poorer for it.

The beak-nosed lady-in-waiting pressed a tray on me. I accepted a watercress sandwich politely and resisted the urge to ask if she happened to have a bit of stag's heart. I was hungry but not intolerably so. The thought that I might become human again was enough to hold my appetite at bay.

Marco had sent word back to the Golden Dawn that Her Imperial Majesty was aware of the threat and prepared to meet it. Another message was dispatched to the Serjeant's Inn.

Then there was nothing to do but wait in the Crystal Palace, where rainbows bloomed and a dead husband still lived, if only in the heart of a queen.

CHAPTER 28

As anxious as I was for evening to come, and as much as I dreaded what it would bring, the hours until then did not drag. Victoria sat—a small, round, still presence—at the center of a maelstrom of activity. A word or a glance from her was sufficient to send men and women scrambling to carry out her every wish. Early on, she met with the head of her household guard to assure that those charged with protecting her knew what was going to happen. The man protested her determination to go forward with the event and to be in attendance herself. But at a look from her, he bent his head in acquiescence.

His mood improved somewhat when Marco tactfully suggested that it might be wise to move the Prince of Wales to a secure location. While no one wanted to think that the queen empress would be in mortal danger, neither could that reality be ignored. Although she had given birth to nine children, Victoria lacked the natural instincts of a mother to protect her progeny. However, she had no difficulty understanding the need to assure the continuity of the succession.

"An excellent idea, Mr. di Orsini. William, send word to Bertie that he is not to come tonight. It is my wish that he depart for Windsor at once and remain there until told other-wise."

What the Prince of Wales, whose relationship with his mother was difficult to begin with, would make of such preemp-tory banishment was anyone's guess. However, he would obey rather than risk the humiliation of being compelled to do so.

The current prime minister, the Marquess of Salisbury, ar-rived, looking pale and harried. He and Gladstone scowled at each other until Her Imperial Majesty called them to heel. Grudgingly, they both got down to crafting a plan of defense.

Meanwhile, Marco and I set out to acquaint ourselves with the area between the encircling stone walls and the palace, where the stand against Blanche and her followers would be made. As we were doing so, Mordred joined us. He came silently and without warning, alighting out of the twilight. His appearance was such that I wondered if he had fed again, hopefully not on Stoker. Perhaps some other member of the Golden Dawn had volunteered. Whatever the cause, he was in good humor.

"I've seen our stalwart lady." As one monarch speaking of another, he did not hesitate to refer to Victoria familiarly. "We are in accord that every effort will be made to stop Blanche and her followers before they can enter the palace. However, we must allow for the possibility that some will slip past."

Marco nodded. "The Protectors will take the first wave. Nicolas knows who to bring and he'll also have his own forces with him."

That Marco would be on the front line was not a surprise. As much as I would have liked to persuade him otherwise, I knew that was impossible. The best I could do was make sure that I was beside him.

"Teams of vampires, werewolves, and Protectors fighting together would have the greatest effect," I said.

"They would," Mordred agreed. "Unfortunately, I doubt that any such cooperation is possible." He paused, then added, "Apart from the two of you, of course."

I was seeing far too much in his quick, sidelong glance and the smile that did not reach his eyes. He could not possibly know what had happened in the bedroom of the Golden Dawn, nor was it any of his affair.

That such dissension should rule even in so dark an hour when the fate of both species hung in the balance angered me deeply. Mordred must have sensed my thoughts. Softly, he said, "It can be different someday, Lucy, but first we have to win."

He was right, of course, though I would not give him the satisfaction of admitting it. As he, who had been born a warrior and never lost the instinct for close combat, turned his attention to the killing ground, Marco drew me a little apart. "I want you to be inside before the attack starts."

I objected vehemently. "For what reason? You and I—"

He gripped my shoulders, compelling me to silence. "If you are with me, I will be too worried about your safety to fight as effectively as I must. Our feelings for each other will endanger us both." When I was still disposed to argue, he added, "Besides, Mordred will be far more concerned with stopping Blanche than he will be with protecting Victoria or her guests. If worse comes to worst, you may be the last line of defense for them."

As much as I longed to deny that possibility, I could not. Even so, I still resisted. "You approved of this. It could have been avoided, another time and place chosen—"

"What time?" he asked. "What place? When else do you think that all the factions—Protectors, werewolves, Mordred and his supporters, ordinary humans—would come together to fight a common foe? The queen empress is right to make her stand here and now. She is the living symbol of the realm we love and for it she is prepared to give her life."

It was on the tip of my tongue to say that was well and good for her, an elderly woman who could look forward to only a handful more of years whereas he—I could not bear to think that he might fall; the pain was too great.

"I do not want to leave you! There are others who can—"

"No," he insisted, "there are not. Do you imagine that Lady Blanche has kept secret her suspicions that you are a halfling? The others will know of that. Until the coming of the next Slayer, you are the being they fear most."

I was disarmed, unable to muster any further argument. My defeat was bitter but, I vowed, it was the only one I would suffer that night. Scarcely able to speak, I murmured, "You will take every care?"

He assured me that he would. We embraced heedless of who might see us. As we stepped apart, the first guests were arriving at the gates. Ahead of them, striding across the lawn, came Nicolas, and he was not alone. A dozen men and women, all lean and agile, followed close on his heels. In their human forms, they were undeniably attractive, but they had about them a feral energy that could not be denied.

The brothers clasped hands. "Are you well enough for this?" Marco asked.

Nicolas laughed. "Would you have me miss it? Besides, I promised Mother that I would look after you." He saw me and grew more serious. "You found Mordred not a moment too soon, Miss Weston. Now let us hope that together we can end this war right here and now."

I was about to reply when the last rays of sunlight slipped below the trees. As they did so, Mordred's legion of vampires arrived, coming out of the sky with dark, sinister strength that reassured me they would be a formidable force.

Everything seemed to speed up after that. Marco and I shared a last lingering glance before his brother dragged him off. Scarcely had I stepped back inside the palace than I was swept away by the beak-nosed lady-in-waiting to, as she put it, "be seen to." When I protested that I had no time for such nonsense, she silenced me in the most effective way possible.

"It is the wish of Her Imperial Majesty."

I yielded. A gown of midnight blue silk of exactly the sort I had coveted, but as an unmarried young woman had been denied, had been found for me. I was slipped into it with admirable speed and efficiency. Embroidered with pearls, the bodice and waist hugged me closely, while the skirt flared just enough for me to be able to dance.

"This won't do," I said. "I may need to move very quickly."

The harried seamstresses, two of whom were scrambling about on their knees trying to finish the hem, looked at me in dismay. Realizing that what I was asking for was impossible, I resolved to make the best of it.

My untamable auburn curls were swept up in a chignon secured by ribbons embedded with sapphires and diamonds. Slippers of absurdly fine silk were placed on my feet. I was tugged at, smoothed, scrutinized, and pronounced fit.

Released, I hurried back to the central hall where Her Imperial Majesty was greeting her guests near the fountain. I hung back a little but had a good view of who was arriving. Truly, the cream of British society was on display with dukes and duchesses all but tripping over one another while baronets and esquires were far too numerous to count. Nor had the new men of science and business been neglected. I saw several who looked familiar. Though I could not yet put names to the faces, I knew that I recognized them from social events at my family homes in London and Whitby.

I was still trying to remember who they were when a flash of violet silk caught my eye. The woman wearing it was in her middle years but still undeniably lovely. She smiled anxiously as she tried to take in everything without appearing to do so. Her escort was a dapper gentleman with a white beard and mustache. With them was a lovely young woman, too thin but beautiful all the same, whose upswept blond hair revealed the purity of her features.

At first, my mind refused to comprehend what I was seeing, but it would not be long denied, the evidence was too clear. My family had withdrawn from society following the events at Whitby. They had picked the worst possible moment to return.

My first instinct was to run to them and tell them to leave at once. But I could foresee all too clearly the pandemonium that would result as they confronted the daughter they had mourned for dead even while fearing that she had met a far more macabre fate. I would have to wait, as difficult as it was, until I could approach Amanda alone. I hoped I could convince her to plead a headache or some such and persuade my parents to end the evening quickly.

The queen empress and her guests proceeded into the gala. Musicians played as waiters circulated with flutes of champagne and trays of canapés. There was a great deal of excitement as people queued up for a turn to have a few "private" words with their sovereign. To be seen in conversation with her and to be able to recount it afterward to the unfortunates

who had not been invited would be the high point of the evening for some.

Shortly, dinner would begin. Until then, I could do nothing but avoid unwanted notice while staying alert for any sign
that the battle had begun.

Struggling to do both at once, I took no notice of Sebastian
de Vere until he was standing directly in front of me.

CHAPTER 29

E asy, Miss Weston," de Vere said when he saw my reaction to his presence. His hawkish face beneath a full head of silver hair wreathed in a mocking smile.

A red mist moved before my eyes. Visions of Mordred chained to the rack threatened to overwhelm me, but so, too, did thoughts of Jack, the lab animals, and the grotesque experiments performed in the perverted name of science. As much as I had been tempted to reveal myself to my family, I felt even more keenly the need to seize hold of the monster before me and rend him limb from limb.

Drawing upon all my self-control, I asked, "You know who I am?"

"Of course, I suspected the moment we met." He tapped the side of his nose. "One develops an instinct for your kind. Although I must admit, Marco's affinity for you is a puzzle. He's always been the predictable one in that family, at least until now. By all rights, he should be your foe, not your ally."

"Perhaps you've missed something." I loathed de Vere and despised everything that he stood for, but as soon as the words were out, I regretted them. It was foolish to say anything that might arouse his interest.

With a flick of my skirt, I said, "You will excuse me."

"Wait. I should be very upset with you but in fact, I'm not. You made a mistake freeing Mordred. He is far too weak to reclaim his power but he will try. When he does, how long do you think the existence of your kind will remain secret?"

Determined to resist the impulse to violence that threatened to overwhelm me, I said, "Why should I care if we are revealed? Humans imagine themselves masters of nature, capable of reshaping the world however they will. They should know that they share it with a species superior to them in many ways."

"Not for long," de Vere said. "I learned a great deal from my study of Mordred. And even without him, I have what I need to learn more. The cellular changes in your kind are remarkable but they will yield to science. We will come to understand how to take what we want from you and destroy the rest."

He leaned closer. The copper scent of his blood made my nostrils flare. Seeing that, he touched a hand lightly to his chest. "Do not challenge me, vampire. You will find me more dangerous than you know."

"Because you possess a stolen heart?" At his look of surprise, I said, "You betrayed the first duty of a Protector, to preserve humanity. Instead, you want to destroy it as surely as you want to eliminate my kind. What will be left in your barren world, de Vere? Only yourself and your 'supermen'?"

Disgust filled me. I whirled away. Several guests stared at us but I ignored them. With a quick glance around, I realized that my parents and Amanda were no longer in sight. The doors to the vast dining room had been thrown open. People were moving in that direction. I went along with them.

The queen empress was seated on a dais from which her loyal

subjects could observe her every move. She was chatting with Gladstone, who was at her left, a place of honor surpassed only by that of the dour Salisbury to her right. Victoria and the lion had their heads together. Others were already wagging at their unexpected accord. Some of the more astute guests had also noticed the large number of grenadiers stationed throughout the room. A gentleman near me opined that the concern no doubt was for the anarchists, who had blown up the foundry.

With a sigh of impatience, I moved on. My family would be somewhere in the crowd, but try though I did, I could not see them. A majordomo approached with an offer to seat me but I brushed him off. In the grip of a desperate need to act, I moved toward the glass windows facing the park.

Bright spotlights of the new fluorescent variety had been lit outside—the Faraday generators again. I was relieved to see that the human defenders would not be taken by surprise by an enemy that could move at will through the dark. Several of the cold white beams had been pointed inward. The glare turned the windows into a wall of light that was impossible to see through. I had to admire the ingenuity of whoever had thought of that. Her Imperial Majesty's guests could dine with no awareness of what was happening outside.

Provided, of course, that Blanche and her supporters were stopped before they reached the palace itself. Frustrated at being unable to learn if the battle had been joined, I debated what to do. I had told Marco that I would remain inside but being literally blinded was intolerable. Surely it would do no harm for me to take a quick look.

Behind a pillar entwined by a fragrant honeysuckle vine was a small door that led outside. Stepping just beyond it, I squinted into the glare. At first, I saw nothing. Hyde Park had boasted a fine herd of deer from the day when it was Henry VIII's favorite hunting ground. The present sovereign had not changed that. Deer fed at night but I could neither see nor smell any. The smaller animals that I also should have sensed—rabbits, owls, and the like—were similarly absent. That could mean only that they had gone to ground.

I stepped farther away from the building in an effort to see better. A flicker of motion caught my eye. Several of the vampires who had gone over to Mordred were keeping watch not far away. Beyond, nearer to the wall, I saw the Protectors. Wolves moved among them.

Reassured that nothing had happened yet, I started to return inside. As I did, one of the wolves threw back his mighty head and howled. The eerie, primal sound raised the hairs on the back of my neck. I looked again to the wall just in time to see vampires soaring over it, their dark shapes seeming to come directly out of the night itself. One by one, dozens in all, they alighted inside the park. First to reach the ground was Blanche. I saw the glow of her pearls before I glimpsed her face taut with the lust for blood. Her fangs were already unsheathed.

The Protectors did not hesitate but moved forward swiftly, the wolves on their heels. Mordred was faster still. He appeared out of the shadows, his cloak streaming behind him and went directly for Blanche.

In an instant, the battle was joined.

The initial clash was furious as the sides came together and foe met foe. Vampires went at one another, fangs tearing, with the same ruthless savagery that I had witnessed at the Bagatelle. But they were far from the worst of it. The wolves hurled themselves at their ancient enemy, the thud of bodies seeming to rock the ground. Through it all, the Protectors advanced relentlessly. I saw one go down when the vampire heart he wielded was knocked from his hand. Blanche's followers would have fallen on him had not a wolf leaped to his defense. A moment later, I gasped as a vampire exploded suddenly into what Marco had so aptly described as a shower of stars. I wondered if anyone would think to recover his heart.

Throughout, I stood frozen, torn between the need to enter the fray and the promise I had made to Marco. The promise won out, if only just. I picked up my skirts and raced back toward the palace. My intent was to find the head of the household guard and warn him, but before I could do so, I ran straight into de Vere. Too late, I realized that he must have followed me.

Gripping my shoulders, he demanded, "What is going on out there? And why are you in such a hurry?"

"Get out of my way!" Without pausing to think, I brought both my arms up and broke his hold with such force that he staggered backward. Wincing in pain, he thrust his hand under his shirt and drew out the glowing red heart that he had concealed there. Holding it up, he advanced on me.

"You will regret that, vampire!"

For all that he had turned his back on his duties as a Protector, de Vere had been trained as one. He knew how to direct the energy of the heart in the most lethal way possible. Even as I recognized the deadly danger that I faced, the air between us rippled. I saw the blast coming, felt it move through me, and then . . . nothing.

De Vere shook his head in disbelief that was equaled, did he but know it, by my own. Again, he raised the heart toward me. Again the air rippled and . . . nothing. "This cannot be," he said. His brow furrowed in calculation. "How could you be unaffected . . . ?"

I had no idea how long it would take him to realize that I was different in some way from other vampires or what he would do once he understood that. But now was not the time to find out. While he was still staring at me in blank amazement, I ran.

Outside, a battle raged, but inside the Crystal Palace the privileged elite chosen to share the final celebration of the queen empress' Diamond Jubilee were enjoying a first course of scalloped oysters. Conversation was robust, no doubt aided by the steady flow of champagne. The music still played; I could just make out Mendelssohn's "Spring Song," one of Her Imperial Majesty's favorites.

While most of the guests had no idea that anything was amiss, at least a few knew better. Gladstone saw me as I entered. With a quick word to his sovereign, he stood, looked in my direction, and left the dining hall. I followed. He was waiting for me directly beyond.

"Our own troops are reinforcing those outside. From the report I just received, the enemy has come but not in great number. There are no more than a hundred or so."

"A hundred or so vampires," I said. "Have you truly no idea of what they are capable of doing?" Belatedly, it occurred to me that Mordred had kept the balance between the species for so long that neither side really understood how dangerous the other could be.

"You presume," I continued, "that you will be able to destroy Blanche and her followers, but if you are wrong, those people in there will meet terrible deaths. I do not fault the queen empress' personal courage, but she's using her court as nothing more than bait."

I thought he might dispute my characterization of the

situation but he was too intrinsically honest for that. Frowning, he said, "Every man and woman in there is a loyal subject of the crown and as such is expected to defend it. Moreover, they have benefited from the best that Britain has to offer in opportunity and freedom, not to mention hereditary privilege. Who do you think should protect her? Those poor benighted Brownshirts who are out there right now, by the way, fighting a foe they didn't even know existed? Is it all right for them to die while we hide behind them?"

"No," I said, "but no one should die for their country without knowing why they are doing it."

"You may be correct," he allowed, "but that must be a subject for another time. All any of us can do is make certain this comes out right." He looked at me gravely. "We are counting on you, Miss Weston. If Lady Blanche does get through, can you stop her?"

"She won't . . . Mordred—"

"If she does, what will you do?"

Straightening my shoulders, I gave the only answer I could. For Marco, for my family, for the legacy of all those who had gone before me. Whatever doubts I harbored about my own powers, I kept to myself. Quietly, I said, "I will defend my sovereign."

I remembered those words a short time later when I finally managed to find Amanda. She was seated at a table of other young people whose company she appeared to be enjoying. I started toward her only to stop abruptly when I saw the young lord with whom she was conversing.

CHAPTER 30

M y stomach clenched as I recognized Edward Delacorte, the golden-haired vampire I had encountered outside the Bagatelle the night I had arrived there and who had tried more recently to sniff out my intentions on Lady Blanche's behalf. I, in turn, had done my best to sow doubts in his mind about her ability to survive the return of a vengeful Mordred. Whatever concerns he might have had about that, his presence at the Crystal Palace left no doubt which side he had chosen.

He was there, past all the guards, within hand's reach of my sister. My only thought was to wrest her from his side at once, but the moment I moved to do so, I feared what his reaction would be. He was so much closer to her than I was, and he could move as quickly and lethally as I could myself.

I needed a ploy, a diversion, something to gain me even a few seconds in which to reach her. But before I could even begin to think what that could be, a grenadier burst through the side door into the dining hall. Blood sputtered from a great wound on one side of his neck, splattering the gowns of the ladies and causing the gentlemen to stiffen in shock.

The screams began just as the lights went out.

In the mad scramble in the darkness, I tried to reach

Amanda, but the panicking crowd racing for the exits held me back. By the time I was close to where she had been sitting, she was gone. So was Delacorte.

I had absolutely no doubt where he had taken her or why.

"It was a diversion," I said a few minutes later as I stood outside with Marco. The fighting was over, Lady Blanche and her followers having withdrawn as suddenly as they had appeared. Gladstone was helping to restore order within. Word had been passed around that the grenadier had been attacked by a Brownshirt who was in custody. Why the attack had occurred was not explained, but the queen had gone so far as to reassure her guests that the fine young officer would recover fully. At her insistence, dinner was continuing in the glow of candlelight as the sabotaged Faraday generators were repaired.

"The intent all along was to seize Amanda," I said. "And to make certain that we all knew she had been taken."

Despite the warm evening, I was very cold even for me. Since realizing the truth, a terrible rage had been building that was matched only by my fear. I saw the stone table . . . saw Amanda . . .

"She is of the same blood that I am, the blood of Morgaine, Anne Boleyn, and Elizabeth Tudor. None could serve Blanche's purposes better." Why hadn't I realized it sooner? Lady Blanche had even sought out Amanda, but so great was my preoccupation with myself I had assumed that was only because of her interest in me. Loathing threatened to choke me as I considered what my folly had led us to.

"We will find her," Marco said. He had suffered a gash down one side of his face but was otherwise unhurt. Nicolas was also well. Felix, too, was unharmed and helping to care for those of Mordred's followers who had been injured. What casualties had occurred among the defenders were mostly survivable. Only a few Brownshirts had died.

"I promise," he added, and opened his arms to me. I went into them gladly, needing his warmth and strength as I had never needed them before. But as much as I longed to, I could not tarry.

I stepped back swiftly. "Where is Mordred?" Unspoken was the question of why Lady Blanche had been able to get away from him. Why hadn't he destroyed her?

"He'll be here," Marco said. "I think he may be a little hesitant about facing you."

The idea that the king of the vampires would feel any such qualms surprised me, but I had my suspicions as to the cause. "Why didn't he kill her?"

"He intended to, but he . . . was distracted." Marco looked at me, his eyes dark and shadowed. "De Vere suddenly appeared. You know what he did to Mordred. What man—vampire or otherwise—would be able to resist going after his torturer? Unfortunately, that gave Blanche the opportunity to escape."

I could have killed de Vere the moment I realized that he could not harm me. Instead, I had let him go while I tried to protect Victoria, who had never been a target.

"And de Vere? What happened to him?"

"He got away." It was Mordred who spoke, his voice low and husky. At a glance, I saw that the battle had cost him much of what strength he had managed to regain. "He turned that damn heart on me, screaming all the while about it having no effect on Lucy."

"What does that mean?" Marco demanded. He looked at me. "De Vere tried to kill you?"

"Tried and failed, so what does it matter?"

"He will be interested in you now," Mordred said. "He won't rest until he discovers what makes you different."

"I don't care." Truly, I did not. Nothing mattered except finding my sister. "They have taken Amanda to the Bagatelle, I am certain of it." At the thought of what would happen to her within those walls, I shuddered. "I am going in there and I am bringing her out, and do not either of you dare to tell me why I cannot."

"Wouldn't dream of it, dear girl," Mordred said. He lifted into the air. Looking down at Marco, he said, "I'd offer you a ride but I'm not quite up to it at the moment."

"Never mind," Marco said. He put his arms around me again, touched his hand lightly to my face, and smiled. "I'm sure that Lucy can manage it."

I did, if with a great deal of nervousness lest I drop him. I hadn't flown very much, after all, and never such a distance, let alone carrying another person. Yet I managed it well enough, no doubt fueled by a combination of terror and anger that casts out all weakness.

Certainly, I could afford none of that as we set down on Fleet Street near the griffin statue. "Blanche will be expecting a frontal assault," Mordred said. "She is wrong to do so. As much as I've avoided the Bagatelle, I know this area very well from long ago. The buildings that used to stand hereabouts form the foundations of those that are here now, and they are linked by buried passages that at one time were alleyways running between them."

"How do we get into those passages?" Marco asked.

Mordred managed a faint smile. "I'm surprised you don't know."

The Serjeant's Inn was closed for the night but Marco's

key unlocked the side door to Nicolas' office. He had yet to return, but at least I knew that he had survived to do so. We descended quickly into the passage where Cornelia had left me sitting in a circle of salt. The flecks of dolomite in the stones shone dimly in the light of the electric torch Marco took from his brother's desk. I spared a moment to wonder how well Nicolas and his pack knew what lay beneath them.

"This same stone was used throughout this area," Mordred said. "People thought it would protect them from vampires. Actually, all it does is protect us from each other."

"As long as we remain surrounded by it, we can't be sensed?" I asked.

"That's right, and if my memory is correct, we will be able to follow these passages right into the Bagatelle."

"Lady Blanche knows nothing of this?" Marco asked.

"I neglected to mention it."

The battle at the Crystal Palace might have weakened him, but his recollection of ancient streets in a vanished London remained intact. Within minutes, we had passed beneath half a dozen buildings and reached the basement of the club. Rats scurried before us, and here and there we had to step over dank puddles, but overall the passages were in good repair.

"These have never been abandoned, have they?" I asked.

Mordred waved a hand negligently. "All sorts of the city's inhabitants have reason to want to get about unobserved. You'll even find the occasional human down here, although not often and not usually twice."

We had come to a broad oak door studded with iron nails. It looked as though it had stood undisturbed for centuries, but when Marco inched it open, the hinges did not so much as creak.

"Beyond here is the Bagatelle," Mordred said. "Lucy, once we enter, can you find the room with the stone table?"

I truly did not know if I could but I nodded all the same. The room might elude me; Amanda would not. We proceeded, Mordred in the lead. I expected to hear the sounds of a victory celebration, prelude to the bloody sacrifice to come, but all was strangely quiet. The fear began to grow in me that I had made a terrible mistake. Could Amanda have been taken elsewhere?

I was about to ask Mordred that when a faint moan silenced me. Leaning forward, I strained to hear it again.

"She is here," I whispered. Going very carefully, I turned a corner in the passage and found myself in front of a narrow opening. Slipping through it, I entered the room where I had seen Harley die. No trace of him remained save for bloodstains on the floor, but by the light of fires in the iron lattice baskets, I could make out my sister bound to the stone table.

Amanda was conscious, her eyes glazed with terror. When she saw me, she cried out, "Don't . . . oh, God, don't!"

Having made so many mistakes that night, I made one more. I thought that she did not realize who I was and was crying out in fear. In fact, she knew me at once. As I ran to the stone table and began trying to free her, she cried out again.

"It's a trap!"

They came from all sides, shielded by the same dolomite that had kept them from sensing our approach. Lady Blanche was there and Delacorte as well, but so were several dozen others, all those not nursing their wounds. I was gratified to see that their number was so much smaller than when they had come over the walls, but that hardly mattered given that we were only three.

Lady Blanche was smiling. "My dear lord," she said to

Mordred. "I fear that you have fallen under the sway of this"—
her mouth curled in distaste—"this halfling. Surely as unnatural a creature as has ever lived. She is attempting to turn you
against those who love you most. We must not allow her to do
so."

"She is attempting," Mordred said coldly, "to preserve my
rule in order to prevent the war you and certain foolish humans seek. A war that will destroy us all."

"Will it? I think not. Much has changed since you were
captured. We"—she gestured at her followers—"we have realized that we must take a stand against the humans now, before
it is too late. Their power grows daily, exceeded only by their
arrogance. They believe themselves the rightful masters of this
earth and will never be content to share it with us."

"Whereas you," Mordred said, "are happy to share it with
them, or at least enough of them to keep you well nourished?"

Lady Blanche shrugged. "We are as we are. I accept that.
You would be wise to do the same."

He was silent long enough for me to fear that he was considering what she had said. Nor was I reassured when he spoke.

"What do you want?"

She did not hesitate. I suspected that the answer had been
uppermost in her mind for years. "Name me your queen consort, then withdraw to regain your strength. I will guide us
through this turbulent time."

"You would rule in my stead?"

Her head lifted. She stared at him coldly. "You are hardly in
any position to do so yourself."

Rather than dispute her, he said, "What of these others—
the halfling, the Protector"—he gestured at Amanda—"this
unfortunate human you've seized."

Blanche waved a hand dismissively. "That one can go. I have no interest in her. Provided . . ." She turned to me. A red glow burned in her eyes. "Take your sister's place, halfling. Lie on the stone table and give up your blood."

"No!" Marco stepped forward furiously. He held the vampire's heart and was clearly prepared to use it. Several of Blanche's followers, those most eager to demonstrate their loyalty, stepped in front of her, shielding her from him.

"Try that, Protector, and you will all die," Blanche warned. "You can kill one or two of us before we overcome you but in the end you cannot win. The halfling or the human, those are my terms."

"Don't listen to her!" Marco shouted at me, but I scarcely heard him. My attention was focused on Mordred. He was looking from me to the stone table and back again.

Quietly, he said, "I suggest you do what she wants, *halfling*."

I frowned, trying to understand what I was certain he was trying to tell me. *Halfling*. The creature spoken of in legend who could destroy all the vampires. But how? I certainly knew of no such power within me. But did Mordred? Had he withheld that knowledge simply because he did not trust me to have it?

Before I could decide what to do, Marco took the matter into his own hands. Ignoring the odds against us, he raised the heart, took aim at Lady Blanche, and let free a blast of energy. At once, the vampire directly in front of her splintered into a thousand shards of glowing light. Another fell as quickly, but true to her word, before he could fire again, a dozen vampires threw themselves at him. He managed to kill one more as he went down beneath a savage attack.

I screamed and tried to reach him but it was too late. At

Blanche's command, the vampires rose. Marco lay bleeding out onto the floor.

"You cannot save him," she said. "Any more than he could save you. But you can save your sister." She came closer to me. The chill of her body made me feel encased in ice. Despite myself, I trembled. "Take her place on the stone table," Blanche said. "I will sate myself but you may somehow manage to survive. A human certainly will not."

From behind me, Mordred said, "Do it, *halfling*. There is no other way."

Amanda was crying softly. I wanted to go to her but Marco's blood was flowing away across the floor, his life vanishing with it. I knelt beside him for a moment and touched his face softly. So that only he could hear, I whispered, "Don't die, my love. Hold on. I will not fail you."

Even then, I wasn't sure what I was promising. I knew only that all other choices were gone. Curtly, I nodded. Amanda tried to resist when they cut her from the table but Mordred put his arms around her and held her close, turning her head into his shoulder so that she would not see.

With a last glance at him, I laid down on the stone table. When Delacorte approached to bind me, I snarled at him. "Do not. I am here of my own choice."

He looked to Blanche, who nodded. She approached swiftly, hunger stark on her face. But even so she lingered a moment, tracing the line of my throat with a slender finger. "You are actually rather beautiful," she said. "Did you know that?"

I averted my gaze and did not answer her. She laughed softly and unsheathed her fangs. As they thrust into me, I stiffened. My back arched off the table but quickly fell back.

I laid quietly, staring up at the ceiling high above. Distantly, I thought that Mordred was right, after the first bite there was no pain. But neither was there the sense of dark intimacy that he and I had shared.

Blanche sucked ravenously, avid not only for my power but also for the power of the one who had incarnated me. She would emerge the strongest of all vampires who had ever existed. Mordred would never be able to reclaim his throne. The war would come and bring devastation. All would be lost—

Halfling. I heard Mordred's voice in my mind, as though the connection between us remained as strong as ever. Strength stirred deep within me. A bright, pure energy began to flow in my cells, in my veins . . . into Blanche.

She gasped and sat up suddenly. Her hands flew to her throat. She stared at me in horror. "You . . ." I saw what was happening to her before the others did, but they saw quickly enough. Several screamed and tried to run but Mordred was having none of that. Having set Amanda aside gently, the king of the vampires proceeded to have his revenge against those who had betrayed him.

While he was so occupied, Blanche's skin turned yellow and began to flake away. Her lips pulled back, revealing black-ened teeth. Her hair, that stunning white, thinned and fell out, revealing her mottled skull. In minutes, the centuries of her long life overtook her. She perished, not as a vampire does in shards of light, but as a shriveled old woman whom Death had long ago claimed but only now come to collect.

When it was over, only her pearls remained. In what I thought was an odd but somehow touching act, Mordred care-fully collected each one.

I knelt beside Marco, holding his body in my arms. Amanda tried to offer what comfort she could but my devastation was complete. Despite my promise to him, it was too late. He was as pale as I. No sign of life remained in him.

"You can still save him," Mordred said.

I met his eyes across the bloodstained room. Hope stirred but feebly in me. "How?"

"The only way it can be done. Transform him."

I stared in disbelief. "Transform a Protector? You are mad."

Mordred shrugged. He rose, holding the pearls in his hands. "It's the only way. Otherwise, he dies. Of course, if you do it, you'll be taking another very large step yourself toward completely becoming a vampire. I'm not sure that you'll ever be able to go back from that. I'd do it myself," he added, "but unfortunately I'm too weak right now." He gestured to the bodies littering the floor. "You understand."

I wasn't at all certain that I did or even that I believed him. It was perfectly possible that Mordred had never intended to allow me to become human again and that this was simply the most convenient way of stopping me.

I gazed down into Marco's beloved face—so strong yet capable of both gentleness and passion. My lips brushed his. I thought of his courage and his sacrifice, his honor and his commitment to humanity. He had given his life trying to protect me. What could I give him? Softly, I touched my mouth to his and whispered, "I'm sorry."

EPILOGUE

I called on Nicolas a week later. He was fully recovered from his injuries at the battle near the Bagatelle and later at the Crystal Palace. We spoke in his office at the Serjeant's Inn. Cornelia was not in evidence. I had been given to understand that she was in the country, caring for her son.

After a brief encounter immediately after I transformed him, Marco refused to see me. I understood, or so I wanted to believe. The shock of finding himself changed into the very creature he was sworn to defend against was profound. He might never recover from it.

"Be patient," Nicolas counseled. He gave me tea, the same kind Cornelia had brewed. It helped a little with the hunger that stalked me constantly but that I could not bring myself to satisfy. Since wading through Marco's blood, I had lost my appetite. Mordred had mentioned a doctor in Mayfair who was studying the science of transfusion and who might be able to help me.

"After I turned," Nicolas went on, "I refused to have anything to do with anyone for months. But eventually I realized that I was only hurting those who cared about me. Marco will do the same."

No doubt he would, but I had no confidence that he would ever forgive what I had done to him.

"I couldn't let him die. Of course, that was completely self-ish on my part. The thought of losing him—"

"You did what was right," Nicolas said. "Someday, he will understand that." Leaning back in his chair, he looked at me gently. "What are you going to do now? Stay here in London?"

I could, of course. Mordred had asked me to do so, but I was not sure that I saw a place for myself in his orbit. He was occupied accepting the protestations of loyalty and devotion coming from all those who somehow had been so unfairly suspected of being followers of Lady Blanche. Felix was there to help him sort the wheat from the chaff. I didn't think he needed me as well.

Amanda was home and recovered. I had no reason to believe that my parents had any idea of what had happened. Certainly, no public notice had been given to the events at the Crystal Palace. With her Jubilee celebration finally over, Victoria had startled her subjects by announcing her intention to visit Scotland. She was there now. Gladstone had returned to Cannes where he had suggested I might like to join him. I think he still felt guilty for his efforts to consign me to the grave.

"I may travel for a while," I said.

Nicolas raised a brow. In his own fashion, his face was as kind as his brother's could be. "De Vere?" he asked. When I nodded, he added, "Is that wise?"

"He isn't going to stop. He's too mad or determined or whatever to do that. And wherever he goes, he'll find others seduced by the notion that they can become supermen and rule the world. The very idea of that is an infection that will spread on the heels of science until we find a way to eradicate it." I managed a smile that I was far from feeling. "Eventually, he will come after me. I would prefer to take the battle to him instead."

Nicolas nodded in understanding. As I stood, he did the same. "You know that if I can ever be of any help, you must call on me," he said.

"I do know that and I thank you." I turned to go but paused and looked back at him. "Actually, there is something you can do, if you will. When you see Marco next, tell him to please remember that for all the deadly power within a vampire's heart, it is also very beautiful. He convinced me of that and I would not have him forget it."

Nicolas inclined his head gravely. "I will tell him."

I smiled again and stepped outside. Dusk was settling over the city. I moved through the soft light silently. All around me the hidden world rippled and stirred, drawing me deeper into it. Welcoming me home.

INCARNATION

Emma Cornwall

SUMMARY

In the steampunk world of Victorian London, Lucy Weston, a character in *Dracula*, seeks out Bram Stoker to discover why he deliberately lied about her in his popular novel. With Stoker's reluctant help, she tracks the creature who transformed her from the sensual underworld where humans vie to become vampires to a hidden cell beneath a temple to madness and finally into the glittering Crystal Palace where death reigns supreme. Haunted by fragmentary memories of her lost life and love, Lucy battles her thirst for blood as she struggles to stop a catastrophic war that will doom vampires and humans alike. Ultimately, she makes a choice that illuminates for her—and for us—the true nature of what it means to be human.

DISCUSSION QUESTIONS

1. Even as she longs to recover her lost humanity, Lucy finds herself increasingly seduced by her new powers as a vampire. If you could trade your humanity for an existence of endless youth and beauty, would you do so? What do you think you might lose in the process?

2. The British government goes to great lengths to conceal the truth about the existence of vampires and their role in history. Are they right to do so? What might be the consequences of revealing such a frightening truth to the public?

3. Lucy is furious at Bram Stoker for his role in the cover-up of what happened to her. Is her anger justified or is he, as he claims, a patriotic man doing what he believes is necessary for the safety of the realm?

4. Lucy's world is being transformed for both better and worse by advances in science and technology. What changes in our own time are having the greatest impact on how we live? Are there advances in science and technology that should be outlawed or otherwise prevented?

5. In this story, the British government is using the increase in social unrest as a rationale for heightened surveillance of subjects throughout the realm. Should people be concerned about this or should they accept it as a necessary price for public order and safety?

6. Lucy is susceptible to being transformed into a vampire because of her bloodline. Could she have exercised free will and changed her fate? Which do you think is a more powerful influence on the choices we make—nature or nurture?

7. One of the consequences of her incarnation as a vampire is that Lucy has only fragmentary memories of her human existence. How important is memory to our sense of who we are?

8. What do Lady Blanche and Sebastian de Vere have in common? What parts do ambition and the lust for power play in the brutal acts they commit?

9. Marco believes that a war between vampires and humans would lead to the destruction of both species. If humans ever do face competition from a superior species, would we survive?

10. Does Lucy make the right decision about Marco? Is her act to save him justified? What does that act say about her "lost" humanity?

Tips to Enhance Your Book Club Experience

Watch movies that have a retro-futuristic (steampunk) setting similar to that found in *Incarnation*.

The Prestige starring Christian Bale and Hugh Jackman

Hellboy starring Ron Perlman and Doug Jones

The League of Extraordinary Gentlemen starring Sean Connery and Stuart Townsend

Van Helsing starring Hugh Jackman and Kate Beckinsale

The Time Machine starring Rod Taylor and Alan Young

Sherlock Holmes starring Robert Downey Jr. and Jude Law

Enjoy these classic vampire and steampunk novels:

Dracula by Bram Stoker

Anno Dracula series by Kim Newman

The Parasol Protectorate series by Gail Carriger

Leviathan series by Scott Westerfeld

The Infernal Devices series by Cassandra Clare

A CONVERSATION WITH THE AUTHOR

Q: **What inspired you to write *Incarnation*?**

A: I spent quite a bit of time in London when I was a child. Moreover, I was left free to wander about on my own in a way that I suppose would shock many people now. The result is that I fell in love with the city that Samuel Johnson correctly said no man can tire of without being tired of life. The London explored in *Incarnation*—a city of buried rivers, haunted lanes, and shadowy denizens— enthralls me. I wanted to share it with others.

Q: ***Incarnation* is set in 1897, but the world you depict has some uncanny parallels to our own. Was that deliberate?**

A: Yes, it was. The story asks questions about what it means to be human, and about the impact technology has on our humanity. There aren't any easy or glib answers but the questions themselves are worth pondering, especially right now when we're on the verge of breakthroughs that will transform what we think of as "human."

Q: **Should we conclude from the opening scene that you're an opera lover?**

A: I love stories told through music, whether that's opera, light opera such as Gilbert and Sullivan, or musicals. Give me a bowl of popcorn and a rerun of *South Pacific* or *Brigadoon* and I'm happy. My absolute best opera experience was attending a marathon of Wagner's Ring Cycle—four operas, fifteen hours, two days. Nothing will ever beat that.

Q: **What made you decide to become a writer?**

A: I can't do anything else. Seriously, I've tried and the results aren't pretty. I'm the fourth generation of my family to write, which leads me to think that we're wired for it. When I was twelve years old, I taught myself to type for the specific purpose of writing a novel. For a while, I made a living in advertising and public relations. That was okay because most of what I was called on to write was fiction. When I sold my first book, I wept with relief. Publishing is a tough, tough business but I'll take it over everything else.

Q: **Tell us about your writing process.**

A: I sit down in front of a blank screen and I stay there until I write something. It may be two paragraphs or two pages but it has to be something. I do this pretty much seven days a week all year long. Some days are a lot better than others. When I'm really having trouble figuring out a character, I walk around the house having a conversation with that person. Out loud. Amazingly, my family has adjusted to this and ignores me.

Q: **What's the hardest part of being a writer?**

A: Rejection, of course, I don't think anyone ever gets used to that. But it's never, or at least rarely personal and it really is just part of the job. Being able to accept that and carry on is what separates would-be writers from published authors. Beyond that there's the struggle to tune out all the distractions of life and focus on an inner world of the imagination, which then has to be captured in a form that can be shared with others. Communicating face-to-face is difficult enough, but a writer has to get inside the head of a reader. That's a rather intimate relationship and it has to be treated with great respect.

Q: **What have you got against Bram Stoker?**
A: Aside from a healthy dollop of professional jealousy, not a thing. I'm actually a huge fan, which is why I'm delighted that he plays such an important role in *Incarnation*.

Q: **Why are people so fascinated by vampires?**
A: Because they're gorgeous and sexy, and they live forever. They tap into our deepest fears and longings. Sex and death—eros and thanatos—drive human existence but vampires have found a way around that. It's a dreadful bargain in some ways but it works, at least in our imagination.

Q: **Is there anything else you'd like to tell us?**
A: Come visit me at http://www.facebook.com/emmacornwall author. We'll talk.